FAIL-SAFE

Compound Series Book 2

by Katy Morgan

Dedication

To the betas: Bee, Emily, Nannah, Sarah, Sophie, Shayla,

and the parentals.

And to the phenomenal students of

the University of Southern Queensland's 2021 Editing & Publishing program:

Anya, Camilla, Cassandra, Melissa, Natalia, Sabrina, and Siobhan.

Thank you for all your hard work—and for making me feel like a

Real Author with a proper Editing Team.

Prologue

THERE'S SOMEONE FOLLOWING him.

Henry's known this for the past five minutes or so, but he's been too pre-occupied to do anything about it. Roaring sirens and epic amounts of smoke will do that. The throbbing in his head, he thinks grimly, could be due to either imminent hearing loss or lack of oxygen. Good to have options.

His line of sight down the compound hall is limited by flames—unnatural flames that are burning the stone just as well as the wood. Flames that have at least one asset still trapped. Better than the first count Michaels gave him, but still one too many.

Henry's lost track of the number of times he's been back in by now. Every time gets a little harder: harder to see, harder to breathe, harder to keep a low profile so the emergency team doesn't tackle him and keep him from doing his damned job.

(He was supposed to protect them, how many assets and staff members are dead now, he was supposed to—)

He shakes his head, irritated and suddenly dizzy from more than just the smoke. Now isn't the time to think about how catastrophically he's failed. Or how much the person following him—if it's who he thinks it is—would enjoy reminding him of that failure. There's only one mission now: to save as many people as he can for as long as he can.

Michaels shouldn't have told him about the stragglers, he thinks as he carefully navigates the debris-filled hallway. At best, she'll get an official reprimand for letting him back in. At worst, aiding and abetting a criminal will mean the end of her career.

But it's not like Henry could just sit around and wait for someone else to take care of things. They can cuff him and lock him up again once it's done.

Only one left now.

Henry takes a turn too quickly and stumbles over a pile of burning stone, nearly falling flat on his face. He manages to stay upright by grabbing the nearest thing: a training room window sill made of wood. Which is on fire.

Cursing and snatching his hand back, he tries to catch his breath and gets a mouthful of smoke instead.

"Sir?" Michaels's voice is in his earpiece, difficult—but not impossible—to pick out from the sirens. "You're close now. The last ID pinged a little further down this corridor."

Henry finishes a cough and squints through watering eyes. "Noted. No more after that one, right?"

"None that we're aware of."

"Good. Then get off the line."

"Sir, Mr. Turner assures me this channel is secure—"

"Nothing is secure anymore, Michaels. Not even if Kent says it is."

A pause. "Yes, sir."

The line goes dead.

Straightening up and covering his mouth and nose with his arm, Henry presses forward as quickly as he can. There's broken glass and some splintered beams here and there—and the ever-present burning stone—but otherwise, not much to impede his progress. For now.

He finds what he was looking for around the corner: a caved-in wall with a chunk of the ceiling balanced on top. The arrangement of cement and wood creates a sort of tent with plenty of holes to see through but none big enough to crawl out of.

"Angelica?" Henry calls, struggling to be heard over the sirens.

He sees a hint of movement, and then a pair of eyes peeks through a tiny opening. "Oh," says a voice, barely audible. "Hello, Major."

She's talking, so that's a good sign. "Are you all right?"

"I'm stuck."

Henry chokes down a slightly crazed laugh. The world is practically falling down around her ears, and she's as calm as ever. Calmer than he is, that's for sure.

"You going to help or what?" Henry yells over his shoulder and into the smoke. He's not expecting an answer, and he doesn't get one. Possibly it's because he can't be heard over the alarms, but equally likely, it's because the asshole following him is the reason they're all here in the first place.

"Hang on," Henry says to Angelica. Then he takes a step back to survey the situation.

The pile of debris trapping her is enormous, heavy-duty masonry and bits of the inner structure of the compound, all straining under the unnatural heat. If the exterior is any indication, Angelica's got a little bit of room to move in there, but not much. And with everything around her on fire, visible only through a haze of smoke, she doesn't have much time before she asphyxiates.

Henry coughs and calls out to her again, scanning the rubble as he does it. "Angelica, do you see any loose stones on your end?"

"No." Her tone implies that she's beyond unimpressed. (Don't think about who that reminds him of.)

Henry's eyes fall on a promising chunk of burning debris.

This is going to hurt.

"I'm going to dig over here, all right?" Henry tells her. "I need you to come through as soon as you can see me."

There isn't anything he can use to wrap his hands—he gave up his jacket ages ago—but he grits his teeth and gets to it anyway, clawing at stone, mortar, and wood. At least things set on fire by an asset's power are less hot than things set on fire the usual way.

Less hot, but still hot. So much for avoiding third-degree burns.

The smoke is everywhere, and his sweat has become a physical weight on his skin. It's an eternity of pushing and pulling and prodding, trying to clear enough room for Angelica. The one saving grace is that partway through, the alarms short-circuit, leaving them in a sudden, ringing silence.

At length, Henry realizes that Angelica is trying to dig out on her end, too. He wants to tell her to stop so she doesn't hurt herself, but realistically, there's no way they have time if they only rely on his exhausted muscles.

Then there's a chink in the stone, and half of a small, soot-stained face appears. "I can see you," she says, like she's commenting on the weather.

Henry digs faster, fighting to ignore the pain. The hole is slowly getting bigger, especially once Angelica starts digging again. Henry is relieved to see that she looks unharmed—even her long, dark braid has survived with only minimal singeing. And she's tiny for a child her age, so it shouldn't take much longer to . . . there.

He reaches through the opening and gives her a small smile. "Ready to get out of here?"

"Yes, please." Her voice is steady, but her eyes are wide, and she's shaking slightly as she takes his hand. He notices that the watch that serves as her asset program ID is still strapped to her wrist. The plastic face is cracked, but the chip must be online if Kent was able to use it to track her. Henry gives silent thanks to whoever first decided younger assets should have wrist band IDs rather than cards.

Because cards can easily get lost in a crisis, Henry thinks, his chest tightening from more than just the smoke. And the compound is a big place. There could be hundreds of assets and officers trapped on lower levels with malfunctioning or missing IDs. People they won't find until it's over, if then.

He forces himself to refocus on Angelica. Even with the opening they've created, it's a bit of a squeeze. But between her pushing and his pulling, they get her through.

And then it all goes to hell.

An ominous groan comes from the beams above them as the flame finally burns through whatever was holding up the rest of the ceiling. Then there's a sharp *crack* and a rush of hot air.

It's not even a conscious choice.

Henry shoves Angelica away from him as hard as he can. He's vaguely aware of trying to move himself, too, but there's no time, and all that matters is getting her out of harm's way, never mind the ceiling coming down on him with a burning crash—

(Surely this is the part where the person who's been following him steps up, where it doesn't matter anymore how this started—)

Henry lies there for an interminable moment, stunned and buried in burning stone and wood, unable to process anything. He thinks the alarms might have started up again, but that and the smoke and the screaming (can't be Angelica, she's always so poised) all fade away.

He's pretty sure he ought to be feeling some sort of pain, but there's nothing. Nothing except a single thought:

Bastian is going to kill him.

Chapter 1

Two months ago

"THIS IS STUPID," Bastian says, frowning at himself in the green room mirror.

"I think you mean *amazing*," Laurel corrects him. "Why don't you know how to tie a tie?"

"When have I ever needed to tie a tie?"

"How about now?"

Bastian gives her—and the tie—a withering look. Not that it makes much difference. He can feel the amused-eager-excited coming off of her at a rate that isn't going to stop in the face of his irritation, no matter how justified. Especially since she's used to it.

Bastian undoes the knot at his throat and tugs at his stiff shirt collar. "Forget it. I prefer breathing. Did I mention this is stupid?"

"Thirty-two times, including that last one. I was counting." She elbows him away from the full-length mirror, grabs the tie from his hand, and ties it expertly around her own neck, patting it when she's done. "Don't worry; it looks better on me."

Bastian smiles slightly. "Yeah, it does."

"Anyway," Laurel continues, fussing with her hair, "I don't know why you're so nervous about this—"

"I'm not *nervous*—"

"Fine, being an empath makes you an expert on emotions, whatever. You know those people in the auditorium are here to see you, right? They're very excited about it. They've been here for actual minutes! And they're sitting down and everything!"

"That's the stupid part."

"What, that they're sitting down?"

"No." Bastian sighs, picking up his gloves from a nearby table and putting them back on. They've stopped blocking his power as well as they used to, but today, he'll take what he can get. Even if it's just the comfort of familiar black leather against his skin. "It's stupid that they're here to see me. Us. That they think we can actually do this. That we *should* actually do this."

Laurel frowns. "What's the alternative? Kick everyone out and let the compound gather dust? Send all the assets out into the world without any kind of help whatsoever? Some of them have been locked up in here and experimented on for most of their lives. Some of them don't have any memories of their lives before this. We can't just tell them to get lost and hope everything works out."

Bastian shakes his head. "You sound like Henry."

"Good!" Laurel grins. "He's right."

For a very brief moment, Bastian lets himself desperately wish Henry were here. Preferably getting ready to give this speech, so Bastian doesn't have to. Even more preferably, standing near enough that he could accidentally-on-purpose brush his hand against Bastian's while laughing at something Laurel said, and Bastian could lean into him, into the calming little bubble of negation that dims Bastian's power, and . . .

But there are rules now about leaning. Just like there are rules about Henry negating anywhere someone might realize he's doing it.

"Not everything can be remade into something that isn't awful," Bastian says. "If we had a chance to rebuild your compound, would you want that? Knowing what happened there?"

Laurel hesitates, her gaze sliding away from his. "I don't know. But that's not an option, is it? The resources are here. The people who need our help are here, too." She looks back up at him. "I know how you feel about this place. What happened to you here. But—"

"You don't know," he says, more viciously than he meant to. "You don't know what Valentine told Wright to do. What he—"

"Oh, right, I forgot. I have no idea what it's like to be experimented on by Dr. Wright and told by Major Valentine that nothing I experienced ever happened and that I should shut up and go along with it because *science*, while everyone I love is hurt and dying and oh, right, they *did* die, didn't they? All of them but me. And I just get to, you know, live with that. Forever."

Her hands are clenched, her nails—specially done up for this thing and sparkling silver—digging into her palms. The level of fury-hurt-loss coming from her is intense enough that he doesn't even have to read it; he can see it in her eyes.

"I'm sorry," he says quietly.

She smooths down the material of her dress even though there aren't any wrinkles. "Yeah, well. I forgive you. Maybe." She pauses, then adds, "I don't forgive you for vetoing my idea to fill the auditorium with some of my plants, though. They were really upset when I told them they weren't invited. Have you ever tried to explain to a fig tree that it's not wanted?"

Bastian hasn't formulated a safe answer to that before there's a knock at the green room door. Without waiting for a reply, an officer opens it and sticks her head through. "They're ready for you," she says, her bored-pleasant-calm grating on Bastian's nerves. She ducks out again just as quickly, leaving the door open.

Bastian and Laurel look at each other. Then Laurel grabs his hand, squeezes it once, and drops it to do her not-quite-skipping thing out into the hall.

Bastian sighs and follows her.

"You don't have any notes," Laurel says as they walk. "Did you memorize your speech?"

"Yes," he says. Which is a lie. Sort of like if he said he actually prepared for this or has any idea what he's doing.

Laurel isn't buying it (skeptical-questioning-concerned), but she doesn't bother to reprimand him in the short amount of time they have before they reach the stage door to the auditorium. The officer is waiting for them, her bland smile still in place, and she opens the door as they approach. "Ready?"

"Yes!" Laurel replies, sweeping past. "I'm especially ready for the part where I sit there and look nice. I'm really good at that."

Bastian rolls his eyes and follows her onto the stage.

He doesn't know what this room was originally. When the staff started doing inventory, they came across rooms like this on every floor of the compound: locked up, dusty, and obviously not in use for years. Apparently, Valentine and Wright only needed so many locations for conducting life-threatening experiments and training officers to abduct people with powers.

This particular room is a good size for an auditorium, so that's what it became. A place for Bastian, Laurel, and the rest of the asset program committee to welcome the first voluntary group of assets.

Bastian still can't quite wrap his head around the idea that there are assets who might actually *want* to live and work in a compound rather than just getting snatched up off the street and forced into it. He has trouble shaking the idea that this isn't just the same Compound Network con, only in a slightly different wrapper: the compound as a place to live and learn as part of a community; a place where assets and potentials can feel safe while they figure out how they want to use their powers; a place where the focus is on training people rather than experimenting on them behind closed doors.

Maybe it doesn't matter if he believes it's possible, though. Not when other people do. People like Laurel and Henry.

Bastian's seen the paperwork, so he knew how many people would be here, but it's still startling to actually be standing in front of them. The room is packed, the collective curiosity-wariness-anticipation pushing against his mental shield, some of it seeping through and setting off yet another headache. He resists the urge to pat his shirt pocket and make sure he still has painkillers left. Probably not a good idea to be popping pills in front of hundreds of people when you're supposed to look capable and in charge.

(Don't think about how it's working less and less, how the headaches are more frequent than ever, sometimes so bad he can't think straight, even when there's no one around to feel—)

Laurel nudges him slightly, nodding toward the podium. Then she goes to sit with the committee, who are all looking expectantly at him. Like he's got something worth saying. Or he better have.

They're going to regret that.

He goes over to the podium, looks out into the crowd, and tries to keep his shield steady. After a moment, he clears his throat and says into the mic, "If you don't want to be here, get out."

There's an awkward silence.

"He means welcome to the compound!" Laurel says cheerfully, appearing at his side.

"No, I don't." Bastian glares at her, then turns back to the audience. "If you're here," he says over the confused murmurs, "it's because you've heard about this place. What happened here. Probably not through official channels because the Compound Council likes to keep things hushed up. But you've heard."

"Bastian," Laurel says in a low voice, "you might want to—"

"We've cleaned it up, of course. It looks a lot better than it did when I was growing up. The assets aren't hidden away on the lower levels anymore, and the officers actually know what's going on."

They *mostly* know what's going on, Bastian amends to himself. Except about Henry. For however long that will last.

"If you've heard the rumors, you know what it was like before," he continues. "People were tortured and experimented on without their consent. A lot of them died. Most of the officers in charge were complicit. Everything you've heard—from wherever you heard it—is true."

More muttering and a rising tide of alarm-confusion-unease. Bastian forces himself not to close his eyes against it, opting instead to tighten his grip on the podium. At least the gloves are protecting him from the small bits of emotional residue clinging there like dust.

"That's what it was like then," Bastian tells the crowd. "You're here to decide what it's going to be like now."

He gestures to the staff sitting behind him, unified in their varying shades of concern-irritation-embarrassment. Captain Smith is offering him one of her more vitriolic glares. "These people have spent the last six months cleaning this place up and fighting to take the asset program from a massive human rights violation to an opportunity to help and support people like us," Bastian says. "If you decide to stay, your job is to make it worth their while.

"Laurel and I and the rest of the staff will support you while you learn about your powers and find good ways to use them. But you're really here to decide what this compound is going to be. Whether it deserves to keep existing.

"And yes, some of that will probably involve experiments that help our medical team understand your powers. But those experiments are *voluntary*. You won't be disqualified just because you don't want to donate some blood."

More whispers and wide eyes, which he tries to ignore, along with Laurel's tenseness as she stands next to him. "This is the important part," he says loudly. "If you're here, it's because you want to be. Because you *choose* to be, and you're willing to do the work. If that doesn't sound like you, get out. We're through holding people here against their will."

He turns and walks away, but not before he hears Laurel scramble to take his place at the mic. "Please speak with one of the staff members on either side of the stage to confirm your enrollment," she says over the chatter. "We're very glad to have you here, despite what that sourpuss just said. I'm Laurel, the assistant director. If you have any questions—"

"Who was that guy?" someone calls.

"Oh, that's Bastian Lucas. He's the director of the program. I promise he's much nicer than he sounds."

"He's the *director* of the *program?*"

Bastian's almost made it back to the side door when his retreat is blocked by a familiar strain of apprehension-worry-disapproval. The middle-aged woman standing in front of him wearing a white lab coat and a frown looks like she'd be delighted to send him to bed without supper—or at least give him a stern talking-to for being the reason behind most of her gray hairs.

This is what comes of putting competent doctors on the asset program committee, Bastian thinks grimly.

"Director Lucas," she begins.

"I have an appointment, Dr. Rowe," Bastian says, his head throbbing hard enough that walking in a straight line is becoming problematic.

Rowe crosses her arms over her chest. "I don't suppose you'd like to explain your . . . interesting recruitment approach first?"

"I'll put it on the agenda for our next committee meeting. Did I mention that appointment is with the major?"

Her frown deepens, but she steps aside. "If your health is causing—"

"It's not. Excuse me."

Strictly speaking, he doesn't have a meeting with Henry for another hour. But he *does* have an appointment with the largest dose of painkillers he can stomach and anywhere that isn't here.

Chapter 2

"I'M NOT SAYING it's an *issue*," Kent is saying in Henry's earpiece. "Our security is way too good for that. But three attempted breaches of the compound mainframe in one week shows they're determined. Pathetic, but determined."

"That we can tell they tried at all means they made it through five layers of protection," Sybil argues. Henry can hear her fingers typing at light speed even as she speaks. "That definitely counts as an issue."

And it's a fantastic issue to raise less than thirty minutes before the liaison committee meeting, Henry thinks as he pushes past several officers on his way down the hall. "Let's move the chatter to a more secure channel," he tells the others. "Keep your hackers monitoring the situation and set up an appointment with Michaels so we can—"

"Sir?"

Officer Michaels herself appears at his elbow like she was summoned by the sound of her name. Henry's never heard of anyone, asset or not, who could do that. But if anyone could, it'd be Michaels.

"How are you at stalling?" Henry asks her.

"Exceptional, sir." She glances at her ever-present tablet, then looks up and quirks a dark eyebrow at him. "Is the director still unavailable?"

Henry sighs. "I'll take care of it. But if you could keep the liaison committee from killing each other until we get to the meeting, that would be great."

"Yes, sir. I'll make sure all sharp objects are removed from the meeting room."

Henry's too tired to play his usual game of trying to decide if she's joking or not. "Thanks. You're a lifesaver."

"I accept payment in the form of macchiatos, as I'm sure you recall, Major."

"Earn yourself another by setting up a meeting with Kent and Sybil as soon as possible to discuss this security situation."

"Yes, sir."

"You copy that?" Henry refocuses on the hackers' back-and-forth, which has continued without him. "Take this to channel six and arrange things with Michaels."

"Honestly, it's probably just a pathetic wannabe trying to gain some cred by sneaking into our system," Kent says. "They should've done their homework and realized that Sybil's security maze is too tough to break. It's a work of art, really. The sort of thing that deserves a very large raise, don't you think, Major?"

"Kent," Sybil begins, doing a remarkable job of infusing one syllable with an equal amount of amusement and exasperation.

"Look, I just think my girlfriend is the most brilliant woman in this compound, and I want that quantified by management in cold, hard cash."

Henry does a poor job of quashing a laugh. "If we're still a viable operation after the liaison committee eviscerates us in today's meeting, I'll seriously consider raises all around. In the meantime, get things worked out with Michaels."

"Yes, sir," Sybil says.

Their voices go silent as they switch over. Henry nods to Michaels, who nods back before turning down a different hallway, already arranging the meeting particulars through her headset.

Henry sets his shoulders and moves on toward his destination.

The traffic in the Level 6 halls begins to thin out as he hits the western side. While most of the area is made up of training rooms, there's one large exception: a pool that is, strictly speaking, open to all compound officers. In practice, no one uses it much—probably because Bastian scared them all off.

That's not how he tells it, of course. When Henry asked, Bastian just said something vague about how the officers decided to train elsewhere.

Henry thinks it's more likely that Bastian got rid of them so he could have sole access to a place that's empty of people and full of water. That seems to be the only thing that helps when his headaches get bad. Not that Henry's supposed to notice the headaches. Or rather, when he *does* notice, because he's not completely dense, he's not supposed to say anything about it.

(Unless he could somehow think of the right thing to say, something that would fix everything, something better than what he's already offered and what Bastian refused—)

Henry sighs and pushes open the door to the pool area. The lights have been dimmed, leaving everything in partial shadow. The humidity envelops him, making him desperately wish he could take off his dress uniform jacket. Bad idea, though; he'd never be able to convince himself to put it back on in time for the meeting.

He walks to the edge of the pool and squints into the murky depths, but what he can see of the water is completely still. Did Bastian not end up here after all?

"Pretty sure this is a top secret area. You should ask the major for clearance."

Henry starts and nearly falls into the water. He's managing an undignified crouch when he catches sight of Bastian lurking in a darkened corner, smirking, with only his head and part of his shoulders above the waterline.

"The lights *are* working, you know," Henry says without much heat.

Bastian shrugs and swims forward a bit, creating ripples in the water. "I like it better this way. Fewer idiots wandering in if they think it's closed."

"I wandered in. Are you saying I'm an idiot?"

"Not on the record. I don't want my boss to fire me." Bastian narrows his eyes. "Speaking of bosses, did Dr. Rowe send you? You know you're *her* boss, too, right? Not the other way around?"

There's no good way to answer that. Even if Dr. Rowe hadn't contacted him with her concerns about Bastian's speech, Henry would have heard about it eventually and managed more than enough concern on his own. But saying anything to that effect will just piss Bastian off.

"The meeting's in half an hour," Henry says instead. "Are you going to have enough time to get ready?"

Bastian's irritation shifts to a dangerous sort of amusement as his lips turn upward. "Major, are you implying I'm not dressed appropriately for a committee meeting?"

Henry *really* shouldn't encourage him—not when chewing him out for that cute speech is more in order—but this is the first time in ages that Bastian's come close to a genuine smile, let alone straight-up flirting, and the words are out of Henry's mouth before properly consulting his brain. "I don't know. What are you wearing?"

Bastian doesn't answer, just dips down under the water and swims over to the stairs. By the time Henry stands up and locates a towel, Bastian is climbing out of the pool. Even in the low lighting, Henry can just make out the scars on his back.

That's why they're doing this, Henry thinks, gripping the towel more tightly than the situation warrants. So no one ever has to go through what Bastian did. What all of the assets did. Does Bastian ever stop to think about what will happen if they screw this up? If anything they say or do makes it look like the compound isn't up to standard?

Henry shakes his head, walks over to Bastian, and hands him the towel. And then tries not to look anywhere distracting—which is difficult, since everywhere is distracting. Some people should not be allowed to stand around sopping wet, wearing only swimming trunks.

"Verdict on the attire?" Bastian's smirk is still there, but the hesitation is starting to creep in.

(Henry hates that hesitation, hates that it's increasingly permeating what little time they have alone together these days, but now really isn't the time to—)

He clears his throat. "Definitely not appropriate." He meant it to sound stern, but that's not at all how it comes out. He needs to move away, or to at least start in on the stuff that matters, but he's much more interested in the amusement that hasn't quite faded from Bastian's face and the unacceptably long amount of time it's been since Henry could touch him.

Bastian reaches out toward Henry but stops himself a split second before Henry says quietly (regretfully), "Cameras."

Bastian's hand drops. "Right."

While their relationship is hardly secret—Henry's pretty sure it's been the backbone of the compound rumor mill for quite some time—their agreement is to keep things as professional as possible in public. And in a heavily monitored compound, public means just about everywhere. They're under intense scrutiny already in their comparatively untried leadership roles; if they let it, their relationship could easily be picked up as proof of misconduct. There's only so much an official appointment from the Compound Council can do on its own to lend legitimacy.

But it's more than that, Henry thinks. Bastian's always been endearingly awkward about showing affection, at least as long as Henry's known him. But he's been even more guarded about it in the last six months since they got back from Council HQ, where Bastian read Major Valentine for her trial. It's been this weird dance of Bastian increasingly holding himself back, even in private, while Henry struggles to figure out what he's supposed to do about it.

(And he can't shake the feeling that something happened during that read, that Major Valentine did or said something that—)

"I'll meet you outside," Bastian says, already drying his hair and turning away.

Henry lets him.

***

They pass several groups of new assets on the way to the meeting room. Bastian doesn't even look at them, but Henry can't ignore the way they're sneaking glances. As the commanding officer of the compound, Henry wonders if he should be insulted that their awe has nothing to do with him.

"I heard about your speech," he says after another group passes and nearly walks into a wall in an effort to keep moving while also peeking at Bastian at the same time.

Bastian sighs. "Laurel is going to give me an earful. I don't need one from you, too."

"I'm your boss, remember? If anyone is going to be providing an earful, it's me."

"Better get in line."

It's about what Henry was expecting in terms of a response. But he can't exactly give Bastian a dressing down in the middle of a hallway. Particularly when he's still vacillating between dreading how the liaison committee will respond and being disappointed that he wasn't there to see every authority figure in the auditorium have a heart attack.

Focus on the mission; too much is at stake. "You know how closely we're being watched," Henry says. "You can't do things like that."

"Like what? Tell the truth?" Bastian stops and turns to Henry. "What would you like me to do instead? Welcome them to a happy little magic school where everything is perfect, and they'll never be hurt again?"

"Of course not. It's just—"

"If you don't like the way I do things, maybe you shouldn't have told them to put me in charge of the program in the first place."

Henry takes a breath, then grabs Bastian's arm and hauls him around the corner. This hallway is less populated than the last one, but Henry's not taking any chances. Ignoring Bastian's sputtering, Henry herds him into an empty meeting room and shuts the door firmly. Then he reaches into his jacket pocket and flips a switch on the device he's hiding there.

Bastian cuts off his own protest and eyes the jammer as Henry takes it out and tosses it down on the table. "Seriously? You're using a jammer just so you can yell at me without the security cameras recording it?"

"I'm using a jammer because we clearly need to talk about this, and we don't have enough time before the meeting to do it the right way."

"There'll be plenty of time for you to chew me out and for me to not listen after—"

Henry sighs. "I get what you were trying to do. You're right that we have to tell the new assets the truth about the compound. But we can't just ignore etiquette, either. This has to look like a legitimate, professional program."

"And we show that how? With vapid speeches you can use to suck up to the people who were perfectly happy until now to let assets disappear and die when they stopped being useful?"

"You know I hate this as much as you do," Henry says, trying to swallow his frustration. "But if we want to help them, we have to play nice with the Council and the liaison committee. There's no room for error. If the Council changes their mind about putting us in charge, the compound and all its resources will get redirected to who-knows-where. Maybe to someone who would start up the experiments again. We can't let that happen."

Bastian looks steadily at him for a moment, then away. "No," he agrees quietly.

"I mean it," Henry continues, alarmed at the desperation he hears in his own voice. "The committee's already talking like we're a liability, and the program's barely started. If they decide we can't handle—"

"You think they've already decided, don't you? And you agree with them."

Henry laughs humorlessly and runs a hand through his hair. "I thought you were an empath, not a mind reader."

"I've told you, don't be an idiot about this. Assuming it's even possible to make the compound into something worth saving, the only person who could do it is you."

Henry reflects that Bastian has an exceptional talent for making a compliment sound like an insult. "You mean I'm the only person crazy enough to want to."

"That, too." Bastian hesitates, then adds, "But it matters. That you want to."

The tightness that's always in Henry's chest these days, constantly reminding him that every mistake he makes could cost lives, releases its choke hold a bit. "Don't say things like that."

"Like what?"

"Supportive stuff. Makes me want to kiss you, and you know I can't right now."

The corner of Bastian's mouth twitches upward. He starts to say something, then clears his throat instead. "Aren't we going to be late?"

Henry sighs inwardly and picks up the jammer, returning it to his pocket. "Michaels is stalling them, but yeah, we should go." He narrows his eyes. "Seriously, though—"

"Seriously, I get it. Dignified restraint." Bastian gives him a half-assed salute that isn't terribly reassuring.

"Bastian—"

"What, you want to risk Michaels running out of jokes?"

Henry rolls his eyes, turns the jammer off, and leads the way back into the hall.

It's a short elevator ride up to Level 3. As they get closer to the meeting room, Henry feels himself tense up again. This meeting shouldn't be much different than the others they've had over the past few months, though. The senators, representing the city, will ask questions about the compound's progress. Henry and Bastian, representing compound leadership, will answer.

According to General Carter, head of the Compound Council and the chair of these meetings, the liaison committee is supposed to allow for mutual understanding and collaboration between city officials and compound staff. In practice, these meetings are more like grilling sessions during which Henry, in particular, is taken to task for all of the compound's failings until Carter decides he's been flayed enough for one day and calls it off until next time.

Of course, city officials have every right to be dubious about compound activities. Given how closely Henry and Bastian worked with Major Valentine, who spent years keeping dangerous secrets, it's understandable that the senators would demand more transparency. They're all supposed to be working together toward more open partnerships between the Compound Network and the various city leaders, after all.

In the interest of said transparency, Henry has been spending most of his days putting together endless reports on programs and processes, especially with regard to today's official inauguration of the new asset program.

Given Bastian's handling of that so far, Henry expects this meeting will be . . . interesting.

"Henry." Bastian has halted them just around the corner from the meeting room.

Lost in thought, Henry nearly bumps into him. "Hmm?"

"You need to stop."

"What?" Henry grimaces. "Oh."

He's gotten much better about controlling his negation, but when he's particularly anxious or stressed, he has to be especially careful. Bastian's power is strong enough to work through the low-level negation field Henry sometimes still puts up without meaning to. But if anyone else realized they couldn't use their power around Henry, it would be problematic, to say the least. He got away with it in the heat of the moment in the forest last year, but that isn't likely to fly in a compound hallway.

Technically, there's no rule against a compound commanding officer being an asset—even one like Henry, who was never officially made a part of the program, since Valentine was too busy using his power for her own purposes to tell him he had one. A commanding officer who might have the ability to remove the powers of everyone in his compound, though . . . that's a different story. One best dealt with once the new asset program is steady enough to stand on its own.

For now, Henry's power is just one more secret. Sometimes, he wonders how they're any different from Major Valentine.

"Henry." Bastian has a hand on his arm.

"Right. Hang on."

Henry closes his eyes, takes a deep breath, and focuses on dissipating the negation field he inadvertently put up. It only takes a few seconds, but he has to concentrate. When it's done, he feels more tense than ever. "Better?"

"Yeah." Bastian removes his hand quickly and starts walking again.

Michaels is waiting at the door. As they approach, she looks up from her tablet and nods a greeting. "The committee is assembled, Major."

"Any trouble heading off disaster?" Henry asks.

"No, sir. Although Senator Nunez was looking for you."

Great. "What does she want?"

"Probably to update us on a list of things we're doing wrong," Bastian mutters.

"If such a list exists, Director, I haven't seen it," Michaels says calmly. "She did mention that she would like a word with the major at his earliest convenience, though she didn't say why."

"Let's survive the meeting first," Henry says. One headache at a time.

"A worthy goal, sir." Michaels opens the door for them and steps aside.

The meetings Henry used to go to were usually in an office or a meeting room not unlike the one he and Bastian were just in: large tables, chairs, and maybe a screen for projecting things, if necessary.

This room is different.

Level 3 has been cleaned up and made the meeting center of the compound, with this room at its core. It's not meant to be a courtroom, exactly, but there's no denying that the remodel was based on the tribunal rooms at Council HQ. Rows of seats are arranged for guests—in this case, the city officials who make up most of the liaison committee. They face the front, where a long table includes a seat of honor for General Carter. On either side of him are chairs for compound staff, which, for this particular meeting, means Henry and Bastian.

In theory, this setup is supposed to allow compound staff and officers to present to a large number of visitors and field their questions while a Compound Council representative oversees the process. In practice, it's been the perfect environment for making Henry feel like he's on trial for every decision he's ever made.

And the med tech with his needle doesn't help.

No one here, besides Bastian, knows that Henry's an asset, so he could just walk past the med tech stationed at the doorway. That's exactly what Bastian has told him to do from the beginning, pointing out that having the commanding officer of the compound stop and stand around irritably every time he enters the meeting room is a bit awkward.

Henry doesn't care. Today, just like always, he crosses his arms over his chest and waits.

Bastian has stopped arguing about it. He wordlessly unbuttons a cuff, rolls up his sleeve, and holds his arm out to the tech, who injects the serum with practiced ease. Bastian doesn't even flinch when the needle pierces his skin.

The serum's better than it was when Henry used it on retrieval missions. Now it just dims an asset's power rather than knocking them out entirely. A little something to assuage the city officials who were nervous about having a powerful empath in the room.

(But it's still wrong, acting like you trust someone enough to run a top secret program while simultaneously refusing to let them have full control of their power; it's an extra hoop Bastian has to jump through, one Henry should have to jump through, too, and if they knew what Henry is and that the serum was originally made from his blood—)

Bastian fixes his sleeve and walks over to their part of the table like getting an injection every time he enters a room is completely normal. Maybe under Dr. Wright, it was.

Henry sets his jaw and goes to sit down, too.

"Good of you to join us, gentlemen," says General Carter. His booming voice echoes off the walls and stops the chatter coming from the gallery.

"We appreciate everyone's patience," Henry assures the general, keeping his tone pleasant. Michaels has left a tablet with his notes on the table, so he picks it up and swipes to the right files. "We're ready to start whenever you are."

"I'd like a word before we begin," says a familiar voice.

General Carter sighs. "Of course you would, Senator Nunez."

Nunez, stiff and dressed impeccably as always in a severe navy suit, gets to her feet. She addresses the general directly, as if no one else is in the room. "Once again, I'd like to express my concern about having an asset present who could potentially use his power to influence this meeting."

"What, sticking a needle in my arm every time we do this isn't enough insurance for you?" Bastian says under his breath.

"The time for objections is long past, Senator," Carter says. "And even if it weren't, this committee has already agreed to allow Director Lucas to attend these meetings so long as he undergoes the compromise we just witnessed. He couldn't use his power here even if he wanted to."

Having seen how powerful Bastian can be when cornered, Henry isn't sure that's true. But now probably isn't the best time to mention it.

"The director *may* have good intentions," Nunez says, "but I think we all know there is substantial evidence that an empath can do more than just passively feel people's emotions. The reports regarding the incident in the forest last year—"

"—are already a matter of record, as are your misgivings about the director. Do we really need to do this at every meeting, Senator?"

Normally, Nunez seems content with this token protest. Today, however, she pauses to give Henry an odd look. Or at least, he thinks she does; it's over too quickly for him to be sure. "The Council still has no qualms about the leadership of this compound, then?" she asks. "They stand behind their appointments?"

"As the head of the Compound Council, I can assure you we do," Carter says. "Just as we did the last hundred times you asked. Can we move on?"

Someone else clears their throat. "What I believe my colleague is trying to say is that, while the city fully accepts the Council's decisions with regard to staffing this compound, we do have some remaining concerns about how its leadership might function in a crisis."

Senator Donnigan, small and bland enough to appear unassuming, waits until all eyes are on him before he stands to continue giving his unsolicited input. "An empath who is able to not only experience other people's emotions but also manipulate them could cause confusion in an already fraught situation," he says, his reedy voice perfectly modulated to make optimal use of the acoustics of the room.

As usual, most of the other senators and aides are nodding in agreement, causing a small ripple across the gallery. The biggest exception is Nunez, who's busy glaring at Donnigan, just like she does every time he steals her thunder. Which is often. She's probably the only person who consistently wants to punch him as much as Henry does.

At least General Carter cuts in this time. "As I just stated, Senator, this matter is closed. I suggest we proceed with the task at hand, especially since we're already behind schedule."

"Excuse me, General. I was under the impression that the purpose of these meetings was to candidly review this compound's efforts to determine if it should be allowed to continue."

Nunez might be the one objecting fastest, but Donnigan has her beat when it comes to aligning the crowd to his whims. He shows just the right amount of respect for Carter's authority while also implying that he understands his fellow committee members' concerns better than the leader of one of the most powerful organizations in the world ever could.

"I'm happy to answer any questions you have about our work, Senator," Henry says, hoping his voice hits somewhere between polite and pointed. He'll never be as good at it as Donnigan is, but someone has to keep the meeting moving along.

"Thank you, Major." An aide hands Donnigan a tablet, which he takes, scrolling a bit before looking up at Carter. "If I may, General?"

"I wish you would."

Donnigan turns to Henry. "Major, since our meeting last month, you and your staff have begun implementing the new asset program, correct?"

"Yes. The program officially launched today." Henry forces himself not to glance at Bastian. "We should have data for you on the initial groups and their progress within the next few months, as I mentioned in my last report."

Donnigan smiles thinly. "Yes, thank you. The report was . . . adequate, if light on detail."

Henry smiles back and tries to ignore the way Bastian tenses beside him. "I'm sorry to hear that forty pages describing our goals, oversight structure, and methods of data collection weren't detailed enough for you, Senator. Is there something you'd like me to elaborate on?"

"Quite a few things, actually." Donnigan glances at his tablet. "Let's begin with the living arrangements for your charges. It says here that the assets who were part of the previous program will live and work alongside assets who have just joined. Is it wise to combine these groups, particularly when some of them might still be unsettled from their past experiences?"

"You mean the experiments that nearly killed them?" Bastian says. "The ones you senators and General Loudmouth over here didn't bother to do anything about until the major and I brought you evidence on a silver platter?"

Henry groans inwardly. So much for dignified restraint.

General Carter glares at Bastian. "Director Lucas—"

"Sorry, General. Just trying to candidly review the senators' efforts to determine if they should be allowed to continue."

Tittering from the gallery.

Senator Donnigan's smile turns frosty. "Major, perhaps you could share some of the thinking that went into making these housing arrangements."

"The compound has always been both a home and a place of work for on-duty staff and officers," Henry says. "The asset program committee saw no reason not to extend that offering to assets as well, and I agreed. Most of them have nowhere else to go."

"Yes, and that's very unfortunate. But housing them here significantly increases the funding required to keep the compound running."

"You're right," Bastian says. "It *does* cost more money to keep people in rooms rather than in jail cells."

Henry presses his lips together. Bastian's not wrong, of course, but this isn't helping their ability to present a professional front—or Henry's ability to keep his blood pressure from skyrocketing. And they literally *just talked about this.*

"Senator," Henry says after shooting Bastian a warning look, "most assets, not to mention the potentials who become assets when their powers manifest, have been abused or neglected their entire lives, including here at the compound. If we truly want to earn their trust and make the compound a place they can rely on to help them understand their powers, we have to create an environment that supports them. Forcing an at-risk population to fend for themselves doesn't help build that trust."

He pauses, then adds, "As for the cost, you'll find several pages of financial options in the report I mentioned a moment ago. And we can certainly review them if you had trouble following the details."

Damn, he's as bad as Bastian. Who just made a noise that's more of a laugh than a cough.

"Thank you, Major. That won't be necessary." Donnigan meets Henry's gaze, apparently unperturbed. "It's a fine notion, this cooperation and desire for trust. But trust must be earned. While some individuals might be willing to overlook problematic behaviors,"—he throws a glance at Bastian—"others don't have that luxury. Without enough data to assure the populace that these assets are safe and willing to work with us, how can we assume they won't act out?"

"And how do the assets know *you're* safe and willing to work with *them*?" Bastian demands. "Major Mortimer is the only one here who's shown any interest in—"

"I think we're all aware of the importance of safety for everyone involved in this," Henry says firmly. "Senator, if you have any suggestions, the director and I would be happy to hear them."

Bastian looks the opposite of happy, but he clamps his mouth shut and sits back in his chair.

"Well," Donnigan says, "I've never worked for a compound, of course. But I *have* worked for my constituents for over thirty years, and I know they'll have concerns about people who could, say, manipulate them into committing suicide. That was the charge brought against John Doe, wasn't it?"

"John Doe has been incarcerated for his crimes and can no longer hurt anyone," Henry says quickly. "He's an atypical example of an asset."

"Really? If I recall correctly, the man sitting next to you is equally dangerous, if what we've seen of his file is any indication—"

"Okay, stop." Bastian leans forward again. "You have questions about assets and their powers? Ask me. I'm the head of the program, after all."

Donnigan turns to him with a calculating look. "Yes, you are, aren't you? Yet you're not an officer. You've had no training. Can you remind us what qualifies you to run this program? I'm still a bit unclear on that point."

And they're back here again. At least this time Donnigan made it more than five minutes before questioning Bastian's credentials. Henry opens his mouth to respond, but Bastian beats him to it.

"Well, I don't run illegal experiments, which puts me one up on the last guy. And I'm an asset myself, so I know more about what that means than you do. If you want an official seal of approval, you might remember that General Carter and the Compound Council appointed me. I'm sure they'd be happy to show you my resume if that's what you're looking for."

Henry frowns at Bastian, who notices and gives a small sigh. "There's also the asset program committee, which includes officers, medical staff, and scientists involved with the experimentation process. I'm not making any decisions for the program without their approval. And no higher-level actions are taken without the major's say-so."

Senator Donnigan nods. "About that. How would you categorize your relationship with Major Mortimer?"

Henry clears his throat. "Senator—"

"The major runs the compound, including the asset program," Bastian says. "I may not be an officer, but that makes him my boss."

"And is that the extent of your relationship?"

General Carter finally cuts in, his voice steely. "Since everyone seems to have forgotten, I'll just remind you all that the Compound Council has jurisdiction over the appointment of compound leadership, not the city. If anyone has evidence that either Major Mortimer or Director Lucas have engaged in activities that would prevent them from doing their jobs, you're welcome to present it. The Council, however, has no concerns in this area at present, so I suggest we refrain from prurient lines of questioning and get back to discussing this compound and its programs."

Donnigan barely misses a beat. "Very well." He turns back to Henry. "Let's return to the topic of living arrangements, then. Major, you mentioned that on-duty officers and staff both live and work at the compound. But they've been through rigorous training regarding decorum, among other things. Assets, I understand, have not."

"Afraid we're going to throw parties after curfew?" Bastian asks.

"I'm afraid the lack of separation between personal and professional spaces could cause conflicts of interest," Donnigan says pointedly. "Without boundaries, what's to stop the residents of the compound from fraternizing?"

Henry laughs before he can stop himself. "You obviously haven't lived in a compound, Senator. 'Fraternizing' happens whether or not it's officially sanctioned. But you're right that officers and staff are encouraged to keep its effect on their duties to a minimum."

"And you're not concerned about the assets' lack of training in that area?"

"Assets are trained in lots of areas, Senator," Bastian says. "If you're that interested in fraternizing, I'm sure we could find someone who—"

General Carter sighs loudly. "This is deteriorating quickly. Let's take a ten-minute recess while everyone remembers how to behave like adults. After that, if any of you would like to have a *legitimate* discussion about the state of this compound and its programs, I'd be delighted to facilitate."

As the general and the senators file out into the hall, Henry turns to Bastian, who's slouching in his chair like a petulant little kid. "Really? Antagonizing Donnigan? Were you asleep before in the hallway?"

"I'm not the one who basically told the entire liaison committee that we condone 'fraternizing.'"

"Bastian—"

"Look, I'm sorry, all right? It's just . . ." He crosses his arms over his chest. "They have *no idea* what it was like, and now they get to tell *you* how to do this?"

Henry sighs. "I told you, we have to work together."

"You going to remind Donnigan of that?"

"Maybe after I punch him."

Bastian's snort is definitely more of a snicker this time. Henry looks over at him, latching onto the way amusement lights up his eyes. It's tentative but still there, like he knows on some level that it's okay to have an emotion in front of Henry, no matter how ridiculous he might think that emotion is. It makes Henry almost wish General Carter hadn't cut off that "prurient" line of questioning because every damned one of them should know how Henry feels about this idiot.

"Major. I need to speak with you." Senator Nunez has stopped at their table. Her face is even more pinched than normal, deepening the dark circles under her eyes.

Henry glances at Bastian, but he's just looking at the floor and scratching his arm, apparently not in the mood for more snide commentary.

"What can I do for you, Senator?" Henry asks.

"Not here." Nunez eyes the doorway: empty now, but the others are milling around just outside. "After the meeting. Your office."

Henry raises his eyebrows. "If you want to make an appointment—"

"There's no need for that."

"Senator—"

A messenger wearing the dark green uniform of the Council HQ steps into the room, and Henry's heart immediately plummets.

"Major Mortimer." The messenger salutes. "May I have a word?"

Henry tries not to immediately perish from the venom Senator Nunez is sending his way. Or maybe the messenger's way; honestly, there's enough for both. "Excuse me, Senator," Henry says. "Michaels can set up an appointment for you, or maybe Director Lucas can—"

"Fine," Nunez says stiffly. "I'll speak with Officer Michaels." She brushes past the messenger and heads out into the hallway without another word.

"Go after her," Henry tells Bastian.

Bastian frowns. "Why? She wanted to talk to you, not me."

"Make sure she gets that appointment. It seems important."

"I'm sure it is. Her list of things we're doing wrong must be getting too heavy to carry around. She needs to unload some of it so there's room for more."

"Bastian. Just go."

Bastian looks at him, making the face that means he's trying to read someone. Which he can't do with the serum in his system. Probably. Henry's relieved to be escaping the scrutiny . . . and disgusted with himself for being relieved when Bastian gets to his feet and goes after Nunez.

"How bad is it?" Henry asks once he's gone.

"Dr. Westbrook requested that you come immediately. She estimates the window has closed to somewhere between twenty-four and forty-eight hours."

"Shit." Henry rubs his eyes, then stops, realizing he just spoke out loud. "Sorry. I'll get a jet prepped. You want a ride back to Council HQ?"

"Yes, sir. Thank you."

He'll have to ask Michaels to work her magic here and find some believable excuse for why Henry has to leave in the middle of the meeting.

He glances at the door, struck by the need to . . . no. He knows what Bastian will say—what he's been saying ever since his last tests came back. It'll have to be one more secret for now. Just until Henry's sure they're completely out of options.

He turns his comm back on and speaks into it. "Michaels? Once you've got that appointment set up with the senator, I need you to do something else for me."

Chapter 3

BASTIAN SUSPECTS IT was Laurel's plan from the beginning to carve out the best portion of the compound grounds for her garden. She probably had a whole set of arguments prepared to convince Henry to allocate her some space, but all it really took to get him on board was the promise of vegetables that might end up in the kitchens and make compound food edible for once.

Henry even offered to get the staff to help her arrange things. Bastian didn't have a chance to tell him how useless that was before Laurel explained that she could do it better and faster than mere mortals—not her phrase, but essentially what she meant. In a matter of minutes, she had the land cleared, seeds starting to sprout, and trees stretching themselves out toward the sun.

She accepted the offer of help with digging the pond, though. Not really something she could ask the plants to do for her.

Even Bastian has to admit the garden has come out nicely. In addition to the vegetables, there are flowers and shrubs everywhere, including varieties he's pretty sure shouldn't be blooming this time of year.

And there are trees. *Lots* of trees.

There was some consternation about that at first. The compound is right near a forest, after all, so why would the grounds need even more trees? Laurel's official response was that the trees in the garden could provide a safe training space for assets who would otherwise have to use a simulation or go into the unpredictably wild forest. Bastian's private theory, though, is that she wanted to recreate her favorite environment closer to home.

Assuming she even thinks of this place as home.

Today, she's sitting with a small group of assets near the pond. As Bastian watches, she flicks her fingers sharply downward, and a small patch of grass shoots up from the dirt. She nods to the girl across from her, who hesitates, then squeezes her eyes shut. A moment later, wisps of condensation come together above the grass to form a tiny storm cloud, which erupts into a rain shower, dousing the grass with tiny droplets of water. Laurel bursts into applause, and the rest of the group join her, laughing and clapping the stormmaker on the back.

Laurel's good at this, Bastian thinks. Some of the people sitting with her are new to the compound, but no one's scared or worried. This is exactly what they're hoping for: compound staff who can guide and train others within a structure that's less regimented than a school or government-run program. A place where assets can learn without the fear of life-threatening experiments.

This is what matters. What Henry and Laurel are fighting for. What Bastian needs to remember before he opens his damned mouth in committee meetings and risks ruining everything.

Laurel sees him approaching and shoos her group away. As they scatter, Bastian's attention is drawn to a girl, maybe fifteen or sixteen, whose dirty blonde hair and slight build are oddly familiar. As if feeling his eyes on her, she stops suddenly and looks up (fear-alarm-embarrassment).

"Who are you?" Bastian demands.

"Hey!" Laurel hurries over and elbows him in the side. "Don't scare the students."

"I just asked—"

"Yeah. Scaring. Like I said."

Bastian rolls his eyes and turns back to the girl, trying not to tense up at the feel of her anxiety-hesitation-tension. "What's your name?" he tries instead.

"Chloe. Sir." She glances at Laurel, then back at him. "Sorry—am I supposed to call you 'sir'?"

"No," Bastian and Laurel say together.

"Although it'd be hilarious if you did," Laurel adds, grinning.

Bastian ignores her. "Bastian is fine. Why do I recognize you?"

"What, you don't remember Chloe? Rude." Laurel has her hands on her hips.

"It's okay," Chloe says quickly. "He wouldn't. I mean, he probably had other things on his mind, and he was hurt, and—are you all right now, by the way? Oh, of course you are, that was awhile ago—"

"You're the tracker," Bastian says slowly. "The one who stood up to Valentine when we cornered her in the forest last year."

She ducks her head, fingers tightening on the strap of the shoulder bag she's carrying. "Well—yes. I didn't really do anything in the end, but—"

"Don't be silly," Laurel scoffs. "You were very brave."

"Yes, you were."

Laurel and Chloe stare at him, a duet of startled-confused-surprised.

"What?" Bastian asks, suddenly self-conscious.

"You said something nice!" Laurel's eyes are still wide.

"I'm always—"

"Rude! I know!" She claps her hands and turns to Chloe. "This is so exciting! We should take a picture to commemorate the occasion."

"Um—"

Bastian sighs. "Chloe, can you excuse us for a bit?"

"Yes, of course. Nice to meet you. Again. Sort of." Chloe gives them an awkward little wave and hurries away.

"See you tomorrow!" Laurel calls after her. Then she looks back at Bastian, crosses her arms over her chest, and opens her mouth.

"I know," he says immediately. "I'm sorry about leaving you to deal with the assembly yesterday."

"If the gossip I heard from the potted plants on Level 3 is true, I hope you apologized to Henry for what you did in the liaison committee meeting, too."

"I didn't mean to—" Bastian makes a face. "I'm not good at this."

She doesn't seem too impressed with this response. "Hmm. What did Henry say?"

"Nothing. He's at an off-site meeting." Bastian decides not to mention that he has no idea where Henry went. Or that he left before the meeting was over.

Laurel gives Bastian an uncomfortably penetrating look. "Did you read the book I gave you?" she asks after a moment.

He frowns at the sudden change in topic. "What does that have to do with anything?"

"I just figured if you got one part of your life sorted out, you might be better at the other parts." Her eyes are not-so-subtly dancing.

"There isn't anything that needs to be sorted out."

"Right. That's why you came to me months ago, moping about how you're sure Henry's keeping something from you."

Bastian absolutely does not do anything related to flushing. (Or thinking about how Henry obviously wanted to get rid of him before talking to that messenger yesterday, or how he was a complete idiot at the pool, or how so much is riding on Bastian not messing this up for Henry and the others, except he's probably already done that a thousand times over—)

"I don't *mope*," Bastian says irritably.

"Oh, right. Because you went directly to Henry when you thought there might be an issue, and you idiots *talked to each other about it*, so there was no need to involve your superior-in-every-way, best-and-most-long-suffering friend."

Bastian is about to say something appropriately cutting in response to that, but he gets distracted by the odd set of feelings coming from her (amused-frustrated . . . sad?). He's felt them all from her before, of course, but there's something strange about that last one. Like she's purposefully trying to keep it hidden underneath the others. "Laurel?"

She blows a stray strand of hair out of her face. "Look, you know I love you and Henry very much, but we don't have time to fix your lives right now—"

"There's nothing to—"

"We have new assets to welcome, and there are new algorithms to put into place for finding potentials, and we have to figure out what to do about General Carter and that awful committee—except, wait, that's *your* job, so maybe you should actually do it."

"I know, but—"

"But you're too busy mouthing off to worry about what sort of effect it's going to have on people like Chloe, who are relying on us to give them a safe place where they can—"

"I *know*." He narrows his eyes. "What's wrong?"

"What's wrong is you're a—"

"Laurel."

She clenches her jaw and looks away (awkward-embarrassed-frustrated, with the sadness seeping in around the edges). "It's stupid."

"Emotions generally are." When she glares at him, he adds, "I said 'generally.'"

Laurel hesitates, then straightens her back and turns on her heel. "Come into my office."

It takes him a moment to realize she wants him to go sit by the pond with her. There's no real need for manufactured privacy, since the garden is empty now, but it's a nice stop all the same: tiny waves on the water, the grass soft but not too damp, the trees giving just the right amount of shade. Even the usual chatter of animal emotions is dull background noise rather than an irritant.

Bastian sits down next to her and leans back against the crooked trunk of a tree bending out over the pond. For some reason, Laurel looks extremely amused by this.

"It likes you," she says.

"What?"

"The hornbeam. You're kind of making its day right now."

"You're . . . talking about the tree?"

She sighs and gives the hornbeam an exasperated look. "See? I told you, he's not very smart. You deserve better."

"Laurel."

"I'm just saying—"

He raises his eyebrows at her. She deflates and turns away.

(He hates this, hates feeling the multilayered whatever-it-is underneath her usual cheerfulness, like she thinks she has to hide it, and how has he not even noticed it until now—?)

"Do you remember when we sat like this in the clearing, and I told you about what happened at my compound?"

It's not really a question, because of course he remembers, but he answers anyway. "Yes."

"This is better than then," Laurel says, more to the pond than to him. "I want to help you and Henry and everyone else make this place less awful. Like working with Mariah just now to figure out how to do the localized storm—that was really neat, and not just because I can get her to do all the garden watering from now on. But . . ." Her sadness-loneliness-guilt breaks the surface.

"You miss them," Bastian says.

She gives him a small smile. "See? It's stupid. They've been gone a long time now. And we made Valentine and Wright pay, just like Vanessa asked. But I still . . ."

When it seems like she's not going to say anything else, he asks quietly, "Do you want to go back to the clearing?"

Helping her with Vanessa's body in the wreckage of her old compound hadn't been pleasant, but it did seem to give her a sense of closure. He'd thought she might start seeing her clearing as someplace simple and peaceful again, not just the facade hiding the ruins she barely escaped. But maybe it wasn't enough.

She shakes her head. "No. I mean, yes, but not like you think. I don't want to live there or ask Henry to have his minions build a shrine or something." She pauses. "You realize *we're* Henry's minions now, right?"

Bastian snorts. "Speak for yourself."

"Well, maybe you get some extra perks; you're more of a consort."

"Can we please stay on topic?"

"This *is* on topic. Sort of." She reaches over and pats the gnarled trunk of the tree. "There's something for you here, Bastian. Work only you can do—if you get your head out of your ass and do it. People are depending on you. You can *fix* things. I can help—I'm amazing, so obviously you need me—but it's not the same. I can't do anything to fix what happened to *my* compound. I can't help my friends because they're all dead."

She runs her hand gently through the grass. "The people here are really great, but they're not *my* people. Except for you, obviously. But you have Henry, so—"

"I don't *have* Henry."

"Really?" She grins. "I mean, to each their own when it comes to what you get up to in bed, but if you wanted to, I bet you could ask him—"

"I *meant* it's not one or the other. It's . . ."

She's hurting again, the amusement sinking back down underneath the wistful-melancholy-pain, and he's suddenly desperate to think of the right thing to say.

"You're good with them," he tries. "Mariah and Chloe and the others. They need someone who will listen to them and help them get comfortable with their powers and with each other. All I see here is Valentine and Wright and the people they killed. But you . . . you saved my life back then. You didn't have to, but you did. I think you can save this place, too. You and Henry."

"And what are you going to do while we're busy with that? Stand around and terrorize people?"

He thinks about the headaches and the tests and just looks out at the pond, feeling the tree trunk against his back, bumpy and solid.

"Bastian," Laurel says, then stops. After all the plant-based remedies they've tried, she knows enough of his medical history to be aware of how things stand.

"I get that it's not the same," Bastian tells her after a moment, "but there's a place for you here, too. If you want it. That doesn't mean you're stuck here, though. If you'd be happier somewhere else . . ."

He makes himself look at her. "It's your decision, what you do from here on out. You should know, though, that if it were up to me, I'd want you to stay."

Her sadness is still front and center, but the surprised-grateful-affectionate knocks it off balance. "Well," she says, "I obviously have to stay after a speech like that. Not that I was planning on leaving." She elbows him gently. "Good to know you realize that I'm in charge."

"Of your own actions? Sure."

"Of everything, and you know it. But don't worry; I'll let Henry stay where he is for now. I can rule from the shadows."

"Shouldn't I be ruling from the shadows if I'm the consort?"

"Nope. You just get to sit there and look pretty."

They fall silent for a while, watching the leaves shift in the wind. Bastian's not convinced he's helped beyond giving her a chance to laugh at him, but he doesn't know what else he can do. This is why emotions are useless: You can't fix the bad ones, no matter how much you want to.

But sometimes, you're moronic enough to try. "What I was saying before. About Henry."

"Yes?"

"It's . . . I meant . . ."

"You should try using words. They can be helpful sometimes."

Only sometimes. "Henry is—he means a lot to me. There aren't really words for that."

"There's one good one."

"But that doesn't mean you're not, you know. Important, too."

She's laughing at him again, at least on the inside, but the amusement-relief-gratitude is much better than the dragging despondency, so he'll take it, even at his own expense.

"Thanks," she says. "That's—"

Bastian jerks his head up a split second before the sound of shouting reaches them (alarm-confusion-fear). Then he's on his feet and running out of the garden, peripherally aware that Laurel is right behind him.

At the edge of the compound property, just in front of the forest, a small group of officers is brandishing weapons at someone staggering out of the trees. The guy looks like he's been wandering around in there for weeks: His clothes are tattered and dirty, and there's a vacant look on his scratched-up face.

"Identify yourself immediately!" yells the security captain.

The man lifts his head and stares blankly at her, twigs standing out in sharp relief against the dark snarls of his hair. It's almost comical. Until he raises his hand and generates a flame in his palm.

Firestarter, Bastian thinks, tensing. How long has he been wandering around the outskirts of the compound? He should've pinged the hackers' algorithm long before he showed up here.

At the appearance of fire, the officers' fingers tighten around their weapons. The captain's anxiety-apprehension-focus spikes so much that it takes her a moment to realize Bastian is standing there. "Director Lucas, I—"

"Oh." Laurel is standing with her hands covering her mouth, her eyes impossibly wide. Bastian flinches at the enormous wave of emotions coming off of her, so many he can barely keep track, everything sublimated by one: shock.

She steps forward in a daze. The captain moves to intercept her, but Bastian shakes his head. He wants to stop her, too—everything in him is screaming that he needs to stop her—but she'd never listen, and any movement could spook this guy. Which isn't likely to end well, given how close he is to releasing that fire.

"Laurel?" Bastian says carefully, eyes on the firestarter.

"I know him."

At the sound of Laurel's voice, the man's expression shifts from vacant to confused. (Except something about it isn't right; it doesn't feel like—how is that even—?)

The fire in the man's hand goes out abruptly. "Laurel?" he says, his voice rough from disuse.

Laurel smiles tentatively at him. "Hello, James."

Chapter 4

BY THE TIME Henry gets to the Council HQ medical facility, he has a headache, the onset of severe exhaustion, and the misfortune of running into General Carter just outside of the restricted wing.

"Sir," Henry says, swallowing his alarm, "there was no need for you to—"

"I got the message not long after Officer Michaels broke up the meeting," Carter interrupts him. "If Dr. Westbrook is right, we don't have time to debate who has a need for what." Nodding briefly to the security guard at the desk, he taps his ID against the door and moves on through without waiting.

Henry grimaces, waves his own ID at the recorder, and follows.

"Messy business, this," the general says, shaking his head. "It was the right call, of course. But you realize how this would look to the committee if they knew, not to mention the rest of the Council."

"We've gathered useful information by studying him as he deteriorated. That's all they'll care about, right? Not that a murderer is dying, and there's nothing we can do about it." Henry's startled by the bitterness in his own voice.

Carter grunts. "John Doe isn't the only one. You're naive if you think they won't put two and two together."

"The compound has excellent security," Henry says, deciding now isn't the time to mention the issue Kent and Sybil brought up. "There's no reason anyone outside of this project would know about Bastian's health if he hasn't told them."

Henry didn't even mean to tell Carter. But it was clear from the start that he wasn't going to get access to what he needed if Carter didn't at least have an inkling of why Henry needed it. Add it to the list of things Bastian will be furious about.

"In case you didn't notice, your compound is being heavily scrutinized right now, Mortimer. Any records, top secret files included, will be open game soon enough. Particularly if they pertain to the most powerful assets in your facility."

Or that facility's commanding officer, Henry thinks.

They're taking precautions, of course. Kent and Sybil have been through all the compound's data on Henry, and nothing unusual showed up. There doesn't seem to be any official record of Henry's power anywhere—Dr. Wright and Major Valentine made sure not to leave any evidence where someone else might find it and make use of Henry before they could. Which is just as well, since it means the hackers don't know the truth, either. Though they're probably wondering why Henry's so paranoid about his personal data.

But Carter is right. If that liaison committee meeting was any indication, it's only a matter of time before everyone knows about Bastian. And Henry's power isn't something they can keep secret forever, either. If they haven't figured out some sort of damage control by the time the truth comes out . . .

Henry stops, turns to Carter, and opens his mouth before he's had time to think better of it. "And you'd just let them take whatever files they wanted. Even the ones pertaining this."

Rather than take him to task for his tone, Carter just raises his eyebrows. "I have my limits, Major."

"You outrank everyone on the Council, sir. Unless they brought in another general—"

"Don't think they wouldn't."

Henry squeezes his eyes shut for a moment. He knows the liaison committee, not to mention everyone else, is just waiting for him to screw up. And as screwups go, this one could be big. Even so, if he's being completely honest, he can't really bring himself to care. Not as much as he cares about getting the information they need. Because even if the tests keep saying the same thing, and even if Bastian's already given up, Henry can't. Not yet.

"We did our best to help John Doe," Henry says. "To understand why this is happening. It was better than throwing him in prison to rot."

"Which you did to the other two parties involved, if I recall correctly."

"I offered evidence, and so did Bastian. But the final decision was up to you and the rest of the Council."

"True. But this isn't what the Council agreed to for John Doe, is it?"

"It's what *you* agreed to, sir."

Carter smiles thinly. "Yes, I did. Are we going to see the bastard or what?"

There are several more security checkpoints before the observation room. At first, Henry was concerned about having his ID on record for so many visits when he had no official reason to be visiting the medical facility. Carter came up with the multi-compound research project as a cover, and by now, both of them are common faces in this area.

Only the research project isn't really a cover. Everything they're observing here will be used to help other assets. It might not be much, but being able to identify the symptoms of this kind of illness could be the first step in finding a cure.

Dr. Westbrook and her med techs look up when Henry and General Carter enter the observation room. The techs go back to work almost immediately, but the doctor sets her tablet down and comes over to greet them.

"How is he?" Carter asks.

Dr. Westbrook shakes her head. "The deterioration is getting worse. I apologize for the dire wording of the messages I sent, but I know you wanted to speak to him at least one more time, and this may be your last opportunity."

Henry swallows. "We appreciate it. Has he said anything?"

"He asked for you a few hours ago."

Definitely not creepy. "Anything else?"

"Some mumbling in his sleep. Nothing coherent." Westbrook looks over at the two-way mirror. "He's awake now, if either of you would like to go in."

"I'll review the recordings out here," Carter says a bit too quickly. Though the general is usually the most imposing person in the room, he's never seemed particularly comfortable around assets. Henry is always the one who speaks directly to John Doe.

Probably just as well. If John Doe somehow overcame all the meds in his system and tried to convince someone they felt like killing themselves, it would be useful to have a negator close by. Even if it's a negator no one knows about.

Henry leaves his gun with one of the techs and checks to make sure his negation field is as low as possible. Then he pushes open the door to John Doe's room.

It looks like any other med bay room, with the exception of the mirror for observation. Otherwise, it's comfortable, if plain. The walls sport generic pictures of ugly flowers and pastoral scenes meant to convey the warmness of soothing tones rather than lifelike objects. There are a few chairs, the bed, and the surprisingly inconspicuous medical equipment keeping John Doe alive.

Barely.

(Bastian won't end up like this, they'll think of something, it doesn't matter what the tests say, there has to be something—)

"Hello, Captain," says a groggy voice. "Come to shoot me again?"

"I think they frown on using firearms this close to oxygen tanks," Henry says dryly. He's never bothered to correct John Doe on his new rank, which

John Doe either remembers or pretends to forget depending on his own unfathomable whims. "How are you feeling?"

"Great." John Doe's face is even more gaunt than Henry remembers, practically the same color as the pale sheets. His hair has mostly fallen out, but a few wisps still cling to his scalp at odd angles.

His grin, on the other hand, is the same as always. "*You're* not great, though. Are you, Captain?"

"I've been better." Henry grabs a nearby chair, pulls it over, and sits down next to the bed. "Any chance you want to help with that?"

"After you had me locked up in here? Probably not."

"Three squares a day, people waiting on you hand and foot, and *not* wasting away in prison like you deserve? I'd hardly call that locked up."

"I see a lock on the door, don't you?"

Henry manages to keep his voice level. "Did you really think there weren't going to be consequences for your actions?"

John Doe shrugs weakly. "I seem to recall you followed orders just like I did, and the only consequence for your actions was a promotion."

"I didn't kill people."

"No, you just collected them off the streets so Valentine and Wright could kill them with their neat little experiments. That's, what, indirect murder? Circumstantial murder? I'm sure there's a phrase for it, but my brain just isn't what it used to be . . ."

"About that." Henry takes a breath. "Dr. Westbrook might not have told you, but—"

"I'm dying. I noticed."

It's not that he says it with any particular emotion. No, what makes Henry recoil is that it sounds exactly the same as it did when Bastian said it. *I'm dying. I noticed. Stop trying to do something stupid about it.*

"We've tried everything we could think of," Henry says. "I'm sorry it's ended up like this, but you have a chance to—"

"To what? Do one good thing before I expire? Possibly the only good thing I've ever done?" John Doe's lips quirk upward. "Any particular good thing you're hoping for, Captain?"

Telling Carter about Bastian was necessary, if dangerous. Telling John Doe, on the other hand, was a catastrophically stupid act of desperation. Seeing his tight-lipped refusal to give them any information about what he might have learned while working for Valentine, Henry thought it might make a difference.

And it did. Just not the difference he was hoping for.

"Maybe you'd like a magical solution, so your own beloved empath doesn't end up lying in a bed, plugged into machines as he exhales his last breath?"

John Doe lowers his voice, like he's sharing a particularly delicious secret. "It hurts, you know. All the time. The headaches at first are nothing compared to—"

"Dr. Westbrook says you have days left, if that. I wish we could've done something for you, but we ran out of time. That doesn't mean you can't still do something for someone else, though. Think of it as a slap in the face for Major Valentine. She'd want everyone to die, wouldn't she? But you can save them."

"Them? Or him?"

Henry clenches his jaw, then meets John Doe's gaze. "This isn't just about you and Bastian. For all we know, any asset could be attacked by their own power at any time. If there's anything you can think of, any research in areas of the compound we might not know about or anything you might've overheard—"

"Oh, I overheard things." John Doe grins at the two-way mirror. "I don't think the general would like me telling you, though."

Henry reacts before he can stop himself. "The general?"

John Doe lifts one shaky arm and crooks a finger at him, beckoning him closer. Henry grimaces but scoots in a bit.

With surprising strength, John Doe grabs the front of Henry's shirt and pulls him down. "He knows," John Doe says, breath hot on Henry's face. "The Council knows, too. All the good secrets."

Henry holds out a hand toward the mirror to keep the med techs from calling in security. "What secrets?"

"The big ones. What caused us. What you are. What will save him."

"And what's that?"

John Doe gives a breathy laugh and pushes Henry away. "I'm glad we got to have these talks, Captain. It's been good to hear about how Bastian's getting on."

"If you don't tell me what you mean, you're letting her win," Henry says, trying to keep the panic out of his voice. "Major Valentine—"

"—is locked up somewhere, isn't she? So she can't win. I can't win, since I'm dying and all." He grins slowly. "But you and Bastian, you're going to lose more than any of us. Because you'll know there's something you could have done, but you won't know what. That's a better high than killing senators for sure."

He laughs, and it turns into a phlegmy cough. "Tell Bastian I hope it's slow. I hope he suffers. I hope he realizes he was never better than me, that we're both going to die from this—"

John Doe's eyes suddenly roll back into his head, and he starts convulsing. The monitors go wild.

Dr. Westbrook and her techs rush in, shoving Henry aside the moment he stands. The shrill beeping makes his head pound. He's backing himself out of the room and into the observation area before he realizes what he's doing.

"What did he say?" General Carter demands. "The audio cut out when you got too close."

Henry shakes his head, willing his heartbeat to slow down. "Nothing that makes any sense." Nothing he's willing to share, anyway.

It's only a few minutes before the activity in John Doe's room slows to a halt.

"We'll need to figure out what to do with him," Henry says, rubbing his eyes and feeling sick. "Is there protocol for something like this?"

"Most assets die in the line of duty, not in a top secret hospital bed," Carter murmurs as they watch a med tech turn off the monitor.

"You mean most assets die using their powers to help an organization that's spent generations trying to kill them."

Henry doesn't realize he's spoken out loud until he lifts his head up and sees General Carter raising his eyebrows. Henry backtracks quickly. "I meant—"

"I know what you meant." Carter actually looks a bit concerned, despite his habitually stony face. "You're tired, Major. Go home. I'll take care of this."

Henry glances back at the other room, where Dr. Westbrook is sighing and taking off her gloves. John Doe didn't ask for this, Henry thinks. What the compound did to him . . .

"Mortimer."

Henry blinks, then shakes his head. "Right. Sorry, sir."

He hasn't quite made it to the door when Carter's voice comes again. "There's still a lot we can learn from the data we collected here, but we need time to fully review it before we bring it to the rest of the Council, and they start grilling us about our methods. So I'm sure you understand why this entire initiative needs to stay top secret."

He means Henry shouldn't tell Bastian.

So far, General Carter's security concerns have dovetailed nicely with Henry's desire to avoid Bastian's wrath. But now . . . How can Henry possibly go on not telling him? Especially when there might not be much time left?

"Understood, sir," he says. Because there's really nothing else to say.

"Good. You can expect a call from me in a few days so we can debrief and discuss next steps."

"Yes, sir."

Henry takes one more look at the room. There's a dull ache in his chest as he watches one of the med techs pull the bed sheet up over John Doe's face. Henry doesn't feel sympathy for him, exactly—hard to feel bad for a guy who tried to kill you repeatedly. But it can't have been much of a life. His whole existence was based on doing Major Valentine's dirty work. And he had no memory of his past before that. Where can they even start trying to find next of kin?

"One more thing, Major."

"Sir?"

General Carter flicks a glance at Westbrook and her techs, who will be coming back into the observation room any moment. "You should know that

I intend to defend the Council's decisions regarding compound appointments for as long as seems appropriate, but no longer."

Henry frowns. "I don't—"

"Let me be clear." The general fixes him with a stern look. "I understand that the main impetus behind this particular project has been personal. Because I believe the research will also benefit the Compound Network, I've been happy to lend it my support. However, given what we've just witnessed, I want to be sure you and I are in agreement about the top priority here. I still think you and Director Lucas are the right people for the jobs the Council has assigned you, but if at any point either of you show signs of being unfit for duty, whether that's due to health issues or an inability to separate your personal and professional lives, I will have the Council reassess the leadership of your compound."

Donnigan's performance in the meeting must have gotten to him, then. Carter has never said much about Henry and Bastian's relationship beyond gruffly demanding they keep it confined to non-work hours. And he's been perfectly willing to let Henry make most of the calls about this thing with John Doe. But he's clearly noticed Henry's growing desperation, and after what just went down, he probably wants to cover his own ass. Henry can't really blame him. "I understand, sir."

"Good. Then get out of here."

It's an easy enough order to follow, since all Henry wants to do right now is get back to the compound and figure out how the hell to keep this from happening to Bastian.

Chapter 5

"WHAT DO YOU mean, you want to interrogate him?"

Laurel takes Bastian's ID out of his hand, taps it against the reader, and opens the door. Then she walks through without looking back at him, probably assuming he'll just follow her into the office. Which he does because it's *his* office.

"I didn't say 'interrogate,'" Bastian reminds her, snatching his ID back. "I said I want to ask him some questions. How did you get here so fast, anyway? The med bay just told me they were releasing him, and I hadn't called you yet."

"I'm very nice to med techs, so they keep me up to date on things. I think they want to stay on my good side until they can figure out why my tinctures work so well." Laurel frowns. "But you *were* going to call me, weren't you?"

Bastian's pretty sure every living green thing within a fifty-mile radius would immediately answer Laurel's request to strangle him if he said no—and anyway, he really *was* going to call her as soon as he got to his office—so he gives her the only appropriate answer: "Yes."

Laurel narrows her eyes at him, then turns away and starts pacing. "James has already been through so much. And yesterday, we just let the med techs take him—"

"That's what you're supposed to do with an injured person, Laurel: Let the med techs help them."

"*I* could help him! My plants are way smarter than the med bay tech."

"You're not exactly objective here. We need—"

"What's objective got to do with it? He's my friend, and I thought he was dead, and now he's not—"

"And we don't know how or why." Bastian pinches the bridge of his nose. "Henry said he saw the place in your compound where James lost control of his power, remember? We need to know how he could have survived that kind of explosion—and why he doesn't remember any of it."

"And we figure that out by locking him in a scary room and being horrible to him?"

"I told you, I only want to ask him some questions. Make sure he's not a danger to the other people here or to himself, now that the med techs have him patched up."

Laurel purses her lips. "Couldn't you just bring him in here like a not-horrible person?"

It's not an unreasonable request. But . . . "He's an unaccounted-for asset. The asset program committee will want a recording. We've got rooms already set up for that."

Said rooms are also better equipped to handle an asset on a rampage. Not that Bastian would care if someone destroyed his office. Or his ID. Or anything else that makes him feel like a stupid kid playing dress-up.

Henry should be doing this. He'd know what to say and how to be a proper, not-awful person like Laurel needs right now. But he's busy doing something he won't tell Bastian about. Again.

Maybe Laurel's right, and Bastian should just ask and not let Henry sneak out of the conversation like he usually does. But there never seems to be a good time to do it, and Bastian can't shake the idea that he doesn't want to know the answer anyway. Henry isn't the sort of person who keeps secrets, so if he thinks this one is worth keeping . . .

"Sure, we've got rooms," Laurel is saying. "Scary interrogation rooms. Which you wouldn't need to use unless you were interrogating someone. Like an interrogator." She gives him a very pointed look.

"I *was* an interrogator," Bastian says. "Now I'm the director of the asset program, and I'm supposed to deal with this kind of thing."

"Sure, *now* you take responsibility," Laurel mutters.

Bastian loses what little patience he still had. "What do you want from me? He's a firestarter. He *burned down your entire compound* and killed nearly everyone in it!"

"That wasn't his fault!"

"We need to be sure of that."

Laurel stares at him, her anger suddenly going cold. "You don't know him. James is my friend."

"Yeah. And he could also be a threat to everyone here, whether or not he intends to be."

"James is my *friend*," Laurel repeats. "The med techs say he's stable. So instead of treating him like a time bomb, I'm going to give him the benefit of the doubt. Like a friend would."

"Laurel—"

"Go ahead and ask him your questions. But I'm going to watch and break him out the minute you do anything horrible."

Bastian doesn't have a chance to ask her to define "horrible" before she's out the door.

***

Twenty minutes later, Bastian finds himself in a Level 2 interrogation room. Sitting across the table from him is a pale, malnourished man about Bastian's age who's covered in healing scrapes and who, so far as Bastian knows, should be very, very dead.

"So," James says, tapping his fingers on the table in a repetitive way that isn't annoying at all. "Laurel says you're the director of the asset program."

Someone found him a razor and tamed his hair, so he looks a bit tidier than he did yesterday. He's wearing a gray t-shirt and pants provided by the med techs from wherever they get clothing for random, not-dead assets who wander onto compound grounds. The clothes hang off of James's body in a way that implies he might've been fit at some point, but that point definitely isn't now.

"That's right," Bastian tells him.

"You're a very important guy, then. Shouldn't someone have cuffed me before I got an audience?" The ghost of a smile crosses James's face.

"We don't cuff assets here," Bastian says. *Not anymore*, he doesn't add.

James raises his eyebrows. "This *is* a compound, isn't it?"

"New management."

"It would have to be."

"You remember your compound, then?"

James hesitates, glancing at the two-way mirror. "Sort of. I remember Laurel. I remember there were others. I remember the experiments and a man in a lab coat. And then there was a lot of light, and I was burning up, and . . ."

He starts rubbing his right thumb and middle finger together, an involuntary gesture, like he's trying to ignite a flame. The trace amounts of serum still in his system from the med techs' examination should prevent him from being able to actually set anything on fire, though. He seems to realize what he's doing because his fingers still after a moment. His expression, which was steadily growing darker, flattens out into something that's almost a tired sadness.

And there's the real issue, the reason why Bastian insisted on an interrogation/questioning/whatever:

Despite his body language, and despite what he appears to be feeling, James doesn't have any emotions at all.

His body language says confused-wary-frustrated with an overlay of bravado. That all fits with Dr. Rowe's initial analysis: evidence of minor physical trauma due to wandering in the forest for an indeterminate amount of time. Accompanying dehydration. Unexplained but significant memory loss. Enough charm to have had several med techs fighting over who got to check his vitals, even though he's only been at the compound for a little over twenty-four hours.

Physically, things check out. Emotionally . . . not so much.

When Bastian first realized it yesterday, he spent a brief, stupid moment thinking Henry was around somewhere, negating at astronomical levels. But it's not that kind of nothing. It's a dull blankness, an empty hole where an emotion should be. Like someone very meticulously erased his capacity to feel anything.

Something must have happened in the forest. There's no asset on record who could do anything like this—none that Bastian knows of, anyway—but James could have run into a weird plant or bumped his head or . . .

Or it's not James at all. Because it could just as easily be the continued deterioration of Bastian's power. Why not lose his ability to function as an empath after months of headaches and nosebleeds, just to make things even more fun?

Except that can't be it, either, because Bastian has no trouble feeling the thundercloud of Laurel's protective-disapproving-disgusted coming from the observation room. Or the alert-careful-tense of the techs observing with her.

"Hey, do I get to ask a question?"

Bastian snaps his head up and finds James looking at him, smirk back in place.

"Sure," Bastian says.

"What's with the gloves?"

"Fashion statement."

"Really?"

"No. Tell me what else you remember."

It's just as well that Bastian doesn't need to wear an earpiece to get instructions like he did during Valentine's interrogations. If he had Laurel in his ear right now, she'd probably be regaling him with a few choice words. Maybe she's sharing those words with the unfortunate techs right now.

James shrugs and leans back in his chair. "I've told you everything I can. What, you think I'm holding out on you?"

Bastian should be feeling something from that, maybe defensive-wary-cocky, but . . . still nothing.

(He can practically hear Valentine in his head, the way her voice sounded coming through his comm during an interrogation—*We don't have all day, Sebastian; Stop stalling, Sebastian; I need more from you, Sebastian*—knowing that all the criminals he sat across from would never be punished if not for the compound, for him and what he can do, and he's screwed if he can't do this anymore because what else is he good for—?)

"Put your hands on the table."

James blinks. "What?"

"You heard me." Bastian takes off his gloves.

James glances at the two-way mirror again with something that's almost, but not quite, alarm. "You're obviously not the brawn, so if this is some prelude to bringing a guy in here to slam my head into a wall, you should know that that's probably not going to jog my memory."

"I'm not going to hurt you."

"You realize that's what people say before they hurt you, right?"

Bastian rolls his eyes, leans forward, and grabs James by the wrists.

If James were at full health, there would be no way Bastian could hold him—James is very right that Bastian is as far from brawny as it gets. For now, though, James is too weak to be able to pull out of Bastian's grip. At least not right away.

And not right away is all Bastian needs.

Still, it doesn't make much sense; just *miles of nothingness washing over him, darkness and nothing, but that can't be right because how can you feel absolutely nothing at all, no images to connect it with except the faint memory of blinding light and heat, a voice that should have been soothing but wasn't soothing at all, strug- gling against restraints—a bit of panic there, the first hint of an emotion he's felt, so he tries to* push *at it—*

—and slams into a wall.

Muffled voices on the other side of the door. Someone's yelling.

Not a real wall, Bastian thinks, dazed and unable to wrap his head around it. No bricks in someone's brain. But . . . metaphorical bricks? A shield? An asset's power? It's unlike anything he's ever felt during an interrogation.

His eyelids are almost too heavy to pull open, but he manages it, slowly. He's vaguely aware that his nose is bleeding profusely, dripping blood on the table. He stares dumbly at it for a moment until he realizes he's still holding James's wrists.

And James isn't moving.

(Like Snyder, eyes vacant after Bastian interrogated him, back when Bastian had no idea what he was doing to the people he questioned, when every time he used his power, there was a chance he'd completely destroy someone's mind, accidentally manipulating their emotions to the point where they just sat and stared like James is doing—)

Laurel slams open the door just as Bastian shudders and drops James's hands.

"What did you do?" she demands, hurrying over to James, who seems to be coming out of his stupor.

"I'm fine," James says, sounding a bit shaken (but not feeling it). He smiles reassuringly at Laurel (also not feeling that). "Not that I mind beautiful women rushing to my rescue."

Bastian makes the mistake of trying to snort, which doesn't improve the nose situation. He stands, wobbling a bit, and realizes he has no idea where to find anything to staunch the blood without calling the med techs. Laurel must have ordered them to stay put, or else they'd be in here whisking James away. And probably Bastian, too, if he doesn't stop bleeding all over everything.

"Here." Laurel hands him a small handkerchief, a stony look still on her face.

"Uh," Bastian says thickly. "I don't think that's going to do much—"

"Shut up and take it. The herbs I soaked it in will help."

Bastian's had enough experience with Laurel's remedies to know when to just do what she says, no matter how smug she gets about it. This time she barely reacts when he shoves the handkerchief against his nose, and the blood slows. It's dried since Laurel did whatever she did to it, but the overpowering herbal scent is still there.

"I told them you don't need to go to the med bay, since I know how much you hate it." Laurel gives him an appraising look. "Do I need to go back and tell them I was just kidding?"

"No," Bastian says around the handkerchief.

She frowns, then nods once. "Do you have any more questions for James?"

He's got plenty, but none he can ask. Not yet. "No."

"Good. I'm going to take him away now." She pauses, then adds in a lower voice, "Are you all right? I mean, I don't really care right now because I'm angry. But are you?"

Bastian doesn't know how to answer that. "Get him out of here."

Laurel helps James to his feet. Despite what he said, James seems to need the help. Or he's pretending he does. "Here I thought I was the one who was going to get beaten up," he says. "People are going to say your interrogation techniques suck if you let the prisoner win."

"You're not a prisoner," Laurel says.

"Oh, sorry. That wasn't an interrogation?"

Laurel gives Bastian a pointed look, then turns back to James. "Come on. I'll show you my garden."

Bastian lets them go, mostly because there's no good reason to stop them. Even if he really wants to.

Chapter 6

THE TROUBLE WITH men, Laurel thinks, is that they're idiots.

James gets a bit of a pass, since he's still recovering. Recovering twice over now: once from whatever happened to him in the forest and once from an extremely rude empath who should know better than to do things that hurt him as much as they hurt other people.

But she's only supposed to care about what Bastian did to James right now. (Never mind Bastian's pale face and shaking hands or how quickly he started to bleed—seriously, don't think about that; he's a jerk who did it to himself, it's not like he doesn't know what happens when he pushes too hard—)

At least James seems all right. He's showing nearly the correct amount of interest in Laurel's garden, exclaiming over how well the petunias and water lilies have grown even though it's not the right season. He gravitates toward the conifers, mostly. They were always his favorites. He said he liked the way the pine cones smelled when he burned them. Laurel is generally against burning trees—it's just as well she, Henry, and Bastian didn't have to make any fires when they were on the run last year—but she'll make an exception for pine cones now and then. Assuming she's already had a word with the seeds about getting off the pine-cone-shaped bus.

It's taken a bit of walking around for whatever Bastian did to James to wear off. Laurel knows it must have hit him hard because he didn't even try to smile, let alone smolder, at the pretty officer they passed on their way out.

His head appears to be in order now that they're sitting together near the pond. Other than the lost memories, of course. The scratches on his arms and face could still use some work, though.

Laurel sets down her messenger bag and takes out a salve. She gets a little more evidence that James is feeling better when he lets out a very energetic yelp as she applies some cream to a cut on his arm.

"What *is* that?" he demands.

"This," Laurel says sternly, "is an extremely potent mixture made from seventeen different plants that were very nice about contributing their oils and leaves so you can feel well enough to whine rather than appreciate their sacrifice."

"Does their sacrifice have to smell so weird?"

"Yes. Weird is the most important ingredient."

James frowns and starts to say something, but he gets distracted by the rapidly fading cut. He looks up at her with a smile—not the smarmy one he uses as part of the smolder campaign, but the smaller one Laurel's always liked but never got to see much. "I forgot how fast you work."

"Yes, well. I'm very amazing. I'm also very insulted that you forgot that."

James shifts his arm back and forth, watching the cut disappear, while Laurel dabs at another one on his cheek. "This is a relief, really," he says. "I was worried when you seemed fine with the med techs' work, but it turns out you were just as concerned about my looks as I am."

Laurel rolls her eyes and shoves the rest of the cream at him. "I couldn't be as concerned about your looks as you are if I tried."

"It's not just me," James says, sniffing at the bottle. "A lot of people are very concerned about my looks. Really, you're doing the world a favor by preserving them."

"I remember Esther and Natalie were very concerned about your looks. Didn't turn out so well for them, though."

"I don't know what you're talking about."

For half a second, she thinks he really doesn't. Then she sees the innocent expression on his face. "Your memory loss is very selective," she says, narrowing her eyes.

"I remember the important stuff. I remember Esther freezing the training room floor and laughing when the techs fell on their asses. I remember Xavier holding midnight poker games in his room."

He turns to her with a vaguely sad expression that doesn't quite fit his face. "I remember you sneaking plants into the compound against regulations and nearly breaking some officer's face when he took them out again."

Laurel picks at the grass, which shifts slightly toward her fingers like a cat leaning into its owner's hand. "He was very rude," she says quietly.

(Don't think about how there was no sunlight for days when they didn't let her out or how the metal gurney felt against her skin just before they put her under for the experiments or how Alice's face scrunched up when she tried to use her power to help them remember because they had to remember, they had to write it down, it was the only way—)

"I also distinctly remember that I've always been a gentleman," James continues.

Laurel raises her eyebrows. "Did you ever tell Esther and Natalie that you were dating them both at once? Or did they just figure it out on their own and decide to ice you and dump you in that trash can?"

"How was I supposed to know they both wanted exclusive access?"

"You could've asked." Laurel knows she should probably still be insulted on their behalf, but mostly she was—and is— impressed that two assets managed to use their powers in tandem and accomplish their smackdown before the officers could stop them. "You have to admit, Natalie's telekinesis was pretty amazing. She'd been working on increasing her strength for weeks."

James scratches gently at a healing cut on his chin. "So really, I did them a favor."

Laurel makes a face. "Honestly, I think you're the most self-absorbed person I've ever met. Except for that maple over there."

"Laurel, trees aren't people."

"You're right. They're better than people."

They sit in silence for a while, and it's good. James was never one to stay still for long, but it feels natural now. Like his edges have been smoothed away. Like a tree that's spent years growing toward a particular patch of sky, and now that it's gotten into the right position, it can slow down a bit and enjoy the view. Maybe James is at a point where he can appreciate being calm and quiet and not feel like he has to—

"Why are you here?" James asks.

So much for that. "Well," Laurel says, "you'll have to ask someone who knows more about physics, or maybe philosophy, but—"

"You know what I mean."

She looks at the ripples on the pond and considers. "What else was I supposed to do? I stayed in the clearing for ages after . . . everything. And then I met Bastian, and he needed my help because he's stupid, and then there was everything with putting Major Valentine away, and then they started rebuilding this place, and how could I not help?"

"You could have gone anywhere. You didn't have to wait in the clearing, and you don't have to help these people now." James's face goes dark. "They're trying to save something that nearly killed us."

"It nearly killed them, too, you know," Laurel reminds him. "But they're still here, trying to make it work."

"Because they're idiots."

"Because they're brave. And they believe in something. Well. Henry believes in something, and Bastian believes in Henry."

James frowns. "Henry . . . that's Major Mortimer, right? The guy you said runs this place? The one who was Valentine's crony before he kicked her out so he could take over?"

"Rude. And inaccurate."

James waves a hand. "Fine, whatever, he's a hero. But you still need to seriously reconsider your choice of lost causes. You can't just wiggle your fingers and make something awful into something good."

"Wow, did you guys coordinate that?"

James blinks at her. "What?"

"You and Bastian. Being all doom and gloom about the compound. Lost causes, can't remake something awful into something good, blah blah blah." She pauses thoughtfully. "Maybe this is our cue to deeply consider how you're both more similar than you realize."

"I'm not—"

"Well, except that you think you're a much better person than you are, and Bastian thinks he's a much worse person than he is."

James narrows his eyes. "I think that's an insult. Was that an insult?"

"More like an observation by a very astute person who thinks you're both pretty moronic when you want to be."

"*That* was definitely an insult."

"You don't *have* to be moronic," Laurel points out. "You could be nice instead."

"What, like he was?" James picks up a twig and jabs it into the ground. "It's not like I *want* these big gaps in my memory, you know."

"Do you really not remember anything about how you got here?" She wants to follow that up with a question about what, if anything, he remembers about being dead—or becoming not-dead—but maybe that's not something to bring up when someone's already having a tough day.

"*No,*" James says, an edge in his voice. "I don't remember any of that. I can see flashes of things from earlier, from our compound, but they're messed up, too. I don't get it."

"The med techs think you were in the forest for a long time," Laurel says carefully. "For people who aren't good at speaking tree, that can be—"

"Do you remember everything?"

Laurel frowns. "What do you mean?"

"From back then. Before I . . . you know. Before."

(Vanessa sneaking them calligraphy of their names and looking embarrassed when Laurel told her how beautiful it was; Andrew and Xavier arguing about who really lost their card game, the cards scattering when Andrew got irritated enough to accidentally shift the air around them; Alice holding their hands, her eyes going blank, her voice monotone as she told them their memories, the ones they were glad to forget, the ones they had to remember now or else they would die without anyone ever knowing the truth—)

"Yes," Laurel says. "I remember everything."

"Well, I don't. And whatever your buddy did to me back there didn't help. What *did* he do, by the way? He's obviously an asset, but what kind?"

"Oh." Laurel hesitates, and then hesitates some more because she's not entirely sure why she's hesitating. "I thought you knew. But of course you don't. How could you?"

"Know what?"

"Bastian's an empath."

James drops the twig he was holding. "He's *the* empath. The one they spliced us with."

Laurel suddenly wishes they could go back to the part where James was being amusingly self-centered and not . . . whatever he is now. Now is an unfamiliar sharpness behind his eyes, a clenched jaw, a hunch to his shoulders like he's about to lash out at her. Now is bad.

"Well," Laurel says as calmly as she can, "there's only one empath in the world, as far as we know, so . . . yes. That empath. But it's not like he had a choice. They took his blood without asking, and—"

"And now he's rebuilding the program."

"He's building a *better* program. We all are."

"Not me." James gets to his feet.

Laurel flinches, then jumps up as well. "James—"

"I'm not waiting around for your friends to decide they liked it better when assets were kept in cages."

"They wouldn't do that!"

"No? How about interrogating assets without their consent?"

"That's—"

"After everything that's happened to us, how can you think—?"

Laurel swallows her nervousness and glares at him. "Because they're my friends, and I believe in them. And *you're* my friend, and I believe in you, too."

She pauses, then adds, "And I believe you're all being stupid about this. Instead of getting upset with each other, we should be working together to help the other assets and to get your memory back and to show the Compound Council that we can run this place better than they ever could, so they should just leave us alone and let me get on with orchestrating the most amazing garden that's ever been seen. You know. The important stuff."

James looks at her, his expression unreadable. "You don't orchestrate a garden."

"Maybe *you* don't."

"Are we talking about growing plants or plotting a revolution?"

"What's the difference?"

She's pretty sure he's on the verge of laughing at her as she sticks her nose in the air and brushes past him, but it's better than him being angry, so she's calling it a win.

Chapter 7

BASTIAN IS ON Level 7, trying to shake a persistent aide, when he turns a corner and sees Henry for the first time since the aborted committee meeting. Between the pounding of his headache and the blabbing of the guy who's been following him for six floors, the last thing Bastian needs is the punch to the gut of Henry's weariness-relief-longing when his eyes catch Bastian's.

"Sir," Fenmore says in his nasal voice, "the monthly budgets still need to be approved. If you'd just—" He sees Henry and starts. "Oh! Good evening, Major."

"Hello, Fenmore. Is the director giving you trouble?" His tone is serious, but he's doing a crap job of keeping the amusement off his face.

"Ah—no—that is—" Fenmore's flustered-nervous-embarrassed makes Bastian's head protest even more insistently.

"Send me the files, and I'll look at them in the morning," Bastian tells him.

Fenmore gathers his wits again. "I did that two weeks ago, Director, but you never—"

"Ask Irfan to take a preliminary look, then. She knows about budgets, right?"

"Yes, sir. That's why she wrote these."

Henry does a poor job of turning a laugh into a cough. Bastian valiantly resists the urge to kick him.

They turn another corner and reach the door to Henry and Bastian's living quarters. Without waiting for the dramatic conclusion of the discussion, Henry taps his ID card against the lock, opens the door, and goes in. Bastian catches the door before it can close, then turns back to the aide.

"Office hours are over, Fenmore. Flag it as important, and I'll look at it tomorrow."

Fenmore lets out a sigh (reluctance-concern-reconciled). "Yes, sir. I just wanted to remind you that materials and accommodations for the program are dependent on these budgets, and with the new influx of assets . . ."

"I understand. Really." Bastian pauses, then adds, "Is there a line item for a new air hockey table for the teen dorm?"

"Yes, sir. And another for the funding needed to repair the walls if any wind-movers get overzealous again."

Femore's beleaguered expression is understandable, Bastian supposes. But that's only because Bastian hasn't had time to properly explain that it was more of an accident than wanton destruction of property. Gabe just got a little too excited about how bad Bastian is at air hockey, and the table paid the price. "Good. I'll look at the report first thing tomorrow."

"Yes, sir," Fenmore says, looking dubious but resigned. He turns and goes back down the hallway.

"I don't think he was regarding me with the appropriate amount of respect," Bastian says, walking into the suite. "I realize I'm not an officer, but—"

Luckily, the sentence isn't worth finishing because he's definitely not going to get the chance. As soon as the door closes behind him, Henry pushes him against it and kisses him, hard. Bastian immediately forgets what he was going to say and pulls Henry closer, hands going under his jacket and clinging to his shirt.

And for a moment, it doesn't matter that Bastian utterly failed to keep it professional at the committee meeting, or that Laurel's irritated with him, or that Henry never says where he disappears to. Because all that matters right now is Henry's mouth on his and the calming nothing-nothing-nothing of Henry's negation field as he lets his guard down, and if Bastian can just ignore the extremely familiar voice in his head that reminds him he's not supposed to want this—

Henry pulls away, but only so he can rest his forehead against Bastian's. "Hi."

Bastian laughs and tries to catch his breath. "Hi, yourself." He touches Henry's cheek, then winces.

(Guilt-worry-stress through the fog of negation, just like always when Henry goes off for a day or two, but also a new desperation-fear-determination underneath it, and the *love* and *want* over everything, a jumble of emotions Bastian wants to lean into but also run the hell away from, and it wouldn't be so bad if he were wearing his gloves—wait, why isn't he—?)

"Headache?" Henry asks, frowning.

"It's fine." Bastian forces himself to slip around Henry and head for the bathroom.

Calling their quarters an officer's "suite" makes it sound much more luxurious than it is, but the term is correct, more or less. It has an open floor plan with a bedroom, a bathroom, and an unimpressive kitchenette/living area. Light on the appliances, but there's enough room for a small table and a decent couch. Henry says it's the sort of thing higher-ranking officers used to have. Suites are also used to put up compound visitors, probably to downplay the fact that the compound is mostly made up of harsh lighting and concrete.

In any case, Henry commandeered it as soon as they started reorganizing the compound living arrangements. Then he awkwardly asked Bastian to share it, which took Bastian a very long moment to process. Moving from a jail cell to an officer's suite was a bit of a jump, after all. He still has trouble remembering that he can go wherever he wants in the compound now, and he doesn't have to trick the security cameras in order to do it. Having an ID card like a normal person is better than being a secret weapon with only a code to his name, although it feels strange.

Of course, navigating hallways is one thing; navigating everything else is a bit more complicated.

The suite is definitely better than the cell block, in large part because of who he gets to share it with. But sharing means Henry knows how often Bastian takes painkillers and how many times he wakes up during the night. He knows when Bastian paces the suite, reading a report and then rereading it several times before he can even begin to understand what all the jargon means.

Being expected to give speeches and look at budgets and face down committees is bad enough. Having to pretend he has any idea how to do whatever it is he and Henry are doing on top of that is one thing too many.

It's also the only thing that matters.

(Except it can't be because even if it weren't inevitable that Bastian's going to mess this up, it's only a matter of time before their relationship erodes Henry's credibility, until Donnigan's pointed digs make everyone reconsider their tacit agreement to let it slide, so Bastian needs to stop awkwardly flirting in pools and letting himself gravitate toward Henry whenever he's in a five-mile radius and desperately missing him when he goes off on stupid, secret errands because Valentine was right, damn her, and—)

Bastian shakes his head, flinches against the pain, and rummages around in drawers for more painkillers.

"You've been taking a lot of those lately," Henry says from the doorway, watching as Bastian locates a bottle.

Bastian shrugs. "You can take up to 2,400 milligrams a day."

"And how much have you taken?"

"Not enough." He shakes out several pills and swallows them dry while trying to ignore the feeling of Henry's eyes on him.

"Bastian . . ."

"What, you've never gotten a headache?"

"Not like you do." Henry continues blocking the doorway for a moment, then sees the look on Bastian's face and steps aside. "Can you just—?"

"I said it's fine."

Bastian goes back out into the living area, scanning until he sees his gloves on a side table. He quickly puts them back on, trying to remember when he took them off in the first place.

"No gloves today?" Henry asks, his voice carefully neutral.

"I must've forgotten them here after—lunch." After the interrogation, more like. He vaguely recalls coming back to the suite to look for more painkillers. That doesn't explain how he could possibly have forgotten to put his gloves back on, though.

"You never forget," Henry says, echoing Bastian's confusion and politely sidestepping the part about Bastian coming back to the suite in the middle of the day, which he never does.

Bastian frowns. "I forgot today."

He takes off his shoes and flops down on the couch, mostly to distract himself from Henry's pregnant silence. No, not silence; hesitation.

This is where Bastian's supposed to know the right thing to say. How to explain that he's tired of secrets, tired of feeling like there's something he's missing, like there's something Henry needs that Bastian can't give him. (Although really, he's not supposed to care at all, not supposed to want—)

Henry blows out a breath. "You hungry?"

That's it, then. Moment passed. And Bastian's still too much of a coward to do anything about it. "Not if we're talking about something from the cafeteria."

Henry laughs, and Bastian tries not to lean into the sound. "Let's see if we can find anything around here, then."

He starts to go into the kitchen, but Bastian stops him. "Henry?"

"Yeah?"

Bastian can't do the stuff that matters, but he can do this, at least. "You didn't, um. Tell me about . . . uh . . . How was your day?"

Henry pauses, obviously confused. Then he gives Bastian a tired smile. "I spent far too long on an uncomfortable jet, came back to the work backlog from hell, and then got a very interesting report about an interrogation that took place while I was away."

Well, that backfired. Bastian grimaces. "We agreed not to talk about work after hours, right?" They'll have to talk about it at some point, of course. But maybe by then, Bastian's headache will have retreated into a dull roar rather than a sharp pain.

"Convenient."

"Pretty sure the no-shop-talk rule was your idea." Bastian gets up and heads for the kitchen. He opens the fridge and frowns at the nearly empty shelves. "Not promising. One of us should learn how to cook."

Henry, who's followed him, leans over his shoulder. He's standing too close—or maybe just close enough. "We'll figure it out."

Bastian decides not to think about whether he means dinner or something else.

Chapter 8

HENRY CAN TELL what sort of afternoon it's going to be when he enters the meeting room and sees that someone's given Senator Nunez a cup of coffee.

To be fair, Nunez's face always looks pinched and irritated. But the almost entirely full cup of acrid sludge on the table in front of her probably isn't helping.

The point of having a meeting room attached to Henry's office is so that official visitors can feel comfortable—more comfortable than Major Valentine ever made them feel, anyway, what with her penchant for keeping people standing in front of her desk until she was ready to deal with them.

Henry opted instead for a small room adjacent to his office to meet with guests. The room features a rectangular table in the center accompanied by a collection of chairs that probably won't kill your back if you perch on them just right. It's hardly in keeping with the sort of grandeur Senator Nunez is probably used to at City Hall, but it's better than nothing.

Keeping the lumpy couch in here was probably a bad idea, though, Henry thinks as he glances at it longingly. It was meant to give him the option of closing the door and taking a quick nap as needed, but that would only work if he ever had the time. And now he's not going to be able to think about anything else during this meeting.

Well. Anything except the details he finally dragged out of Bastian about the appearance of a firestarter who should be dead. Whose remains Henry found in the burned-out shell of Laurel's compound last year. Or at least, that's what they'd all thought.

But maybe it's better to think about that instead of the part where Henry still can't figure out how to tell Bastian about John Doe.

"Sorry to keep you waiting, Senator," Henry says, forcing himself back on task. "I didn't realize you were going to take another trip out here so soon."

"Neither did I."

Henry frowns. "Michaels said—"

"I'm here today on behalf of the liaison committee. Senator Donnigan suggested I convey the message, though why he thought *I* should be the one to—well. The others agreed, so here I am."

Henry sits down across from her, resisting the urge to ask if Donnigan is familiar with the concept of conveying information via email. "I see," he says, though he doesn't. "What's the message?"

Nunez glances at the clock on the wall above the door through which Henry entered. "It's who, actually. And since he's never late, I can only assume your security is holding him up. You should call—"

"No need."

Henry turns to see Michaels opening the meeting room door. A middle-aged, uniformed man is standing next to her, holding a thin white cane and wearing a pleasant smile that Henry finds extremely familiar, even though it's been years since he's seen it. "Increased security is understandable, given the new asset program participants coming in. Hello, Henry. Ah, excuse me. Major."

Henry realizes belatedly that he's gotten to his feet. "Major Alexis! What are you doing here?"

"This is your message, Major Mortimer," Nunez says. She's standing as well, though she doesn't seem particularly pleased about it. "Major Alexis has been assigned to this compound to . . . observe the implementation of the new asset program as a representative of the liaison committee."

"Senator Nunez enjoys the irony of a blind man being assigned to observe," Major Alexis says lightly.

Nunez pales. "I wouldn't—"

Alexis waves a hand, apparently amused at Nunez's discomfort. "Never mind, Senator. I'm sure Henry and I will do just fine. Officer Michaels, what's the best seat in the house?"

"To your left and a little forward, sir. Ten o'clock. May I help you?"

"Yes, thanks."

Michaels offers him an arm and gets him situated at the table kitty-corner to Henry's chair. Then she nods to Henry and leaves the room.

Once they're all seated, Nunez clears her throat. "Major Alexis was recommended by the Compound Council as an expert who can assist with getting operations off the ground, now that the asset program has officially been restarted. He'll be providing you with whatever support you need."

"Support, but not orders," Alexis clarifies. "I'm quite aware that you've been out of my training program for quite some time, Henry, and my days of being your commanding officer are more than a little over. I've made it clear to the Council—and they agree—that this compound is already being run by a competent leader who's shown extreme valor in protecting his charges and reporting the frankly alarming abuses this compound was perpetrating."

He smiles at Henry. "You hardly need a babysitter. I'm just here to help."

Hearing the approval in Major Alexis's voice takes Henry back to when he was a teenager training at Alexis's compound, desperately trying to live up to the inexplicable idea that an adult could give a damn about anything Henry did. While all compounds have basic training programs, Alexis's is more robust than most. Alexis has never served in the field himself, so far as Henry knows, but the caliber of his compound's training program has earned him great respect and more than a few accolades over the years. And his reputation for being able to navigate complex compound/city interactions without bloodshed, metaphorical or otherwise, is far more impressive than Major Valentine's ever was.

"I'll be making reports to the committee on your progress," Alexis admits, "but really, I'm here to be a resource for you—and to see if there are any changes being implemented here that can be applied to the rest of the Compound Network. We could all stand to throw out some archaic practices and serve our assets and officers better."

Henry finally manages to find his voice. "Not that I'm not grateful for your support, sir," he says carefully, "but don't you have your own facility to run?"

"That was my concern as well," Nunez says, her tone implying it was more than just a concern. "It also seems not entirely aboveboard to put a former mentor in this position. You'll forgive me, Major Alexis, if I point out that you'll hardly be an objective observer."

"I certainly won't," Alexis agrees. "But objectivity isn't really the point here. As you no doubt remember, the committee is more interested in the opportunity for collaboration than anything else. Regardless, we're both a bit beholden to the general's wishes, wouldn't you say, Senator?"

That gives Henry pause. If this was General Carter's idea, why didn't he mention it at Council HQ? Was he pressured into additional accountability by Donnigan and the rest of the committee? Or was he planning to send Major Alexis all along?

"In answer to your question, Henry, my compound has just as many committees as yours," Alexis says ruefully. "I think they'll manage without me for a while."

"A while" isn't much of a timeline. They'll definitely have to circle back to that.

Nunez is pressing her lips together like she has to physically keep herself from further commentary. "The official order with the details of this arrangement will have been sent to you by now, Major Mortimer," she says at last. "I trust you'll follow Major Alexis's guidance and keep the liaison committee informed."

"Of course. If you can wait a little, I'll get Major Alexis set up with a room, and then we can discuss that other—"

"I don't have anything else to discuss, thank you." Nunez gets to her feet. "Excuse me, gentlemen."

Henry watches her walk out of the room and wonders whom that lie was supposed to benefit.

"I'll have security release your things so we can get you settled," he tells Alexis. "Parts of the compound are still being inventoried and refurbished, but you'll have plenty of options."

"No need to go to any trouble," Alexis reassures him. "I'm guessing you have better things to do than wait on an old man."

"Don't be ridiculous, sir. It's a pleasure."

It is, actually. Henry's always liked Alexis's calm demeanor and wry sense of humor. Other officers trained by stomping and shouting, but Alexis mostly just asked the right questions at the right time. Henry's known him to be the sort of person you could go to in order to get advice without anything getting awkward.

No, it's not the advice that's going to be awkward. It's the part where Alexis almost certainly knows Henry's a negator.

It's *possible* he doesn't, Henry supposes. No official records means it probably wasn't common knowledge. But Major Alexis was there twenty years ago, standing on Henry's doorstep with Major Valentine and inviting him to the compound. If Valentine knew then, how could Alexis not know, too? And even if he didn't know at first, surely he would've looked into why Valentine would bother to personally track down a fourteen-year-old boy who wasn't even a registered potential.

Henry doesn't know anything for sure, and he can't risk asking. Not until he knows where they stand.

"We're the same rank now; you might consider calling me Gideon," Alexis says.

Henry blinks, then lets out a short laugh. "Sorry, it's just—I realized I never even considered that you'd have a first name. You know, when you're a kid, you just assume authority figures are all automatons until you see them in a grocery store . . ."

Major Alexis smiles. "I'm afraid you'll find I'm as human as anyone else."

"If that's true, you're probably exhausted from your trip. Let me make that call to security, and then you can tell me how I can convince you to say nice things about us in your reports."

"You could start by not giving me any of that coffee I smell." Alexis wrinkles his nose. "It's clear why Senator Nunez was in such a foul mood."

Henry laughs again. "Deal."

Twenty years ago

IT'S BETTER THAN hearing Mom and Dad shouting at each other all the time, Henry reminds himself as he sits on the floor of the empty classroom. This way, he's not just something they can leave behind while they go on another trip to try to "fix" things. Not anymore. Major Valentine and Major Alexis brought him here for a reason. He can help people.

If he survives training, that is.

Part of him still thinks it's a mistake, that they got the wrong person. There's nothing special about him, after all. No reason to think he'd be able to wrap his head around this stuff about people who can light a fire just by thinking about it or cause earthquakes by blinking or make stuff float by sneezing. Those things are just rumors, stupid stories made up by the kids at school. They're not real.

Except that apparently, they are.

"It's a lot to take in, isn't it?"

Henry jerks his head up and jumps to his feet before he's even gotten a good look at whoever is standing in the doorway. He didn't bother to turn on the lights when he sneaked in here, but even in the dimness, he recognizes the willowy build of the man in the doorway.

He is so screwed.

"Major! I was just—"

"Avoiding training? Already?"

Major Alexis guides himself by trailing his hand along the edges of the precisely placed desks as he walks over. "I don't blame you. Lieutenant Ryan's courses can be . . . uninspiring."

Henry stands rigidly and wonders if he's supposed to salute. Does it matter, since the major can't see it? But everyone saluted at orientation, so maybe he should anyway. Or maybe he's spent too long worrying about it, and now it's too late. Is there a time limit on saluting? Lieutenant Ryan definitely hasn't covered that yet.

Major Alexis stops in front of Henry and tips his head thoughtfully. "You know, when I was first brought here, I was incredibly homesick," he says. "I thought I'd made a horrible mistake, agreeing to come to the compound. I even considered asking to be let go."

"Really?" It would be safer to play it cool, pretend like it's no big deal that the head of the entire compound is talking to him. But the word just slips out, and now Henry can't take it back. Just like everything else he's gotten wrong. Getting beaten up in training, saying stupid things to his classmates, being the only person who didn't know what an asset is . . .

Major Alexis reaches out to the table behind him to position himself, then rests his lower back against it. "I was sure there was no way I was supposed to be here," he says. "Do you know what I mean?"

Henry swallows. "Yeah."

"Here's the thing, though." Alexis leans forward, like he's about to tell Henry a secret. "I wasn't taking into account what other people were thinking."

"I thought you weren't supposed to care about what other people think."

Major Alexis laughs. "Yes, I suppose that's true. But sometimes, when we're really unsure of ourselves, it helps to believe in the people who took a chance on us."

Henry looks at the floor and doesn't say anything.

"Major Valentine and I saw something in you, Henry. That's why we asked you to join us. That's why we thought you should come to my compound." Alexis smiles slightly. "Valentine and I argued a little about that, actually. We both wanted you. But we finally agreed that my compound is best suited to giving you the data you need to move your career forward. That said, when you're done here, I have it on good authority that there will be a place for you with Major Valentine. If you want it."

Henry blinks. "She wants to give me a job?"

"If you earn it, certainly. She and I both believe you have the capacity to excel at this work. We weren't lying when we stood on your doorstep and told you that."

Something in his face gives Henry the impression that this isn't just feel-good bullshit. Whatever doubts Henry has, Major Alexis doesn't seem to share them.

"Our belief in you isn't enough, though," the major continues. "You need to decide that this is what you really want. You need to decide that you're willing to put in the work and learn what you need to learn so you can protect the people you'll be in charge of. And you have to start thinking in terms of what will serve everyone, not just yourself. In order to be a successful officer, you'll need to set aside what you want for the greater good. What you want doesn't matter anymore."

Henry's never heard the major say so much all at once before. Major Alexis doesn't usually interact directly with officers in training—except for the speech he gave when the new class began. This is like seeing a very prominent and well-respected statue suddenly come to life.

It's probably the unexpectedness that makes Henry act like an idiot. Or maybe he just is an idiot. "What if I want a piece of cake or something? Does that matter?"

Major Alexis considers this solemnly. "Well," he says after a moment, "I happen to know that the cafeteria does a pretty good dark chocolate cake. But they only put it out for dinner, if they have it at all. That said, I do pull some weight around here. If someone were to go back to training and really apply themselves, I could probably make sure they got a piece tonight."

Like all grown-ups, he takes everything way too literally. Still. Not like Henry's stomach is going to let him pass up cake. "Done."

Major Alexis holds out a hand. "I always shake on deals."

It reminds Henry of shaking Major Valentine's hand on the doorstep, the little gesture that started everything. Something about it makes Henry hesitate, though he's not sure why. Then he mentally snaps himself out of it and shakes the major's hand.

"Good." Major Alexis nods. "Now, I think you have somewhere to be."

"Yes, sir."

Of course, Henry doesn't get back to class without being seen, and that causes a bit of hubbub and earns him a very stern word from Lieutenant Ryan, who demands to know where Henry went over break and why he's taken so long to get back. Henry gives him an honest, if pathetic explanation and then stands silently through the dressing down, ignoring the stares and giggles of his classmates.

Then he gets back to it. He's only got four years to make it through training, after all.

And he wants that cake.

Chapter 9

"TELL ME WHY I have to be here again?"

Laurel frowns at James, who's leaning back far enough in his chair that he should have tipped over already. "You're here," she says, "because we are very open about our policies, not to mention efficient in enacting them."

"Uh-huh. Is that why your committee is late? Efficiency?"

"Everyone is very busy this morning. I'm sure they'll be here in a minute—probably right around the time you fall over and crack your head open. There aren't any plants that can fix that, by the way."

James rolls his eyes but rights his chair. "I'm just saying, a *real* committee wouldn't talk about me while I'm in the room. You'd be meeting secretly in the dead of night, distressed about having to make tough choices about the future of someone as attractive as me, but ultimately resigned because at least it'll give you an excuse to be in my presence—"

"We could make you stand in the hall if you'd rather," says a dry voice as its owner steps through the meeting room door.

Granted, Laurel's spent the last few days too grumpy with him to have an unbiased opinion on the subject, but she thinks it's fair to say that Bastian looks awful. He's even paler than usual, and the huge shadows under his eyes imply that he hasn't slept well in months. Which is probably true, given that he's refused her sleeping tinctures since day one. If she hadn't promised not to make suggestions anymore . . . Well. Then she'd have to admit that she and the plants don't have any more suggestions to make.

"Tough call," James says as Bastian sits down at the head of the conference table. "I mean, the plotting in secret would be comforting and familiar, but Laurel might get upset if you just reinforce old stereotypes."

"Laurel might get upset if you two don't behave," Laurel says.

"Unrealistic expectations." James looks around. "Is this it? A committee needs more than two members, doesn't it?"

Bastian looks up a split second before the rest of the team comes in.

The med techs take their places at the table quickly, Dr. Rowe giving Laurel a quick nod in greeting.

Dr. Rowe is generally okay, as medical staff goes. She still doesn't understand the importance of talking to plants before you grind them down into medicines—honestly, why doesn't anyone get that it's only polite to ask permission before you demolish a living thing that's probably much smarter than you are?—but she usually listens to Laurel's suggestions, and she's much less scary than Dr. Wright. Also, she's quite good with assets who get nervous about coming in. Chloe told Laurel yesterday that she doesn't mind seeing Dr. Rowe for check-ups, which is saying a lot; Chloe usually goes nearly catatonic at the mere mention of the med bay.

Anyway, good people deserve a nod back, so Laurel gives her one.

Next comes Captain Smith and several other retrieval officers, who make sure to position themselves between the assets and the door. They're followed by Mr. Fenmore and Ms. Irfan, who has always impressed Laurel with how quickly she can take notes and how serious she seems to be all the time, especially when someone mentions money.

Henry comes in last, which means everyone who was sitting has to stand up again, and there's a lot of saluting. Laurel thinks this part is pretty silly, but officers seem to like saluting before meetings, so if it makes them happy, why not? Henry looks like he's enjoying it even less than normal, though. Probably got about as little sleep as Bastian did, and not for any good reason the two of them might have for losing sleep. Clearly, Bastian hasn't been reading the book Laurel gave him—or if he has, he's failed utterly at implementing its suggestions.

"Wow," James says, treating them all to a grin. "I'm flattered that this many people have gotten together to talk about me."

"We want to talk about budgets—or Irfan does, anyway," Bastian tells him. "But you come first."

"Lucky me."

"Before we get started, I'd like a word, if that's all right?" Henry's looking to Bastian. Although Henry is the highest-ranking officer in the room, the committee is still, strictly speaking, Bastian's.

Bastian waves a hand, so Henry continues. "I want to thank you all for taking care of things the last few days while I've been getting details worked out with Major Alexis. He'll want to meet with each of you about your work with the asset program, so please be prepared to make yourselves available."

He gives James a small smile. "I'm sorry I haven't properly welcomed you to the compound yet, James. Are you settling in all right?"

"Oh, sure," James says, sending Bastian a less-than-polite glance. "Just like home."

"And where did you say that was again?" Captain Smith asks.

Henry frowns at her, then looks back at James. "We may have some questions for you today, but this isn't—"

"An interrogation?" James supplies helpfully.

"We wanted to give you the courtesy of hearing us talk about what we're going to do with you," Bastian says. "Dr. Rowe and her team have reviewed your tests and cleared you medically, for the time being. Based on the recording we took"—he doesn't mention what he did while that recording was being taken, Laurel notes—"there's no need to hold you as a security risk. So that means—"

"We need to focus on helping him get his memory back," Laurel says.

"I agree," Captain Smith says, to Laurel's surprise. "We have no idea how this asset even ended up here. And we have documentation suggesting he destroyed an entire compound. Frankly, I question whether the director's assessment of the security risk here is accurate. If the asset really has no memory—"

"'The asset' has a name," Laurel reminds her. "And what do you mean, *if* he really has no memory?" She decides not to get into the part where Captain Smith likes to find lots of reasons why assets shouldn't be trusted. It's a wonder Henry didn't spend all his time demoting her back when he was her captain.

"We do have resources here that might help with memory reacquisition," Dr. Rowe says. "Given the number of assets who were involved in memory-related experiments under Dr. Wright's tenure, we've made it one of our top priorities. I can't say we have any methods with a guaranteed outcome attached to them, given how new the science is, but if James would like to—"

"James would *not* like to," James tells them, his smile gone cold. "I'm very done with experiments, thanks."

"Do I need to requisition a gavel or a megaphone or something?" Bastian says irritably. "I wasn't finished."

He waits until everyone's eyes are back on him before continuing. "We've cleared James according to compound rules, so he's free to go. But that doesn't mean I think he should."

"Does that mean it's chains and lockup after all?" James grins at Captain Smith. "You wanna cuff me, Captain?"

Laurel elbows him in the side, but Bastian's still talking. "If you ask any other compound in the Network, they'll tell you they're in complete cooperation with their neighboring city governments, and there are never any incidents. Leaving aside whether or not that's bullshit—and it almost certainly is—that's not the case here. After everything Valentine pulled, the city isn't going to welcome you with open arms if they find out you're a firestarter, whether or not Dr. Rowe's signed off on you."

"Aw, are you worried about me?"

Bastian skips it. "I can think of two options here. One: James leaves the compound with the understanding that he'll be expected to come back for regular check-ins with our medical team. Then we'll be able to back him up with evidence if someone claims he's causing trouble in the city."

"Director," Smith says, "for security reasons, that's not—"

"Or two: James stays at the compound until we're able to get his memory back, and Laurel takes full responsibility for him."

Oh. And here Laurel thought this was going to be difficult.

"The assistant director has history with the asset," Smith protests. "You can't—"

"Done," Laurel says.

Even James seems startled by that. "What, really?"

"Yes." Laurel locks gazes with Bastian. "I take full responsibility. Can we move on to the money stuff now? I'm meeting with some new assets in an hour, and I need time to remind the snapdragons that it's rude to bite people."

"What if I don't like either of these options?" James asks. "Would that mean we're back to the locking up thing?"

"You seem awfully interested in being locked up," Captain Smith says, smiling in a weird way that looks nothing like a smile. "I'm sure we can arrange that."

"I'm open to discussing other possibilities," Bastian says. "I'm *not* open to squabbling. We've all got too much to do."

"James does appear to be in good health at the moment," Dr. Rowe says slowly. "But we haven't been able to determine what caused the memory loss or what side effects, if any, might be associated with it. I'm not sure I can recommend the first option in good conscience."

"We drafted bylaws when we started this thing," Bastian reminds her. "If an asset doesn't want to stay here, they can go, unless they pose an immediate threat."

"Maybe it's time to draft *new* bylaws," Captain Smith says. "Ones that will actually keep everyone safe."

James snorts. "Safe how? By holding assets in the jail block indefinitely?"

"I'm not saying it was handled the right way before, but you can't deny that with the most dangerous assets under observation here at the compound, we didn't have to worry about the potential security issues we have now."

"Oh? What about the undocumented serial killer who was wandering around in the forest last year?" Laurel demands. "Or the officers in this compound who were plotting things and hurting people?"

Captain Smith frowns. "If we'd known—"

"But you didn't, which is my point. Safety isn't just about what an asset can do; it's about what *anyone* can do. You can't just go around blaming assets for everything." She pauses to consider. "Well, I suppose you *can*. But that would be stupid."

"It's all right, Laurel." James grins at the captain. "I'm flattered to be considered a security issue."

Captain Smith makes a face. "That's not something to be flattered by."

"Isn't it? Lots of people like dangerous men, so I just thought—"

"Never mind," Bastian says, rolling his eyes. "James, it sounds like Laurel's willing to take responsibility for you if you want to stay here. Otherwise, you're free to go under the previously stated conditions. Unless anyone has other ideas?" When no one speaks up, he adds, "And for the record, you'd be lucky to end up on Level 15 with Prison Officer Templeton. Although she deserves better than to have to put up with you."

Henry clears his throat. "Maybe we should take a quick break? Give James some time to consider what he'd like to do?"

"Five whole minutes to decide my future? Great, thanks."

"You can consider your future while we consider the budget. Let us know after the meeting." Bastian sighs. "But Henry's right; let's take five first. Laurel, Dr. Rowe, I need to talk to you for a minute."

The others file out into the hall, Captain Smith giving James a glare when he holds open the door for her. Which isn't really fair, since he's just being polite. Sort of. Laurel feels like she should give him some sort of warning, but she can't think of anything beyond "don't be you" and "she has a gun," so she skips it and goes over to where Bastian and Henry are sitting.

"We can't keep him here against his will," Bastian is saying. "Not unless we want to look like total hypocrites."

"Also because he hasn't done anything wrong," Laurel reminds him, crossing her arms over her chest.

"Sure. Except for the part where he burned down your entire compound, which you seem to keep forgetting."

"That wasn't—"

"—his fault. I know. Dr. Rowe's tests agree with you." Bastian turns to the doctor. "But his power is stable now? You're sure?"

Dr. Rowe shrugs apologetically. "I sent you my report, Director. As far as my staff and I have been able to determine, his power is under control. I'd feel more comfortable if we could do additional tests over a longer period of time, but the few days we've had to work with him indicate that there's no immediate threat."

"Then there isn't even a good reason to make him come back here for more tests, except to keep the liaison committee from freaking out, which is hardly his problem. But since we have to play nice . . ."

Bastian sighs and rubs his eyes. "There's something else you all need to know that came up during the questioning. I was hoping Dr. Rowe's tests would provide more context, but clearly that's not going to happen. This doesn't make a difference in terms of what we can do here, but it might affect James's treatment plan, if it comes to that."

Laurel tenses. "Did you hurt him? He didn't look hurt, exactly, but—"

"He doesn't have any emotions."

There's a brief silence. Then: "What?" Henry says on behalf of all of them.

"You heard me."

Of course, it makes no sense. James laughs and smiles and flirts and gets sad or angry. Laurel's seen it all over the past few days, and the med techs probably have, too. How could he not have emotions? Unless . . .

"Bastian," Laurel says carefully, "you're not exactly at your best lately. Maybe—"

"That's not it," Bastian snaps.

"Nothing unusual came up in James's tests," Dr. Rowe points out.

"And it was stupid of me to think it would. Not having emotions isn't exactly something you can test for."

"He's definitely been through some trauma," Henry says. "Maybe it's psychological."

"People don't just stop having emotions. Trauma affects them, sure. But it doesn't make them completely disappear." Bastian glances at Henry. "Someone told me once that you can't just shut them off, no matter how much you might want to."

"Maybe you *did* hurt him, then," Laurel says, her chest tightening. "Maybe he was fine, but you—"

"He was like this from the moment he stepped out of the forest, Laurel. Whatever happened to him in there did this."

And they don't know what that was, do they? Not even James knows. But instead of trying to help him figure it out, here they are whispering—okay, talking—in the corner of a conference room, acting like he's a danger they need to mitigate, when he's really just a confused, scared person who's been through something awful. And he has to be feeling *something* about that, no matter what Bastian says.

"We can certainly run some more tests," Dr. Rowe says dubiously. "And I'm sure our psychiatric staff would be happy to help, if James is willing . . ."

Bastian shakes his head. "He won't be. You saw how he reacted to the idea of working with the med techs on his memory."

"Maybe you should do another read," Henry suggests.

"No," Laurel says firmly. "No more reads."

Bastian gives her an inscrutable look, then sighs again. "Look, I just thought you all should know."

"You think it's a security issue?" Henry asks.

Laurel frowns. "Why are we acting like James is so much more of a threat than any other asset here? Or do we all get to be big threats now? Captain Smith will like that."

"Smith is just doing her job," Henry says. His tone is mild, but he sounds like he'd really appreciate it if Captain Smith would not do her job so much right now so he could take a nap.

"I told you the situation," Bastian says. "We don't have enough reason to hold him if he doesn't want to stay. But if he goes, we need to convince him to cooperate so we can make sure there aren't any issues."

"No convincing required."

Laurel turns to find James standing at her side. "Sorry to interrupt the cabal," he says, "but I've made up my mind. I'm going to stay. You all made me feel so welcome, after all."

Laurel grins at him. "I realize you're being sarcastic, but I'm glad you're staying anyway."

"That's because you always see the best in people. Particularly people who *are* the best people, like—"

"You. We get it." Bastian turns to Laurel. "Make sure he gets a guest ID, and keep an eye on him. He's your responsibility."

Laurel frowns. "I heard you before."

"Smith wasn't wrong. The fact that you two have history could cause problems."

"It won't."

"Even so, I think you should schedule regular check-ins with Dr. Rowe. James's memories could start coming back at any time, and he may need help."

"I'll be the judge of that," James says.

"No, you won't." Bastian gives Laurel a stern look. "Your call. But I'm definitely recommending it now rather than waiting until it's an issue later."

Laurel hesitates. She doesn't like the idea of forcing James to do anything—not after all the forcing he's already been through. But Bastian's right: People who need help aren't always great about getting it. Bastian would know.

"I think it's a good idea," Laurel says to James. "But we can talk about it some more if you're not sure."

James sighs. "Fine, I'll do it."

"One more thing." Henry waits until they're all looking at him. "I'm on board with all of this if the asset program committee agrees to the terms. But James, I want you to understand how important the security of this community is. You're welcome to be a part of it, and we'll do everything we can to help you. That said, if any of your actions threaten anyone else here, there will be consequences."

James meets his gaze solemnly, then nods. "Very good job being scary, Major. I'm going to start quaking any minute here."

"He means that very respectfully," Laurel says, her cheerfulness a bit pointed. "Right, James?"

"Actually—"

Bastian pushes back his chair and gets to his feet. "I'm going to grab some water before Irfan puts us to sleep. If you all could keep from inciting Smith to shoot you in the meantime, that'd be great."

The fact that he reaches into his shirt pocket and pulls out a bottle of pills as he turns away leaves nothing to the imagination regarding why he wants that water. Laurel notices Henry noticing, too, but neither of them say anything.

Chapter 10

BASTIAN PRETENDS NOT to be jealous when Henry ducks out of the asset program committee meeting early. It's not unusual; Henry frequently gets called away from meetings for one reason or another, and he always does his best to make it as minor a disruption as possible.

But when he leans over during Irfan's budget presentation to whisper an apology, the blip of curiosity-excitement-wariness catches Bastian's attention.

There isn't time to talk about it, though. Henry's gone before Bastian can safely divert his attention from the numbers he's struggling to keep up with.

Bastian manages to hold it together through the meeting and even through a bit of follow-up clarification from Irfan, whose curious-surprised-pleased in response to his questions gives him the brief illusion that he's not a complete idiot.

That illusion is shattered pretty quickly over the course of subsequent meetings and the ensuing paperwork back in Bastian's office. He gives the files on his tablet about ten minutes of valiant effort before the pain starts pounding its way back into his head, and all he can think about is hiding somewhere dark and quiet, preferably with at least eight feet of water in the deep end.

His vision is starting to blur by the time he makes it into the Level 6 pool, but he can't be bothered to care because the relief is almost instantaneous. The quiet becomes even more all-encompassing when he dips his head underwater, and the vague mishmash of emotions from outside of the pool fades away. All that's left is *the feeling of being in a dream that isn't quite a dream, opening his eyes to see the painted lane on the bottom of the pool merging with the shadows, everything squirming away from him in a not-quite-real way, and then chills on the backs of his arms, a sudden tingling, like someone is breathing down his neck—*

Bastian propels himself back up above the water, the sound echoing along with his startled gasp. He wipes his hair out of his eyes and turns in a circle, visually checking every corner while also reaching out with his power. The pool is empty, of course. Even the hallway outside is empty at the moment. No reason to be a paranoid idiot. Except . . .

(Except the last time he wasn't alone in his own head, it was because John Doe was there, projecting enough fear to cut through Bastian's shield, keeping him from being able to think straight or breathe himself back into reality, and there was nothing but the panic—)

Oh, come now. It's not that bad, is it?

Bastian starts, fumbling for the side of the pool to keep himself afloat.

(concerned-embarrassed-soothing) *Sorry! I didn't mean to alarm you. I was just so pleased that the connection works, I got ahead of myself. Are you all right?*

This isn't quite like what happened with John Doe, Bastian realizes. It's more like the empath link with Laurel, the one she created to communicate with him while he was stuck in the compound, and she was in the clearing.

Yes, it's a bit like that. She showed remarkable skill for someone whose power only came from being spliced with yours.

"How do you know that?"

(relieved-amused-harried) *If you're asking questions, you must be all right. But we both know that's not going to last.*

"Who are you?" Bastian demands. "How are you doing this?"

With some help, I admit. But that's not what matters right now. You know what I'm talking about, right? The disease is spreading. Just because you've been hiding from it doesn't mean it's not going to kill you.

Bastian can't stop the thought from rising to the surface: Maybe he should just let it.

(sympathy-worry-sadness) *No, you shouldn't. You're attached to the life you have now, and with good reason. People depend on you, and you depend on them. It's symbiotic. Remove yourself from the equation, and the system suffers. Which would be a waste, since there's no need for it.*

"You don't know anything about me," Bastian snaps, willing his heartbeat to calm down. "I—"

No need to get worked up. You know how dangerous that is, especially now.

"Oh, sorry. I'll try not to get upset about a stranger barging into my head, then."

(regret-frustration-awkwardness) *I wish I could explain this better, but there isn't time. Your compound security may notice the amount of power being used here, and I can't risk it. I wish there were another way to contact you.*

"Have you tried the phone?"

I've been waiting a long time to meet you. I know you don't believe it, but you're important. You deserve to be saved, and saving people is what I do.

"Is digging around in people's brains part of that?"

I only want to help. You'll need help, Bastian. The players are in motion, and it won't be clear who you can trust.

"But I can trust you, right? Because nothing says trust like someone who creates an empath link with no explanation and then tells you to watch your back."

A pause, then: *Goodbye for now. You'll know where to find me when the time comes.*

"Hey—" But of course it's too late.

The moment he feels the presence leave his mind, he closes his eyes and bolsters his shield with everything he's got. He'd thought it was holding just fine before, but now he takes several moments to pull it tighter around himself, pretending that it'll be enough to keep out someone who is clearly able to connect through it without any trouble.

When he opens his eyes again, the pool is quiet, the water lapping gently against his skin. Just the way it was before. The way it always is when he comes here to calm down.

Except it's different now. The quiet is deafening, the shadows have eyes, and at any moment, someone could barge into his head.

Bastian grimaces and decides he's done with the pool for the day.

*** *

After showering and leaving the pool area, Bastian allows himself a moment of relief. The halls are empty, and he seems to be the only one in his head. All that's left now is to go down a level and hopefully find Henry in their suite. If he's particularly lucky, maybe the headaches will hold off for the night, and . . .

He perks up at the emotional signature coming toward him until he realizes it's not alone. When Henry turns the corner, Bastian sees he's walking with a vaguely familiar middle-aged man in a major's uniform who's carrying a long white cane. They're both laughing as they walk. Bastian feels himself tense for no good reason.

Henry notices him and smiles, which reminds Bastian that they're going to have to have a very serious conversation about how Henry's not allowed to do that crinkle-around-the-eye thing when he smiles because it's extremely distracting.

"Bastian, I'm glad we caught you," Henry says. "I haven't had a chance to properly introduce—"

"Major Alexis," Bastian says, matching the face to one of the many personnel files he's had to review over the past six months. He's known the name for a lot longer than the face—Valentine mentioned him a few times—but they've never met.

Alexis's smile is nowhere near as appealing as Henry's, but it's pleasant enough. "It's Director Lucas now, isn't it?"

"That's what people keep telling me."

"I've been showing the major around," Henry says, "which is why I had to duck out of the committee meeting earlier. The hackers are setting him up with security clearance so he can review our work so far, but I'll need you to let him sit in on one or two of the asset program committee meetings as well."

"Why would I do that?"

"Possibly because your commanding officer asked you to?" Alexis suggests mildly. Bastian looks for the hidden layer of judgment—or even just sarcasm—but it all just feels like calm, patient politeness. Maybe a little amusement. Either Alexis's shield is almost as good as Valentine's, or he really is that innocuous.

"Major Alexis needs to review our work and report to the liaison committee, as we've discussed," Henry says in a tone that borders on warning. "That means we need to—"

"I'm not sure we should be helping a spy."

Alexis laughs. "I assure you, Director, I'm only here to do my job. Which is beneficial for you, believe it or not."

"I'm sure Bastian isn't about to make any judgments about the situation before he's had a chance to get a good read on it," Henry says. He sounds like he's just barely winning the battle against his irritated-embarrassed-frustrated.

"There's an idea." Alexis holds out his free hand toward Bastian. "Would you feel better if you read me, Director?"

It's a good play. Henry's got his negation firmly stowed right now, so reading through it wouldn't be a problem. It would be easy to take Alexis's hand and see if touch can get him a better handle on Alexis's intentions.

But if Bastian does a read, it'll make him look paranoid and unreasonable— just what Henry doesn't need. And with the compound already on shaky ground, having the director of the asset program grill a visiting dignitary isn't likely to go down well, either.

And then there's the look on Henry's face: annoyed but hopeful. Slightly hesitant. He wants to please Alexis, like a kid wants to please a grown-up they really admire. Because—oh. Right.

"You should come to our place for dinner," Bastian says.

Henry stares at him. "What?"

For a split second, Bastian wonders whether he's made a horrible misstep regarding pronouns. But it's not like it's a big secret that they live together. Alexis can't possibly have gone several days in the compound without hearing the gossip.

"You trained with Major Alexis, right?" Bastian says to Henry. "So you'll want to catch up outside of all the red tape involved with him not being a spy. I'm guessing you haven't had much time for that so far."

There's an awkward silence. Then Alexis retracts his hand and smiles broadly. "That's very generous of you, Director. But I'd hate to intrude."

"It's not an intrusion," Henry says quickly. He gives Bastian a skeptical look, then returns to Alexis. "We'd be happy to host, if you're up for it."

"Well, in that case . . . certainly."

Bastian nods. "Good. You two work out the details. Meanwhile, I'll get you the date and time of the next asset program committee meeting. But I warn you, it's just a short follow-up on budgets and supply allocation. Bring a pillow if you want to take a nap."

He starts to move off toward the stairs, but Henry murmurs something to Alexis and catches up. "What was that about?"

Bastian puts on his most innocent look. "You said to tell him about the next meeting."

"You know what I mean. Why dinner?"

Bastian sighs. "I don't trust him, so obviously, I don't want him anywhere near our home. But *someone* said I shouldn't jump to conclusions, and anyway, he might be more willing to open up about his intentions somewhere less public." He frowns. "What?"

Henry's smiling slightly, just enough for the damned crinkle-around-the-eye thing to start happening again. "You called it 'our home.'"

Bastian hates himself for flushing. So much for his handle on pronouns. "Yeah, well."

Henry takes pity on him and doesn't press it, although the amusement is clearly still there in his eyes. Jerk. "Do we even have any food?"

"I can figure something out with the cafeteria. Though that'll probably just put Alexis off ever eating with us again. Maybe we can disgust him enough to leave the compound alone."

"I'm not sure we want news of our substandard food service getting back to the liaison committee, but we'll have to deal with that fall out when it comes." Henry hesitates, then adds quietly, "Thank you."

"For what?"

"This thing with Major Alexis. I don't know what his being here means or how it's going to affect us, and you're probably right to be wary, but—"

"It matters to you. I don't want to mess up the stuff that matters."

Of course, he's already done that a thousand times over, but it's out of his mouth before he has time to consider just how stupid it sounds coming from him, of all people. He's not sure what to think of the wave of Henry's startled-fondness-love in response. Seems like an overreaction to Bastian indirectly apologizing for being an idiot, but it feels . . . good. Embarrassing, but good.

Bastian clears his throat. "If Alexis turns out to be a problem, though, I'll do more than just say I told you so."

"I think there are a few steps we can take before threatening a high-ranking officer who's only doing his job."

"Let's just get clear on what that job is."

"I don't suppose taking him at his word is good enough?"

"Nope." Bastian looks back at Alexis, who's standing right where Henry left him, tapping a finger thoughtfully against his cane.

"Go on, then," Henry tells Bastian, giving his arm a quick squeeze. "I'll see you at the suite when we're done here."

Bastian suddenly wants to refuse to leave Henry alone with Alexis. Which is stupid, particularly since Henry has a gun. So he just nods and continues on toward the stairs, mind lingering on the feel of Henry's warm hand on his sleeve.

Chapter 11

LAUREL KNOWS THIS is a dream, which is exceptionally annoying. She's already given herself a stern talking-to about how she's not going to have this dream anymore.

She's home again (don't call it that; it was just a squat and ugly thing in the middle of her forest that she kept safe and hidden for more than a year). She's standing at just the right place, flicking her fingers to ask the sod to break apart, revealing the stairs that lead down to the entrance. The dented door is staring at her, and the twenty small gravestones she set up nearby are almost completely covered with grass and dirt. Barely visible. Like this whole place will be once the forest takes it back.

She walks down the stairs, stopping in front of the door and resting her hand on the metal. It grows warm against her palm, getting warmer as she stands there. Dream logic (stupid logic) tells her that if she doesn't push it open now, she'll never be able to get back in.

She pushes, and it opens.

Inside, the compound is just as Laurel remembers it: dull gray corridors dimly lit with sickly yellow lights. She walks past officers and technicians going about their business, none of them looking at her. (Shouldn't they be worried about an asset wandering around without a security contingent?)

Esther and Natalie appear from around a corner, giggling to each other. They're followed by a security officer in a black coat who looks less like giggling himself, especially after Esther purses her lips, and he stumbles on a patch of ice that definitely wasn't there before.

Except . . . this isn't how it was. Esther would never have been allowed to use her power outside of a training room. And assets were always cuffed in the hallways.

Unless . . . was that the dream, and this is the reality? Why does she ask herself this every time, and why doesn't she know the answer?

Esther, Natalie, and their black coat disappear down a side hall without noticing her. Laurel keeps moving forward, past the closed doors of officers' quarters and training rooms where assets and staff are working together. Everyone she passes has a fuzzy, out-of-focus face, like they're more fragments of people than real people. But that's dumb; there were only twenty-one assets, including Laurel, and she remembers all of them, along with most of the staff. She can't have forgotten.

At the end of the hall, she comes to the door to the stairwell and pauses. If she stays here, she'll be able to hear people chatting and going about their business. She might even see more of her friends. Maybe she'll be able to stop and say hello. Everything will be like it (maybe) was.

Down the stairs . . . well. She knows what's down there.

She doesn't have to do this. Except of course she does, because dreams are like that. So she takes a deep breath and, just like always, opens the stairwell door.

In here, it's no longer the compound that's (maybe) from her memory. This is the burned-out stairwell from when she, Henry, and Bastian were here last year. The walls are scarred with scorch marks, and she has to navigate carefully around broken and uneven areas, her hand clinging to the railing even though she knows it'll fall apart if she holds too tightly. She can feel the uneven grains of the charred wood digging into her palms and sense the faint echoes of the voices these trees used to have.

The lower she goes, the hotter her face gets and the faster her heart beats. There's no need to panic in a dream, of course. There will be plenty of plants and sunlight when she wakes up. None of this is real.

(But the steel and stone and wood feel real—her imagination is just that amazing, apparently—and there's no green because there wasn't any in her compound, and she strains to hear something other than the dying wood, even something as small as a root left in the wall or the sod above, but no one's talking even though they should be talking, some plant is always talking somewhere, and if they aren't, that means she's really alone—)

At Level 4, she leaves the stairwell and follows the wall into the training room where she and Bastian found the opening to the secret passageway. It's not as fun this time without him, Laurel thinks a bit sadly before she remembers she's too busy being irritated with Bastian to miss him, even in a dream.

There's no need to figure out how to reach the button this time because the door is already open. She goes through, even as the urge to stop gets stronger. She knows what's in the room at the end. Not what—who. Vanessa, dead and lying on the floor, a note pinned under her body, begging whoever finds her to finish putting together enough evidence to lock away Dr. Wright and Major Valentine for what they did to her. To all of the assets here.

Only it's not Vanessa this time.

There's someone sitting on the gurney in the middle of the room, and when he turns, Laurel sees that it's James. He's smiling and holding a bit of fire in his right hand, making the room much brighter than it was in real life.

"Hello, Laurel," he says.

Laurel pauses in the doorway. "I'm supposed to ask what you're doing here. But that's silly, since this is my dream, and neither of us are really here. So why don't you just tell me what happens next?"

James laughs—his old laugh, the one from before things got bad, the one that lights up his eyes and makes it obvious why Esther and Natalie and who knows how many others were into him. "Shouldn't you be telling me?" he asks. "You did say it's your dream."

Laurel crosses her arms over her chest. "Dreams don't make sense. You should start an argument about something like what you think the acidity of the soil outside is, and then I can win because I can ask the plants growing in it, and then I can wake up."

"I don't think you want to wake up." James extinguishes his flame and jumps down from the gurney. With him out of the way, Laurel can see there's something on the floor a little beyond where he was sitting.

"Why wouldn't I want to wake up?" Laurel demands uneasily. Her skin feels prickly, like she walked through a patch of burrs and can't convince them to jump off until she's taken them where they want to go.

James's eyes are dancing. "Maybe you'd rather stay here than go back out there."

"And why would I want that?"

"Because if you remember in here, you can pretend it's just a dream. If you remember out there, you have to admit it's real."

"I don't know what—"

"Go look."

Well, now she obviously has to. Giving James the glare he deserves, Laurel brushes past him, walks over, and looks down.

There's a dead officer on the ground.

The smell of decay that Laurel remembers from the real version of this room hits then, forcing her to cover her nose and mouth with her sleeve.

The officer is on her stomach with her head turned sideways at an awkward angle. Her skin is greenish and mottled with weird bruises and bumps that make it impossible to identify her. She's not bleeding or anything, so . . . poison?

"She doesn't look too good, does she?" James is standing at her shoulder, looking where she's looking, clearly not concerned about dead people.

"What happened to her?" Laurel hears herself ask. Which is a stupid thing to ask when she doesn't really want to know the answer.

"You don't remember?"

Laurel considers explaining that of course she doesn't remember because she's never seen this officer before. Except she can't seem to drag her eyes away from the body.

In fact, she keeps squinting, trying to make out more details. But everything's going blurry and getting darker, so she leans forward and—

—wakes up lying on her bed, the tablet with the files she was reviewing slipping from her fingers and hitting the floor.

The aloe plant on her nightstand sits with its thick, waxy leaves exuding judgment.

"I know," Laurel grumbles. "You *did* warn me that those reports were going to put me to sleep. No need to be all smug about it."

The aloe doesn't have time to respond before there's a sudden pounding on the door. "Laurel?" calls a familiar voice.

Laurel grabs her dropped tablet, checks it for damage (none, thankfully), and sets it aside. The commotion at the door comes again, and she takes a quick look at the tablet's clock: after midnight. Not at all the time for door-pounding.

Shaking her head to clear it, she rolls out of bed and goes to the door, flinging it open. "Shush and get in here," she says, squinting against the hallway lights.

James, one hand raised to knock again, lets it drop and grins at her instead. "You sure you want to invite an older man into your room in the middle of the night? People might talk."

"Oh, all right." Laurel yawns and starts to close the door.

"Hey!"

"Coming in, then?"

They still haven't found him decent clothes, Laurel notices. His nearly shapeless shirt and pants, both dull gray, make him look like a ghost who could easily blend into the stone walls around him.

(A ghost like when she catches something out of the corner of her eye—an elaborate hairstyle that looks like Alice's; a deep laugh that sounds like Xavier's; a shadow that seems to shift on its own like Kabir's—and it's all so silly because of course you have to remember, but how does it help to see things that don't exist—?)

"You really shouldn't be out of your room," Laurel says, closing the door once he's through. "We agreed you weren't going to go wandering around the compound without supervision, remember? So Officer Smith doesn't get anxious?"

"Yeah, but rules are boring. Why aren't you on a residential floor, anyway? I had to flirt with three different officers just to find—shit!"

Laurel barely manages to get between him and a rhododendron before he can knock over the pot. "Careful!" she hisses, gently pushing it aside.

"Thanks for the warning." James looks around. "How many plants do you have in here?"

"The correct amount. Which is to say, as many as were willing to come inside with me."

"And what, you couldn't get a bigger suite for all your, uh, friends? Couldn't Lucas have pulled some strings to get you something better than this closet?"

Laurel steps around a pair of large strelitzia, ignoring their attempts to show off their sharp-edged, fluorescent blooms as she heads to the kitchenette. "First of all, closets are useful, so I'm taking that as a compliment. Second of all, Bastian's not in charge of housing. And third of all, if you're mean about my room, I'll send you back down to Level 8 without making you tea first."

"I'm just saying, the least they could do is find you bigger living quarters." James gingerly sidesteps several more pots and sits on one of her only two chairs—torture devices, really, and only worth their continued existence because they're the same brown as the tiny table. "Aren't you important enough for that?"

"I'm very important," Laurel says, rummaging around in a cupboard until she finds the sachet of tea she was looking for. The chamomile plant gave her the flowers as a thank-you for the small field Laurel set up to one side of the garden. Which she really ought to remember to tell Henry about before the officers who were using it as a training ground get upset. "And because I'm so important," she continues, "the housing staff naturally offered me any room I wanted."

"And you wanted this one?"

Laurel gets down two mugs, taking slightly longer than is necessary. "It turned out all right once we fixed it up a bit. And Level 1 is a lot closer to the outside than any other floor."

There's a long pause. "Oh," James says. "Right."

Laurel finishes making the tea in silence. Then she hands James a mug, takes hers, and sits down across from him.

"Aren't you going to ask me why I'm here?" James asks.

"Obviously, you were very lonely and decided you couldn't wait until morning to see your incredibly kind and patient and most important friend." Laurel frowns. "You realize you probably shouldn't have done that, right? Wandering around the compound at night on your own, I mean. The officers are pretty good these days about not shooting people, but if you don't have your ID on you—"

"I don't care about IDs," James snaps. Then, seeing her expression, he softens. "Anyway, you're not my most important friend. You're my *only* friend."

"That's because you haven't taken the opportunity to make new ones. Lots of people would be your friend if you'd give them a chance. The other fire-starters I introduced you to seem to like you pretty well, and the plants would probably like you pretty well, too, if you stopped trying to knock them over."

"Everyone likes me pretty well. Everyone with good taste, anyway. But what's the point of making friends? It's not like I'm going to stay here forever."

He leans back in the chair. "Although I wouldn't mind being friends with some of the black coats who've been glaring at me today. There's that one patrolling Level 8 who's got a really great pair of—"

"Yes, she does. But also, *rude.*"

His smirk fades, and he drops his gaze to his tea, which he's left on the table, barely touched. "Look, I know it's weird, me being here. It's like old times, except . . ."

"Except you don't remember old times," Laurel says quietly.

He runs his hands through his hair. "It's like . . . flashes. I remember one person, but only part of them. Like, I remember Vanessa had really good handwriting—but why do I know that? Did I see her write something? Why wouldn't she just type it? I don't even remember her power or what she looked like."

Laurel thinks of the shy way Vanessa laughed, like you had to startle the amusement out of her. The way her long, dark fingers curled around a pen, turning cheap plastic and ink into something beautiful just as quickly as she spoke to a hard drive. The way her decaying body looked, sprawled on the experimental room floor, her hands stilled forever.

"She was a cyberreader," Laurel hears herself say.

James throws up his hands. "See? How could I forget that?"

"We don't know what happened to you," Laurel reminds him. "Maybe all the stuff you've forgotten will come back if we just—"

"What, sit around and wait for my memory to jog itself? Hope that doctor has a stroke of genius? Maybe I can bide my time making some nice friends while the new management screws over the next generation of assets."

Laurel debates getting up, grabbing his tea, and dumping it over his head. "There's nothing wrong with nice friends," she says instead. "You just don't get it because I'm the only nice friend you remember having. And because I'm nice, I'm going to ignore the part where you just implied that Henry or Bastian or I would ever allow something as awful as what happened to us to happen to anyone else."

"You're acting like you have a choice. What if that's just how compounds are? What if there's nothing you can do to make it any different? What if—?"

"You think we haven't asked ourselves those things? That we're not *still* asking ourselves those things?" Laurel glares at him. "I know it's not perfect. It takes a long time to make things that were that bad into things that are even a tiny bit better. Longer to make them actually good. But we're trying. Have *you* done any trying lately?"

James frowns. "What do you mean?"

"I mean, what if you stopped complaining and tried to think about how you actually got here?"

James blinks, then gives her an innocent look. "I got here thanks to a deep-seated desire to see my favorite plantspeaker and have her make me tea."

"That's why you came to the compound? That's why you decided to not be dead? So you could have tea with me?" Oh. She didn't mean to bring up the not-dead thing. His fault for being annoying.

"Obviously not," he says, looking confused. "I—"

"No? Too bad. That would've been a really cool reason."

"Laurel—"

"If it wasn't about tea, then what was it?"

"I don't—"

"Remember, yeah. You said. But have you *tried?* Like, really tried?" She sets her mug down and waves a hand at him. "Go on. Try to remember."

She thinks he's going to keep protesting, but to her surprise, he succumbs to the calm of chamomile—or the eloquence of her request—or both. He blows out a breath and closes his eyes.

He looks like a little kid this way, she thinks. Like when she found him after training that one day, cowering in a corner away from everyone else. She'd only ever seen him flirting and being a smartass up till then, but there he was, begging her not to tell anyone how upset he got after the last round of tests. He never told her what happened, but she recognized the too-smooth redness of recently healed burns on his hands—hands that shook when he tried to hide them.

"I was in the experimentation room," James says slowly. "I knew something was wrong because the fire wasn't cooperating. It just kept getting bigger, and ..."

(Firestarters don't burn themselves, not once they've gained control of their power, and James was always in control until Laurel found him that day, and then she couldn't stop seeing it, the shadows like bruises under his eyes, the sallow tinge to his skin, the way he stopped meeting anyone's gaze—)

James swallows. "I think they—I was on the table, and then someone was yelling, and there was too much—" He shudders and falls silent.

(Laurel definitely doesn't think about how he looked in the interrogation room, slumped in his chair with Bastian clinging to his wrists, all the life sucked out of his eyes—)

James shakes himself. "I was on fire, and then ... I wasn't. There was someone there, and then there was a whole group of people, and we were supposed to go somewhere safe."

"Here?"

"I doubt it." James opens his eyes. "But it's all mixed up in my head. All I know is that we were trying to get somewhere. There was someone we had to meet."

"Hmm." An idea is taking form in her mind, just starting to put its leaves out, and nothing silly like the skeptical look on James's face is going to stop her from being brilliant. "You were trying to get somewhere, but you ended up here. So that means there has to be a path somewhere around here that goes wherever you were going."

"Laurel, there are hundreds of paths in the forest. Maybe thousands."

"Or more. But that's fine."

"How is that fine?"

"Because," Laurel says, smiling broadly, "I know exactly who to ask when you need help finding a path."

Chapter 12

HENRY SUPPOSES IT ought to be concerning to come back to the suite and find Bastian messing around in the kitchen with a large knife, but honestly, that's the least surprising thing he's had to deal with in the past week or so. Certainly less surprising than Bastian's suggestion that they do this in the first place.

"I don't care what the cafeteria told you; human fingers aren't an acceptable source of protein," Henry calls as he closes the suite door behind him.

Bastian looks up from massacring vegetables and frowns. "Didn't you forget something?"

"Major Alexis had some questions for the med techs about compound healthcare. He'll be by when he's done."

Henry comes into the kitchen area and surveys the assortment of plates: rubbery-looking chicken that probably smells better than it tastes; vegetables that must be from Laurel's garden, given that they appear to be the right colors and consistencies; and, to Henry's delight, a small chocolate cake. There's even a bottle of wine. Alcohol isn't available in the compound (at least, not through official channels), so Bastian must have made a special effort to get someone to bring it in from the city. Or to con someone out of it.

"I can't vouch for the cake," Bastian warns as he continues to haphazardly demolish carrots. "Or any of it, really."

Henry takes the knife from him to avoid further culinary disaster. Or blood loss. Or both. "Did you make sure to ask the cafeteria for the most edible stuff from today's menu?" he asks, setting aside the knife when it becomes clear, on closer inspection, that the carrots are beyond saving.

"This was the best they could do with only a few days' notice," Bastian says. "This is the best they can do in general, really, until you fire people and get us some competent cooks."

Henry gives the cake a foolish but hopeful look, then spies some unfamiliar utensils on the table. "I didn't realize we had a third set of silverware."

"We don't. I stole those from the cafeteria while they were getting the food ready."

Henry rolls his eyes and wonders if it's too early to open the wine. "You could've just asked."

"Do you know how many people in this place are eating right now? They barely wanted to part with the chicken. Probably had it lined up to poison someone else."

"They'll want a meeting after this, you know," Henry says, sighing as he grabs some dishes and puts them on the table. "I'll have to spend a whole day fielding questions about why the director of the asset program goes around stealing silverware."

"You're assuming they'd notice." Bastian pauses. "How was it, by the way?"

"How was what?" Henry's busy trying to arrange things in a way that won't make them look like two adults who utterly fail at everything related to entertaining.

"Your day."

Henry gives Bastian a sidelong glance. Asking about Henry's day has apparently become Bastian's thing, which is weird; it's the inane sort of question he'd normally hate.

No time to follow up on it, though, because there's a knock at the door. Henry goes over and opens it.

"Hello," Major Alexis says, smiling broadly. "Is that chicken I smell? Did you cook?"

"Ah, no." Henry scratches his head awkwardly. "The cafeteria did. But I'm sure they put special effort into this meal."

"The utensils are clean," Bastian calls. "That doesn't mean the food is edible."

Alexis laughs. "There's a similar problem with my compound's cafeteria. Perhaps the struggle is universal, Director."

"Bastian." To Henry's great surprise, Bastian comes over to the doorway. "Can I offer you an arm? The table's forward and a little to the left around the couch. But don't say I didn't warn you about the food."

With Bastian's help, Major Alexis gets situated at the table and sets his cane aside. Henry, still a bit bemused by the pleasantries, makes sure everything else is arranged. There's a little back-and-forth about drinks, but before long, they're all seated at the table like a proper dinner party, Bastian across from Alexis and Henry to Alexis's left.

"So," Bastian says, ignoring his food. "Did you find anything good to spy on today?"

Henry chokes on his wine. So much for Bastian's attempts at civility. "We don't usually talk shop at dinner—"

"It's fine." Alexis sets down his fork. "I understand your concern, Bastian. We're all in a strange position here. But I meant it when I told you both that my work will be beneficial to you and to the program."

"Sure, but you weren't very specific. So you can see how that answer might not be believable no matter how many times you use it."

"Bastian," Henry warns.

"I see you haven't given up your penchant for interrogation," Major Alexis says, his tone light and amused. "Let me put your doubts to rest, then. According to the liaison committee, my job here is to collect data they might not otherwise get and report back so they can feel more comfortable about how decisions are being made in this compound. But that's not the only reason I'm here. It's not even the most important one."

Bastian raises his eyebrows. "There's something more important than getting in good with the Compound Council and the liaison committee?"

"I think so. Believe it or not, my real goal here is to support this program in whatever way I can."

"And how would you do that?"

As much as Henry wants to remind everyone present that there's a difference between an interrogation and a dinner party, he can't help but think Bastian might be able to get something from Major Alexis about his motives that Henry hasn't been able to prise out. And even if the major walks away at the end of the night without having revealed anything, just being around him could allow Bastian to get an empathic read strong enough to give them some more data—so long as Henry can keep his negation field low enough. They probably should've had Michaels bring the machine so they could record after Alexis leaves. If Henry hadn't been so busy earlier hounding Kent for more information on that not-quite-security-breach—

Henry frowns inwardly. Wait, what is he thinking? The major has only ever been thoughtful and professional, the sort of adult Henry desperately needed during training. Yes, there should be some boundaries while he's here, given his position with the committee and his somewhat ambiguous role. But that doesn't mean they need to be immediately suspicious of everything he does, especially since he's only asked polite questions, gone on tours, and taken notes since he's been here. Hardly criminal offenses.

Then again, Henry spent years believing Major Valentine had his best interests at heart, that her guidance meant something, when all she'd wanted was his power—and even that became much less of a priority once he stopped being blissfully ignorant about everything. So maybe Henry isn't the best person to judge.

"Well," Major Alexis is saying, "my reports could be very helpful to you, for a start. In fact, I just sent the first one to the committee earlier this evening. Shall I tell you what I wrote?"

"That's not necessary," Henry says quickly. He'll likely find his own copy of the report waiting in his office tomorrow, and anyhow, pestering Alexis for details at dinner doesn't seem quite fair.

Alexis smiles, and Henry can see the weight of his pity in the curve of his mouth. "While you may be the trusting kind, Henry, it's clear Bastian isn't. So let's cut to the chase. I told the committee that I'm pleased with the progress this compound has made so far. Despite the odds, restructuring efforts seem to be going well. New staff and officers are being adequately trained, and while the introduction to the asset program was a bit . . . unorthodox, it doesn't appear to have done any harm."

Bastian grimaces but says nothing.

"Of course," Major Alexis continues, "there are elements of the situation here that I haven't had a chance to properly review yet. For example, I believe an unregistered asset appeared on the grounds not long before I got here. I'll need to be brought up to date on how you're handling that situation—though I'm sure you've followed protocol to the letter."

There's a pregnant pause, during which Bastian narrows his eyes at Alexis but stays silent. Henry considers stepping in, but what they share with the major is really Bastian's decision at this point. At least until official requests are made.

Unfazed, Alexis goes on. "I'll also be expected to report to the Council on your progress with the compound inventory. I understand it's still taking place?"

"Yes," Henry says, glad there's something simple in this conversation that he can navigate. "Major Valentine wasn't, er, focused on facility maintenance, so we've been inventorying every floor to get an accurate assessment of the available space and supplies. We've finished most of the areas, but there are still a few of the lower levels that need to be cleaned out and refurbished."

"Would Level 49 be one of those levels?"

Henry tenses, and Bastian asks a little too sharply, "Why?"

"Dr. Wright's records are spotty at best," says Major Alexis, "likely because he destroyed as many as he could before they were confiscated by the Council last year. But based on what we have, it appears that a significant number of experiments took place on that level. You didn't find anything relevant during your inventory?"

"Plenty of bad things happened on plenty of levels in this compound," Bastian says. "There's no reason to think Level 49 is different than any other level."

Alexis shrugs. "True enough. But according to the compound schematics Henry shared with me, Level 49 does seem to have more experimentation rooms than any other level. And there's far less data available about it." He pauses, then adds, "The records we do have indicate that you spent quite a bit of time there yourself."

"Maybe that's enough shop talk," Henry says quickly. "Major, can I get you something else to drink?"

"This must be difficult for you, Bastian," Alexis continues, his voice softening. "To live and work in a place where—"

Bastian pushes back his chair and stands. "Excuse me."

Henry starts to get up as well, but Bastian's glare is enough to keep him in his seat.

"I hope I didn't offend him," Alexis says after Bastian leaves the dining area, and they hear the bathroom door close. "I realize it's a touchy subject, but we can't just ignore it if we want to convince the committee of our intent to provide them with any and all relevant information. A level of professionalism—"

"You know he almost died there, right?" Henry snaps. "Any helpful tips on how to be professional about that?"

In the awkward pause that follows, Henry realizes what he said and is immediately mortified. "Sorry, sir. It's just—"

Major Alexis shakes his head. "I understand. I shouldn't have pushed. But you must realize that the committee won't treat this lightly. The fact that both of you have such difficult pasts with this place makes it hard for the committee to see how you could possibly run it effectively."

"Maybe we can't," Henry says in a low voice.

"The Council disagrees, and I do, too. If anything, I think your pasts make you uniquely qualified to do it. But we won't be able to successfully turn this compound around if we can't all communicate openly and honestly."

Henry doesn't have time to answer before Bastian comes back to the table and sits down, his face carefully blank. He's barely had time to pick up his fork before Alexis says cheerfully, "Did you know I was with Major Valentine when she recruited Henry?"

Bastian pauses his fork's descent into chicken territory. "No," he says after a moment.

"He was barely fourteen, courteous and incredibly wary. Made us show him our IDs and refused to let us into the house." Alexis chuckles.

"To be fair, I'd already taken a beating that day," Henry says, vacillating between being glad the previous conversation has been dropped and worrying about where this one will lead. "I wasn't about to make it easy for me to get another one."

Bastian frowns. "Beating?"

"There was a dog on the school grounds. One of my classmates was hurting it, and none of the teachers were doing anything."

"So Henry rushed to the dog's rescue and got a black eye from the other boy for his trouble." Alexis eats a bite of chicken. "Even back then, it was a bit of a problem for him—wanting to save everyone and everything."

Henry shrugs awkwardly. "I just did what anyone would've done."

"That's what you used to say when you diffused tense situations during training, too. But obviously not everyone would have done it because no one else did." Major Alexis takes a sip of his wine. "What do you think, Bastian? Does he still have a hero complex?"

"Not my area," Bastian says. "Ask a psychologist."

"I'm not looking for an official diagnosis. I just thought you might have some insight, given your history together. I suspect Henry's saved you a time or two, hasn't he?"

Henry assumes Bastian will make some sort of rude comment—or not answer at all. Instead, he glances at Henry, then away, before saying very quietly, "Yes."

Alexis nods. "He has a way of doing that. I was always disappointed Valentine didn't see it because it's a huge part of what makes him such a good officer. He's willing to do whatever needs to be done to protect people, no matter what the cost."

It's meant to be a compliment, Henry supposes, but something about the way he says it makes it sound like a joke. "Maybe we can move on to a different embarrassing story now?"

"Oh, well." Alexis beams. "I could talk about the time I found you and that girl—Farrah? Fiona?—in a very secluded part of the grounds during what was supposed to be a training period, and—"

"Would anyone like dessert?" Henry asks quickly.

They stick to lighter topics for the rest of the evening, to Henry's relief. Bastian exerts the smallest possible effort to support the conversation, but at least he isn't openly hostile.

"I apologize for the awkwardness earlier," Alexis says later when Henry leads him to the door. "But I hope we'll be able to do this again sometime soon. And I hope you know how proud I am of you and all you've accomplished here."

"Thank you, sir," Henry says, trying unsuccessfully to quash the little bubble of pride at the major's words. "And thank you for coming tonight. We'd love to have you again."

He puts a bit of emphasis on "we" to make up for the fact that Bastian is standing in the kitchen, leaning against the counter with his arms crossed, watching them. Not quite belligerent, but also obviously not as inclined toward pleasantries as he was at the beginning of the evening.

"Gideon," says Major Alexis.

"Gideon, sorry. Old habits die hard." Or not at all; Henry can't see himself ever getting used to referring to Major Alexis by his first name.

Alexis smiles, then calls toward the kitchen, "Good night, Bastian. It was good to have a chance to get to know you better."

"Good night."

Alexis's smile becomes wry as he turns back to Henry—like he's aware of what a pill Bastian's being and how long-suffering Henry is. He's not wrong, exactly, but something about it annoys Henry. He was sort of hoping this dinner would show Alexis what Bastian is really like. That his irritability is (usually) a bluff. That there's a truly decent person on the inside.

Which is a lot to ask of a dinner, really. Maybe Henry should just be pleased everyone made it out alive.

"Henry," Alexis says quietly. "I know you're in a difficult position, and I appreciate your continued candor in spite of that challenge. Please remember that I'm here to help you in any way I can. I mean that."

Henry swallows. "I know. Thank you."

Major Alexis—Gideon—confirms that he can find his own way back to his room, and Henry lets him go.

"He's lying," Bastian says as soon as the door closes. "Or at least, he's not telling the truth."

Henry sighs and walks back over to the dining area to clear the table. "You're going to have to be more specific."

"He *was* sent by the liaison committee to gather information and report back to them. But that's not the only reason he's here."

"I don't suppose the other reason is that he wanted to catch up with an old student?"

"It is, actually. Sort of."

Henry pauses in the act of setting a dirty plate on the kitchen counter. "What, really?"

"Sort of," Bastian repeats. Then he makes a face, turns around, and starts doing the dishes. "He's calculating when he talks to you. The story about saving the dog, talking about how you're always heroic and hardworking, then mentioning that girl in passing—he says what he thinks you want to hear, then adds something that will make you uncomfortable, just to see how you'll react. It's an experiment. He's testing you, seeing how far he can push, so he can collect the data."

Henry grimaces. He supposes Bastian would know all about experiments, having undergone plenty of them himself. "And where do you fit into this? Is he testing you, too?"

"Not exactly. He was obviously fishing for information about Level 49—he's *much* more interested in it than he let on—and he was trying to get a rise out of both of us by name-dropping your teenage girlfriend—"

"I'm not sure 'girlfriend' is really the term for someone I only knew for a few months before she got transferred to a different training facility."

"Fine. Someone you fraternized with."

Henry's not sure that quite covers it, either. Felicity (nowhere near Farrah or Fiona, but at least Major Alexis tried) had a great laugh, a truly epic mischievous streak, and absolutely no interest in a long-term relationship. In her defense, she and Henry were teenagers at the time, and with officers frequently being sent to different assignments across the country, the outlook for longevity was pretty bleak. Some did manage to pull off having partners and families they rarely saw in the areas surrounding their compounds, but generally, the practice was discouraged. Quick indulgences of hormones: frowned upon but mostly tolerated. Permanent plus-ones you might leak top secret information to: not so much.

So when Henry finally got up the guts to tell her that sneaking off into darkened corners wasn't really cutting it for him, he wasn't surprised that Felicity was quick to call everything off.

Afterward, it had been surprisingly easy to give up that sort of thing altogether. After all, there were final exams to take and ranks to achieve and missions to go on. Hoping for anything other than a life of service was stupid, naive, and self-indulgent—unless you were prepared to give the compound less than your full commitment, and Henry wasn't. Not when there were people who needed his help. So he locked away that part of himself and focused on the mission.

(But then he got orders to bring in an escaped asset who turned out to be irritating and charming and far braver than he gives himself credit for, and now Henry's gotten caught up in sharing a suite and trading pointed looks in long meetings and waking up in the morning with someone curled into his side, and what's the point of finally having what he always wanted if he doesn't know how to keep it—?)

He clears his throat. "We haven't really talked much about . . . past fraternizing. Should we?"

Bastian rolls his eyes and hands Henry a dish towel. "I grew up in this compound. Just because I wasn't interested in that stuff doesn't mean I don't understand how it works. If Alexis thought he could shock me by pointing out that you did what most teenage recruits do, he's an idiot."

"Okay. And while we're on the subject, how do you feel about *us* fraternizing?"

As soon as he says it, Henry realizes it isn't quite as silly and off-handed a comment as he meant it to be. Because he *has* been wondering.

Bastian is silent for a long moment, giving Henry plenty of time to mentally kick himself for bringing it up in the first place. Then he says awkwardly to the glass he's washing, "It's . . . good. All of this is . . . good. I just wonder if—"

He presses his lips together, then looks up and glares at Henry. "Weren't we talking about Alexis?"

Henry sighs inwardly and takes the glass out of Bastian's hands to dry it. "Yeah, I suppose you'd better finish accusing him of whatever you're accusing him of. You said he's doing some sort of experiment? Like, literally? What's the point?"

"I don't know," Bastian says, moving on to a plate. "He isn't wrong, though."

"About what?"

"About how you help people. How you try to save everyone. Still annoying, by the way."

Henry turns, both so he can put the glass away and so Bastian can't see his face. "Yeah, well. It's great being such a hero," he says, not quite as lightly as he meant to. "Especially when other people think it's a joke."

"Henry." His subsequent silence forces Henry to turn around again. "Alexis is wrong."

"You just said he wasn't."

"No, I mean—whatever he's doing, whatever information he's trying to find, he's counting on you to go along with it no matter what because you don't want to risk rocking the boat and hurting someone. He thinks you're still the same person you were when he met you. He's not taking into account what you've been through since then."

"He's probably read reports."

"Reports written by Valentine. So they're shit."

"She wrote pretty comprehensive—"

"Yeah, your problem is that you actually read them. That's why everyone thinks you're so willing to put up with anything."

Henry lets out a less-than-enthusiastic laugh. "That's what he should be taking into account, then? That I read Major Valentine's reports?"

"Granted, those reports took a heroic amount of patience to get through, so that does speak to your character. But that's not what I'm talking about." Bastian clears his throat. "It's just—I know you think it's a weakness, but it's not."

"What's a weakness?"

"You know." Bastian waves a hand, getting soapy droplets of water on the counter. "Wanting to do good. Getting angry when other people don't. I'm guessing Valentine liked to make you think trying to do the right thing was stupid. Like Alexis trying to make a joke out of your hero complex."

"You know you're basically confirming that I have one?"

"I'm confirming that it's not something to feel bad about. Like when we were working the John Doe case, and I said all that stuff about how you should stop trying to help people. I was wrong."

Henry barely manages not to flinch at the mention of John Doe, choosing instead to focus on the most important part of what Bastian just said. "Hang on, can you repeat that bit about you being wrong? I need to record it for posterity."

Bastian rolls his eyes. "Anyway, just because some assholes took advantage of you being you, doesn't mean you have to feel ashamed of it now."

"I'm not feeling ashamed."

Bastian raises his eyebrows.

And there's the downside of living with an empath. Henry sighs. "Okay, maybe I'm feeling a *little* ashamed. Look, compound officers aren't really encouraged to be nice. We've got a job to do, and we do it. Sure, the rhetoric sounds good, but no one actually believes it."

"Except you."

Henry sets down his dish towel and rubs his eyes. "I think this compound is capable of doing good. I think the entire Compound Network is capable of doing good, as much as it's tried not to. And I think there are people out there who need help: potentials who don't know about their powers yet, assets who need training, people who would make really good officers or staff if they knew that the compounds exist. Our job is to find them and help them. I'm not blind to the politics involved or how completely this compound screwed things up, but I think we can do better. I *know* we can. We owe it to the people who were hurt here to turn this thing around. And if thinking that makes me an idealistic idiot, then so be it."

"You're not an idiot, Henry. Not even Major Alexis thought that."

"Oh, you're a mind reader now?" He doesn't mean to sound so stung, but there's something about this whole day—wrestling with himself over how to tell Bastian about John Doe; balancing politeness and firmness as the liaison committee fills his email inbox with their demands; trying to understand his former mentor's murky intentions—that has Henry on edge.

Bastian shuts off the water and leans over the sink. "I'm messing this up. I just meant—"

"It's not like I've forgotten about what happened with Major Valentine," Henry continues, gathering steam. "How I let her make me think I had to play along in order to keep my team safe. But what would Major Alexis get out of doing something like that? He's flat-out admitted he's reporting back to the liaison committee, and they're the ones asking him to be here. Who's to say he *doesn't* want to help us?"

"Maybe he does. But it's not top of mind for him—or at least, it wasn't tonight. Not if his feelings are any indication. And they usually are for this kind of thing."

"Fine. Duped by one more person. Great."

"That's not—"

Henry sighs. "Never mind. What do you want to do, then? I can't just refuse to work with him. Not unless there's some actual proof of wrongdoing."

"All I can say is, I think he's searching for information beyond what the liaison committee has said it wants. So be careful what you share with him."

"Sure," Henry mutters. "I'll just tell the visiting dignitary that he can't have access to certain information. That'll go over well with the committee."

"You're the commanding officer of this compound. Your rules, remember?"

"Hardly."

Some secrets are necessary, Carter said when they started the John Doe project. *Some data needs to be kept secure in order to achieve the best outcome for everyone involved.* But how can the best outcome be never knowing whether you can trust someone? How can it be keeping things from someone you love, someone who deserves to decide his own fate?

That last bit is all Henry, though. He can pretend he's keeping secrets because he's concerned about the safety of the data and feels obligated to follow Carter's lead on when and how they tell the Council about John Doe. But the real reason for the secrets is that he knows what Bastian will say when he finds out Henry's still looking for a way to save him. And Henry isn't ready to have that conversation yet.

Maybe he really *does* have an unfettered hero complex.

"Another thing," Bastian says. "If Alexis was there when Valentine first recruited you, do you think he knows about you?"

"You couldn't tell?"

"Empath, not mind reader, remember?"

Henry shakes his head. "I'm not sure. And I can't exactly ask, can I?"

"No, I suppose not." Bastian hesitates, then adds, "If he does—"

"We'll deal with it." Not that he has any idea how.

They're silent for the rest of the clean-up procedure, after which Henry escapes to the bedroom on the pretense of turning in early. Of course, he's too agitated to do much other than toss and turn for several lifetimes while his brain shows no inclination toward anything resembling sleep.

Eventually, Bastian comes in and lies down next to him. After a brief pause, he scoots very deliberately into Henry's space, which gives Henry an excellent excuse to put his arm around him. It doesn't solve anything, of course, but Henry can't pretend it doesn't make him feel a little bit better.

Six months ago

THEY START WITH Major Valentine's office.

"Will you want different furniture, sir?" Michaels asks Henry, taking notes on her tablet as they go. "The desk and chair are perfectly serviceable, but—"

"Burn it," Bastian says.

Privately, Henry agrees. But . . . "We can't burn everything in the compound, Bastian. It would be a waste of resources."

"There are five firestarters on the asset roster right now. We can call it training."

"I'm glad you're taking an interest in your work, but I really think—"

"A different room, perhaps?"

They turn to Michaels. "There's no particular reason to continue using Major Valentine's office in the same manner," she says. "Might I suggest designating it for storage? There are several other rooms that would serve just as well for your base of operations, Major."

"Sold," Henry says.

"Yes, sir."

They've spent the last few weeks inventorying rooms, halls, entire floors. Other staff will do the actual fixing up, but Henry needs to know where things are and what updates are necessary for the various spaces. It feels important for him to see the rooms and floors he had no idea existed because he was so much in his own insular world. It's all going to be his responsibility now. He needs to be prepared.

Nothing could prepare him for the lower experimentation rooms, though.

The day they hit Level 19 is bad enough. Being back in the blue-lit room where he found Bastian nearly catatonic—never mind finding a member of his team dead—makes it hard to breathe. It's not like there's blood on the walls or anything macabre like that; just well-worn instruments in innocuous drawers and vial upon vial of *blood in refrigerators, some of which probably belongs to assets who didn't make it. Whose bodies will never be found.*

Then they get to the levels below that.

Bastian's held up pretty well, but the farther down they go, the shallower his breathing gets. His gloved hands reach out to grip the wall when they turn corners, like he can't keep standing without the extra help.

By Level 47, things are so bad, Henry can't stop himself from commenting. "You don't have to do this," he tells Bastian quietly.

"Shut up," Bastian snaps, not looking at him. "And don't negate."

Negating isn't the problem, of course. Henry's getting used to the constant strain of keeping it in check even when he'd prefer to be using it to help someone. The real problem is that he hates seeing Bastian like this, unable to keep from sucking up all the emotions around him because there's too much of it, even for the strongest of shields. A parting gift from Major Valentine and Dr. Wright: all the things they did, all the people they hurt, soaked forever into the walls so no one will ever forget. Especially not an empath.

Henry desperately wants to put his arms around Bastian, to hold him and kiss away the lines on his forehead. Maybe that would be enough to get rid of the sick feeling in his own stomach. It'd probably be the wrong side of professional, though.

By Level 49, Henry's decided it's not necessary to be an empath to feel the fear and hurt left over from what went on here.

On the surface, this floor looks like every other level they've inventoried today, except that there are more experimentation rooms. And more sharp objects in drawers, clean but obviously having been in regular use. Everything is pristine and perfectly arranged in a way that makes Henry's skin crawl. There's an overwhelming sense of wrongness that has even Michaels looking a little green in the face.

"Have the cleaning teams start here," Henry tells her, fighting to keep calm. He flicks a glance at Bastian and adds, "But tell everyone to take a break first."

"No." Bastian looks down the hall, a determined set to his shoulders. "Finish the floor."

"Bastian—"

But of course he ignores Henry and keeps going.

Henry sighs. "We'll finish it and then take that break after. Make sure they clean this level especially well."

"Yes, sir." She makes a note on her tablet and gestures for the rest of their team to follow.

The next room is a repeat of what they've seen plenty of already: recovery beds, some storage units, machines with monitors gone dead.

Something must be different, though, because Bastian hasn't moved more than a few steps from the doorway. He's staring at the far wall, entire body rigid, like he's forgotten how to start moving again.

Henry walks quickly over to him. "What is it?"

"There's a room. Behind the wall. It—I have to—"

He clenches his jaw and practically runs out of the room.

Henry immediately follows after him, ignoring Michaels and the rest of the staff. Bastian's fast enough to get around the corner before Henry can catch up, so it's the telltale sound of retching rather than a visual that clues Henry in to what's happening. Grimly, he reaches into his jacket pocket and flips a switch on the jammer. As soon as he sees Bastian, hunched over and wiping his mouth, Henry puts up a negation field.

Bastian turns, breathing heavily, eyes darting back and forth. "Don't—"

"Shut up."

His heart is beating wildly when Henry hugs him. Henry does his best to keep the negation field contained—just enough to protect Bastian from whatever's immediately around them. It must be working because while Bastian is still clinging to Henry, he's also (very slowly) starting to relax.

"You want to know about the room," Bastian says, voice muffled against Henry's shoulder.

Henry shakes his head. "I'm more interested in you remembering how to breathe. That can wait."

"It's where Wright . . . Just before I escaped, that's where . . ."

Shit. Henry swallows and pulls Bastian closer. "We'll burn it. We'll burn the whole damned floor."

Bastian laughs half-heartedly. "Waste of resources."

"Don't care."

"I think you're abusing your authority, Major."

"Wouldn't be the first time someone in this compound has." Henry kisses the top of Bastian's head. "You're done for today, by the way. Get out of here. That's an order."

Bastian pulls back to look at him, mouth open to protest. Then he frowns. "Did we decide to give Kent and Sybil a show? I thought the idea was to keep incriminating actions out of the security footage." He says it lightly, but Henry can feel his body tighten at the idea that he might've been caught on camera getting the stuffing hugged out of him.

"I kiss everyone I order around," Henry assures him. Then he takes the jammer out of his pocket. "Also, I have this."

"Remind me why we're not using those all the time?"

"Because it would get suspicious. But I'm willing to take the risk at the moment." Henry touches Bastian's cheek. "Are you all right now?"

"No." Bastian looks away. "I hate this. They're gone; it shouldn't be—" He shudders.

"I'm not an expert," Henry says slowly, "but I don't think it just goes away like that. Everything that happened here, everything that happened to you . . . Just because Major Valentine isn't in charge anymore, doesn't mean her actions don't have lasting repercussions. For all of us."

"And you think we can fix it."

"I think we can try." Henry regards him sternly. "I mean it. Go see how Laurel's getting along with the garden. Pester your staff about getting ready for the inauguration. Do something that isn't this."

"Only if you stop negating."

Henry hesitates. "Are you sure—?"

"Getting caught with the jammer would be bad enough. We've talked about what happens if someone sees you negating—or if the power trackers in the security cameras pick it up."

Henry drops the negation field and immediately hates the way Bastian winces. But he seems less pale and wobbly, at least.

"I love you," Henry says quietly. "Go."

"I'm actually—" Bastian sees the look on Henry's face and sighs. "Fine."

He glances at the security camera, then back at Henry. "I . . . you know."

"I don't know. I'm very stupid. You'd better spell it out for me."

Bastian rolls his eyes and flushes a little. "I mean—I thought you should know that I'd really like to be kissing you right now, but I just threw up, so that would be disgusting."

"Definitely the most romantic thing I've ever heard."

"Forget I said anything."

"Never." Henry kisses his forehead. "I'll see you back at the suite. Brush your teeth before then."

Bastian snorts, leans into him for a moment, then moves past and heads for the elevator.

Henry turns off the jammer and, setting his shoulders, goes back to Michaels and the others.

Chapter 13

"I CAN'T WORK with you breathing down my neck like that," Kent complains.

"Would you prefer I have Captain Smith breathe down your neck instead?" Bastian mutters, trying to understand what he's seeing on the computer screen in front of him.

Kent scoffs and turns partway around in his chair to glare at Bastian. "I resent the insinuation that I could ever be interested in having someone other than my extremely brilliant and attractive girlfriend come anywhere near my neck."

From where she's leaning against the door jamb, Smith heaves a loud sigh, exuding a wave of annoyed-bored-fatigued. She and Henry's team—*her* team, Bastian reminds himself—have spent the past week pursuing potentials all over the city and surrounding area as they test the hackers' new algorithm. So far, she hasn't drawn her weapon on anyone, but Bastian suspects it's only a matter of time if she has to keep interacting directly with Kent.

"She has a gun," Bastian reminds him. "What's that red thing?"

"Ugh, not something for you to put your finger on! Now I have to clean the screen again."

"Kent." Sybil, who's been sitting next to him and ignoring his indignation in favor of working, is now frowning at her monitor. "Are you seeing this beacon? It's in quadrant C, right?"

Kent immediately sobers and cross-references with his own program. "Yeah, that's—oh."

Smith straightens up and comes over. "Designation?"

"It's—" Sybil blinks several times and narrows her eyes. "It's an error. Has to be."

"Why? What is it?" Smith is at full alert now.

Sybil turns around, eyes finding Bastian's and then sliding away (startled-confused-flustered). "I'm sure it's not—"

"What?" Smith sounds like she's moments away from getting that gun out and using it in non-sanctioned ways.

"An empath," Kent says.

Bastian goes cold. "Where?"

"Center of quadrant C. Intersection of 8th Avenue and 17th Street."

Bastian turns on his heel and switches his comm to the right channel. "I need a car. Now." Over his shoulder, he calls to Kent and Sybil, "Send the directions to the vehicle GPS—I'll have the driver let you know which one it is. Then stay online and direct us in case the potential moves."

Smith trails him out of the room, her irritated-defensive-concerned a palpable cloud above her head. "My team can handle this," she says. "And anyway, you heard them—it's probably just an error. There's no need for you to—"

"We really don't have time for your territorial bullshit, Smith." He realizes even as he says it that it's not really fair; she has every right to question why the director of the asset program would want in on this. It's probably just another miscalculation by Kent's algorithm, like when it didn't catch James before the perimeter security did. Unless it actually *is* an empath. In which case . . .

She doggedly follows him onto the elevator. "You're welcome to accompany us, but it seems like a waste of your time. Director."

Only Smith could use titles in a way that sounds more insulting than omitting them.

Bastian takes a breath to calm his nerves, then turns to her. "Look, if this is an empath, they'll be terrified. It's extremely unlikely that anyone's ever told them what they are or how to shield. Even a team coming in with the best of intentions is going to spook them, and they'll lash out. You remember what happened in the forest with John Doe? Please tell me that's a report you actually read."

"Of course. But I still think we can handle—"

"—a lot of things. Just not this. Get your team and follow."

She says it around gritted teeth, but she still says it: "Yes, sir."

They split when the elevator opens on Level 1, Smith heading for the training rooms to collect her team, while Bastian hurries to the loading dock. He switches to a different comm channel as he does it. "Laurel?"

There's a moment of silence, some shuffling, and then: "What? Yes? Sorry?"

Her harried-distracted-irritated is vague from this distance but still notice-able, especially since he has her tone of voice to go on, too. But he doesn't have time to press. "I'm going into the city for a retrieval, and I need you to look after things here until I get back."

"Okay, no prob—wait. Why are you going on a retrieval?"

Bastian blows out a breath as he pushes through a collection of officers exiting the building. "Can you just—?"

"I thought we agreed that you weren't allowed to terrorize new assets until they got to the compound."

"I'm not going to—"

"Actually, I don't think you should be terrorizing them here, either. No terrorizing, full stop. We can put that in a contract somewhere, right? Or Henry can make it an official order. Which reminds me, have you told him about this not-terrorizing-people field trip?"

"He's busy." Busy with Alexis, which means that if Bastian tried to contact him about this, Alexis would hear about it, too. And Bastian can't shake the feeling that they shouldn't be telling Alexis any more than they absolutely have to.

"Of course he's busy!" Laurel says. "That doesn't mean he won't want to talk. *I'm* busy, and I'm still talking to you."

"Busy doing what?"

"Things! Important things! And now I guess I'm busy with your things, too. Didn't you say you were leaving?"

"Yes. I'll catch you both up when I get back."

Bastian cuts the line and heads for the vehicle loading dock.

He spends the entire trip into the city drumming his fingers against his leg and glaring at the back of the driver's seat. Not for the first time, he wonders if he should learn how to drive, just so he can get places without having to wait around for other people. He mentioned it once to Henry, who looked horrified and told him there was absolutely no way he was ever going to sanction Bastian taking a compound vehicle anywhere without someone else doing the driving. He must've found the note in Bastian's file about the incident with the electrocutor asset and the five-car pileup, which isn't really an accurate representation of Bastian's driving capabilities. He was only behind the wheel for about thirty seconds, and the explosion wasn't his fault. Also, he was twelve at the time. He'd be much better at driving now. Probably.

At least his driver gets him to the scene before Smith's vehicle, which is saying something. From what Bastian's heard, Smith tends to think of speed limits as mere suggestions.

The intersection is undamaged and fairly quiet. The police haven't been called, and none of the passersby seem particularly alarmed, even when Bastian's vehicle drives up. This is part of the reason compound vehicles aren't painted in camouflage or anything similarly ostentatious: makes it easier to get where they need to go without causing any disruption of city life. Or whatever it says in the bylaws.

And the fact that no one's screaming or causing a ruckus means no one's caused any harm. Yet.

"Is the potential still here?" Bastian asks Kent, jumping out of the car without waiting for it to come to a full stop.

"Should be," says Kent's voice through Bastian's comm. He pauses, then adds, "Look, I know our algorithm is amazing, but do you really think—?"

"I don't know what I think. Shut up until I do."

Bastian stays next to the car for a moment, closing his eyes and feeling out, trying to filter through the usual noise of the city. Morning rush hour is mostly over, so the crowds aren't as bad as they could be, but there are enough people around that he has to concentrate to feel his way through the tired-sad-anxious of people late to work.

His head starts to pound, which is when he remembers that he left his painkillers back at the compound. Clenching his jaw, he tries to focus on pinpointing the most likely emotional signature. The one with the most fear.

Kent and Sybil's algorithm *is* pretty amazing, but it's not always precise, which means the potential could be anywhere in the general area. Bastian wasn't expecting it to be in the exact alley it turns out to be, though. He frowns and looks over at the street signs, really seeing them for the first time: 8th and 17th. *That* 8th and 17th.

Oh.

"Director?" Smith is in his ear. "We're positioned around the block. Give the word when you want us to move in."

"Stand by."

There's going to be so much emotional residue in that alley, some of it very familiar, and . . . well. Too late for cold feet. He squares his shoulders and walks over.

The fear becomes clearer as he approaches, but there's no indication that it gets any worse as he gets closer. If it's an empath, they're not very strong. Or they're so far from full manifestation that their power isn't impacted by other people yet. Except that makes no sense; being impacted by others is pretty much the whole point of an empath.

(He remembers this alley, remembers holding his head like it was going to crack open, the fear running through him, hot and cold, like a fever—he was shaking and unable to stop, closing his eyes against the intermittent sunlight until he heard the noise, boots on the ground, someone coming closer—)

"Hello?" He narrows his eyes, trying to see through the scattered shadows between the buildings. The nearly caved-in old restaurant door, the dumpster covered in graffiti, the mildewed posters on the brick walls—everything is where it should be. He scans the area, looking for anything unusual, and . . . there. The potential isn't shielding—probably doesn't know how—but the power is there, jerking in and out, like they're still getting the hang of it. Another point for the recently manifested column.

He feels the fear coalesce at the end of the alley just before he sees what he's looking for.

Sitting wedged between the wall and the dumpster is the dirtiest child Bastian has ever seen. She's less of a human being than a tiny ball of mud and misery curled in on itself.

And she's hiding in the exact same place Bastian hid all those years ago.

He walks over to her, careful not to make any sudden movements. Sharp, dark eyes look up at him from behind a curtain of matted hair. She doesn't move when he crouches down in front of her, but her eyes lock onto him and never waver.

"Are you all right?" he asks. Which he realizes is a colossally stupid question as soon as it's out of his mouth.

"It got too loud," she says, her voice impossibly soft.

Bastian swallows. "Yeah. It'll do that."

Her hand suddenly snakes out of nowhere and grabs his wrist. "You remember being here," she says in an oddly calm voice. "You remember feeling everything, all over. It was too loud for you, too. It was like it would never stop. Until—"

Bastian jerks his arm away—more of a reflex than a conscious decision. He immediately hates that he did it because her reactive resignation-hurt-sadness settles heavily in his temples. Just like the realization of what this really is.

"They don't like it when I touch them," she says. "I don't mean to, but . . ."

"You can't help it." Bastian sighs. "What's your name?"

"Angelica. What do you mean I can't help it?"

"Touch activates your power. You're subconsciously drawn to it."

"My power?"

"Director?" Smith in his ear again. "We can move in on your position in—"

"Not yet. Kent, you there? I need you and Sybil to look for missing children under the name Angelica—" He looks at the little girl, who's still watching him carefully. "What's your last name?"

"Pinelli."

"You got that, Kent?"

"Yup. We're on it." He pauses, then adds, "But you know we've been having trouble finding—"

"Just do it."

"I'm not missing, though," Angelica says when Bastian turns back to her. "I know where I am. I went where the feeling was."

Bastian looks up sharply. "What?"

"I was walking, and then I felt the feeling, and then I remembered this place, so I came and sat down." She frowns. "Why can I remember things that didn't happen to me? Like when I touched you?"

"You can do a lot more than that," Bastian says. Which is even truer than it should be. Remembering is one thing, but being drawn to an emotion that isn't hers . . . ?

"Do you have a power, too?" Angelica asks. "Does it get stronger when you touch things? Is that why you wear gloves?"

"Yes."

"Can I get some gloves like yours?"

Bastian smiles slightly. "If you want."

"What's *your* name?" Angelica asks, suddenly more on the suspicious side of curious-thoughtful-suspicious.

"The memory didn't tell you?"

"No. Was it supposed to?"

"I don't know, actually. I've never met one of you before."

"One of me?"

"She's not an empath?" Smith asks.

"No," Bastian says. "She's a memor."

Twenty-three years ago

BASTIAN CAN'T REMEMBER *how long he's been in the alley, hiding in the shadows, scooting backward whenever someone walks by. Luckily, no one comes in. Makes sense; there's nothing here to see. Cracked brick. A rundown restaurant side door that isn't used anymore. Rusted-over trash bins with nothing in them except stains.*

If he curls himself up as tightly as possible and holds his head through the worst of it, it's not so bad. Except during rush hour twice a day, when the emotions of the crowds passing by assault his mind, and he makes embarrassing sounds he's glad no one is around to hear. The hurry-irritated-worried-anxious-bored claws at him, worse than how it felt when his mom slapped him for spacing out too much. This isn't just a sting in his cheek; he can feel it everywhere, and when it fades, everything's still sore. If they would just stop, *give him a chance to catch his breath—*

He raises his head and frowns at the alley opening. The traffic has died down for today, but there are still people walking by. Except one of them feels . . . different. Harder to read (calm-determined-something else) because there's a barrier around them. They're coming closer, and he should be getting overwhelmed again, only he's not.

He doesn't really know what he's doing, but he reaches out with his mind to touch this weird feeling that's not anywhere near as painful as everything else . . .

A woman walks into the alley.

She's thin but looks strong, her reddish hair pulled back severely. She's wearing a buttoned-up jacket and pants that make her look like the people with guns on TV. She comes toward him, not at all surprised to see him there, and he notices two things: Her hands are perfect, like she's never done anything with them in her entire life, and her eyes are icy blue.

"Hello, Sebastian," she says.

He stares at her but doesn't ask how she knows his name. "You don't hurt," he says instead. His voice sounds strange in his own ears. He can't remember when he last spoke out loud.

She smiles. "Don't I? Good. I've tried very hard not to. Would you like to know how?"

He nods.

"It's called shielding. Anyone can do it, but for someone like you, it's very important because it can make things hurt less. I can show you, if you'd like."

He wants to know how to do it, of course. But it's not like he can just trust some random lady who showed up in his alley. He hasn't been sitting here long enough to get that stupid. Yet.

She must see something in his expression because she crouches down to be at eye level with him—but far enough back that she's not in his face. Like he's a wild animal she's trying to keep calm. "You have a very special gift, Sebastian," she says. "Where I'm from, we teach people like you how to use that kind of gift to help people."

"There are other people like me?" It just slips out.

She smiles again. "Well, no one quite *like you. But yes, there are people who would understand what you're going through. They were hurt and sad when I found them, too. But now they're happy in a place where they can learn about who they are and what they can do. Where people care about them and want to keep them safe. What do you think of that?"*

He thinks it sounds like a place that doesn't exist. His mom, his school, his doctors— they all say there's something wrong with him. No one's ever said that he has a gift, that he could do something good with it. They just want him to forget about it and act normal.

"Where is it?"

She gets to her feet. "Outside the city. It's a special place where no one bothers us unless we'd like them to. Do you want to see it?"

He hesitates. "I should ask my mom first."

"When was the last time you were home, Sebastian?" There's a sad look on her face, like she knows exactly when and how he ran away. But it doesn't seem like she's going to make him go back because she adds, "Maybe you didn't know . . . your mother left."

He blinks at her. "What?"

"She moved out of your house a few weeks ago. My people have been trying to trace her, but we haven't found anything yet. So you won't be able to ask her permission right now." Her piercing eyes look into his. "That means it's up to you."

It's never been up to him, not in his whole life. Mostly, it's been trying to do what other people wanted him to do and failing because the pain got too bad, or he was trying to avoid it altogether. That's why he ran away in the first place: to get away from it. Because curling up in a dark alley is better than disappointing everyone.

But now he gets to decide.

He looks up at the woman and says, "Okay." After all, there's nowhere else to go, is there? Unless he wants to stay here forever.

He tries to stand on his own, but he starts wobbling right away (When was the last time he ate?), and she grabs his elbow to steady him. It should hurt even more—it's always worse when people touch him—but it doesn't. This shielding thing must really work.

As they walk slowly toward the alley opening, he looks up at her and finally asks, "Who are you?"

She smiles. "My name is Major Valentine."

Chapter 14

THEY'VE ONLY BEEN going through files for a few hours so far today, and Henry already desperately wishes someone in the compound knew how to make a cup of coffee that doesn't kill people.

Of course, all the coffee in the world wouldn't change the fact that he's spent almost two weeks with Major Alexis going over everything from plans to bolster overall compound infrastructure to specific goals and parameters for various training and experiment programs. Today, for a slight change in the stressful tedium, they've taken a deep dive into every financial decision Henry's made or overseen since his promotion.

As boring as it is, it's just as well they're focusing on it. Otherwise, Henry's pretty sure they'd have to discuss things like dead serial killers and memory-challenged firestarters. Henry hasn't had to deal with the former just yet—General Carter has kept it quiet, and anyhow, it doesn't officially have anything to do with this compound. Nor has it resulted in anything that could help Bastian, according to Carter's somewhat sporadic updates as he and the Council HQ medical team review the data.

As for the latter, Major Alexis has been content so far with the update that James is being monitored by Dr. Rowe and her team while he works with Laurel to regain his memories. Henry doesn't expect Alexis's complacency to last, though. And when it runs out, he doesn't know what, if anything, he'll need to hold back.

Which is a stupid thing to worry about, given the complete lack of evidence that the major is up to anything other than taking inventory of what's going on at the compound and writing back to the liaison committee about it. But

Bastian seemed so sure there was some ulterior motive, something they need to prepare for. Even if Henry can't see it himself yet, he's hyper alert to every question, every pause, every slight twitch or sigh that could be an indicator of . . . something.

Maybe he doesn't need that coffee after all. He's probably jittery enough as is.

"Everything seems to be in order," Major Alexis says, fingers flying across the keys of his touch tablet as it converts the files into something he can read. "Frankly, I'm impressed that you've managed to document so much."

Henry laughs half-heartedly. "Michaels is the organized one. The rest of us just try to keep up."

Alexis raises his head and smiles. "I find that hard to believe. I have it on good authority that you were a model student."

"I was good at not getting caught doing things I shouldn't. Usually."

"Hmm. Or you were an upstanding officer who was good at following orders."

Something in the way Alexis says it gives Henry pause. (Because that's what he did: took orders and nodded and saluted and pretended that was enough, that he didn't need to know what happened after he and his team brought in all those potentials, that he didn't need to question what he was helping Major Valentine do, until—)

Alexis sets his tablet down on the meeting room table. "Well, I suppose it's time I had that chat with the mechanics over at the loading dock. Of course, I can wait here if you'd like to have them hide anything first."

Henry reminds himself that it's a joke. "In that case, I'll just—"

There are loud voices outside of the room, coming closer. Henry's barely gotten to his feet when the door bursts open.

"I get that there's protocol," Kent is saying as he adjusts his shoulder bag, "but this is important."

"Important enough to interrupt a meeting?" Henry asks, crossing his arms over his chest.

"Sorry, Major," says a calmer voice from behind Kent. Sybil steps around him, putting her hand on his arm.

"Don't 'sorry, Major' me," Kent tells her, frowning. "It was your idea to come up here!"

"After we finished the write-up on that retrieval. And definitely not while the major has a guest!"

Kent notices Alexis for the first time. "Oh. Um."

"Sir?" Michaels suddenly appears, causing both Kent and Sybil to jump. "Is there something I can help with?"

Henry considers the crowd and sighs. "It's fine, Michaels. Major Alexis, Kent Turner and Sybil Tassos run our hacker team and oversee security at the compound. Kent and Sybil, this is Major Alexis. He's the liaison committee representative who got network access from you a few weeks ago."

"Nice to finally meet you in person," Alexis says, smiling politely. "It seems Major Mortimer's given you the most difficult job in the compound."

"And the best," Kent says smugly.

"I'm sure you have something important to discuss, so I'll leave you to it. No doubt I can get an update later if it's relevant." Alexis stands and picks up his things. "Maybe I can meet you at the loading dock, Henry?"

"We can come back," Sybil says quickly. Her tone is falling over itself with deference, but her hand has tightened on Kent's arm, the silver rings on her fingers standing out against his dark shirt.

"That's all right; my exploration of the exciting world of vehicle maintenance doesn't require the major's presence just yet." Alexis reaches for his cane, then guides himself out of the meeting room. Michaels joins him, closing the meeting room door behind them and leaving Henry, Kent, and Sybil alone.

Sybil's apologetic demeanor completely evaporates, and she tugs at Kent's bag. "Do you have the security upgrade we promised the major?"

Kent looks about as confused as Henry, who definitely wasn't promised anything. "Do I—? Oh! Yes, of course I do. Let's get that installed."

They brush past Henry, taking something—several somethings—out of the bag and letting it drop to the floor as they go. Kent climbs onto the couch, facing the wall. There's a flash of metal in his hand as he reaches up toward the security camera.

Henry opens his mouth to protest, but Sybil turns back to him and shakes her head once before going over to the camera on the other side of the room and mirroring whatever Kent is doing—in her case, aided by standing precariously on a chair. They're not messing with the cameras themselves, Henry realizes; they're attaching little metal boxes to the walls just below them. That done, they stop to look at each other and nod. Then they both push buttons on their respective boxes at the same time. Henry might be impressed by their coordination if he wasn't pretty sure he knows what just happened.

Kent hops down. "Okay, we're good for—"

"Did you just install jammers on those cameras?" Henry demands.

"We augmented the cameras in here with extended jammer capacity," Sybil explains before Kent can do anything other than open his mouth. "Sorry, sir, but we don't have time. And Major Alexis was right: It's important."

"It had better be, if it meant you needed to burst in here and mess with security without warning me first."

"So, funny story," Kent begins.

"There've been developments since we last talked about that security issue," Sybil cuts in. "It'll be safest if we do this quickly." She gives Kent a pointed look.

"Right, sorry." Kent goes over to the bag he dropped earlier, takes out a tablet, and sets it down on the table, gesturing for Sybil and Henry to get closer.

"Sybil's enhancements to the jammer tech mean anyone who gets hold of the footage your cameras are taking right now won't see or hear what we're doing . . . *and* they won't be able to break the encryption down later and see that we augmented anything. It'll be clean even to the best hackers out there. Totally safe."

"For five minutes," Sybil says.

"Better than zero minutes, which is what we had before your beautiful brain came up with—"

"You were telling me why we need this level of security," Henry reminds them firmly.

"We told you someone's been trying to break into the compound mainframe, right?" Kent starts tapping on the tablet, too fast for Henry to keep up.

"Yes. That's why you've been making appointments with Michaels as needed to keep me updated. You know, those appointments that are supposed to be planned ahead and don't involve interrupting me when I'm with a guest."

"Er. Right. Except—"

"We weren't sure until now," Sybil says, "but it's not just that someone's been trying to get in. They've also been leaving presents on our virtual doorstep."

"We found packets of coded data at the entry point," Kent explains. "Despite our very busy morning, we still took a look and found something we thought you should see."

Sybil reaches around Kent's arm and taps on a file. "Does this mean anything to you, Major?"

The file name—FSP6342867—pings something in his brain, but he can't place it. Kent is scrolling too fast for Henry to read much of the content, but he does notice one important detail: "Your note says that some of it's missing."

"Yeah. They're only leaving us bits and pieces at a time. And it's heavily encrypted, so it takes awhile for us to fit everything together and decipher it." Kent doesn't look too worried; he's acting like it's a tough game he's enjoying rather than a potentially catastrophic security issue.

"Is this all we have?" Henry asks.

"There are a few pieces we haven't decoded yet, but that's most of it." Sybil shakes her head. "They seem pretty determined, so I'm betting we'll get more."

"All right, it's definitely weird," Henry admits. "But they haven't breached our system yet, right? So why all the urgency?"

"Well," Kent says, "there's the part where some of this stuff has your name on it." He scrolls through the file a bit more, then points to a line.

Subject H. Mortimer brought to Level 49 observation lab xx.xx.xxxx. Fail-Safe Protocol test to be initiated asynchronously with research regarding subject AP367284. See also: splicing initiatives.

As soon as Henry's finished reading it, he says sharply, "I need to know where this came from. And I need a secure way to read through everything you've got."

Kent and Sybil exchange glances. Then Kent shuts the tablet down and hands it to Henry. "You should be good on this. But I wouldn't use it anywhere other than here, where the relays can give you some added protection."

He hesitates, then adds, "We were right on the security level for this, weren't we?"

"Probably," Henry says grimly.

After an awkward silence, Sybil clears her throat. "We'll keep tracking the activity and let you know when there are updates."

"The cameras are going to come back online in a minute here," Kent warns them. "We should—"

"One more thing." Henry gives them both a stern look. "Have you read the full file? Or whatever you have of it?"

"Not . . . really," Kent says, his tone extremely suspect.

"From here on out, you read none of it," Henry tells them. "Do you understand?"

Kent frowns. "You can't just—"

"I *can* just. Boss, remember?" Seeing their dubious faces, Henry sighs. "Look, I know you need to read some of it in order to get your programs to decipher the code. Just keep it to a minimum, and get it off your hard drives after you've sent it to me. I want the smallest number of data paths possible leading back to you or to this compound's mainframe."

"You think it's dangerous, then." Sybil doesn't make it a question.

"Maybe. I don't know for sure." Henry rubs his eyes. "I need your help with this, but I also need you two to be safe. So stay out of it as much as you can."

Kent's frown deepens. "But we don't even know—"

"No time." Sybil nods to Henry. "We understand, sir. And Kent promises not to get so overzealous about going over security updates with you next time," she adds loudly, flicking a glance at the metal boxes on the wall, which are now sporting blinking green lights.

"Enjoy your upgrade, sir!" Kent says cheerfully. "We're honored to be doing our part to keep the compound safe!"

Henry makes a face at him, but Sybil's already dragging him out of the room.

"Wait," Henry calls. "You mentioned you were just working on a retrieval. Anything there I need to know about?"

Sybil and Kent stop and turn, glancing at each other in a way that pretty much answers Henry's question. "I . . . think the director can answer that better than we can," Sybil says carefully.

Great. "I'll ask him, then. Thanks for the—upgrade."

When they're gone, Henry walks over to the couch and sits down. He wants to read the rest of the file—and doesn't. Because anything connecting Level 49, Bastian's ID number, and the splicing experiments at Laurel's compound can't be good. And while he doesn't know what the Fail-Safe Protocol is, he's guessing that isn't good, either.

And something else about it makes him deeply uneasy; a nagging feeling, like there's something important he can't quite remember . . .

Henry glances at the clock. Major Alexis will be waiting.

He should tell Alexis about this, of course. A security breach, or even the threat of one, could affect the entire Compound Network. And as the liaison committee representative, Major Alexis will expect Henry to report anything unusual.

But if this information is important enough that someone is trying to break through one of the most intricate security systems in the country to deliver it . . .

He's stashing the tablet in an unobtrusive file cabinet on the far side of the room before he realizes he's decided to do it.

Because he can't tell Alexis, can he? Not when Bastian felt something off about him. And even if Bastian's wrong, how can Henry justify getting someone else caught up in a potentially dangerous situation before he even knows what this is? After all, isn't a commanding officer supposed to gather data, make an informed call, and then determine who acts and how?

Henry shakes his head and closes the drawer. Better to keep it to himself until he knows what they're dealing with. Add it to the pile of secrets he's still not sure he should be keeping but can't justify telling anyone about, either. Once he's reviewed all the fragments they have, he'll sit down with Laurel and Bastian and figure out what to do about it. Until then . . .

He forces himself to turn away and not look back as he leaves the room.

Chapter 15

"WHY DID SHE register as an empath?" Smith asks as she and Bastian wait outside the med bay.

"Because Kent's algorithm is crap," Bastian says absently. He's leaning against the wall and trying to refocus his shield enough to stave off another headache. Failing that, he's prepared to compromise: a modicum of coherence for as long as he has to deal with people, and then total collapse later. So long as Henry's late enough getting back to the suite that he doesn't notice.

There's a shuffling noise in Bastian's earpiece, and then: "Hey!" Kent squawks, shattering any hope Bastian might've had for concentration. "Sybil and I spent months augmenting that algorithm. Let's see you find potentials without it."

"Where have you been?" Smith demands. "I need the data you collected on this retrieval right away." She turns to Bastian. "So? It was just a mistake?"

"Not exactly. Memors are drawn to people and places with significant memories. The algorithm must have pinged a combination of her power and the alley."

Smith frowns. "Why does the alley matter?"

"It doesn't," Bastian says quickly. "Not really. It just happens to be where she was drawn."

It's more than that, though. Angelica is clearly a memor, based on the way she uses her power: channeling memories, gravitating toward touch to enhance them, relaying what she sees in that strangely calm voice. All things Bastian's read about because sometimes he actually does his homework.

But memors aren't supposed to *feel* things. They're not drawn to emotions the way empaths are. She must have meant that the memories left in the alley caught her attention. Though if she can feel memories that strongly from a location rather than a person, that would still make her a remarkably sensitive memor.

"An untrained memor could be a security risk, particularly if she's picking up on classified information," Smith is saying. "We should have a detail of officers—"

Bastian raises his eyebrows. "What, you think a little girl is dangerous? Got some memories you don't want anyone to know about, Smith?"

"It's not unreasonable to be concerned," Smith says stiffly. "We can't just ignore—"

"She's a *child*. A child who's been hiding in that alley for who knows how long, terrified—"

"She didn't *look* terrified, though, did she? Did you see her face when you brought her out? She didn't look like she was feeling anything at all."

For a brief moment, Bastian considers telling her about James, just so she can have something real to be concerned about regarding emotionless assets. Instead, he says, "Between the two of us, I think we can agree on who's more likely to know what someone's feeling. As for which of us gives a shit—"

Kent coughs loudly. "Um, Captain? I can give you that data if you'd like to stop by hacker HQ."

"Thank you," Smith says. "I'll do that." She tosses Bastian another glare, then turns on her heel and heads for the elevator.

"So, I'll just—go get that stuff ready," Kent says. His line goes dead.

In the ensuing silence, Bastian takes a breath and lets it out slowly. There's no telling how long it will take Dr. Rowe and her people to finish with Angelica's intake examination, and he has plenty of other work to do. He should go back to his office and check in with Laurel. Let the med techs contact him when they have updates.

Instead, he shifts his weight against the wall, crosses his arms over his chest, and settles in to wait.

***

She's different, isn't she?

Bastian starts and nearly falls over. Thanks to the sharp pain in his neck, he deduces that he's somehow managed to drift off while standing.

And the voice is back.

"What do you want?" Bastian demands, immediately trying to strengthen his shield.

The girl. How do you think she ended up in that alley?

"I suppose you're going to tell me you know?" Bastian's mind starts racing through the possibilities: Security breach? Retrieval caught on city camera? Rumors already spreading through the compound?

(amused-concerned-tired) *It's complicated. And right now, it isn't important.*

"Right. A stranger with up-to-the-minute access to confidential information is no big deal." He expands his shield a little, pushing at the place where the voice has seeped into his mind. Nothing happens.

What matters right now is that you found her, the voice says. *You see the significance of that?*

"What, you think someone should give me a medal for doing my job?"

(thoughtful-calculating-curious) *But it wasn't exactly* your *job, was it? And yet you still went. You made the extra effort when you realized someone might've been suffering in a way that only you would understand. Why do you think that is?*

Bastian wonders if he should look for a conference room so he isn't caught standing in a Level 14 hallway talking to himself. "What's that supposed to mean?"

If you don't find people like that little girl, who do you think will?

"Smith, probably. Or one of the other retrieval teams."

And you think they'll do a good job?

Bastian starts pushing against the intruder in his mind, slowly putting more force into it, trying not to let the headache take over. "I think you'd better tell me who the hell you are and how you're getting this information."

The focused-determined-resolve presses back against Bastian hard enough that he flinches. *There isn't time for this*, the voice says with a tinge of irritation. *You know you're dying, but there's still work to do. You need to make a choice.*

"And you need to *get out of my head*." Bastian shoves his energy outward, but it's like trying to break down a brick wall with a sponge.

You need to make a choice, the voice says again with no indication that it even noticed Bastian's attempt at defense. *What are you willing to do to keep this work alive? To keep your place in it?*

"My 'place'? What does that even mean?"

It means that it matters that you're doing this. That you're *doing it. Surely you can see that.*

Laurel said something similar in the garden the other day, about how there's work here at the compound that only he can do. But that's ridiculous—unless she and the voice are referring to Bastian's uncanny ability to make things worse. "If you're talking about running the asset program, pretty much anyone could do it better than I can. Except the last guy, obviously."

A pause. *You really don't see—?*

"What I see," Bastian says, squeezing his eyes shut, "is that you need to get out. *Now.*"

He *pushes* as hard as he can, and he's suddenly alone in his head. It happens so fast, he barely has time to register it—or the resulting small drip of blood from his nose—before a new wave of very familiar excitement-indignation-determination comes bounding closer.

"Bastian!" Laurel maneuvers around a group of med techs and comes to a stop in front of him. "I just heard you brought in a memor. Why didn't you call me? Also, why are you bleeding? We've talked about how you're not supposed to do that."

"Where's James?" Bastian demands.

Laurel huffs. Reaching into her pocket, she pulls out a handkerchief and waves it in his face until he takes it and applies it to his nose. "It's very nice that you're concerned about James," she says, "but it's also very rude that you're ignoring my questions. See how you like it." She smiles at something over his shoulder. "Hello, Henry."

Bastian turns to find Henry approaching—without Major Alexis, for once. "I thought you were busy giving tours to spies today," Bastian says.

"Major Alexis had a few more questions for the mechanics at the loading dock." Henry frowns. "Are you all right?"

"Fine." Bastian returns his attention to Laurel. "I didn't call you because I'm waiting to hear Dr. Rowe's assessment. And you're supposed to be busy babysitting a firestarter and covering other program duties."

"I was! Well, not the babysitting part, but the other stuff. Then I heard about the memor, and James agreed to stay with the students while I came down here to see what's going on." She narrows her eyes. "They said it's a little girl. You didn't scare her, did you? Being brought in can be scary, and add to that your you-ness . . ."

"I'm not *that* scary."

"No, you're mostly grouchy and unpleasant. But that could be scary to a kid."

"Laurel," Henry says, finally managing to get a word in, "I'm sure Bastian was going to meet with you as soon as things got settled. Just like he was going to report this directly to me, so I didn't have to hear about it from someone else while I was over at the vehicle loading dock."

"Okay, but this is really important! A memor could help James!"

"No."

Their combined startled-surprised-miffed makes it impossible for Bastian to keep holding back the headache. He feels it intensify and slide through his temples, tightening like a vice around his forehead.

"Bastian," Henry says carefully, "it's not a bad idea. A memor might be able to—"

It's taken even less time than it did when Valentine first brought him in, Bastian thinks. At least he got a few days before people started asking him to use his power for them.

"No," Bastian says again, but he doesn't have time to say anything else before a small cloud of concentration-tension-resolve starts heading their way, and Angelica appears across the hall.

She must have come around through a side exit from the med bay to get past the med techs. She's walking slowly and carefully, one hand sliding along the wall as she goes. The hand, Bastian notices, is clean—and so is the rest of her. They obviously held onto her long enough to apply some soap and water in addition to Laurel's fast-acting hydration solution, though it's still quite early for her to be up and moving.

"Oh," Angelica says, spotting them. "Here you are."

Dr. Rowe bursts through the exit door. "I guess we can confirm the new healing protocol is working," she says wryly through somewhat ragged breaths. "Angelica, you should be resting. Why don't you come back with me so we can help you feel better?"

"I feel fine." Angelica turns to Bastian. "They left me and went away. I don't think they like being around me."

"They're very silly if they don't want to be around a nice person like you," Laurel tells her. "Want me to go have a word with them? I'm good at having words."

"That's because you like to threaten violence," Bastian mutters.

"What was that?"

"Nothing."

"I'm Laurel," Laurel says. "This is Henry. And you already know Bastian and Dr. Rowe. I'm definitely the nicest person out of all the grown-ups here, but we all want to help you. If Dr. Rowe says you should go back to bed, then she's probably right."

"You might feel fine now, Angelica, but it will take you awhile to heal completely," Dr. Rowe explains. "You were in that alley for a long time."

"I know." Angelica drops her hand away from the wall and looks at Bastian, her gaze intense enough to be moderately disturbing. "You were there longer," she says. "I remember from when I touched you. When she came and took you away, she said she'd teach you something to make it hurt less. Will you teach me?"

"Of course he will!" Laurel says immediately. "He's been making me teach everyone how to do everything up till now, so it's about time."

Bastian makes a face. "I can't exactly teach other assets how to be empaths, Laurel."

"You could teach people how to shield, like Angelica just asked. Or how to be grumpy. Or distrustful. Or—"

"You know," Henry says, "it will probably take awhile to track down Angelica's family. In the meantime, we ought to make her as comfortable as possible, don't you think? Maybe help her get used to her power a little?"

Bastian can hear an echo of the voice in his head: *She's different, isn't she?* And even if she weren't, she'd still need to know how to protect herself.

Of course, the idea that Bastian should be the one to teach her is ludicrous, and he opens his mouth to say so. But then he catches sight of Henry's almost-smirk, feels the moment when Henry's muted concern-worry-irritation grows an outer layer of smugness-amusement-fondness, and at that point, trying to be anything other than resigned is pointless, really.

"Angelica," Bastian says, "I'll teach you what I can, but for now, you need to go back to the med bay with Dr. Rowe. All right?"

She holds his gaze for a long moment, then nods solemnly and lets Dr. Rowe lead her away.

Henry turns to Laurel and Bastian, all amusement gone. "Do either of you want to explain why I heard about this from Smith rather than one of you?"

Bastian grimaces inwardly. Point to Smith for doing what he should've done as soon as they got back to the compound.

"I didn't know!" Laurel protests.

"Exactly." Henry raises his eyebrows at Bastian. "Well?"

"What, you want us to get permission from you before every retrieval? I thought you were busy giving Alexis top secret things to report back to the liaison committee."

The blip of guilt-frustration-embarrassment is there and gone so quickly, Bastian almost thinks he imagined it. "If the retrieval is serious enough to warrant you going along, I need to know about it," Henry says. "Your assistant director does, too."

"I told her. Sort of."

"Calling me just to say you're running off and not telling me why doesn't count," Laurel says.

"Yeah? You sounded a little busy yourself. Should I ask what *you* were doing?"

Henry sighs and rubs his eyes. "Look, we obviously need to talk about communication and make sure we're all on the same page." He hesitates. "And I think there's something else we need to—"

"Sorry, am I interrupting?"

Major Alexis approaches from a side hallway, smiling his usual guileless smile, his cane tapping gently on the floor as he moves toward them.

Bastian frowns; he should have felt Alexis approaching. Alexis's subdued emotions are hard to pick up, but even his current deferential-apologetic-curious shouldn't have flown completely under Bastian's radar.

Bastian glances briefly at Henry, but he can't detect any significant negation that might've masked Bastian's ability to feel Alexis's approach. Which means Bastian's just getting slower as the headaches get worse. Great.

"I finished at the loading dock," Alexis says, "so I was hoping to review the latest liaison committee communication with you, Henry. Unless . . . ?"

For a split second, Bastian thinks Henry might refuse and go back to whatever it was he almost said.

But the moment passes.

"Of course," Henry says. "Bastian and Laurel have things to discuss, and I can catch up with them later." He looks pointedly at Bastian.

"Right," Bastian says quickly. "Laurel, come on. I'll tell you about the retrieval."

Laurel, who was eyeing Alexis thoughtfully, turns back to him. "Yes, you will," she says. Then she frog-marches him in the direction of the elevators.

Bastian manages to focus on her indignant-curious-concerned as they go rather than trying to figure out what Henry wanted to tell them—or why he apparently wanted to hide it from Alexis.

Chapter 16

"I GET THAT you wanted to spend more quality time together," James says to Laurel, slapping at a bug that lands on his arm. "And really, who could blame you? But how much longer are we going to be out here? And do we really need the third wheel?"

Crouched on the ground between James and Laurel, her hands in the dirt, Chloe mumbles to herself, "There are new paths in this section, too. The animals have been busy."

They've spent weeks trawling through the forest, looking for a path or landmark that James recognizes. Laurel maintains that asking Chloe for help was a brilliant move, even if they haven't found anything yet. Well. Anything other than the thirteen hidden animal paths Chloe's uncovered as they wander deeper into the forest.

"Maybe we're not getting anywhere because you're not a very good tracker," James mutters, kicking at the ground.

Chloe flinches. "I'm sorry! It's just—there are a lot of options. It helps that you said you think you came to the compound from the north, but there are lots of paths coming from the north."

"Don't be rude to Chloe," Laurel says sternly, poking James in the arm. "And don't take your anger out on the moss just because it's much smarter and more observant than you."

"What are you talking about?"

He's like a cranky little kid who missed his nap, Laurel thinks. "I'm talking about how we've both been relying on Chloe all day, and now it's time to ask someone else so she can have a break."

Laurel follows the path of moss to the place where it hits an oak and starts going up the trunk. "Well?" she asks it. "You *are* more observant than James, aren't you? I mean, that's not saying much because anyone would be more observant than James when he gets all grouchy."

"Hey!"

"Anyway," Laurel continues, "we've asked a lot of your friends in other parts of the forest, but they haven't been able to help. Can you?"

The moss seems hesitant to reply to her vocalization—moss tends to be pretty shy—so she decides to try something different. She goes quiet enough to feel the roots moving sugars beneath her feet, then sends out a mental greeting to all the plants in the immediate area and a request for information. *Anything new in this part of the forest?*

Beetles, says the oak sluggishly.

Laurel strokes the tree's trunk. *I'm sorry. I'll show them a thing or two when we're done here. Nothing else?*

Ask Mother.

The trouble with trees is that their familial ties are mostly knots. "Mother" could be any number of ancient trees for hundreds of miles. Still, it's not a bad idea; Laurel should have thought of it before. If she's lucky, maybe she'll be able to find this mother as easily as a human one.

Laurel goes back over to the main path where she was standing before. She plants herself right in the middle, clears her throat, and makes a sharp downward gesture with her right hand, asking the forest's root system to carry her message.

MOM?

At first, there's no response other than a tiny rustle of wind in the tree branches. Out of the corner of her eye, Laurel sees James about to open his mouth, probably to say something impatient that doesn't show anywhere near the appropriate amount of appreciation for all of Laurel's hard work. Luckily for him, Laurel has other things to pay attention to right now, such as the several trees that start to call out: *Yes?*

The polite thing to do would be to talk to each of them individually. But that would take days, given how large the forest is. And Laurel has a meeting later. Or several. She's lost track of what she's supposed to be doing today, actually.

James and Chloe are talking in low voices—or rather, James is saying something, and Chloe is quietly demurring. Laurel does her best to tune them out and focus on the underground chatter of the fungus and roots relaying the messages between trees. *We're looking for a path*, Laurel says. *Someplace where something unusual happened.* She hesitates, then adds, *Maybe something dangerous.* James did say he was trying to get to safety.

No response, so she adds, *Can you think of anything new that's happened in the forest recently?*

The slow murmurings begin again.

Too much water.

Not enough water.

Beetles.

Bad mushrooms.

And then, from somewhere far off: *Humans.*

Laurel latches onto that voice. A fir of some sort, too far away to be sure. *What kind of humans?* she asks.

They come on the path from the mountains. Mark us with something sharp. Then they go away. They try to hide, but the forest sees them. Even in the not-seeing place.

Doesn't sound like the usual compound operatives who patrol the forest. They've all gotten very detailed descriptions of what will happen to them if Laurel finds out they've done something to harm the woods in any way. *What's a not-seeing place?*

The place they don't want others to see.

Well, that's not terribly specific.

Rather than risk getting into a fight over semantics with a fir, Laurel takes a moment to consider the rest of the information. The only people who have official access to the forest are people who arrange it with the compound first. If there's a group of people hanging around without permission, compound scouts ought to have caught them by now.

She turns to James. "You said you were traveling with other people. What do you remember about them? How many were there?"

"I told you, I don't know. Aren't your plants giving you anything?"

"They're giving me ideas about how to deal with rude people."

"If it helps," Chloe says quickly, "a bunch of the paths farther out have been trampled down by stuff that isn't animals. So if James was traveling with a group, it might've been on one of those trails."

At least one of those trails leads to the clearing, Laurel thinks, feeling a sudden, sharp pain in her gut. (The place she can't stop dreaming about, where she and James and the others had a life until they didn't, until they realized what Valentine and Wright were doing to them, and then it was all hiding coded notes and talking in whispers after dark and trying to piece together enough evidence to add up to something that would save them, something that would stop the compound staff from hurting them, until the night Laurel woke up to the cries of *danger* from the plants outside, the smell of hot metal and smoke already choking her—)

"So we know James was traveling with a group, probably on a path that runs north to south," Laurel says a little too loudly. "And we know from the fir I just spoke to that somewhere in the forest, there's a path that a group of people have been using for nefarious purposes."

"What nefarious purposes?" James demands.

"Hurting trees, for one. Is there anything more nefarious?"

"Actually—"

"There's something else," Chloe says. "I've been thinking . . ."

She pauses long enough that James has time to mutter, "Don't hurt yourself," and Laurel has time to elbow him in the side.

"I should have been able to see the path Laurel's tree is talking about," Chloe says. "I mean, there are a lot of paths, but we've been out here off and on for days, so—"

James rolls his eyes. "Do we need to revisit my comment about how you might not be the world's best tracker?"

"Only if you want me to smack you upside the head," Laurel says sternly. "I'll refrain if you apologize to Chloe for that. And for interrupting."

James opens his mouth, then sighs and runs a hand through his hair. "Sorry. I'm just frustrated."

"It's okay," Chloe says in exactly the way you say it's okay when it isn't.

She hurries on. "Anyway, I think there's something wrong. When I see the paths, they usually sort of . . . glow. Every one of them, all the way to the end, and especially where they intersect. But there are a few in this forest that come together and just go dark. Like a dead zone where my tracking stops, and everything around it goes really fuzzy. Maybe the path Laurel's tree was talking about is in that dead zone, and that's why I didn't see it. Maybe that has something to do with why James can't remember it, too."

Laurel frowns. Powers not working in the forest sounds an awful lot like Henry using his negation in here last year when they were facing down John Doe. Maybe something he did is causing whatever it is Chloe's talking about. That doesn't really fit with what they know about negation, though.

"The fir said something about a 'not-seeing place,'" Laurel says. "That could be where your paths go dark."

"If the problem is darkness, I can fix that." James grins, snaps his fingers, and ignites a tiny ball of flame in his palm.

"Um. I don't think that's how it works," Chloe says, obviously missing the part where she's supposed to be impressed.

"And stop trying to burn down the forest," Laurel adds, pushing James a safe distance away from a low-hanging branch.

James sighs again and snuffs out the flame. "How do we get past the dead zone, then?"

"We could check the library database," Chloe suggests. "If we compare the maps we've put together out here with the maps on file, we can see where there are gaps, and—"

"And you expect the data in the library to be accurate? You remember how much compounds like to hide information, right?"

"But we could—"

"Why don't we just requisition a vehicle and go find this tree of Laurel's? Isn't that faster?"

Laurel gives him a stern look. "When you say 'requisition,' you mean 'steal,' don't you? Not 'go through the official request process, which could take several weeks'?"

"Well, if you want to be technical—"

"I can help," says a small voice from behind them.

Laurel whips around to see a child staring up at them. A single strand of brown hair has fallen out of her tight braid and is stuck with a bit of sweat to her tawny skin, but otherwise, she might've just strolled up and stopped to chat—after escaping her med bay handlers. Which she's been doing every day since she got to the compound.

"Hello, Angelica," Laurel says a bit wearily. "Does Dr. Rowe know you're out here?"

"I can help," Angelica says again, more firmly this time.

Inexplicably, Laurel finds herself unnerved by those eyes, which is awfully rude of her. It's not like Angelica can help her eyes being her eyes.

"I don't have to remember you," Angelica says, as though she's read something in Laurel's face and is trying to be reassuring. She turns and points at James. "I can just remember him."

James glances between them. "What is this kid talking about?"

"She's a memor," Laurel tells him. "But that doesn't mean she has to—"

"You had a memor lying around, and you didn't tell me?"

"She wasn't *lying around*. I mean, she probably was lying down while the med techs looked at her, but otherwise, no lying. Oh, except for sleep, I suppose. But other than that—"

"We had an easy option for getting my memories back, and you just decided *not to mention it?*"

There's something about James in that moment that puts Laurel on edge. For a split second, she wishes Bastian were here so she could show him that James absolutely *does too* have emotions. How else could you describe the whatever-it-is that's pushing through his eyes and pinching up the skin around his nose? Clearly, James is frustrated. And stupid.

(Doesn't explain why she tenses and suddenly feels like backing up when he's like this, why she almost doesn't want to look at him, like everything is balanced precariously on a weak branch that could break at any moment—)

"It's not like I didn't think of that," Laurel says slowly, "but like you said, she's a *kid*. And recently manifested, so far as we can tell. So she wasn't just an 'easy option.' Plus, she only got here a few days ago."

It's a little disingenuous, Laurel supposes; James is only having the same reaction that Laurel did when she first heard about Angelica. But as Bastian pointed out to her when they talked about the retrieval, there's only so much you can ask of an asset before things get rude and awkward. Especially when the asset is a dehydrated and malnourished little girl who's just trying to recover.

"I can help," Angelica insists. "I want to help."

"If she wants to help, I say let her." James holds out a hand and smiles broadly. "Go for it, kid."

James may have forgotten a lot, but apparently he still remembers that touch makes it easier. Maybe he still remembers Alice holding their hands, trying to help them remember what Wright did to them during the experiments so they could write it down.

(Maybe he still remembers the way her voice went monotone as she described needles and blood and shocks, none of which they remembered themselves, but she remembered for them, *had* to remember for them—)

Chloe clears her throat and glances at Laurel. "Maybe we shouldn't . . ."

But Angelica has already taken James's hand in both of hers and squeezed her eyes shut.

There's a moment of calm in which Laurel hears a few birds flitting between the trees and the whispers of the moss as it munches contentedly on sunlight. Then Angelica starts speaking in an even, emotionless tone.

"You remember running," she says. "You woke up in the forest, and then you were running, and there were people helping you run, and that was good because it hurt"—she sucks in a breath—"it hurt a *lot* because you still felt like everything was on fire. Like *you* were on fire."

Laurel sneaks a peek at James. He's kept his eyes open, but his gaze has gone glassy, and there's a tendon standing out on his neck. He doesn't seem to be in pain, exactly; it's more like he's experiencing the memory of pain. Laurel's heartbeat speeds up as she looks back and forth between them.

"When you couldn't run, they carried you," Angelica continues. "They fixed you some but not enough, and they said they knew someone who could help you. Your skin was red, and everything hurt, and you shouldn't have been alive, but they said it would be okay. And then—"

She makes an agonized little noise, and it goes straight through Laurel's chest. "That's enough," Laurel says, so quietly she has to repeat herself. "That's—"

"Keep going," James says over her. "What happened next?"

"I can't. There's something in the way."

"Angelica, you can stop," Laurel says, desperation clawing at her throat.

"No." James's eyes have focused again, and he's clinging to Angelica's hand. "It's almost—I remember—"

(Keep going, Dr. Wright said in the experiments, the little bits and pieces Laurel remembers. Keep the lights off, keep the door shut, keep the needle in her arm, keep the dying plants all around her, the shattered wailing of the chlorophyll desperately trying to absorb sunlight and failing because there isn't any light, not anymore, not ever—)

"*Stop*," Laurel snaps, forcing herself forward just as Angelica gives another whimper and lets go of James's hand. Laurel manages to grab her arm and keep her from falling, though they both stumble back a bit.

"Sorry," Angelica whispers. She's leaning heavily into Laurel, steadying herself with a grip on Laurel's forearm.

"*You* don't have to apologize," Laurel says, glaring at James, who's shaking himself. "*You're* not the one who—"

"No. I'm sorry you . . . your memories are messed up, too. There's something . . ."

"I think we should go back now," Chloe says. Her hands are clenched at her sides, and she seems a little scared. But she's taking them all in, and her face looks like it did in the forest last year when she disobeyed Major Valentine and offered to help them. She looks like she's standing up to the bad guys.

Which makes Laurel and James the bad guys.

Laurel swallows, then says with a little too much brightness, "You're absolutely right. I don't know about any of you, but I could use a nap."

James, who seems to have regained his composure, immediately starts protesting. "But—"

"Are you okay?" Laurel asks him.

"Yeah, but—"

"Good. Then I don't feel guilty telling you that you've lost the right to have any buts." She turns to Angelica. "Ready to go back?"

"Yes, please." Angelica moves far enough away from Laurel that they're no longer touching, but no farther.

James narrows his eyes. "What about—?"

"Later. We've done enough for today." Laurel turns on her heel and starts walking back to the compound. Chloe and Angelica fall in line with her, and after a moment, she hears James follow them.

Chapter 17

STRICTLY SPEAKING, THERE'S no reason for Henry to be walking the grounds at sunset. He's made up a few paper-thin excuses just in case anyone asks, but other than the occasional salute from officers going about their business, he's been left to his own devices. Still, he knows it's only a matter of time before someone needs him for something, so he's making the most of a quick walk, trying to prolong his freedom for however long he can.

He knows he should just go back to the suite, but he also knows why he's not: because then it would be harder to avoid the conversation he really, *really* needs to have with Bastian.

This way, he can just drive himself nuts trying to remember where he's seen that FSP6342867 number before. The more file fragments he reads, the more he's certain this Fail-Safe Protocol has something to do with him. Some sort of training, maybe? He can't imagine he'd forget something that seems so important—but then, Major Valentine was taking his blood without him knowing for years in order to make the serum used to bring in assets. So who knows what else she—or Major Alexis—might have decided to use him for?

Passing by Laurel's garden, Henry tries to distract himself by wondering whether she'll keep the plants going year round. Having a perpetual source of greenery is an appealing idea, not only because of the potential for fresh produce but because the compound itself is so gray and dull. But he can practically hear her lecturing him about how plants need rest, and it's really rude of him to even consider asking them to—

Henry frowns and stops near a line of bushes. He *does* hear a voice, but it isn't Laurel's.

He backtracks slightly and sees Bastian and Angelica sitting cross-legged underneath a gnarled tree next to the garden pond. They're facing each other, eyes closed. Henry's familiar enough with the body language to recognize that this must be Angelica's shielding lesson.

"It's not working," she says. Her eyes are still closed, and she sounds placid enough, but Henry thinks he sees a bit of frustration in her rigid posture.

"You're not trying," Bastian tells her, barely moving.

"You don't know that."

"You're feeling bored and irritated and annoyed. I wouldn't know any of that if you were at least trying to shield."

"Yes, you would. You can feel through it. You remember when you first knew you could feel more than you should. You remember . . ."

She's sitting close to Bastian but not actually touching him, which makes her ability to read his memories quite remarkable, especially in someone so young. Memors usually need training before they're able to read without touching a subject, and even then, very few can manage it.

Bastian did mention some irregularities in her power, though he didn't elaborate, either in his report or to Henry directly, claiming he wasn't ready to commit to anything official. At the very least, if Dr. Rowe's initial data is anything to go by, Angelica is likely the strongest memor this compound has ever had. And the most prone to escaping adult supervision.

None of that seems to impress Bastian, though. "I remember when I said I'd teach you to shield, and you said you wanted to learn, not waste time reading me."

Angelica opens her eyes and regards him gravely. "You're mean."

"Yup. Are you going to try this or not?"

"I did. It doesn't work. You're bad at this."

Henry chokes on a laugh.

"I never said I was good at it." Bastian opens his eyes and frowns at Angelica. "Look, when you remember things, do you see them?"

"Sometimes."

"So see your shield like it's something you're remembering. See everything that makes up *you*—your body and the bubble of space around it."

"What space?"

"The part that's yours. There's you, and then there's the space around you. If someone else stepped into that space, it would make you uncomfortable."

"I don't feel uncomfortable. Other people feel uncomfortable around me."

Bastian sighs. "All right, try this, then: Imagine you're being squeezed until you can't breathe. Like in the alley, when you were hiding behind the dumpster."

Henry frowns. Reminding someone—especially a little kid—of a recent trauma goes a bit beyond Bastian's usual rudeness. But Angelica doesn't seem to mind. If anything, she's more focused now, her eyelids falling half-closed.

"What did it feel like when you came out of the alley?" Bastian asks after a moment.

"Like there was more space. Like I could breathe."

"That's what you need to see: the amount of space it takes for you to feel like you can breathe. Then you build your shield around that."

"How?"

"However you want. However you see it in your mind."

"What does yours look like?"

Bastian hesitates, then says, "A wall."

"Like a stone wall?"

"Yes."

"Why?"

Henry expects Bastian to brush the question off. Instead, he answers it carefully, like he's never been asked to articulate it before and wants to get it right. "When I learned how to do it, my power was . . . Everything hurt. All the time. I wanted to shut out as much of it as I could. Making my shield a thick wall meant it was easier to keep more out."

Angelica's eyes open. "Does it still hurt?"

Henry clenches his jaw. He knows the answer to this one.

"Not like it did," Bastian says, much to Henry's surprise. "The shield still helps, though."

"Is yours still a wall?" Angelica asks.

"Yes. But I let more through now. You can always change what your shield looks like. You just have to decide how much to let in and how much to keep out."

Angelica appears to consider this for a moment. Then she asks, "Why would you let in anything at all?"

Henry thinks of working the John Doe case with Bastian last year and how Bastian claimed he'd just decided not to have emotions anymore—as if shutting everything out would somehow protect him from Major Valentine and the asset program and what his power was doing to him.

Except of course it hadn't. Henry still found him barely conscious and almost bled dry in a Level 19 recovery bed, and even though Bastian kept claiming that emotions were bad and that he'd somehow risen above it all, it was obvious he hadn't, that the pressure of feeling so much all the time was taking its toll on him. And then Dr. Rowe officially diagnosed what they already knew.

"It's not a bad thing, exactly," Bastian tells Angelica. "Being an asset, I mean. Having a power. You don't need to shut *everything* out. You just need to be able to protect yourself. And sometimes other people, too."

He flicks a glance at the bushes, and Henry is belatedly reminded that he's very much within the range of Bastian's power.

"So if you learn how to shield, it gets better?" Angelica looks dubious.

"Yeah. Eventually."

Angelica sits quietly, absorbing all of this. Then she leans forward. "You remember when it *wasn't* enough, though. It helped for a while, but it never really stopped the hurting. Like it isn't now. Like—"

She snaps out of her daze. "You just did it, didn't you? The shield?"

"Yes." Bastian gets to his feet, putting a bit more distance between them in the process. "You're going to have to learn about tact, too."

"What's tact?"

"Something I'm definitely not qualified to teach." He raises his head and glares at the bush Henry's standing behind. "If you're done eavesdropping, maybe you can call someone to come pick her up."

Henry moves sheepishly into view just as Angelica protests, "I don't want to go back." To Henry's great surprise, she clutches at Bastian's shirt. To Henry's even greater surprise, Bastian lets her, despite having moved away from her before.

"We're just going to find someone to take you to the children's dorm."

"*You* could take me."

Bastian makes a face. "If I show up there, they'll think I'm the one who wandered off with you in the first place."

Henry, who was about to switch his comm to the right channel to call the children's staff, stops and raises his eyebrows. "I take it this wasn't a planned lesson, then?"

"Angelica might've had a plan, but as far as I can tell, it was just to ditch the adults watching her, show up in my office, and refuse to leave until I brought her out here."

Henry immediately begins plotting to get the security footage for Bastian's office from this afternoon so he doesn't have to rely on his imagination for how that went down. First things first, though. "Angelica," he says, "I'm sure Bastian called the children's staff before bringing you out here"—Henry gives him a pointed look—"but I'm betting they'd like to check in with you and see how you're doing. Why don't I tell one of them to come over, and if you decide you don't want to go with them, you don't have to. All right?"

She looks at him for a moment, then nods.

He makes a quick call, then turns back to Angelica. "While we wait, why don't you tell me about what Bastian was teaching you? Did it make sense?"

"Sort of. But he's not very nice about it."

Henry can't quite make his laugh into a believable cough, especially after he catches a glimpse of the sour expression on Bastian's face.

"It's okay," Angelica continues. "He can be mean if he wants to. But he has to teach me because people don't like it when I remember. If I can act more normal, maybe I can stop making them mad."

"No." Bastian's frown has gotten deeper, and there's a sudden urgency in his voice. "It's not—you don't learn to shield for someone else, to make them happy. You learn because you have a right to that boundary. You're not protecting other people from you; you're deciding how much of *them* you want to let in. You're deciding what feels good for *you*."

Angelica gives him an intense, silent stare. "I'm not very good at it," she says at length.

"No, you're not."

"Bastian," Henry warns.

"You're not," Bastian repeats, "because you just started to learn today. And everyone starts out not very good before they get better."

Angelica nods slowly. "Okay. Thank you."

"You're welcome. I think."

"Are you not very good at teaching because you just started today, too?"

There's absolutely no chance of Henry pretending his laugh is anything other than what it is, especially given that the exasperation on Bastian's face is cut through with amusement.

It's the kind of expression Henry so rarely sees these days, not since Bastian's headaches got worse and the tests got more conclusive, and they shifted into this double life of pretending everything is okay and not talking about anything. Seeing Bastian's self-conscious but genuine smile makes Henry's chest hurt, a visceral twinge, like he's been stabbed. And he suddenly knows that no matter what General Carter might say about it, he has to stop messing around and tell Bastian everything.

"Sorry to keep you waiting, sir." A housing staff aide is hurrying toward them, slightly out of breath. "Hello, Angelica."

Angelica nods once in greeting.

The aide smiles at her. Despite having been dragged away from whatever he was doing on short notice, he seems unruffled and genuinely pleased to see her. "I'm David," he says. "I can take you to the dorm if you're done talking to the major and the director. Has anyone shown you where we keep all the extra treats that we steal—uh—receive from the cafeteria?"

"You shouldn't poison children," Bastian mutters.

The aide grins with the ease of someone used to not lingering on comments from grumpy children. Even if they're shaped like adults. "Don't worry; the director is teasing. I'd be happy to show you if you'd like. I think you've earned a treat for all your hard work today, don't you?"

Angelica narrows her eyes. "If I go with you, do I have to talk to people?"

"Nope. Not if you don't want to."

"And I still get a treat?"

"Yup. As long as you come back in with me so I can show you where they are."

"All right."

David turns to Henry. "Sir?"

"Go ahead," Henry says. "Good night, Angelica."

"Good night, Major. Good night, Director."

David holds out his hand to her, but she hesitates. "I shouldn't."

"It's all right either way," David says.

Apparently, it really is. Angelica doesn't take his hand, but she stays close, talking comfortably as they head back inside. David doesn't push her to get closer, and he doesn't shrink away from her, either. Not having had much direct contact with the children's housing staff when he led a retrieval team, Henry's never gotten to see how well-trained they are in dealing with touch-sensitive assets.

"I wonder if it was always like that?" Bastian asks quietly.

Because of course he wouldn't know, Henry thinks. Not when Major Valentine kept him locked away from such a young age. Not when keeping your valuables safe and secure was more important than remembering that they're also human beings.

"We need to talk," Henry says.

Bastian looks at him for a moment, then says, "I'm not going to like this, am I?" It sounds like he's trying to be flippant, but there's an edge to it. He's known this conversation was coming, too.

"No." Henry clears his throat. "But I'm going to need you to let me tell you everything before you call me an idiot."

"Well, that's not ominous." Bastian glances around. "Are you sure you want to talk about it here?"

"Yes." Sharing top secret information anywhere isn't a good idea, but security in the garden is looser than it is in other parts of the compound. And Henry can't risk either of them coming up with a reason to keep avoiding this. "You remember last year at Council HQ, when I told you the Compound Council decided to incarcerate everyone after the trial?"

"I remember when you and Carter hid yourselves in a meeting room and made me sit in an aide's office for an hour, and then you came out and said he'd told you it was taken care of." Bastian eyes him warily. "Are you saying it wasn't? Because if Valentine and Wright and John Doe aren't locked in a deep, dark dungeon somewhere having their toenails slowly ripped off—"

"No, they are. If by 'deep, dark dungeon' you mean 'a secure holding facility even Prison Officer Templeton would approve of.' And minus the toenails part."

"But?"

Henry takes a breath. "That's what the Council did with Major Valentine and the doctor. John Doe was . . . different. The Council made their determination, but General Carter and I determined differently. He was transferred to the Council HQ medical facility."

"Why?" It's not really a question; more like a clipped statement—a threat that demands an answer immediately. It reminds Henry a bit of Major Valentine. Not that he's going to say that.

"The Council wanted to execute him," Henry says. "They said he was too dangerous. Too unstable. But he's an empath—a person genetically modified to be an empath, anyway. We don't have a lot of data on empaths. Carter talked them down to lifetime incarceration, and then I suggested to him that John Doe might be willing to participate in some studies to help us understand how Wright created him. It wasn't exactly on the books, but we hoped it'd be worth it, in the end."

"And how did that go?"

Henry sighs. "He was sick, Bastian. The med techs did everything they could think of, but nothing worked. He got worse, and—"

"He died. When?"

There's really no way to make it sound good, so he just says it: "A few weeks ago."

The silence stretches out. Bastian stays completely still, not looking at him. And even though Henry knows he should keep his mouth shut, he goes on. "I was hoping we could learn something from him that would help you. Something that would help any asset in danger from their own power. But he wasn't exactly forthcoming when we asked him things directly, and Dr. Westbrook's tests only told us things we already knew: that he was artificially given powers, and those powers were causing his health to fail. So—"

"That's where you've been going. Why you left before the end of that meeting. The messenger told you he was dying, and you went to watch."

Henry frowns. "I went to see if there was anything we could do."

"And you didn't think to tell me until now?"

"General Carter said—"

"That's right; he helped you spearhead this nice little experiment, didn't he? Did you tell him about me, too?"

"Not . . . as such. But he's always had access to Dr. Wright's notes—the ones Wright didn't destroy before he was arrested, anyway—and he knows I was trying to help you."

Bastian falls silent again.

"I was a coward, not telling you," Henry says quietly. "Carter asked me to keep it secret for security reasons, but honestly, I just—I knew you wouldn't agree to it. And I had to do whatever I could to—"

"Did you even get anything useful out of it? All this sneaking around and experimenting on a dying asset?"

Henry grimaces. When you put it that way . . . "No. Not yet. But we're still going through the data, so there could be—"

"That's it?"

"Yes. Basically."

"Okay. You're an idiot."

It's sort of what Henry expected, except a little lighter on the verbal evisceration than anticipated. After a few more moments of cold silence, Henry decides he'd really prefer evisceration.

(Say something, say anything, say you haven't given up, that you understand why I did it even though it was the wrong thing to do—)

Bastian brushes past him, obviously intending to leave the garden without another word. But then he pauses, his back to Henry. "After everything Valentine did to you, after all those years of keeping things from you and lying to you, you thought it would be a good idea to keep me in the dark, too?"

Henry swallows. "No. I thought it was a horrible idea. But I didn't know what else to do to save you. Not if you won't let me use my—"

"*No.*" Bastian turns on his heel, shoulders hunching with repressed fury. "You can't do that."

Henry understands the irritation, given how Bastian's reacted to the suggestion in the past, but his pure venom seems a little out of place. "I told you before, I'm not even sure if I can, but I'm willing to try if you—"

"I don't care if you're willing; you're not doing it."

"Bastian—"

"There are *consequences*," Bastian hisses at him. "You can't think like this anymore. You can't just break the rules and expect—you're the commanding officer of this compound. That has to come first."

"I'm not proud of how I handled this," Henry says, "but don't think for a minute that I wouldn't do everything I can to—"

"*Stop.*" Bastian is rubbing his temples and wincing. Seeing it, Henry nearly puts up a negation barrier before he can catch himself. Unlikely anyone would notice out here, but they're tempting fate enough as is.

"Bastian," Henry says, struggling to keep his voice steady, "you know how much I care about the work we're doing here. But did you forget about the part where I care about you, too?"

He reaches out to touch Bastian's arm, but Bastian flinches away. With a sinking feeling, Henry lets him.

"I have things to do," Bastian says. "Don't wait up."

Henry watches him leave. Then he stands in the garden for a long while, watching the darkness creep in. Eventually, the compound exterior lights blink to full power, creating cocoons of light across the grounds.

At that point, Henry shakes himself out of his stupor and goes back inside. Because there's really nothing else he can do.

Chapter 18

THE OFFICER ON the floor is lying face up—for a generous definition of "face." She barely looks human; just a mottled mess of green and brown and black and yellow bruises. Her blank eyes are staring dully upward, nearly hidden beneath the puffiness of her skin. The body is, in a word, gross. *In two words,* super gross. *Laurel is definitely going to have a serious discussion with her subconscious about its choice of dream subjects.*

She's just considering how to start that discussion when the officer's head begins to move very slowly. Her sightless eyes blink slowly, and her mouth opens to say—

"Laurel?"

Shuddering herself back into waking, Laurel gradually becomes aware of Chloe, who is sitting on the floor, surrounded by books and maps.

"Sorry," Laurel says, stifling a yawn. "Were you saying something?"

"She was saying this is pointless." Draped across a chair a few feet away, James heaves a sigh. "Or, wait. That was me."

Laurel frowns at him and sits up, nearly knocking over the tablet she was holding when she absolutely did *not* fall asleep. Because falling asleep in the middle of the Level 20 library while doing very important research would be silly. It would imply that she's developed some sort of inability to sleep at night like a normal person, which she hasn't. Much.

"Do we need to have another conversation about how rude it is to not appreciate people who are trying to help you?" Laurel asks James pointedly.

James makes a face, then sighs again. "Sorry. Really. It's just . . . we were so close in the forest, and now . . ."

"We're not asking Angelica to read you again," Laurel says firmly. "And anyway, the library is an excellent place to find information. It comes with a catalogue and everything."

"Oh!"

The kind-but-startled face of Anna, the librarian, is peeking around the bookshelves and into the nook where Laurel, Chloe, and James are working. Her salt-and-pepper hair is pulled back, like always, except for a single loose strand toward the front. Clearly, she's forgotten to fix it again, despite the twenty times she looked in on them, got distracted by her hair, and mumbled to herself that she really ought to fix it.

It's not Anna's fault, of course. She can't help that she forgets everything—that's the whole point of an erasi: to forget things and make other people forget things, too. Henry says Major Valentine put Anna to work here to make people forget about the library, which Laurel thinks was an odd choice. Valentine could've just *said* that this is a non-circulating library rather than making an asset scare people off. Better yet, she could've gone without the restrictions altogether and just opened it up to everyone after putting some rules in place about returning things. Restricting stuff just makes people more interested in getting into it, even if it's nothing but old books and maps.

At least Anna hasn't forgotten the part where she doesn't have to make people forget anymore. Unless she's already made them forget, and they just forgot that they forgot . . .

"You're not supposed to be here," Anna says. "Unless . . . are you? I can't remember."

"It's fine," Laurel says in her best convincing-the-poison-ivy-not-to-attack-people voice. "The major won't mind."

Anna frowns, her gaze flitting nervously to each of them. "She might, though."

"Major Valentine doesn't make the rules anymore," Laurel reminds her. "That's Major Mortimer's job now. You remember Henry, don't you?"

"I . . . yes, of course. Please excuse me." Anna pauses, then smiles. "Would you like some tea?"

James opens his mouth, probably to remark on the fact that Anna's already brought them twenty cups of tea apiece, but Laurel says loudly, "Thank you, Anna. That would be lovely."

Anna beams and hurries away.

James tosses aside the book he was looking at and rubs his eyes. "This is a waste of time, and I can think of better ways to die than drowning in boredom and tea. I'm going to—"

"I think I found something."

Laurel and James look at Chloe, who's scrolling intently through a file on her tablet. She glances over to compare something with one of the large maps open all around her, then pauses and looks up at their expectant faces. "Oh, right. So . . ."

She sets her tablet down next to a highly detailed topography map in an overbearingly enormous, hardbound book. The map in the book and the map on the tablet screen both show the compound grounds and surrounding area.

"These are the places we've been exploring in the forest," Chloe says, pointing at the tablet. "According to the maps, the man-made paths in those areas connect at lots of different points, just like we thought. But if you compare this"—she taps the tablet screen—"with this"—she taps the book—"you can see there are differences."

Laurel slips off of her chair and sits cross-legged on the floor next to Chloe to get a better look at the maps. In addition to a look, she gives each an extra squint, just to be sure. "Unless the forest folded in on itself—which, to be fair, it could totally do if it wanted to—there's something missing here."

"Let me see that." James crouches next to them. Without waiting for permission, he swipes the tablet. His head bobs like a baby bird pecking for worms as he looks from screen to page. "There are more paths in the book than on the tablet," he says at last.

Chloe nods. "And as far as I can tell, the ones that're missing from the tablet are the ones that hit this junction of paths running north and south."

"That's the route we think James might've taken, right?" Laurel asks.

Chloe nods again.

"So why are the maps in that book different than these?" James is still hoarding the tablet and staring at it like he's trying to burn the zeroes and ones into his eyes.

"I don't know," Chloe says. "But there's something else here that's weird."

She pulls over several more books, all just as monstrous as the first one and with older dates on the spines. "I checked all the cartographic data in the library database against all the bound maps of that part of the forest. If the paths did change somehow over time—like new ones were built, or old ones fell out of use—all of the data would've been updated as it happened. There have always been trackers at the compound; they would've known as soon as new paths became usable or old ones became unusable."

James shrugs. "So maybe data just got lost in the transition to digital. Happens all the time."

"It's more than that, though."

Chloe looks at James, then at the tablet. When nothing happens, Laurel rolls her eyes, grabs the tablet out of James's hand, and gives it to Chloe.

"Um. Thanks." Chloe opens several more files as she continues, "So here's the thing: The cartographic data is incredibly detailed going back hundreds of years. Except for this weird jump about fifty years ago, when those trails disappeared. I'd say it was just a clerical error or something, but the only data missing is that very specific section, which is about a day and a half walk from where we were when Angelica—um—where we were the other day. It's also almost exactly where I felt that dead zone when I tried to track, which is probably why I didn't know about it until we started researching again."

The fir's "not-seeing place"—the dead zone—is a real, documented thing, then: an area of the forest that the compound claims doesn't exist anymore, at least in terms of what they put on their maps.

"What were the trails being used for?" Laurel asks.

"Moving supplies, probably. That's what the compound does with a lot of these bigger paths. But I'm not completely sure because that information is missing, too. As far as I can tell from the records we *do* have, the paths in that general area haven't been in use for—"

"—fifty years," James finishes. "Right?"

"Right."

James sits back on his heels. "So either the compound stopped using them for a good reason . . . or they stopped using them for a *bad* reason and hushed it all up, including literally deleting the trails from their maps. Which do we think is more likely?"

"Not *everything* is a sneaky cover-up," Laurel says.

"You sure about that?"

She isn't, really. Compounds are very good at being sneaky, after all. And making it difficult to put all of this information together doesn't point toward a benign explanation.

"Secret paths are pretty good, I suppose," Laurel admits. "Not as good as secret passages, but still pretty good. Where did you get these books, Chloe? Shouldn't we have found this stuff earlier if it was just sitting there on the shelf?"

"Um, well. These books *were* just sitting there on the shelf . . . in the restricted section. Do you—do you think Anna will be upset?"

"She'll get over it," James says, grinning. "And by 'get over it,' I mean she'll forget about it. How did you get them out?"

"I sort of . . . found the best path through the library to get there and back while she was busy getting more tea."

"Chloe." Laurel regards her sternly. "Are you saying you used your power to sneak into a part of the library where you weren't supposed to be and then walked off with these huge books all by yourself? And you didn't get caught while you were at it?"

"Um . . . yes? I know the books back there are supposed to be taken by request only, but I thought—these aren't too old, and I've been very careful, and Anna seems really busy, so—"

Laurel feels her throat tighten and her eyes sting. "I'm so proud of you!" she says in a tone that's not quite a squeal. "Breaking the rules and putting your life on the line to help a poor, defenseless—"

"Hang on," James interrupts. "Who's poor and defenseless? Because if we're talking about me, I'm—"

"—very grateful to Chloe for her death-defying bravery. I know!"

Chloe glances between them. "If I was really defying death, maybe I shouldn't have—"

"Of *course* you should have!" Laurel taps an open book emphatically. "Your walk on the dark side gave us this very important breakthrough! Now we just need to figure out a way to get James to those paths so we can see if he remembers anything."

"Couldn't we ask the major to let us go?"

"Right," James says, "because we're definitely going to be allowed to just waltz into the forest without having to fill out forms in triplicate explaining what we're doing and how many times we intend to breathe while doing it. Or is this the part where we steal a car? I'm still down for that."

Laurel thinks of Major Alexis, who's still asking around about things like budget allocations and research data. He seems like a nice enough guy, from the few interactions Laurel's had with him during asset program committee meetings, but he's awfully curious about a lot of things. Three assets gallivanting into the forest on a hunch seems like the sort of thing that would arouse the major's suspicions. As much fun as gallivanting is, they might be better off being boring grown-ups about it. "I hate to admit it, but James has a point. Not about stealing cars," Laurel adds quickly, "but about needing to do this the right way. If we can present Henry with a specific plan and explanation of what we're trying to accomplish, maybe we'll only need two forms instead of three."

James groans. "Are you seriously saying you want to write a report and submit it to your supervisor before we do anything?"

"No. I'm saying I want *you* to write a report and submit it to your supervisor. By which I mean me."

"What?"

"Chloe can help you. Put together these maps and all the other information that seems relevant: your check-ins with Dr. Rowe, your memories, Chloe's observations in the forest, whatever. We have to have a solid argument for why Henry should let us keep investigating. And more than that, *he* needs to have a solid argument for anyone else who might ask."

"Like who?"

"Like everyone. Henry has a million people to answer to now. He can't just get shot and wander around in the forest for days anymore."

"What?"

"Never mind. Are you two going to work on your report now or what? I'll give you extra points if you can find some pretty stickers to put on the cover."

James and Chloe blink at each other.

"We could go back to the restricted section," Chloe suggests tentatively. "There were other books there related to the compound mapping projects over the years. Maybe we can find some more information on what those paths were being used for."

"We *could* do that. Or . . ." James gives Laurel an appraising look. "Or we could call in the big guns."

Laurel frowns. "I don't have any guns, big or otherwise. And I'm not stealing Henry's, so don't ask."

"But you have higher security access. Perk of being the assistant director of the asset program, right?"

"What exactly do you think I have access to that you don't?"

"Well—"

They're interrupted by the sound of approaching footsteps. James jumps to his feet and moves toward the opening of their nook. "Anna," he says, keeping his voice low. "I'll distract her while you two keep researching."

Laurel narrows her eyes. "This is just your way of getting out of doing the work, isn't it?"

"I have no idea what you—Anna! Just the woman I was looking for." James rushes forward to take the tea tray out of her hands, setting it down carelessly on the small table where the rest of the tea Anna brought is slowly growing cold.

"Oh! Can I help you with something?"

"Absolutely," James says, grinning at her. "Could you show me where that collection of historical data on forest flora and fauna is? I'm sure I'll find it much faster with your help."

Laurel thinks James might be piling it on a bit thick, but Anna seems swayed by the attention. "Well," she says, "of course I want to help, but it would be a shame for your tea to go cold . . ."

"It's fine; Laurel and Chloe can drink it. Or I can warm it up when I get back."

Deciding it would be better for everyone's blood pressure if Anna doesn't know she's got a firestarter with an itchy trigger finger in her library, Laurel adds, "It's all right, Anna. James could really use your help. Chloe and I will be fine."

"Well, if you're sure . . ."

James pats Anna's shoulder and gently, but firmly, turns her away. He sneaks a pointed glance at Laurel before turning back to Anna. "The print books from that collection were on the north side, right? And wasn't there something in the library database as well?"

Their voices fade as they walk away.

"Um." Chloe's voice breaks through the sudden quiet, making Laurel jump. "I guess I'll go back to the map section . . . ?"

Laurel nods. "Good luck. I'll contact your next of kin if you don't make it."

"That's . . . not reassuring."

"Really? I thought that's what you're supposed to say whenever someone goes off on an adventure." She considers for a moment, then adds brightly, "Don't worry! I'm mostly sure everything will be fine. Is that better?"

"I guess so." Chloe gets to her feet in such a way that Laurel only catches about half of her dubious facial expression.

"I'm sorry about James," Laurel says abruptly. "I know he's a little brusque, which is a neat word even though it sort of just means rude, so he really shouldn't be proud to be it. Anyway, I've known him a long time, so I know that even if he's a bit James-like now and then, he really is grateful for your help."

"It's all right," Chloe says. "I just want to help."

Laurel smiles at her. "I know. And I appreciate it. James does, too. Even if he's bad at showing it."

Chloe pauses, clearly a prelude to bolting for the opening in the bookshelves. She seems to be struggling with something—her whole body tenses up briefly like a sapling bracing itself against the wind—and then she says very quietly, "It's just . . . if he really *were* grateful, he wouldn't make you be the one to tell other people, would he?"

"What do you mean?" Laurel's voice comes out a little sharper than she intended.

"I mean, you know him best, of course, but I just noticed he spends a lot of time being sort of . . . self-centered. And then you say something about it, and he apologizes. And then he does it again, and you have to do it again, and . . ."

"That's not—"

"Never mind," Chloe says, quickly grabbing a few books. "I didn't mean to—never mind. I'll go see what else I can find."

Perplexed, Laurel watches her scurry away.

***

Laurel goes through the pre-loaded data on the tablet Anna gave her and comes up with nothing new. She has access to the same maps Chloe was comparing to the books, and there are a few reports about officers tracing various trails through the forest. But nothing screams "super secret hidden paths"—which is just as well, since a screaming fragment of data would probably bring Anna running, and that would defeat the entire purpose of this little venture.

After she's been through all the files enough times that the letters are starting to blur, Laurel taps on a program that opens up a dialogue box asking for her username and password. And then she stops.

Strictly speaking, there's nothing wrong with her using her security access to go deeper into the compound's files. The whole reason she has access is so she can use it when necessary. Sure, her use will be monitored, but she can explain to whoever needs to know that she's been helping James with his memory, and that'll be that. The asset program committee will at least trust that whatever research she's doing is in the best interests of the assets she's supposed to be taking care of. Which includes James.

Still, her fingers hover over the screen. Just because more information is open to those who need it now, rather than hidden away like the compound had it for ages, doesn't mean it's information she actually wants to know.

Laurel sits with the stupidity of that thought for a moment, then shakes her head and puts in her credentials.

Her first few searches don't give her anything terribly exciting: just a few more folders of data and charts and maps. She's mildly interested to see how closely the compound has been monitoring and scouting the forest over the years, but nothing here is anything they didn't already know. No mention of the missing paths Chloe found.

Laurel is about to give up when she realizes there's an additional file on her home screen that wasn't there before. The file name is unwieldy—all numbers and letters jumbled together, starting with FSP. Laurel has to tap it several times before it opens sluggishly. Not that that helps much, since the text is mostly corrupted. More letters and numbers in odd configurations, no spaces, taking up page after page. And no reason for it to be here, so far as Laurel can tell.

Then she sees something that makes her breath catch: an image of a dead compound officer lying on the ground, her face bruised and mottled green.

Laurel swallows and reminds herself that she ought to be breathing. Just because it *looks* like the officer she's been dreaming about nonstop for weeks doesn't mean—whatever her silly brain thinks it means. This is just … something she must've caught sight of before. A misplaced file from somewhere. It certainly doesn't belong in a section of data about the forest, anyway. She should have a word with whoever came up with this organizational system.

She closes the file and looks at the date stamp. This is the first time the file has been opened today. And it was created today, which makes no sense and also makes it hard to believe she could've somehow come across it before.

Laurel glances around the nook. It was a quiet and inviting place to research not too long ago, but now it feels cold and menacing. The back of her neck prickles like someone's watching her. Which is silly because she's alone with the books and bookshelves, and neither of those things have eyes. Probably.

She looks back at the tablet and comes to a decision without realizing she's decided to make one. Very quickly, she opens several programs and sends herself the document over a secure channel. Then, using her administrative access, she deletes the file from the library tablet.

"Well? Did you find anything?"

Laurel starts and looks up to find James peeking his head around the bookshelf nearest to her.

"No," Laurel says. "Nope. Definitely, exactly nothing."

James raises his eyebrows and opens his mouth, but she interrupts him, tossing aside the tablet with what she hopes is the right level of casual disinterest in compound property. "I promise I'll keep looking, but right now, I have to go teach a class. Which means Chloe needs to come with me and attend that class, and you need to go to your appointment with Dr. Rowe. So let's move."

She gets to her feet and hurries him out of the nook. Not because she's done something wrong and wants to escape the scene of the crime, of course, but because she really does have to get to a class, which is far more important than the uneasy feeling in her stomach.

Chapter 19

BASTIAN SUPPOSES THAT he should be glad he finally knows what Henry's been keeping from him. But it's hard to feel thankful when he's spent almost a week completely numb, thinking about Valentine's experimental empath, the guy who tried to kill just about everyone Bastian's ever let himself care about, being dead. After a long period of suffering.

Suffering Bastian's going to have to go through, too.

And Henry, the colossal idiot, not only kept the whole thing a secret, but went there and probably sat in a room with John Doe, who could've killed him at any time, particularly with Henry having to hide his own power. All that for nothing.

Maybe Henry's the one who's sick, Bastian thinks. He can't seem to stop trying to protect people, even if it means putting himself in danger for no good reason. For people who don't deserve it.

"Director? Should I make the call again?"

Bastian starts, realizing he was nodding off with his head resting on his hand. He immediately sits up straight and glares at the nearest person, who happens to be Dr. Rowe.

Meeting, he reminds himself, trying to focus his blurry vision by sheer will alone. Budgets. Updates on asset training regimens and health checks. Collecting notes he'll have to pass on to Major Alexis, whether he likes it or not. Time to forget about how he's barely slept for days and stop acting pathetic, or Dr. Rowe will march him off to the med bay for more tests.

"Director?"

"No, I'll do it." He turns to the rest of the asset program committee, who are waiting for the meeting to start. "I'll be right back. Plot amongst yourselves."

Smith gives him a withering look, which Bastian ignores as he steps out into the hallway, already switching his comm to a different frequency.

"Laurel," he hisses, "where the hell are you? At least send me a plant to put in your chair or something."

There's no response. He wasn't expecting one, really. She's been flighty for weeks, dodging calls, showing up late to meetings, skulking around the compound with James doing "research."

He ought to be able to use his power to find her, but just thinking about sifting through all the emotional debris in the compound makes his head throb.

The last time Laurel was this late, Bastian tried the empath link she set up between them last year. But he couldn't get anything on that, either. He wonders if he accidentally severed it in his effort to deter the voice that keeps barging into his head unannounced.

Or maybe Laurel just doesn't want to be found.

Maybe she doesn't want to be found by *him*. They're not fighting, exactly, but she definitely hasn't forgiven him for not joyously welcoming James and instantly trusting him. Like she thinks it's somehow unreasonable to be cautious, particularly when Bastian is supposed to be making decisions that take into account anything that might be a danger to the assets in this compound.

He waits another pointless minute before going back into the meeting room, closing the door, and sitting down again at the head of the table. "We'll have to do this without the assistant director for now," he says.

"This is the third meeting she's been late to this week," Smith points out.

"Yes, thanks. I can count. Fenmore, about that report—"

"If the assistant director has something better to be doing than coming to these meetings, I think we should know about it."

Bastian blows out a breath and turns back to Smith, ignoring Fenmore's awkward-worried-embarrassed as the aide glances between Bastian and Smith.

"You're right," Bastian says, lacing his fingers together. "If there *were* something going on, you would need to know. But there isn't. So if we're done with unfounded accusations—"

"She could be doing something you're not aware of. That asset she's responsible for—"

"Maybe we should postpone this meeting until the assistant director can join us," Dr. Rowe suggests.

"Not necessary." Bastian nods to Fenmore. "Go ahead."

"Are you sure?" Rowe asks quietly as Fenmore gets out his notes. "Maybe you need some time to—"

"I'm *fine*," Bastian snaps at her. "Waiting for Laurel is pointless. Do you want me to do my job or not?"

But he has to stop because he realizes with a slow, awful burn underneath his skin that Dr. Rowe has gone still, her eyes glassy and staring at nothing.

(The gray *nothing* of muted emotions, just like Snyder in the interrogation room, just like so many others, before he knew what he was doing—but how could he have done it to Dr. Rowe just now when he wasn't even—?)

"Sir?" Fenmore is looking a bit dazed, clutching his tablet full of financial data in front of him like a shield.

"Shut up and stay back!"

Bastian is on his feet with no memory of how he got there. He rips off one of his gloves and feels Dr. Rowe's wrist for a pulse: thready, but it's there. She's still sitting quietly, not blinking, a vacant expression on her face. Not feeling anything.

Struggling to steady and bolster his shield, Bastian turns to the others. "We need to—"

They're all staring at him, their eyes the same as Dr. Rowe's.

(It's like in the forest last year, John Doe laughing while Henry and the others lay on the ground, while Valentine tried to pretend she still had control of the situation, and all the anger and fear and loathing Bastian kept bottled up boiled over—except he'd had to *let* it, he'd had to *want* to use it, and this is just—he was only irritated and tired; he didn't mean to—)

He wants to go around and check on them all, make sure everyone's okay, but he can't risk it. Whatever he's done to them, it'll wear off soon. After all, it did when—

Shit. When he did it to James. Because he's done this before, whatever it is.

He can't just sit here and wait. Not when he doesn't understand what happened or if it'll happen again.

Clenching his jaw tight enough to hurt, he hurries out of the room, knowing how bad it will look but totally at a loss. Should he call the med bay and have someone come for him? Would it be better to get himself away from people first and see if he can figure out what's going on? Maybe he should try the pool . . . No, too many people between here and there. Outside, then. When he's far enough away, he can—

"Bastian? Have a moment?"

Shit shit shit. The forced patient-calm-pleasant does nothing to hide the sadness-guilt-worry underneath, and why the *hell* does it have to be Henry right now?

"No," Bastian says, speeding up and walking right on past.

Henry, damn him, catches up easily and falls into step. "Listen," he says quietly, "we don't have to talk about the other day—"

"Then let's not."

Henry's frown weighs heavily on Bastian's skull. "Fine. But I do actually have to ask you—"

They turn a corner, and it's suddenly far too bright in the hallway. Bastian slows down against his will and squints. Henry says something, but Bastian has no idea what. He's too busy reaching out to steady himself against the wall.

As soon as he touches it, everything in his head explodes.

He drops to the floor immediately. He thinks he might need to throw up, but everything hurts too much for him to do anything besides squeeze himself into a ball and try to remember how to breathe.

(Because he can feel everything ten times, twenty times more than he should be able to, startled-surprised-confused-curious, all the emotions of everyone passing by. And then the rest of the floor, tired-irritated-bored-calm-determined-focused, everything all at once, and somehow it's worse than it's ever been, worse than in the forest or on the gurney for Wright's experiments or even what he felt just now in the meeting room, realizing what he did. It's like every emotion in the entire compound is pressing down on his head and the back of his neck—)

"Bastian, what—?"

"D-don't—"

But of course Henry's kneeling next to him, starting to put up a negation barrier. Trying to protect him.

(But it's not working, it's never not worked before, not like this, Henry's nothing-nothing-nothing just a thin blanket with holes that Bastian can still easily feel through, but it doesn't matter, the important thing is that Henry can't be caught doing this—)

"Get the med techs here *now*," Henry is saying into his comm. "Yes, it's an emergency. Stop talking and *do it*." To someone nearby: "Find Laurel and send her to the med bay as well."

Bastian grabs Henry's jacket. "S-stop—"

"I'll be careful. Just—"

"S'not working."

Henry stares at him. "What?"

Bastian should probably say something appropriately cutting about Henry's inability to hear, but that would be pretty hypocritical, since Bastian's having trouble hearing anything right now, too. Even though it's stupid and pointless, he buries his head against Henry's neck (*fuck*, he is never going to complain about a headache ever again). He's only vaguely aware that Henry is putting his arms around him. It doesn't help with the pain at all—that's still getting worse—but he does enjoy being in Henry's personal space. Except . . . except they said they weren't going to do this, right? Not in compound hallways. They were going to . . . do something. Or not do something. Something that means Bastian can't touch Henry nearly as much as he'd like . . .

"The med techs will be right here," Henry says (terrified-alarmed-confused, still easy to read, jarring with the attempt at a calm exterior). "Can you tell me what's going on?"

That seems like a reasonable question. If Bastian's head weren't on fire, he could answer. He could warn Henry about Dr. Rowe and the others. He could . . .

"Bastian?"

It suddenly seems very important for him to muster up the strength to say that secrets are bad, that they should make a new rule not to have any, that he didn't like finding out about John Doe that way even if he understands the stupid reason behind it, but everything's blurring now, and it's still too bright . . .

"Don't—hey, stay with me—"

Bastian closes his eyes, and then there's nothing.

Seven months ago

BASTIAN DOESN'T PARTICULARLY care about using his power in front of other people, but sitting in an interrogation room at Council HQ, knowing Carter and the rest are on the other side of the two-way mirror and waiting for the show to start, Bastian feels like he's a trained pet on display. The whole Council is watching him fetch. Good boy!

But he said he'd do it, didn't he?

For a brief moment, he lets himself pretend Henry's on the other side of the glass, too, rather than stuck out in the hall. Of course, it's better this way; Bastian isn't sure Henry would be able to keep his negation in check.

Henry has made no secret of the fact that he thinks this is a bad idea. He said as much on the beach yesterday, not to mention several times at dinner. He even started to broach the topic again when they got back to the hotel, at which point Bastian had to awkwardly remind him that there were other things they could be doing besides rehashing this. Henry didn't need any further convincing to drop the subject.

Anyhow, as much as the weak, traitorous part of Bastian wants Henry here, and as much as Henry might be able to stick to stony silence per regulations, the Council was pretty clear that dissemination of the information they get at this interrogation is strictly need-to-know. Of course, since Henry's been all but promoted, he'll be getting the official report—with whatever redactions the Council sees fit to make. For now, though, there's protocol.

Bastian figures Henry can practice holding back the negation while he waits in the hall. He's going to be doing a lot of that. Just like they talked about last night and this morning and will probably continue talking about indefinitely, assuming this goes well. For a certain definition of "well."

"Lucas?" says a booming voice in Bastian's earpiece. "We're ready to start."

The door to the interrogation room opens. Officer Hendricks leads the shackled prisoner to Bastian's table, waits for her to sit down, and then steps back to stand by the machine in the corner of the room.

Major Valentine's face is perfectly calm as she sits across from Bastian, as though she spends all her time in interrogation rooms, cuffed and prepared to be read by an empath as part of a misconduct trial. She even smiles at him, her face a bit paler than it was several weeks ago in the forest, but still just as confident and sharp.

"This is like old times, isn't it, Sebastian?" she says.

"We expect your full cooperation, Valentine," Carter booms through the room's intercom system. "No shielding. Your emotional signature will be recorded afterward. But I don't need to tell you how this works, do I?"

"No, sir," says Valentine. "I'm familiar with the procedure."

"Very well. When you're ready, Lucas."

If they wait till he's ready, they're going to be waiting a long time.

"Afraid, Sebastian? That's not like you." Valentine looks almost concerned. It's the look he's seen a million times: the one she uses when he takes too long. The one she wears when the suspect has too much anger-fear-worry, and he knows it's going to be one of those reads where his nose starts bleeding, and he can't breathe, and he'll have to touch them . . .

He'll have to touch her.

He doesn't at first, though. He closes his eyes so he won't have to look at her, shores up his shield as much as he can, and feels out. Nothing here he didn't already know. Her amusement-calm-curiosity is strong, at odds with the likely outcome of this interview—that she'll be locked away for a very long time. On the surface, being arrested for manufacturing a rare asset and using him to kill senators doesn't seem to be weighing her down much.

"I don't blame General Carter for wanting to send me to prison," she says in a low voice, putting cracks in his concentration. "I told you in the forest: No one ever really understood what I was trying to do. It must look like some sort of devious plan, hurting people just to get what I want. Orchestrating all of the experiments, despite the not insignificant odds."

"Shut up," he says through clenched teeth. (He's going to have to touch her.)

"Valentine," Carter rumbles, "this is a read, not an opportunity to pontificate. Kindly keep the commentary to yourself unless you're asked for it."

"Excuse me, General, but I don't see how my explaining the situation to Sebastian will affect his work. We've done this more than a few times, he and I."

"Not like this," Carter growls.

"It's fine," Bastian says, if only to shut them both up long enough for him to regain focus.

He can feel Valentine's eyes on him—and the bit of thoughtful-condescending-amused that goes with it. She's probably smiling her favorite smile, the one that's genuine enough to make you complacent but fake enough to hide what she's really thinking.

"The problem," she says, "is that most people are too afraid to do what must be done. Not just to further science, like Dr. Wright wanted to, but to further themselves. We're trained to give up everything for the good of the compound, and some idiots take to that, like your Captain Mortimer. So quick to put his brain away and do what he's told—"

Bastian, who's opened his eyes and grimly removed his gloves during this clear attempt at baiting, now reaches forward and grabs her wrists before she can say another word. She goes quiet instantly, but her smug-confident-unimpressed is stronger now.

He doesn't get pictures, exactly, but he can connect the vague feeling with the blurred action: collecting data with Dr. Wright in Laurel's compound (focused-determined-intrigued); working under the direction of Senator Haldis's secret committee, knowing he would be annoying and would assume he was in charge, but also knowing it was necessary to achieve her goals (disgust-irritation-purposefulness). And—

A little boy in an alley.

(Her entire career has led to this, all the searching and putting up with idiots telling her how to do her job when all they've ever done is sit behind a desk; everything—the hackers spending years tracking the data, the officers making sure the parents were dealt with, the timing to make sure he'd be there for several days and get desperate enough that any adult showing up with a way out would be welcome—all of it led to this moment—and it has to be her, not some junior officer or even Major Alexis, because there hasn't been an empath in over two hundred years, and now she's the one who's going to—)

Bastian jerks away without meaning to. He almost gets to his feet before he remembers that he needs to stay calm. Well, comparatively calm. For one thing, it's more important than ever not to let Valentine think she has the upper hand. For another, if he acts too upset, even Carter will notice and terminate the interview. And they really do need whatever Valentine can give them if they want to take her down permanently.

"I'll be very interested to see how it goes," Valentine says, smiling at him and rubbing her wrists as best she can while shackled. "The hubris of believing you can change a system with generations of history."

She knows about the plans to put Henry in charge of the compound, then. It's not something they brought up at the initial hearing, but it's no surprise that rumors are already circulating.

"The Council will guide you, of course," she continues, her tone making it clear what she thinks of that. "But if you'll let me give you some advice—"

"No, thanks."

She smiles. "You don't have time for that, do you, Sebastian? Not if you want to do something about it."

"About what?"

"Lucas," Carter says in Bastian's ear. "You have the read. Stop letting her—"

Bastian holds up a hand to the mirror, his eyes never leaving Valentine's. "About what?" he repeats.

The smile stays in her eyes, but now she's leaning forward and projecting only concern-worry-sadness. "Are the headaches getting worse yet?"

Bastian wishes he had no idea what she's talking about, but she saw what happened to him in the forest when he used his power. And while he can pretend he didn't have to get up last night to down a larger-than-average number of painkillers, he and Henry both know he did.

(But there was also after, when he came back to bed, and Henry didn't ask anything, just put his arms around Bastian and stroked his hair and enveloped him in a low-level negation field that took care of what the pills couldn't, and Bastian felt safe enough to fall asleep again in that little bubble of calm—)

"If you really care about him—if you really care about any of them—you won't let them waste their time on you," Valentine says quietly. "I know that sounds harsh, but the truth often does. If you want this new compound of yours to work, you can't allow the person in charge to be conflicted about his priorities. And you know he will be because your captain is unable to differentiate between necessary objectives and idealism. I think we've both seen that."

"You don't know anything about him," Bastian says before he can stop himself. "You've made that very clear."

Valentine's smile gets fractionally larger. (He should have kept his mouth shut.) "I know you think you're capable of having an emotional attachment to him. And while he may be the worst, there are others, too. Your weakness doesn't have to be theirs, though."

"What's that supposed to—?"

Her face falls into an expression that might look like genuine sadness on anyone else. "I'd hoped Dr. Wright and I would be able to find a way to save you. But we knew a year ago that there wasn't much time left, and after the way you've chosen to use your power since then . . . well. Perhaps if you'd let us continue our work—"

"Lucas," Carter says sternly.

"You forget," Bastian says to Valentine, "I was just in your head. You never gave a damn about saving me or any other asset. We're all just data to you."

"Important data," Valentine amends. "Can you really say anyone you interrogated was any different to you? I'd like to applaud your recently developed sense of honor, but frankly, I think any change in your character lately has been part of an effort to entice a certain—"

"We're done."

He gets up and walks over to the machine waiting for him in the corner, rolling up his sleeve as he goes.

"Sebastian."

He turns back without meaning to. Valentine is looking at him with an unreadable expression, projecting thoughtful-concerned-resigned pretty clearly, but it doesn't add up. She's always been good at separating what her face says she's feeling from what she actually is.

"Think about what I said," she tells him. "You'll have much bigger things to deal with in the coming months. If you've truly become as selfless as you think you are—"

"I never said—"

"—you'll want to consider how to make things easier on the people you claim to care about. Don't bring them down with you."

"That's enough, Valentine," Carter says through the intercom. "Let's finish this."

Valentine smiles thinly at Bastian like they're sharing a secret. "Another bit of advice, Sebastian: Be careful who you trust. Not everyone has your best interests at heart."

"Like you did?"

Valentine shrugs, her smile still irritating and enigmatic.

Bastian lets Officer Hendricks apply the electrodes to his skin. There isn't a good way to deal with the fact that he either has to turn his back to Valentine (uncomfortable) or face her while he does this (also uncomfortable).

He opts for keeping his back to her, making sure to detach himself from the machine and get his gloves back on as soon as the recording is done.

General Carter throws open the door, and several officers follow him into the room. He nods to Bastian, then turns to Valentine. "Officer Hendricks will review the recording and report back to the Council when we reconvene tomorrow morning," he says. "The Council will debate and then decide how to proceed. In the meantime, you will accompany these officers back to the prison level and remain there until you're needed. Is that understood?"

Valentine, Hendricks, and the other officers give their best yessirs before Hendricks herds Valentine out the door. Bastian makes it a point not to watch them go.

Carter gives Bastian a once-over, then sighs. "Go put Mortimer out of his misery before he assumes we've done something nefarious to you."

Bastian takes out his earpiece, hands it to Carter, and tries for something closer to striding with purpose rather than running away as he exits the room.

Henry is leaning against the hallway wall but straightens up immediately upon seeing Bastian and hurries toward him. "What did she say to you?" he demands.

So much for keeping a stoic face. "Not here."

"I told you if she—"

"Henry. Please."

It's probably the "please" that throws him off enough to stop the steady stream of foggy worry-anger-concern that's wafting off of him. Bastian feels a headache coming on, but he can still read through the vestiges of Henry's negation. They'll have to work on making it less obvious. He can't be doing it in public from here on out, even at such a low level. Not when there are going to be even more assets around that he might accidentally negate.

(He can't negate, just like Bastian can't put his arms around Henry's neck and breathe him in and forget the disgust left over from being anywhere near Valentine's mind—because she was right, damn her; everything he does now could ruin Henry's chances of turning the compound around, and if Bastian really does care about him, he'll have to—)

"Whatever you're thinking, stop it," Henry says into his ear, making him shiver (not fair). "Let's take a walk."

Bastian looks around and realizes they've made it outside onto the grounds. There aren't a lot of people here at this time of day, but still . . . "Cameras."

"Oh, you were thinking about doing something we don't want caught on the security feed?"

Bastian tries to give Henry a withering glance but gets distracted by the very poor effort Henry's putting toward hiding a grin. Bastian is torn between reminding Henry about how they agreed to maintain an air of professionalism in public and just kissing him senseless, cameras be damned.

Henry's amusement dissipates as Bastian's silence stretches out awkwardly. He clears his throat. "Do you want to tell me what really happened?"

"No," Bastian says. And then, because he's weak and pathetic and can't stop himself, he grabs Henry's hand. "Can we just—go take that walk somewhere? Anywhere? Now?"

Without missing a beat, Henry laces his fingers through Bastian's. "Yeah. Wherever you want."

Chapter 20

LAUREL ISN'T SURE whether it's the crick in her neck or the fern poking at her ankle that does it, but either way, she jolts awake and nearly falls off her chair.

"Sorry," she mumbles to the fern, whose pot she almost knocked over. *Almost*, but *didn't*, so the alarm pulsing through its leaves is totally unwarranted and just further evidence that ferns are drama queens.

"Oh, hush," she tells it as she crouches down to pat its leaves. "You volunteered to come with me, remember? And then you said it would be cooler if you could hide mysteriously underneath the table instead of sitting on top of it like a normal plant."

She shouldn't have asked, of course, because it's really quite silly. Sure, Level 17 is a bit lower than she generally likes to go in the compound, but there's plenty of artificial light in this meeting room. She's willing to admit that she *might* be a bit of a drama queen herself.

It would've been smarter to stick to her usual haunts on the upper levels, but for the past few days, she's been restless, unable to stay too long in any one place. She knows exactly why, but she's not going to think about it, thank you very much. Instead, she's trying a different tactic: new room, new plant companion, new dedication to reviewing training reports and to *not* thinking about Files That Shall Not Be Thought About.

The first two things have gone fairly well.

The persnickety fern has been a faithful companion so far, really. It doesn't deserve to live in terror of being knocked over, even if it can be a bit of a pill.

"Sorry," Laurel says again with a sigh. "It was very nice of you to come down here with me, and I'll try very hard not to disturb you. Or I can take you back upstairs, if you'd prefer . . . ?"

The fern twitches its fronds very slightly, which is fern-speak for an eye roll and an indicator that it would rather risk toppling over than have to go back to her room and share space with a hosta.

Laurel gets to her feet and stretches, letting out a loud yawn. Her eyes fall on the dark screen of the tablet on the table, and for the millionth time since she got in here, she's tempted to open the file she's definitely not thinking about and scroll through it again, burning the weird letters and numbers into her eyeballs until they make some sort of sense. Not that she wants to look at that picture again. She sees the officer's face out of the corner of her eye all the time now, which is silly because of course she doesn't *really*, except . . .

She shakes her head vigorously and reaches for the tablet—to look at reports and nothing else. Then she notices something else lying on the table next to it: her comm.

Oh.

There are classes. There are meetings. She's supposed to be *doing things*, not hiding in unused meeting rooms and engaging in unscheduled naps. Sleep deprivation is no excuse. At least, it's no excuse Bastian is going to accept for why she's late to yet another asset program committee meeting.

Laurel snatches up the comm, turning it on and putting in her earpiece at the same time. "Hello! Sorry I'm late, I was just . . ."

The time on her tablet home screen finally registers in her staticky brain: It's early evening. She is now *very* late for the morning meeting.

"Um." Laurel clears her throat. "Okay, I've just realized the meeting is probably over, and 'late' doesn't really cut it. Maybe someone can just, er, get me up to speed when they get a chance . . . ?"

The other end of the line is oddly silent. No yelling from Bastian, who's probably got epic frowny lines between his eyebrows by now. Nothing from anyone else, either.

"All right," Laurel says, a bit miffed. She starts packing up her things and putting them back into her shoulder bag. "Bastian, I'll come see you in your office, if you're free. You can yell at me when I get there. You won't have much time to put together your harangue, but I have faith in you."

She's just flung her bag over her shoulder and is about to pick up the fern when there's a beep from another channel. Laurel switches over. "Yes? Are we chewing me out over here instead?"

"Laurel? It's Kent."

"Oh! Hello, Kent. How are you?"

"Busy. Did you know your signal was offline for several hours?"

"Er. Yes. Sorry about that."

"Why would you just turn off—? You know what, never mind. At least now we don't have to send the black coats out to track you down. Anyway, I'm supposed to tell you that you're needed in med bay."

Laurel sighs inwardly. "I'm sorry, Kent, but the yarrow and I haven't finished our rebuttal presentation for the med techs on why their fever reducers are so inferior to my tinctures. We only have a few more slides to finish, but for now, I need to check in with the committee, and—"

"Yeah, I don't think this is about that. The major said it's an emergency."

Fern in one hand, the other poised to open the meeting room door to let herself out, Laurel nearly drops everything literally and her stomach metaphorically. "Is Henry all right?"

"He's fine, as far as I know. But I get the impression that Lucas is . . . not."

Laurel goes hot and cold all at once. "Tell me what happened so I know what herbs to bring. No, never mind; I'll bring everything. Right now." (It won't work, nothing works, and it especially won't work if Bastian's already—)

"I can't tell you anything else for sure right now, but I think you should get over there," Kent says carefully.

Laurel swallows and tries to steady herself. "Okay. Thank you."

"Sure." He hesitates, then adds, "Just—let me and Sybil know what's going on as soon as you find out." He cuts off his line before she can respond.

Alerted by the anxiety in her voice, the fern has draped one of its leaves over her hand in solidarity. Or maybe it's just off kilter because it's been moved around so much; Laurel is too distracted to be sure. She adjusts the pot in her arms, already mentally running through her herb stock as she opens the door and hurries out into the hallway.

"Laurel!"

She turns to find James heading toward her, his eyes bright. "I need to talk to you!"

"Not now." Laurel tightens her grip on the fern and picks up speed as she heads for the elevators. From somewhere far off, her brain reminds her that she hasn't checked in with James in a while and really ought to, since she's supposed to be responsible for him and all, but she tells that part of her brain to shut up because it really ought to be helping the other part of her brain figure out what to do about Bastian.

James gets in front of her. "It's important," he says in a low voice. "I remembered—"

"I need to *go*," Laurel says.

"And *I* said—" James pauses and frowns at her. "What's wrong?"

She manages to hold it together, barely. "Bastian is—I don't know. I have to go help."

James opens his mouth to reply, but she skirts around him and keeps heading for the elevators.

"Wait," James says, matching her pace. "There's something I need to—listen, if you'd just—"

"I *can't* just," Laurel snaps. "I was in that meeting room catching up on work I missed because I was helping *you*, and meanwhile, Bastian was—" She can feel her eyes start to sting, so she digs her nails into the strap of her shoulder bag and tries to focus on the way the fern feels, resting against her chest.

"Okay," James says in a tone implying it's nothing of the sort, "but—"

"Are you actively dying right now? Because I know someone who might be, and that has to come first."

"No, it doesn't."

Laurel glares at him. "Seriously? What could possibly come before saving my stupid best friend's life?"

"You can't save him, Laurel."

Laurel suddenly understands why flytraps feel the need to lash out and kill things that get too close. "You can't know that for sure."

"*You* can't save him," James says, grabbing her shoulders. "But I think I know who can."

Chapter 21

HENRY HAS BEEN pacing the Level 14 hallway outside the med bay for at least seventeen lifetimes. He has no idea what time it is, only that no one's come to tell him anything yet, and at this rate, he's going to punch a hole in the wall in the very near future. Never mind that the walls are stone.

An aide's voice comes over Henry's earpiece. "Sir? Senator Donnigan is—"

"I told you, only emergencies," Henry snaps. His voice sounds oddly loud in the otherwise quiet hallway.

"Yessir, but—"

"Unless Donnigan is actively on fire right now, I don't want to hear about him until further notice."

"But—"

"Sir."

Henry turns around and is about to bite someone's head off when he realizes it's Michaels. "Perhaps you'd like me to take care of communications for the time being," she suggests. "I believe you have more important things to attend to right now."

Of course she looks completely put together, damn her, while Henry is struggling to pretend he even remembers what it means to have a coherent thought. But he's relatively sure she has a point. "Remind me to give you a raise, Michaels," he says, taking out his earpiece, switching off his comm, and handing them to her.

"Unnecessary but appreciated, sir."

He immediately feels guilty. (His job is to make sure the entire compound is running smoothly, he should have found out what the hell Donnigan wants, better that than standing here ignoring all his duties just so he can worry about someone he's already categorically proved he can't help—)

Henry rubs his eyes. "Did I already ask you if they found Laurel yet?"

"No, sir, but I did just get a call from Mr. Turner saying he's located her, and she's on her way."

"Right. Okay. Good."

Michaels gives him an appraising look, then says, "Forgive me if I presume, sir, but I think a brief delegation of your duties is completely reasonable, under the circumstances. I'm happy to do what I can to make sure everything is attended to, and I'm sure the rest of your staff agrees." She pauses, then adds, "Please give the director my best wishes for a speedy recovery."

Henry stares at her and considers asking if she needs to sit down after that uncharacteristic outburst of emotion, but she seems to be in one piece, and his brain can't really handle any response other than a somewhat numb, "Thank you, Michaels."

She nods and walks quickly and efficiently down the hall.

"Major?"

He turns to find Dr. Rowe coming through the double glass doors leading into the main med bay wing. He immediately tries to deduce something from the shadows under her eyes and the way she's holding her shoulders, but of course it's useless; she's a pro.

She's looking a lot better than she did when she rushed in hours ago. Henry didn't realize at first that she wasn't with the initial group of med techs who brought Bastian in from the Level 1 hallway where he collapsed (horribly pale and still and Henry can't think about that right now). Instead, she showed up sometime not long after, a little gray in the face but too focused on her mission to bother doing anything other than brushing past Henry and hurrying into the med bay proper without waiting for the doors to close behind her.

Henry got an alarmed call from Smith about an issue at a meeting or something around then, too, but he wasn't tracking well enough to understand what was going on. He intends to find out, but he'd be lying if he said that's his first priority right now.

Dr. Rowe gives him a quick once-over, just like Michaels did. Then she says in a neutral tone, "Let's go to my office."

Henry considers pulling rank and demanding immediate explanations, but then he decides having a fit in the middle of the hallway probably wouldn't help his reputation any. Instead, he clenches his jaw, nods once, and follows her silently.

At least she makes it quick. As soon as she closes the door behind them— and before even going to her desk—she says, "He's stable."

Henry tries to remember how to breathe. Or swallow. Or do anything other than gape at her as the relief rushes through him.

She gives him a tired smile, then gestures to the chair he didn't notice even though it's right in front of him. "Please have a seat, Major."

He does something more like falling into the chair rather than sitting in it, but the result is the same.

Dr. Rowe moves to the other side of her desk and sits down, facing him. She doesn't exactly flop like he did, but her movements are just this side of exhaustion. She laces her small, compact fingers together and rests her hands on the desk. Henry would feel like he's been called to the principal's office except for the oddly cheerful green plant at the edge of her desk, which implies that she has Laurel's seal of approval. (Where is Laurel, anyway?)

"Have you noticed the director experiencing any memory loss lately?" Dr. Rowe asks.

It takes Henry a moment to find his voice. "I . . . yes, actually. Small things, like his gloves. He's forgotten them in the suite more than once."

"Any other unusual behavior?"

"An increase in headaches, maybe. Not that he tells me anything about that, if he can avoid it. Is he awake yet?"

"Not yet. But we've moved him to recovery."

"Can you—what *was* it?"

"For all intents and purposes, it was a ruptured brain aneurysm."

"Holy shit." Henry's stomach drops. "Those can cause permanent brain damage, right?"

"Yes. And they often do. This one, though . . ." She shakes her head. "It makes no medical sense. An aneurysm of this type should require a craniotomy and a recovery period of at least four to six weeks. But other than the attack itself, nothing has demonstrably changed about Director Lucas's condition. He hasn't regained consciousness, but he also doesn't appear to be injured physically. The best way I can describe it is that his power has been building and just . . . attacked his brain, causing a reaction similar to what we might see with an aneurysm. But otherwise, he's fine."

"Except for the part where he's still dying."

She gives him a wan smile that's probably supposed to look sympathetic but mostly just looks tired. "Yes. But what happened today didn't significantly speed along the likely outcome—at least, not that we can tell. He'll need some time to recover, but he was able to fight it off."

Henry hears himself say what they're both thinking: "This time."

After a pause, he continues, "Tell me about the committee meeting. Smith said . . . I'm not sure, actually; I wasn't tracking well. She was upset."

"That's understandable. I can't be certain of what happened in that room, and of course the director isn't in any condition to explain at the moment. But in the interest of compound security, I suggest you discuss the matter with him as soon as possible."

"What do you mean, you can't be certain of what happened?"

"I mean I'm not prepared to make an official statement." Dr. Rowe hesitates, obviously considering her next words carefully. "But I can tell you that Director Lucas exhibited extreme agitation in the presence of the asset program committee, and then . . . I don't think I'm the only one who lost track of time. When I came back to myself, the entire committee was waking up from a daze, and the director was gone."

Against his will, Henry thinks of the forest last year and how Bastian described what he thought was happening when he used his power as an interrogator. How the people he questioned sometimes went dull and seemed to forget where they were, and suddenly it was easy to get them to answer questions . . . "You think he did something to you?"

"I think there's significant evidence in his file that he can use emotions as a weapon, particularly in times of high stress. And given the fluctuation in his power and its effect on him, I would say he's been under a significant amount of stress for a very long time."

"So, what, you think he *attacked* you? On purpose?"

Dr. Rowe's fingers tighten slightly. When she speaks, it's as if she's trying to calm down a skittish animal. "I think we may need to begin considering what course of action to take if and when the director is no longer able to control his power."

Henry gets to his feet stiffly. "Thank you for your input, Doctor. I'd like to go see him now. Which room?"

She stands as well, her expression part pity, part concern. "Major, I realize this is difficult, but I need you to know that if the director continues to show signs of instability, I'll have to officially recommend he be removed from office."

"I understand." At some point that isn't now, he'll appreciate her candor.

"And will you be able to—?"

"Protect the compound from any potential threat, including its own people? Yes, I think I've proven I can do that. It's how I got this job in the first place."

An uncomfortable silence stretches out for a few moments before Dr. Rowe nods and moves past him to the door. "I'll check on the director's status and run our last tests, and then I'll have a tech come get you. You're welcome to wait here—it won't be long."

She hesitates, then turns back to him. "Just because I think we need a contingency plan doesn't mean I'm giving up."

Henry just barely manages to curtail a crazed sort of laugh. "Whether or not we give up doesn't matter if he already has."

She doesn't try to respond to that; she just nods again and lets the door close softly behind her.

***

Henry waits several more eons, pacing around Dr. Rowe's office, before a med tech sticks her head in. "Sir? Please come with me."

The room she takes him to was probably once an experimentation recovery room. Most of the rooms in this area were, if Henry recalls correctly. This one looks a lot more pleasant now. Personality in the wall art, clearly chosen to be soothing. No windows, since they're on Level 14, but the hackers have set up a screen that could offer an approximation—although at the moment, it's dim. In fact, the whole room is in low light, with the exception of the glow from the machines Bastian's hooked up to, monitoring in case there's a change in his status. They tinge Bastian's skin blue in places.

Henry thinks about another time when he found Bastian unconscious in a recovery room and swallows hard.

Once the med tech is gone, Henry sits in a chair next to the bed and realizes he doesn't know what to do now. This is better than being stuck in the hall or in Dr. Rowe's office, though; at least he can confirm as many times as he needs to that Bastian is still breathing.

But it also gets Henry thinking about things he'd rather not: What Dr. Rowe said. How this may be just the first of many med bay visits as Bastian's condition continues to worsen. That no matter how lost Henry feels about all of this, he still has to run the compound, find a way to get the senators and the compound staff to work together, figure out how to make up for everything Major Valentine did. Maybe it was stupid to think he could ever do this, and what's the point in the end if . . . ?

"Laurel's going to be furious with you," Henry says, his voice puncturing the stillness of the room. "You keep proving that her plants can't solve everything."

Henry clenches his fists and looks away. The machines make several more rhythmic beeps before he takes a breath, turns back, and leans forward to take one of Bastian's hands in his.

"Look, I know you think there's nothing left to do. I know you don't want to talk about this anymore. That's your call, and I want to respect it. But I need to say something, and . . . well, it's not like you can do anything about it right now. So."

He runs his thumb gently over Bastian's knuckles. (Warm, not like before, when Henry found him on a narrow recovery bed on Level 19, almost—no, nothing like that, so stop looking for the quickest way out of the room—)

"I'm sorry about John Doe," Henry says. "General Carter said—no, it doesn't matter. I should have told you from the beginning. But I knew you'd tell me to stop, and I wouldn't have been able to. I can't—"

He swallows and tries again. "I don't know what else to do. Not if you won't let me . . . But we don't even know if I *could*, or if it'd work. And I understand why you wouldn't want to. I just . . . Everything we're trying to do here to save the compound, to help the assets, it doesn't matter if—"

His voice cracks, but he makes himself finish it. "I can't do this without you."

"Yes . . . you can."

Henry raises his head to find Bastian's eyes are open, focusing on the corner of the room, like he can't quite bear to make eye contact.

"Debatable," Henry says. "But I don't want to. Also, I'm done finding you in hospital beds."

Bastian snorts, then cringes like it hurt him. "I'm not . . . too big on it, either."

"Not even when I save you and carry you down a flight of stairs?"

"Especially that part." Bastian finally turns toward him, wearing a glare that isn't very frightening, given how pale and fragile he looks at the moment. "I've told you, you need to . . . let other people save *you* sometimes."

Henry frowns. "Is that why you won't let me—? Are you trying to save me?"

Bastian turns away and starts to drop Henry's hand. Henry doesn't let him. "Bastian."

"I . . . what I'm doing doesn't help," Bastian says, his voice so quiet that Henry can hardly hear him. "The liaison committee is looking for any excuse to get rid of you, and you know it. Things like that speech—I don't mean to make it worse, but . . ."

"Let's get one thing straight." Henry gently turns Bastian's face toward him. "Your work here is as vital to this compound as Laurel's or Michaels's or anyone else's. Sure, it'd be great if you played nice a little more, but what matters is that you get the job done."

"Henry—"

"And since you mentioned it, do you have any idea how many of the new assets decided to stay after that speech of yours?"

"Yes. I actually read that report."

"Do you know *why* they decided to stay?"

"Because they're idiots?"

"Then you didn't really read it. They stayed because of you."

Bastian stares at him incredulously. "What?"

"After your stunt, new assets came to existing assets, to Laurel, even to me," Henry explains. "They said they weren't sure what to think of the new program. They'd heard all the rumors, and they knew what happened here before. Then they heard you speak, and they decided it wasn't the bullshit they thought it was going to be. That maybe they could get something out of the program. So they decided to stay."

There's an odd expression on Bastian's face, and it's enough to make Henry wish he were an empath so he could read it.

"So . . . they're idiots," Bastian says at length.

Henry laughs, but it wobbles a bit under the strain of the hours he's just spent thinking he might never get another chance to be exasperated by Bastian's willful stupidity. "Yeah, all right. Whatever you need to tell yourself. But that's going in your file, just so you know."

"Does that mean I get a raise?"

"After Michaels, maybe. But I might need a really impressive bribe."

"You have something in mind?"

Henry hesitates for a split second, then leans over and kisses him very gently.

"Cameras," Bastian says against his mouth.

"Don't care." Henry kisses him again, nothing near as involved as he'd like. Bastian isn't strong enough to move much yet, but he tightens his hand around Henry's.

"Dr. Rowe will kill me if I don't get out of here and let you rest," Henry says after a moment.

Bastian's expression becomes strained. "There was—at the meeting, I—"

"We'll talk about it when you're feeling better," Henry tells him firmly.

They'll *have* to talk about it, and a lot more besides. Especially if they want to soothe ruffled feathers and keep Bastian in his current position. Assuming that's even safe to do.

He squeezes Bastian's hand and is about to stand when he realizes Bastian isn't letting go. "You could . . . stay," Bastian says, not looking at him. "You outrank Rowe; what's she going to do about it?"

"You mean besides declare me mentally unfit and have me thrown in the jail block if that's what it takes to protect a patient?"

"Templeton would let you out for good behavior. She also caves if you give her chocolate." Bastian glances at him, then quickly away again. "Never mind. It was a stupid thing to say."

He's completely wrong, of course. But if Henry starts thinking about what it means that Bastian almost-sort-of asked for help, he's pretty sure his heart is going to give out.

Before Henry can give that request an appropriate response, he hears a muffled commotion coming from the hallway. Hard to tell from within the recovery room just how much commotion is happening, but it's probably enough to disturb Bastian if it keeps up, not to mention any other patient in the area.

Henry leans back in and kisses Bastian's forehead. "Sleep," he commands. "That's an order from your boss. I'll be right back to make sure it's carried out."

Bastian rolls his eyes but lets Henry go.

Henry has just closed the door behind him when the source of the noise turns the corner and comes barreling toward him, scattering med techs every which way.

"Henry!" Laurel says. "Is he awake yet?"

He starts to ask her where she's been when he registers that she's dragging along two people behind her: James and a mousy teenage girl who looks mortified but determined.

"He's resting," Henry says, frowning at them all. "Which is harder to do when people are making a lot of noise outside his room at—whatever o'clock it is right now."

Laurel scoffs. "Who cares what time it is? We've been talking, and now we need to talk to Bastian."

"Laurel, it'll have to wait. He's—"

"Dying, right?" James says loudly.

Henry glares at him. "How do you—?"

"No offense, Major, but I think you're going to agree that this is more important than Lucas getting his beauty sleep."

All three of them are vibrating with excitement, and although Henry sternly tells himself to ignore the flutter of hope in his chest, he's having trouble doing it just now. "Okay," he says slowly. "What's this all about?"

Chapter 22

BASTIAN WAKES TO a fuzzy taste in his mouth and a pair of hazel eyes glaring at him.

"What do you think you're doing, collapsing in a hallway without telling me?" Laurel demands. "I'm not even going to start on how beside himself your Henry was; we'll get to that when we're done talking about me. I went to all the trouble of saving your life two years ago, and this is how you repay me?"

Bastian blinks several times and realizes after a moment that he's still in his med bay room, and Laurel is sitting next to the bed, arms crossed over her chest, expression murderous. No sign of Henry.

Seeing that he's not going to appropriately respond to her tirade, Laurel sighs and leans back in her chair. "Henry just went to get coffee," she says. "And that should tell you something about his state of mind. You drove him to *coffee*, Bastian. Coffee from the *cafeteria*. I made James and Chloe go with him to make sure he gets back alive."

"Why . . . ?"

"Because you can still hear the coffee plants screaming if you listen hard enough, and—"

"No. Why are you here?"

Laurel stares at him. "Really? You almost—Dr. Rowe said they were trying to stabilize you for hours, while I was—I didn't even realize because I was—"

Her ashamed-worried-frustrated hurts, but not because of an overload of his power. It's the way she won't look at him, the way she's clenching her hands in her lap, digging her nails into her palms.

"Laurel . . ."

"I tried," she says to the floor. "When Kent told me, I got all my herbs together, and the plants shared all their ideas, but it doesn't matter, does it, because nothing I do helps—"

"Laurel—"

"And even if we try something else, it still might not—I mean, you don't even *want* us to try anymore, do you, so—"

"*Laurel.*"

Her waterfall of words pauses, and she finally looks up—which is almost worse than her avoiding his eyes altogether. Bastian makes himself go on anyway. "I'm not asking you to fix this."

She snorts (sadness-irritation-amusement). "Of course you're not asking. You never ask. Because you're an idiot."

"Shouldn't you be nicer to me? I'm convalescing."

"I'm always nice, so I have no idea what you're talking about. In fact, because I'm nice, I'll tell you that Kent and Sybil have called me several times wanting to know how you're doing. And Henry said Michaels told him she hopes you feel better soon."

Bastian stares at her. "That's . . . wow. Is she okay?"

"I can neither confirm nor deny that she has perished from that emotional outburst," Laurel says in an official-sounding voice.

There's a strange tightness in Bastian's chest that he really hopes he won't have to report to a med tech. "I don't . . . you all have things to do. You don't have time to—"

"To what?" Laurel demands. "Watch you implode because you're too stupid to realize we're worried about you?" She pauses, then adds, "Can people actually implode? Do we have an asset who can do that? I don't remember anything from the current roster, but—"

Bastian feels a jumble of bored-placating-anxious-concerned coming quickly toward the room, followed by voices that are probably trying to be hushed but are failing miserably at it. Before he has a chance to separate everything out, the door opens.

"You really shouldn't be bringing so many people in here," a med tech is saying sternly. "The patient needs—"

"The patient is awake," says James, glancing at Bastian as he opens the door the rest of the way and comes on through. "I think we're good."

"There are other patients on this hall," the med tech insists. "This ruckus is really unacceptable."

"We'll keep it short," Henry assures her. He's following James and carrying two paper cups of coffee. With no free hands, he's about to get a door to the face, since James isn't bothering to hold it open.

Laurel jumps up, clearly intending to go help, but before she can get too far, a much closer foot snakes out to serve as a doorstop. Chloe appears from behind Henry, also holding coffee in each hand.

As everyone shuffles in, the med tech is finally able to see Bastian for herself. "Keep it *very* short," she says, voice laced with disapproval. "And I'm getting his vitals first." Clearly, she's only slightly mollified by the leader of the entire compound agreeing deferentially to her demand. Bastian wonders yet again why Henry doesn't just pull rank on anyone who gets in his way. Except of course Bastian doesn't *really* wonder because being infuriatingly gracious until excessively provoked is just how Henry is.

Once the med tech has had her way—including helping Bastian sit up in bed while the others dole out the undrinkable coffee and pretend not to notice how weak he still is—she leaves with only a quick warning glance for each of them.

"Is one of you going to tell me why there's a party in my room?" Bastian asks a bit crossly when she's gone. His throat feels scratchy, his head is sore, and while it's miles better than the excruciating pain from the hallway, that doesn't mean he's having a good time.

Laurel takes a deep breath. "So, you know how I was just saying you're stupid? It turns out that's fine because—"

"We know how to fix you," James says. "And more importantly, we know how to fix *me*."

"There's nothing wrong with me," Bastian says immediately.

"Bastian." Laurel waves pointedly at the machines in the room.

He sighs. "Fine. But I thought we agreed my . . . situation was going to be need-to-know."

"Yeah, well, if you want my help, I need to know," James says.

"Who says I want your help?"

"Bastian." It's Henry this time, giving him a patient look that has no business being on the face of someone who's clearly reached astronomical levels of exhaustion. "Can you just let them explain?"

It's faint, but it's there: a tiny tremor of hope mixed with the low-level buzz of Henry's negation. He's holding both back pretty well—Bastian isn't having any trouble reading him—but they're threatening to break free.

(Bastian hates it, the way Henry and Laurel keep trying when it's clearly a lost cause, *he's* a lost cause, and even though things might've turned out all right this time, more or less, it's probably just a fluke, and whatever scheme they're concocting right now is—)

"Please," Henry says. There's no particularly dramatic emphasis on the word, nothing that makes it stand out from the slightly negation-dimmed emotional landscape he's already projecting. But something about the way he says it makes Bastian wish he were standing close enough to touch.

Bastian clears his throat. "Fine. Explain it."

"I remembered someone," James says. "Angelica must've knocked something loose when she—"

"Angelica?" Bastian glares at Laurel. "You asked her to—?"

"We didn't *ask* her to do anything," Laurel says hastily (impatient-worried-guilty). "She offered. Now shush."

"*Anyway*," James continues, "it took awhile to come together, but what I remembered fits in with all the research I've been doing—"

"All the research *we've* been doing," Laurel corrects him.

"—so when I was chatting with a lovely officer on Level 7 yesterday, I realized what I've been missing. The big question is how I survived, right? Obviously, someone must have realized how important my good looks are to humanity and decided to heal me. But after my power went haywire in the compound, I was nearly dead—maybe I *was* dead, I dunno. So one of the people who found me must have been a fantastic healer. Or"—his eyes are suddenly bright—"*or*, they were an adequate healer who knew an even better one to take me to. Because I think that's where we were headed: to someone who could help. To some*place* that could help."

"And if there's someone who could heal James, maybe they could heal you, too," Laurel adds.

Bastian looks at them all, waiting for the rest. When there's nothing, he says, "That's it? You're excited about a figment of James's imagination?"

"It's not, though." Standing in the corner of the room, Chloe nearly drops her coffee cup when all eyes fall on her. "Um. I mean. James and Laurel and I have been researching the forest paths, and we found some irregularities. I tried looking a little deeper while you were . . . not ready for visitors, and I found some information that I think can help us."

Laurel picks up her bag, which she left on the floor near one of the monitoring machines, and takes out a tablet. Chloe sets her coffee down and comes forward to take it. Then they all cluster around Bastian's bed. The convergence of that much emotional energy in addition to James's odd blankness causes Bastian's head to send out a twinge of pain, but it's nothing he can't handle. Especially when Henry leans in to see the screen and rests a hand on his shoulder.

"We kept seeing discrepancies in the forest maps we were comparing," Chloe says. "Some of the paths disappeared over the years. So I looked into why that might have happened, and I found this."

She brings up what appears to be a survey report from a mission to map the forest and surrounding terrain. Most of it looks like gibberish—odd collections of numbers and letters, like the file is corrupted or written in code. Bastian would assume the whole thing is worthless except that there are a few lines that do make sense, including "FSP6342867.SYN likely deployed in dead zone" and "APxxxxxx last seen in proximity."

Bastian feels Henry's hand tighten on his shoulder, and he catches a tiny jolt of alarm-apprehension-concern. "Where did you get this?"

"Floating around in the library database," Chloe says. "It doesn't have any metadata, so I'm not sure how it showed up in my search, but—"

"Look," Laurel interrupts. "'AP.' That's the prefix for asset program ID numbers. So there was an asset out there."

"What's a dead zone?" Bastian asks.

"When I was tracking, there was this area in the forest that sort of . . . went dark," Chloe says. "My power worked everywhere else, but not there. And as far as I can tell from this file, that area is the same one described in this file and on the maps. Maybe an asset did something there that created the dead zone."

"If you were going to build a place where assets could find help they couldn't get anywhere else, you wouldn't want to just leave it out in the open, right?" James says. "Not with an active compound so close. You'd find a way to keep it concealed. Like behind an area of the forest where something shady went down, and now the compound likes to pretend it doesn't even exist."

"It's a lead," Henry says, frowning at the screen. "But like I told you earlier, we need a little more before we can act on it."

James throws up his hands. "A little more *what?*"

"Information. I'll send a new survey team to confirm what we're seeing in these files as far as the actual location of this dead zone. Maybe we can figure out if any unaccounted-for assets have been seen in the area recently. Meanwhile, what else can you tell us about this healer? And why do you think they might be the one mentioned in this file?"

To Bastian's great surprise, James does an excellent approximation of fighting back some sort of intense emotion. He looks (but doesn't feel) distressed enough that Laurel reaches out to touch his arm, her own concern-sympathy-hesitation taking up enough space for both of them. "It's all right," she says. "You don't have to—"

"He said I deserved to be saved," James says quietly, staring at the floor without seeming to really see it. "That saving people is what he does."

Bastian starts. The voice in the pool, and later in the hall . . . the one that seemed to know him, that told him he's important and that he'd know where to go when the time came . . . that he deserves to be saved . . .

"It *could* be the same asset noted in the file," Henry admits, "but without the ID number or any other solid evidence that this healer exists, we can't be sure."

"Why don't you just let us take a vehicle out there and see if James remembers anything?" Laurel asks impatiently. "We've been trying to do this the super officially sanctioned way, but that takes time, and we don't know how much longer Bastian has until—"

She stops, and the room goes awkwardly silent.

"I can see how this might help with James's memory," Henry says, "so we should definitely look into it. But Bastian gets to decide what, if anything, it has to do with him." His voice is even, but he's backed away from Bastian and is standing with his arms crossed, his mouth a thin line.

James rolls his eyes. "How is this even a discussion?" He glares at Bastian. "Do you want to die or not?"

You're dying, says the voice in Bastian's head—or the echo of it, anyway. *You need to make a choice.*

"James," says Laurel, "you really shouldn't—"

"I want my memories back, okay? I'll figure out a way to do it whether or not this loser is on board, but this would be quicker, so—"

"We'll do everything we can to help you, James," Henry says. "But even I can't authorize resources until we know for sure—"

James jerks his head toward Bastian. "Bet you'd drop everything if *he* said go, wouldn't you?"

(Henry in the garden, soldiering up for the big confrontation, his exhaustion-fear-sadness pressing into Bastian's mind, his voice desperate as he said he would do anything—)

Laurel sighs and waves a hand. "Clearly, Henry is a party pooper, but—"

"I'm the commanding officer of this compound, Laurel—"

(Valentine's smile, the one that never reaches her eyes and makes you feel like you're just an interesting butterfly pinned to a board, telling him that if he really cares about Henry and the others, he won't let them waste their time on him—)

Bastian closes his eyes for a moment, then does what he's always felt is the most important thing to do in life: namely, the opposite of what Valentine tells him to do. "All right."

They all turn and look at him. "Sorry?" Laurel says.

"This healer. Let's find him."

Laurel pauses, then practically sidesteps the laws of gravity to shoot forward and throw her arms around his neck. "You're stupid, and I love you, and we're going to fix this," she mumbles, quietly enough that he's probably the only one who can make out the words.

It turns out Bastian's arms are strong enough at this point to give her about half a hug without informing him of their intention to do so. "I told you, you don't have to—"

"Too late! It's a deal." She breaks away quickly and clears her throat. "Okay, so we'll see what else we can find out about James's healer while the scouts confirm the location of the dead zone, and then Henry will give us a fleet of vehicles—"

"*One* vehicle—"

"—and then we'll find this healer and make him help both James and Bastian, and everything will be fine." She grins broadly. "Let's get to work!"

Laurel shepherds James and Chloe out the door, Chloe rounding up all the coffee cups as they go.

Once the door closes behind them, Henry opens his mouth . . . and is interrupted when the door opens again, and Laurel sticks her head in.

"Just to be clear," she says to Bastian, "in light of all this, I've decided we're okay now. I mean, I hope we're okay now. Are we okay now?"

"Uh—"

"Because I'd like to be okay now. I still don't agree with you about James, of course, but I think being okay is more important than us agreeing on everything. Right?" She hesitates, then adds, "If you change your mind about the not-dying thing, I'll be upset, but I'll still want us to be okay anyway."

Bastian isn't really clear on the definition of "okay" in this scenario, but he thinks he can deduce the general idea from her level of anxious-sad-hopeful. "Yeah," he says, surprised by how relieved he is to say it. "I think we're okay."

"Good." She nods once. "I'll go now so you can talk to Henry. Have you told him about the book yet?"

"What book?" Henry asks.

"Bye, Laurel," Bastian says pointedly, ignoring her laugh as she closes the door.

Henry raises his eyebrows, but Bastian makes no effort to elaborate. Instead of pressing it, Henry lets out a small sigh and sits down in the chair Laurel used earlier. He takes the jammer out of his jacket pocket and taps his thumb against it thoughtfully.

"How long have you had that on?" Bastian asks.

"Since we came in. Which means it won't last much longer. But I need to talk to you about that file Laurel and the others found."

"Did you recognize it?"

"Not exactly." Henry sets the jammer on his knee and rubs his eyes. "Kent and Sybil have been receiving strange bits of data from somewhere outside the compound system. They're corrupted, or coded, or both—I'm not really sure what shape they're in when they hit our mainframe, but I've been getting them as they're deciphered."

"And they look like Laurel's file?"

"Yeah. They seem to be lists of asset numbers and notes about various experiments. Nothing that makes a whole lot of sense yet, but . . ."

"But?"

Henry's anxious-concerned-dread feels like a slap in the face despite his obvious attempt to keep calm. "The fragments mention you," he says. "And the experiments at Laurel's compound. And . . . me."

"And *you?*"

"Briefly, with regard to something called the Fail-Safe Protocol. Does that ring any bells?"

Bastian immediately tries to remember everything he ever heard Valentine say, but of course his brain isn't really up to the athletics required for that at the moment. So he's reduced to just shaking his head. "Does any of the data mention negation?"

"No. Not that I've seen yet, anyway. But that FSP number we just saw shows up a few times."

"Wait, didn't you say these files were coming to you through Kent and Sybil? Why would Chloe have found one in the library database?"

"I don't know, but I don't like it." Henry glances at the jammer. "Look, we're running out of time, and I need to check in with Michaels. She's been holding my calls since last night."

"It's fine," Bastian says quickly. "We can talk about this later. I'll probably still be here."

"You'll *definitely* still be here, unless Dr. Rowe clears you to go," Henry says sternly.

"Right. That." He decides now is not the best time to mention how much practice he's had over the years at sneaking out of med bay and experimentation rooms. And another thing he's not going to mention: the sudden jolt of anxiety in his chest at the thought of Henry leaving.

"I'll be right back," Henry says, slipping the jammer back into his pocket.

"You don't have to. I mean, you're busy; I don't need you to—"

"What if *I* need me to?" It sounds like it was supposed to be a joke, but Henry isn't smiling, and Bastian's having trouble seeing past the relief-fear-desperation lurking underneath his light tone and slight negation buzz.

Bastian swallows, looking at the dark circles under Henry's eyes and not knowing what to say. Since his vocal cords have failed him, he fumbles awkwardly for Henry's hand. It's just as well he's sitting up in bed because Henry's resulting surprised-grateful-affection when he laces their fingers together would have been hard to take standing up.

"I have faith that you'll figure out a way to sneak back in if you have to," Bastian says, finding his voice at last. "You're pretty good at being where you're not supposed to be."

Henry makes a face. "Breaking the rules is definitely a great habit for compound leadership to get into."

"Got you a promotion, didn't it?"

"Go to sleep, Bastian. I'll be back as soon as I make that call." He hangs onto Bastian's hand until the last possible moment as he stands. Then he turns off the jammer and sticks it back into his jacket.

Bastian watches him go, then decides he's going to stay awake out of spite. Unfortunately, his body doesn't seem to agree with him, and his eyes drift closed.

Chapter 23

HENRY STARES AT the tablet in front of him, willing the data fragments to say something other than what he thinks they're saying.

FSP6342867 session xx.xx.xxxx inconclusive. Blood appears stable for serum manufacture, but further testing on active assets required. Continue using FSP6342867.SYN until status confirmed.

Catastrophic failure. Splicing program aborted. Damage contained.

AP367284 AWOL as of 0100. Please advise.

Adjusted FSP Stage 0 initiated. Council apprised.

And the note from Sybil, sent yesterday: *Communications stopped.*

He hasn't found another occurrence of his name, but FSP6342867 has to be him. It's also clearly connected the creation of the serum the retrieval teams, including his own, used to knock out uncooperative assets. Even before Henry had any idea what he is, Major Valentine knew—and she used it to her advantage.

Just like the liaison committee is doing now, using the serum on Bastian before every meeting. This many iterations in, the serum is synthetic enough that no one's bothered to trace it back to its origin. Which would be difficult, given that those files appear to have been some of the ones Dr. Wright destroyed back when he had the chance.

But Henry knows. And so does whoever wrote that fragment.

He's not sure what the "SYN" suffix means—some other version of the serum, maybe? Whatever they used before they had Henry's blood? He remembers it being mentioned in the file Chloe found, but there doesn't seem to be any other record of it. No indication of what, if anything, it has to do with whatever happened in the forest to cause the dead zone.

The notes on splicing have to be in relation to Laurel's compound and what happened to James. These mentions look similar to what he read in the files he found in the burned-out lower level of Laurel's compound. "Damage contained" is a nice way to say "entire compound destroyed, nearly everyone killed, and the whole thing covered up to prevent the perpetrators from having to pay for it."

The second-to-last entry makes Henry's chest ache. "AP367284 AWOL" must be from a record of Bastian escaping the compound two years ago. Having seen Bastian's reaction to Level 49 during inventory, Henry has some idea of how traumatic the events leading up to that must have been. On the other hand, if it hadn't been for that, Henry would never have been sent after him, would never have started questioning everything, would never have fallen in love with him . . .

(Would never have had to sit in that med bay room and realize that James's healer is probably their last chance—)

Henry pinches the bridge of his nose and forces himself to focus on the last fragment in the set. It's not just that he doesn't know what "FSP Stage 0" means; it's that last bit: "Council apprised."

There's only one council worth noting in this context, and that's the Compound Council.

Against his will, Henry remembers that last day in John Doe's room, the glee with which he insinuated that there's something the Council is keeping hidden—"all of the good secrets," whatever that means. Henry had thought it was a bluff on John Doe's part, some random comment to make Henry doubt himself, but . . . What if there's some truth to it? Could the Council know something about this Fail-Safe Protocol and Henry's connection to it?

And if the Council knows, doesn't that mean General Carter knows, too? And Major Alexis?

Henry feels like he's been staring at these letters and numbers long enough to see them in his sleep, to see the rooms where the experiments happened, hear Dr. Wright's voice as he typed away at a computer, feel the cold metal of a gurney, the tightness of a mask over his nose and mouth, the jolt of panic as he went under . . .

There's a beep from his comm. "Major?"

He glances at his jammer, which is sitting on the table. The relays Kent and Sybil installed, combined with the jammer upgrade Kent gave him earlier this morning, should keep him off the security feed for another few minutes. But it would be best not to tempt fate. Sybil will understand if he says they have to keep it short. "Go ahead," he tells her. "You have more data?"

"No, but I've got a line on where it's coming from. Finally."

She pauses so long, Henry has to hold back a sigh. "Sybil? I'm running out of time on the jammer."

"Yes, sorry, it's just—"

He hears some sort of commotion from her end: a harsh knock, then loud voices.

"We traced the messages back to an origin point," Sybil says, her voice lowered. "Not to the actual system, but the general location. They're coming from the Hall."

Henry frowns. "From a senator's office?"

"Probably. I mean, it's possible they're bouncing the signal off something else, but—" More noise from somewhere near her. "Sorry, sir. I have to go."

"What's happening?" Henry's ear buzzes even as he says it; a call on another frequency. "Sybil?"

"Sorry," she says again. "I need to go make sure Kent doesn't get arrested."

Henry bites off a response to that when he realizes she's dropped. He flips to the other channel. "Yes?"

"Michaels, sir. I've received a request for you at security on Level 1."

"I'm in the middle of something. Can you hold them off?"

"I'm afraid not, sir. The city officials are very . . . persistent."

Henry narrows his eyes. Either this is very convenient timing, or . . . "Have any of them entered the compound proper yet?"

"I believe Senator Donnigan requested that security bring our head hackers to meet with him and his party immediately."

"And no one thought to inform him that that sort of request should go through me?"

"I made an attempt, sir, but the senator was quite adamant."

"Of course he was." Henry gets to his feet and returns the tablet to the back of the file cabinet. "Tell them I'm coming now. If anyone requests anything else, shoot them."

"Sir?"

"I meant, tell them I'll be happy to help them when I get there."

"Yes, sir."

***

The idea behind picking an office on Level 1 was for Henry to be easily accessible and close to anything that might need his immediate attention. Unfortunately, this means he's easily accessible and close to anything that might need his immediate attention. Like Senator Donnigan and the small group of city officials clustered around the Level 1 security desk.

At least Donnigan has the decency to stand up straight and look a bit flustered when Henry approaches. Although, as Henry gets closer, he realizes Donnigan might actually be reacting to Bastian, who's blocking the hallway and wearing an expression that implies he wouldn't have a second thought about attacking the next person who gets anywhere near him. Normally, that would be funny, given that Bastian's a scrawny lightweight. At the moment, though, he looks pissed enough to try it. Probably not the best mentality for someone who's only been out of the med bay for a few days—though Henry supposes angry, ready-to-fight Bastian standing in a hallway is better than pale, can't-stay-awake Bastian lying in a hospital bed.

It's also a little better than awkward-and-aloof Bastian, which seems to be his only other available mode lately. Henry would assume Bastian is still embarrassed about having shown the unacceptable weakness of being ill, but as the days go on, Henry's starting to wonder if he's actually having second thoughts about finding James's healer and just doesn't want to bring it up yet.

And now Henry gets to add mediating crises in compound hallways to his list of headaches.

"I apologize if we concerned you, Director," Donnigan is saying. "Our officers are just trying to get some answers."

"By waving their guns around and scaring people?"

Henry realizes the shadows on the wall just behind Bastian are moving, tiny little shivers that don't match up with anything else in the hallway. He tenses for a moment before he registers a barely visible pair of terrified eyes blinking at him from within the darkness. An umbra, then. Probably the asset Donnigan's people scared.

Donnigan is still frowning at Bastian, who's standing between him and the asset Donnigan probably doesn't even know is there. "I assure you, Ms. Pham and I are only—"

"It's Detective Pham, actually, and I can speak for myself."

A woman moves efficiently around Donnigan like he's nothing more than a misplaced chair, her ID out to show Bastian and the black coats at the security desk. Her gaze seems to be cataloguing everything around her in a way that makes Henry suspect she won't need to do it twice.

"I'm here to see your commanding officer," she continues.

"Consider me seen," Henry says, stepping forward before Bastian can open his mouth again. "Though that usually only happens with an appointment."

"Donnigan decided they shouldn't wait for security clearance and already sent their groupies into the compound," Bastian explains. "In case you were wondering why Michaels called you out here. She's gone to intercept the ones headed for hacker HQ."

Donnigan holds up his hands placatingly. "It's been challenging at times to reach you, Major Mortimer, so I thought we should simplify things by coming here ourselves. As a member of the liaison committee, my job is to coordinate interactions between the city and the compound, so for the purposes of this investigation—"

"What investigation?" Henry demands. "And why isn't this happening through official channels?"

"Perhaps we should—"

"Excuse me, Senator, but I'll decide what we should as soon as I know what's going on." Henry turns to Donnigan's companion. "Detective?"

Pham puts away her ID and looks Henry straight in the eye—no hesitation or fear like Henry often sees in city officials dealing with compound officers. "There's been a murder," she says.

Henry frowns. "If you need compound assistance with that, we have those official channels I just mentioned."

"The only assistance I need at the moment, Major, is for you to accompany me back to the city for questioning."

Bastian jumps into Henry's startled silence. "That's not going to happen."

Detective Pham turns toward him and gives him a cool, unfazed look. "This is just a questioning, Director; I'm not accusing the major of anything—yet."

"Although the circumstances are quite concerning," Donnigan says in a tone that is in no way helpful.

Henry opens his mouth to respond but gets sidetracked when he spots Michaels hurrying down the hall toward them.

"Sir," she says, only slightly out of breath. "Several city officers were … encouraging Mr. Turner and Miss Tassos to accompany them to the city to answer questions. There was also a request for some highly classified communications data."

Charming. "Tell the black coats on Level 4 to escort all of the city officers out of the compound."

Donnigan bristles as Michaels nods and moves off to make the call. "Major, that's—"

"Completely within the rights of a compound," Henry tells him. "I'm happy to work with you and Detective Pham to get this resolved, Senator. But if anyone is going to be questioned or taken off of these grounds, it will need to be cleared with me first. I'll make a note of your eagerness to assist."

He turns back to the others, not waiting to see how red Donnigan's face can get. "Detective, there's a meeting room around the corner, if you—"

"I'm coming," Bastian says.

Henry sighs inwardly, but it's not as though he can order Bastian away if this somehow involves assets. And frankly, Henry could use the backup.

"I'll be joining you as well on behalf of the committee," Donnigan adds. "I think we can all agree that clandestine meetings between city officials and compound leadership can become problematic if not accompanied by oversight."

Which is just the sort of insulting interjection Henry expected.

As he turns to lead them down the hall, Henry notices Bastian nod slightly to the shadow, which skitters away in the opposite direction, turning into a twelve- or thirteen-year-old boy as it does.

"All right?" Henry asks under his breath as Bastian falls into step next to him.

"Finneas doesn't like surprises," Bastian says. "Particularly when they come with loud noises."

"Good thing he's got someone looking out for him, then."

Bastian makes a noncommittal noise, but Henry catches him glancing briefly in the direction Finneas escaped, as if to make sure he got away safely.

Henry herds them into a meeting room, closes the door, and gets right to the point. "Detective?"

"I know everyone's time is valuable, so I'll keep this quick," Pham says briskly. "The victim's name is Emily Tezuka. She was an aide to Senator Nunez."

"When?" Bastian demands.

"The body was found on the Hall grounds earlier today, but our initial tests indicate she died yesterday."

"How?" Bastian continues in the same clipped tone. Henry wonders if this is an accurate representation of how his interrogations went.

"We'll need to complete our tests to be sure, but it looks like poison."

"Why do you want the major? Is he a suspect?"

Pham looks a bit exasperated, but she shakes her head. "Not right now. But Tezuka was assisting the senator with her work on the liaison committee, and the last communication Tezuka made was to this compound. So you can see why we're hoping for Major Mortimer's cooperation in determining what that message was and who it might have gone to."

Henry frowns. "I'm not familiar with the name, but if she was working with Senator Nunez, she could have been included on any of the message chains going back and forth regarding liaison committee business. Otherwise, there wouldn't have been any authorized communication between the compound and an aide."

"What about unauthorized communication?"

Of course. "That's why you wanted Kent and Sybil," Henry says. "To see if they'd tracked anything between here and the Hall."

Except the only thing Kent and Sybil have been tracking is the encrypted data, which they just realized is coming from the Hall. Or was, until yesterday. Which happens to be when Nunez's aide died.

It *could* be a coincidence. Hundreds of people work at the Hall, and any of them could have sent the files. Or, as Sybil suggested, the Hall could've just been a location to bounce the signal off of, which would make this murder and the data fragments unrelated.

Unless Tezuka was sending them. On her own . . . or because she was instructed to.

Henry can barely wrap his head around it, but Tezuka was Nunez's aide, and Nunez has been acting strangely for weeks. Requesting meetings and then lying about it in front of Major Alexis; acting like she had something to tell Henry and then refusing to say anything . . .

"I didn't authorize anyone to disturb your team," Pham says, a slight edge in her voice. "You'll have to ask the senator why he chose to bring officers in from City Hall without discussing it with either of us first."

Donnigan has the good grace to look abashed. "I was perhaps . . . overzealous in my desire to be helpful," he admits. "I thought if I had some officers speak directly to the relevant parties, we could work through Detective Pham's questions more quickly."

"If speed was the point of all this, you should've just asked to talk to the hackers ahead of time," Bastian points out. "Then you wouldn't have lost time by getting your officers kicked out for trying to drag people away without explanation."

"I'd prefer to do all of this at police headquarters, actually," Pham says. "You'll forgive me if I'm not particularly comfortable with the way investigations have been conducted at compounds in the past."

Henry flicks a glance at Bastian, but he doesn't seem interested in arguing with Pham on that count, even as someone who took part in some of those investigations. He's still leaning back in his chair, arms crossed over his chest, though. Waiting out the enemy.

"Actually," Donnigan says, "Detective Pham has agreed to the suggestion put forth by the liaison committee, which met briefly this morning when the news of Miss Tezuka's murder first came in. The detective will discuss the situation with Major Mortimer on neutral ground."

"And where might that be?" Bastian's tone that implies he already knows and dislikes the answer.

"Senator Donnigan has offered to host the questioning in his office at the Hall," Pham tells them. She sounds perfectly polite, but in the way someone who has dealt with more than their fair share of politicians has learned to be polite. "I'll be bringing several officers along to record the interviews, and the major is welcome to bring whatever assistance he needs."

"Good. We'll do a read."

Pham frowns. "We're not asking for—"

"You're getting it anyway."

"I think we all want to find out what happened at the Hall," Henry says quickly. "The director's idea for a read isn't a bad one, but unfortunately, he's not available to perform it right now."

Bastian shoots a look at him. "What do you mean, I'm not—?"

"You have that meeting with Dr. Rowe, don't you?"

The look becomes awfully glare-like, which isn't at all surprising. While Bastian has agreed to check in regularly with Dr. Rowe since being released from the med bay, he's made it very clear that he's doing it under duress.

After hearing about what happened at the asset program committee meeting, though, Henry couldn't disagree more with Bastian's assessment. So far, Dr. Rowe's daily reports have given him enough data for a compelling argument in favor of allowing Bastian to stick to his regular duties—though it took more than a little work to smooth over the ruffled feathers of the asset program committee.

They're treading on thin ice with Bastian's health, and Henry is very aware that allowing him to leave the compound—especially to use his power for an intense read at a crime scene—could be a disaster in the making.

Not that Henry's about to say any of this in front of guests. Not unless Bastian makes him.

Bastian glares at him for several more seconds, then says firmly, "Can I speak to you in the hall, Major?"

Awkward, but doable. "Excuse us for a minute," Henry tells Pham and Donnigan.

Bastian barely lets the meeting room door close behind them before he starts in. "I'm coming."

"You've been out of the med bay for less than three days," Henry says, keeping his voice low enough to avoid at least some of the curiosity of the passersby. "Do you really think this is a good idea?"

"I'm not some delicate flower. Reading at a crime scene is what I *do*—"

"It's what you *did*. Now you've got a program to run."

"Laurel can cover me."

"She's working on another project with James and Chloe. Remember?"

Bastian makes a face and turns, paces a few feet away, then back. "I don't want you to go alone," he says quietly. "They're looking for a scapegoat, and you're extremely convenient."

"I'm not about to let them hold me without evidence. Frankly, I don't think they'd be dumb enough to try. Donnigan likes posturing, but we all want to at least look like we're working together. Locking up compound leadership without reason isn't going to help with that."

Bastian hesitates, glancing at the nearest security camera. Then he says, "Fine; you can deal with the idiots. What about the crime scene itself? It sounds like it's connected to the . . . thing Kent and Sybil are working on."

That's where Bastian has a point. Henry might get a chance to briefly walk through, but he's more likely to get tied up with Pham's questions than to have an opportunity to get a good look. And his good look wouldn't be nearly as useful as Bastian's if Tezuka's death has something to do with the data coming in from the Hall.

Henry sighs. "I don't like it."

"I know."

"I really think you should stay here."

"I know."

"I can't even tell you how not okay it would be if you collapsed in public. Or anywhere, ever again. Under any circumstances."

"I know." Bastian's doing a relatively decent job of keeping a straight face. Except he clearly knows he's won because a smirk is getting started at the left side of his mouth. Henry is torn between doubling down on the lecture—he really *is* concerned about the implications of Bastian getting ill at a crime scene—and seeing if kissing someone into compliance works.

Apparently, something about his jumble of emotions must've caught Bastian's attention because he puts a hand on Henry's arm. "Let's make a deal: I'll be careful if you will."

Henry lets out a small laugh and covers Bastian's hand with his. "You're not exactly good at careful. You sure that's a deal you can follow through on?"

"Yes." Bastian frowns. "Probably. Look, is it a deal or not?"

"It's definitely a deal." He almost wishes Bastian had forgotten his gloves again today so Henry could be touching his skin. But even just the warmth through the black leather helps. "And you're checking in with Dr. Rowe before we go."

"That's not—"

"—open for discussion."

Bastian sighs and drops his hand away, and Henry lets them back into the meeting room. "It turns out the director is available to help us after all," he says.

"Bastian, explain the situation to Laurel and tell Michaels to meet us in fifteen at the loading dock with the machine."

"Major," Pham says, "this level of effort isn't necessary. We only need—"

"I realize you didn't make a formal request, Detective, but I think the compound can provide some important assistance here," Henry says. "I promise we won't get in the way of your own efforts."

He turns to Donnigan, who has his mouth open to protest. Henry just manages to get ahead of it. "You were so eager to get started on this investigation, Senator, I know you'll want to make use of all the resources available."

Donnigan goes a bit pinched in the face, but he doesn't offer up any further argument.

Chapter 24

FANCY POLITICAL RAT'S nests have a weird way of staying the same no matter how much new paint gets applied.

The reflecting pool where Bastian did a read for Senator Goldsmith's murder last year has gotten a new plaque and a few benches. Someone apparently thought that cleaning it up would make it more appealing to the current denizens of the Hall, despite the fact that all of them can now read a flouncy bit of chiseled stone and see that something bad happened here. Whether they still think Goldsmith committed suicide or they know that an empath helped her along depends on whether they have access to the right gossip.

Otherwise, not much is different. The Hall itself still looks ostentatious with its marble pillars and gilded windows, and the grounds have been severely manicured to the point where Bastian is glad Laurel's not here to have a very violent reaction.

She was harried when he called her, obviously agreeing to cover program duties just to get him off the line. Bastian can only assume she's on to something with regard to finding James's healer.

He wanted to tell her to forget it, that they're all wasting too much time on this. But it's about James, too. And whether James is a threat or just a self-absorbed asshole, Bastian can grudgingly admit—to himself—that he deserves a chance to regain his memories.

Bastian shakes his head and looks out over the Hall grounds. At least this time he doesn't have to worry about not being able to use his power when Henry's around. For the moment, that's because Henry's behind closed doors—namely Donnigan's, where he's holed up answering Detective Pham's questions.

Bastian wasn't excited about being left out of that, but Henry didn't give him much choice. Bastian is here to do a read, not to be Henry's bodyguard. So Henry gets to sit in a nice office entertaining the enemy while Bastian and Michaels examine the crime scene with one of Pham's officers.

"Sir?" Michaels has stopped beside him, carrying the huge black bag with the machine for recording his read. Better get a move on—not so much because Michaels isn't strong enough to carry it, but because Pham's officer is getting antsy about them lingering by the reflecting pool.

Bastian allows himself to be led away to an unobtrusive side entrance to the Hall. "Nunez's aide was picking up some food handling work?" he asks, noting the "Service Entrance: Cafeteria" sign on the door.

"Not to my knowledge," says the officer, sounding like she's heard it all before and was less than impressed the first time (tired-bored-apathetic).

She opens the door to reveal a long, dimly lit hallway, stone walls washed out with pale fluorescent lights. There are a few doors here and there on either side, but mostly it's just a narrow path with an unfinished ceiling. According to the officer's brief overview when they got to the Hall, this corridor is used to transport food deliveries directly to the cafeteria without offending the sensibilities of the fancy senators in the main Hall areas.

"So Tezuka just liked hanging out in darkened hallways between sessions?" Bastian wrinkles his nose as he gets a cloud of dust to the face. Good to know the Hall cafeteria food gets some extra seasoning when it comes this way.

The officer shrugs, holding the door open to let Michaels through. "Maybe she didn't intend to be here in the first place. The only things this hallway has going for it are inconsistent use and a minimal number of security cameras."

"A good place to kill someone, then."

"You tell me. That's what you people do, isn't it?"

It certainly doesn't look like a crime scene, he thinks as Michaels gets the machine set up off to one side. But there's no mistaking the apprehension-trepidation-dread emanating from the walls. "This goes straight to the cafeteria?"

"Yes. The door at the end of the hall opens to the kitchen."

"And the other doors here?"

"Storage. Nothing leading back outside."

Bastian hangs back for a moment, taking a breath and trying to steady himself. When he realizes he's hesitating, he makes a face and immediately puts a hand on the wall.

It's vague at first, like he's feeling through a mist, and he's just starting to think he'll have to take his gloves off already when *she's choking down her fear, walking fast and trying to text at the same time, her phone the only light in the corridor, her heartbeat fast, but she can't afford to be nervous-uneasy-scared—*

definitely not that last one—she has to stay calm, has to ignore the stupid crawling feeling on the back of her neck, of course there's no one following her, just have to type faster, why is the code so complex—?

"Director?"

Bastian snatches his hand away from the wall. "What?"

The officer has moved a bit further down the hallway. She has her phone in her hand, its glow turning her face slightly blue. "Message from the CSIs. It was definitely poison. No definitive method of entry, but it was likely administered before she got down here."

"And then someone followed her to make sure it stuck," Bastian says slowly.

"There's no evidence of that."

"Not *your* kind of evidence, no."

Bastian walks over to her and looks around, but there's no significant difference here as compared to where he just was. No tape, no scene markers, nothing. Pham's CSIs must have done their job and picked up quickly. "Is this where you found the body?"

"Yes."

"Did you invite everyone in the Hall down here to celebrate the end of your investigation?"

"Sorry?"

"You didn't bother to keep things cordoned off. Did you make sure everyone got a chance to trample all over the evidence before we got here?"

The officer smirks. "We got our kind of evidence collected before you got here. Didn't want police work to get in the way of you touching the walls real hard."

Gone are the days when the city staff defaulted to discomfort and fear versus outright disdain of compound officials, Bastian thinks dryly. Maybe some things were better when Valentine was in charge. No one dared talk back to her.

He turns back to Michaels. "Let's hold off on the recording for a minute." He doesn't usually need to do more than one read, but that last one got interrupted, and the aura of vagueness around here is making him uneasy.

He crouches down, pulls off his gloves, and puts his hands, palms down, on the floor.

Rising alarm-anxiety-fear but she's not running, refuses to run, there's no need to run—it's just that the senator is relying on her to get out this last fragment, the others on the committee are getting suspicious, and it really shouldn't be taking so long except of course the signal down here isn't great, but she keeps thinking she sees people following her, so it didn't seem safe in the office anymore—or maybe she's just paranoid—except, wait, what was that noise—?

An odd, blurry vagueness affects this read as well, but clearly, Tezuka was trying to get information out to someone. And she definitely wasn't alone, though he couldn't say who or what was with her.

He could try shoving more of his power at it—and probably earn himself a nosebleed and a strong word from Henry regarding the definition of "careful"—but somehow, Bastian doesn't think that will work in this case. Something about what was happening at the time means there's less emotional residue than normal for a situation like this. It's not so much that it's been erased as that it wasn't allowed to settle in the first place.

Of course, his first thought is negation. But that's not how negation works— at least, not the way Henry uses it. And it's not like there are other negators Bastian can ask for insight.

"Director Lucas?" It's Michaels this time.

"Hang on." If brute force won't work, maybe finesse will.

Bastian gets to his feet (slight wobble—stupid, it wasn't that intense of a read), walks a few paces toward the kitchen door—the direction Tezuka was headed—and touches the wall there, gently this time.

She's sick to her stomach, can't shake the feeling that someone's following her, but all that matters is that this goes through—it's the last one she could get, so it has to be enough to tie everything together so that the major can take some sort of action because otherwise—

Her desperation bleeds into his, and for a moment, he's not sure where (or who) he is. It's enough of a shock to jolt him out of the read. That and the sudden, excruciating headache.

Bastian pulls back sharply from the wall and swallows a heartfelt curse. The last thing he wants is to look weak in front of a city officer who already thinks compound staff are idiots. So it's just as well that he's facing the wall and not the others. It gives him a moment to compose his face into something resembling a stoic but severe don't-think-an-asset-can't-kill-you-in-an-instant expression.

But the only thing he could possibly do at the moment to kill someone would be to bump them really hard on his way down to the floor. (How can it hurt this much, a read never hurts this much, not enough that he can feel it above the near-constant throbbing he's gotten used to—)

He turns carefully and gives Michaels a look, not even sure what he's trying to say with it. Her eyebrows knit together briefly, but she sticks to professional silence. She doesn't offer to bring the machine over to him, but she says nothing about him taking his time getting to her. And she's particularly careful attaching the electrodes to his arm, waiting for his nod before turning on the machine.

The jolt of energy running from the wires and into his blood feels disgusting, like always. But the familiarity of it is weirdly comforting. His head's still not happy with him, but it quiets down as he stands there.

Michaels has just finished removing the last electrode when a loud buzzing startles them both. Bastian turns to find their companion touching her earpiece.

"What—? Sorry, the signal down here isn't—just a minute—" She looks at Bastian, nodding curtly toward the door to the cafeteria. "Time to go." She opens the door and waits for Bastian and Michaels to precede her.

The kitchen is just starting to get busy for the lunchtime crowd. In a testament to the dedication of food service workers, the buzz of busy-focused-disinterested barely wavers as the officer herds Bastian and Michaels out into the cafeteria seating area and, from there, into the Hall atrium.

"You're wanted at security," she tells Bastian.

Her tone says the time for witty banter is over, so Bastian turns to Michaels. "I'll meet you back at the vehicle with Henry when we're done here."

"Yes, sir."

The officers sitting at the atrium security desk shoot a mixture of relief-amusement-irritation Bastian's way as he approaches. At first, Bastian wonders if he has something on his face; then he realizes the officers are reacting to a series of squawks coming from the comm he had to leave with them when he first arrived.

"I think it's for you, sir," one of them says. "I hope you speak ... whatever that is."

Bastian sighs, picks up the comm, and puts the earpiece in. "I have a cell phone, you know."

The squawking continues for a few more seconds before going abruptly silent. Then: "Cell phones are the most insecure method of communication currently in existence," Kent says.

"And this is better?"

"This signal is encrypted, but it would help if you'd back away slowly from the incompetent security desk before you give me heartburn."

Without bothering to ask for permission, Bastian turns, skirts the edge of the atrium, and walks outside into the sunlight. There are still Hall staff members meandering around, but with most people probably working through lunch or else trying to be first in line at the cafeteria, Bastian has some space to himself, at least for now. "Better?"

"Ugh, not really. I still have to sit with the knowledge that it's this easy to mask frequencies from the Hall's network."

"Can you sit with that knowledge without bothering me in the middle of an investigation?"

"Not really. I mean, I would have, but I can't reach the major, so you'll have to do."

"Thanks. And?"

Kent pauses, then opens the floodgates at rapid speed, even for him. "Okay, you know how Donnigan and Pham were in our faces about unsecured messages going into and out of the compound earlier? Turns out they were right to be concerned."

It takes Bastian a moment to realize what Kent is saying. "So there's a br—"

"Don't say the B-word!" Kent hisses. "Do you *want* me to have a stroke?"

"I *want* you to tell me what's going on," Bastian says sharply.

"It's not a—you know. Not exactly. It's just that we found evidence that a few of those file fragments that were being left for us did make it into the compound mainframe."

"And how is that not a—?"

"I mean, it is. But they didn't do any damage. They just got flung into different sections of the compound system, like whoever was sending them started to get sloppy toward the end and just stuck them wherever they fit. And, uh, some of them disappeared."

"And why are you only noticing this now?"

"Because it's not the sort of thing our computers could pick up. It's not just code, Lucas—if it were, Sybil's security program would've caught it right away. Whatever did this is a *living thing* that just sneaked in and . . . disintegrated as soon as it got the files inside. Code doesn't *do* that. Not unless someone's talked it into life. Someone who can read and write code better than is humanly possible."

"A cyberreader," Bastian says slowly.

"Yeah." Kent's shudder is audible in that one syllable. "We've got some of the best security in the world at this compound—obviously, since I built most of it—but a black hat cyberreader could still bring everything down if they really wanted to."

It must be a big deal if Kent is willing to admit a potential flaw in his work, Bastian thinks. "There are something like five cyberreaders in the Compound Network right now," he says, trying to remember files he barely spent more than a few minutes on. "I don't think there's any record of malcontents in there, but I can check."

"You're assuming whoever did this is a registered asset and not a potential. Or just someone off the grid."

Because if Henry's managed to stay off the grid this long, surely other assets have, too. "All right, so what now?"

"Sybil and I are tracking down anything that's left in our system and keeping an eye out for any holes we can plug. And we've put together this extra secure channel, which is, y'know, extra secure. We think. But we wanted to let you know as soon as we figured out what it was because—"

"—you wanted to talk about highly confidential information in a semi-public setting? Remind me how this is better than a cell phone?"

"*Listen*," Kent hisses. "We're good for now—whatever this cyberreader was up to, they don't seem to have damaged our system. But if they decide they want back in, they could do more than just leave us some weird, encrypted files. They could corrupt everything—asset files, research materials, every communication that comes in and out. An asset-made virus could spread through the entire Compound Network. We're pretty good working with cyberreaders who are on our side, but if there's a rogue one wandering around—or if someone wants to try to come in after them . . ."

Bastian considers silently for a moment. "Henry will want to alert the Compound Council."

"You can't do that," says a low voice that definitely isn't Kent's.

Bastian starts, furious at himself for being too distracted to realize someone has come up behind him. "Someone" being, inexplicably, Senator Nunez.

She looks awful. There are deep shadows under her eyes, and though she's got her usual smart suit and severely tied-back hair in place, she's clearly cracking around the edges: one slightly askew collar here, one smudged bit of mascara there. Her shoulders are even more tense than usual.

But it's her completely uncharacteristic desperation-anxiety-fear that leaves him temporarily tongue-tied.

"You can't tell Carter anything," she says. "Come with me, and I'll explain why."

Chapter 25

HENRY IS ABOUT to explain to Detective Pham for the third time that he has no idea why Emily Tezuka contacted the compound on the day she died when the door to Donnigan's office slams open.

"Playtime's over," Bastian says. "I need the major."

Pham raises her eyebrows. "This is a confidential interview, Director. Whatever you need can wait."

"It's an interrogation. Trust me, I know what one looks like. You've already had, what, three hours? And in case you forgot, the major has a compound to run. So no, this can't wait."

As much as Henry wants to jump at any chance to get out of the chair that's currently trying to dislocate his entire back, it's probably not good form to leave a detective hanging in the middle of an investigation. "Bastian, maybe—"

"It's a code 4357."

Henry frowns. That's not—oh. "Right. We should go, then."

"Excuse me," Donnigan says from where he's sitting behind his desk. He's been holding court there and clearly enjoying it ever since he, Henry, and Pham got to his office. "What's a code 4357?"

"I'm sure it's mentioned in one of those liaison committee reports you skimmed rather than read," Bastian says. To Henry: "Coming?"

Of course he has to. "Sorry, Detective," Henry says, getting to his feet and trying to ignore the twinge of protesting muscles. "If you have any more questions, we'll be happy to receive you at the compound."

"Don't be preposterous!" Donnnigan sputters. "You can't just—"

"Can and will." Bastian backs out of the doorway, apparently having used up his allotment of patience for this social engagement. Henry should probably be irritated that Bastian's assuming he'll up and leave an important meeting just because Bastian tells him to. But in this case, he's right.

"I'll be in touch, Major," Pham says as he heads for the door. It's almost, but not quite, a threat.

Henry nods, then slips out before Donnigan can start pontificating.

He has to take several long strides to catch up with Bastian, who's got his earpiece back in and is handing Henry his before Henry can even ask when he liberated them from security.

"Code 4357 doesn't exist," Henry reminds him.

"Sure doesn't," Bastian agrees.

Henry hears a crackle on the line. "I've worked it out with Officer Michaels," Kent says, a weird tinniness behind his voice.

"Got it," Bastian tells him. "Stand by."

"Bastian," Henry says, "this would be a good time for you to—"

"No, it wouldn't. Let's get to the car first."

Michaels is waiting for them, along with the driver. As Henry and Bastian approach, she offers up a quick salute, then says to Henry, "We'll be taking our lunch break now, sir. Unless you need anything?"

Henry glances at Bastian, who does nothing to explain. "That's . . . fine," he says after an awkward pause.

"I've set up the conference call for you to take in the vehicle, as you requested," Michaels continues.

Henry, who requested no such thing, raises his eyebrows. "All right."

"We'll be back in twenty minutes, sir."

As they walk off, Henry stares after them, bemused. Bastian opens the front passenger side door and gets in, leaving the back seat for Henry. There really isn't anything for it, so Henry opens the door—

—and sees Senator Nunez sitting in the shadows on the other side.

"Get in," Bastian says impatiently.

Henry does, closing the door behind him. "Did you need a ride, Senator?"

Turning around in his seat to face them, Bastian hands Henry a tablet. "Kent, we good?"

"I've jammed everything I could," Kent says, his voice coming through the tablet now. "Keep this tablet running until you're done. Then get it back to me so I can scrub it. Sort of like I'm going to sign off now and go scrub my ears so I can disavow all knowledge of this conversation."

Henry hopes his frown is open-ended enough to encompass everyone in the car, but especially Bastian. "Is this the part where you explain what this is all about, or—?"

"There are things you need to know," Nunez interrupts, leaning forward. At this angle, there's a little more light on her face, and Henry can see how exhausted she looks.

"This has to do with your aide, doesn't it?" he asks.

Nunez's usually brusque and efficient expression crumbles. "Emily was . . . She believed in this. Believed in me. I should never have gotten her involved."

Nunez shakes her head almost violently, and her usual cool mask slips back into place. "It's about the liaison committee," she says, "though it's more than that. There's also the Council."

"If you have a problem with either, there are channels—"

"Not for this."

Henry pauses, then turns to Bastian. "This is why you used the distress code. The one we kept off the books and agreed to only use for something catastrophic."

"I'm reserving the adjective until Nunez comes clean," Bastian says. "But Kent just told me something concerning about the compound's security, and Nunez claims there's a link between that and her dead aide—and that we shouldn't tell Carter. Now she's going to explain."

"I'm the one who's been sending you the encrypted data fragments," Nunez says. "Well. Emily was sending them. Until yesterday."

"Was she a cyberreader?" Bastian asks, eyes narrowing.

Henry frowns. "You think an asset—?"

"I have no idea what you're talking about," Nunez says stiffly. "All I know is that we needed you to get that information, and Emily agreed to make it happen."

"You haven't always been . . . eager to help the compound," Henry says carefully. "Why the change of heart?"

Nunez makes a face. "I know you have very little reason to trust me, Major. The incident regarding the murder investigation last year—"

"You mean when you had me, Director Lucas, and Officer Michaels locked up for doing our jobs?"

She looks slightly abashed, which is an odd look for her face, though it seems genuine enough. "Yes. I was concerned for the safety of the Hall, given the suspicious deaths and the apparent involvement of not only the compound, but Senator Haldis, before his death. That's part of the reason I made sure I was assigned to the new liaison committee. To make sure everything was aboveboard."

"And you suspect it isn't?"

"I *know* it isn't."

Henry refuses to look at Bastian, who's probably exuding I-told-you-so vibes from every pore. "The committee hasn't been easy to work with," Henry admits, "but that doesn't mean someone's out to get us."

"I'm afraid that's exactly what it means." Nunez glances at the tinted window behind Henry's head, then continues. "Senator Donnigan and General Carter have organized a subcommittee. Ostensibly, it's a forum for further discussion of how to coordinate between city and compound officials, but in practice . . . It doesn't exist in any official record, and notes are never taken. Donnigan asked me to join a few months ago, and the content of the discussions I've witnessed has been disturbing."

"In what way?" Henry asks. "And what does this have to do with the data fragments?"

"I believe that data is why the subcommittee was formed in the first place."

Henry steels himself. "Have you read it? The files, I mean?"

"Have you?"

"Yes. As much as our hackers have been able to decode."

"Given the quality of your resources, you probably know more than the subcommittee does at this point. All we've been told is that the data involves some sort of long-standing, unsanctioned experiment called the Fail-Safe Protocol. As the name suggests, it has something to do with controlling assets believed to be particularly significant threats. Carter seems to know quite a lot about it, but not everything. He has a collection of relevant files that he shares with us as the Council hackers decode them."

"Where did they come from?" Bastian asks.

"According to Carter, they're made up of Dr. Wright's notes. I'm unclear on how the general came across them in the first place; they weren't included with the other files we reviewed during the trial last year."

"We've already been through all of Dr. Wright's notes," Henry says, realizing as soon as he says it how stupid it is but plowing ahead with the official line anyway. "Everything else was destroyed before he was arrested."

"Not everything. Not whatever General Carter has. And let me assure you, he's convinced there are more—and he's determined to find them."

Because of course they found something and held it back. And of course Carter lied about it, even if only by omission. Once upon a time, Henry might have given him the benefit of the doubt and assumed there was nothing sinister in this—just a high-level officer doing his job. Now, all Henry can do is think back to John Doe's warning that Carter and the Council know something important that they're keeping under wraps. Was he referring to the Fail-Safe Protocol?

"You have to understand," Nunez says. "It's likely that this data will be used to make an argument for starting a new round of experiments not unlike the ones Dr. Wright and Major Valentine oversaw."

Henry frowns. "Hang on. General Carter put a stop to those experiments in the first place. Why would he want to start them up again?"

"The general seems to think this Fail-Safe Protocol, whatever it is, needs to be tested and implemented without delay. And he wants the Council to closely oversee whoever does it."

She locks gazes with him. "While no one's said it outright, I suspect that the primary mission of the liaison committee has always been to come up with enough evidence to remove you from office and take control of the compound whenever they were ready to."

Henry knows it'll make him sound like an idiot, but he can't stop himself from blurting, "After everything we gave them on how those experiments killed thousands of assets?"

Nunez gives him a thin smile. "Surely you didn't think the purpose of the liaison committee was to help you make the world a better and brighter place?"

"If Carter's been holding back with the subcommittee, how did you get the data you've been sending the compound?" Bastian asks. "And why send it to us?"

"You're not the only one with access to talented hackers. Emily is—" Nunez goes silent for a moment, obviously struggling to get herself under control. "Emily *was* excellent at what she did. She was able to track down some of the original files and copy them in bits and pieces, which we sent to you as we got them."

"That's why they killed her," Henry says quietly.

"I can't prove they did, of course." Nunez sighs. "It was her idea. I never meant to . . . I only asked her opinion on whether it was possible to find the original versions of the files being discussed at the meetings and send copies somewhere for safekeeping. But when we realized this data was part of a plot to overthrow the compound, she suggested we send as much of it as we could to you. She wanted to make it look like she was doing it without my knowledge. To keep me safe. To do some good."

Nunez gives Henry an almost condescending smile. "She was an idealist. You would have liked her, Major."

"How long have you and the others been reviewing this material?" Henry asks, ignoring the jab.

"Carter and Donnigan formed the subcommittee right after Major Valentine's hearing, or so I'm told. The data review is a relatively new addition. My understanding is that it's taken the Compound Council hackers this long to decode what little they have."

So it began right after the hearing, Henry thinks. They didn't even wait to give the new compound a chance. From the start, they were looking for an excuse to take control.

"Why bother?" he says, more to himself than the others. "If they just wanted to start the experiments up again, why go to all the trouble of removing Major Valentine from office and putting someone else in charge?"

"Maybe your efforts to expose her had gone too far, and they needed damage control," Nunez suggests. "What better way to put a more palatable face on the compound and hide their true intentions than to promote someone malleable who was also known for removing corruption from their ranks?"

Her smile this time is genuine, if a bit exasperated. "But you kept refusing to play along or give them a good enough reason to get rid of you once they felt it was necessary."

"So they had to send someone in to *find* a reason," Bastian murmurs. "Someone who had your trust and could tell them where to dig."

Henry rubs his eyes. "Major Alexis."

"I suspected that was his function," Nunez admits. "Not that it was ever openly discussed in subcommittee meetings." She hesitates, then adds, "I have to admit, Major Alexis never struck me as the sort of person who would . . . Well. People often surprise us."

It doesn't make any sense, though. What would Alexis get out of not-too-subtly spying on the compound? The liaison committee could've just requested the financial records and vehicle maintenance logs and everything else Major Alexis has been reviewing. Instead, they sent someone in to shadow the compound's day-to-day operations. What could that possibly give them that they could use to take over?

Unless there's something going on at the compound that Henry isn't aware of. Something Alexis and the committee are interested in but don't want him to know about.

Something Emily Tezuka's files can explain.

"We have to finish decoding the fragments," Henry says. "If there's anything in there that points directly back to the Council or Donnigan or anyone else, we need to—"

"Do what? Take it to the Council? Of which Carter is the head?"

"He's not the only one on the Council. There are others who—"

"—are probably also part of this." Nunez rolls her eyes. "You're naive, Major. Dangerously so. There's a reason I told the director to convince you not to tell anyone about this yet."

Henry swallows his growing irritation. "So what do you suggest we do, then? Sit on our hands while the committee finds a way to remove us? Wait around for more people to die?"

"I suggest you keep these files and this knowledge as secure as possible. I suggest you use every resource at your disposal to maintain your position and power. And I suggest you dedicate yourself to building so solid a case that Carter and the others can't possibly stand against it."

Bastian snorts. "But you don't have any suggestions on how to actually *do* any of that. Or why you think we should."

"You're asking me to do your job for you, Director?"

"I'm asking you to explain why you're telling us all of this. What do you get out of it?"

"I would have thought that was clear." She turns to Henry. "I may not care much for assets or the Compound Network as a whole, but I've read Dr. Wright's notes. I know what he did. What Major Valentine sanctioned. That sort of human rights violation *cannot* be allowed to resume in any capacity."

"Okay," Bastian says. "So you're altruistic. And hypocritical, given that you just mocked Henry for that. But let's not forget the part where breaking up a conspiracy would get Donnigan out of your hair."

Nunez is quiet for a few seconds. Then she says, "You're right. I think anyone who wants to resurrect those disgusting experiments should be permanently locked up. And whoever killed Emily must be brought to justice. But I can't deny that I would also benefit politically from Senator Donnigan's downfall."

She gives them both a hard look. "Is that what you wanted to hear? That I have ambition? Consider it said. But I also believe in doing my job. I believe in protecting my constituents, many of whom work with compound officials or could be potentials themselves. It's clear that whatever Senator Donnigan and General Carter have in mind will be dangerous to everyone. And need I remind you that someone I was responsible for was murdered?"

Watching her, Henry thinks of his team: the years he spent training them, working with them, putting their safety ahead of his own. The dawning realization that in the end, there was only so much he could do to protect them from Major Valentine.

(The way Johnson looked in the Level 19 experimental recovery room, still and pale and very clearly dead because Henry hadn't been able to stop them from taking him away, and it will always be his fault that it happened because that was his job, to train them and keep them as safe as possible, and he failed so utterly and completely that he'll never—)

"No," Henry says quietly. "You don't have to remind us."

"Then you understand why we need to prevent any further damage here." Nunez smooths down her skirt unnecessarily, then reaches for the door handle. "We shouldn't speak like this again."

"Wait," Henry says. "You're just going to go back out there?"

Nunez gives him another thin smile. "I have a job to do, Major. As do you."

"It's not safe. At least let us—"

"I don't need your help with anything other than making sure justice is done here. I know how to keep my head down when I need to."

She starts to open the car door again, but Henry stops her. "Senator. Before, when you wanted to talk to me but were trying to hide it, especially in front of Major Alexis. That was because of this, wasn't it? You didn't want him to know."

She looks at him like he's an idiot. "Yes."

"I'm sorry it's taken us so long to address this," Henry tells her. "And I promise we'll figure it out."

Nunez's face hovers somewhere between exasperation and amusement. "Your chivalry has been duly noted, Major."

Henry frowns. "I'm not—"

"Of course you're not." Nunez glances at Bastian. "Director, please make sure the major's urge to help doesn't get him in trouble."

"Sure, Senator. And make sure you remember that your aide's urge to help is the only reason she's dead right now, and you're not."

Nunez purses her lips, then nods, as if to accept the criticism. She gets out of the car, slams the door shut behind her, and walks back toward the Hall like she didn't just take part in a covert meeting that could get them all killed.

Chapter 26

LAUREL DRUMS HER fingers against the conference room table, then stops when she realizes James is doing the same thing. Someone has to be the adult, after all. And adults don't get impatient waiting for scouting parties to connect their video and audio feeds. Adults remain quiet and still and definitely don't absently reach out to pet the leaves of the snake plant they brought along to the meeting.

Adults also don't spend their waiting time thinking about the three separate coded file fragments they deleted from the compound system and hid on their own tablet, then reviewed a million times.

There's not enough readable information in any of the fragments to create a full narrative, although Laurel has a guess, based on what she's seen:

1. Some sort of property called FSP6342867.SYN went missing, along with an asset.
2. The compound freaked out and sent people after them.
3. Nothing was ever recovered.
4. The compound stopped using the paths in the area where the asset was last seen.

And all of that happened around fifty years ago, when the maps were changed.

She tried asking James if it meant anything to him, but he only said the people he was traveling with wanted to use that specific path because it would keep them safe on the way to wherever they were going. Laurel supposes if a bunch of people were trying to avoid compound scouts, they'd want a "not-seeing place," like the fir mentioned. But that doesn't really explain how the "not-seeing place" came to be—or why the compound would've abandoned it.

Anyway, those files are confusing but relevant to the task at hand—namely, pinpointing the location of this "not-seeing place," which is what Captain Smith and her team are doing. There's no reason at all for Laurel to hide the documents from the compound mainframe, except . . .

Except they also contain bits of information related to the file she found in the library. The one with the dead officer, whom Laurel is definitely not still dreaming about every night. The one that makes something catch in her throat every time she thinks about it, like it puts her on the verge of remembering something she doesn't want to remember.

"Assistant Director?"

Laurel looks up sharply and realizes Captain Smith has finally gotten the feed to work. She's appeared on the projection screen, standing in the forest, the slight sheen of sweat on her forehead the only indication that she's been trekking around, directing both her team and the survey scientists. Behind her, other officers are fiddling with various devices or hurrying past.

"Hello, Captain," Laurel says in her most cheerful voice, elbowing James in the side so he'll sit up straight and pay attention. "Find anything to retrieve yet?"

Strictly speaking, this isn't a retrieval. But since they're trying to find evidence of asset activity, Henry suggested sending the captain and her team.

He wasn't excited about Laurel's counter suggestion that they send Chloe as well, despite the fact that she's the only tracker in the asset program right now, and if you're investigating a path, it really helps to have a tracker around. Henry started in on the whole "but she's just a kid" thing, which meant Laurel had to remind him that compound officers go into the field regularly starting at age eighteen, and Chloe's only a few years shy of that, and honestly, what terrible thing is he expecting to happen while she's surrounded by Captain Smith and her team, not to mention the forest, which is really good at keeping an eye on people if you ask nicely?

Henry eventually relented, but Laurel suspects it was only because he was distracted by wanting to go sit with Bastian in his med bay room some more. Which was adorable and also extremely helpful, since it meant Laurel has been able to elect herself president of this initiative. (President? Commanding officer? Benevolent dictator? She hasn't decided on a title yet.)

"There's nothing here," Smith is saying. "As far as we can tell, this location does align with the missing paths marked on the maps, though. And I can't say there isn't something weird going on out here."

Laurel frowns. "Weird like a new variegation pattern on a camellia or weird like a water hemlock developing a new poison?"

"Weird like your tracker isn't much help. We've had to do everything on our own because she claims she can't use her power. Frankly, I'm not sure why you thought we should bring her along in the first place." Smith pauses, then continues, "Not that I'm doubting your recommendation. Ma'am."

"Actually," Laurel says, "that's exactly what you're doing. And it's very rude, especially because I can see Chloe by the oak over there, so she probably heard everything you said. I bet she picked up on the dead zone before your machines did, right?"

"Yes, but—"

"So we've proved that there really is a dead zone out there where asset powers don't work. Good to know. What else have you found?"

"Evidence of people using this path, although they've done a good job of trying to hide it."

"Recently?"

"Within the last month or so."

James mutters something, derailing Laurel's train of thought. He's been so uncharacteristically silent, she almost forgot about him. "What was that?" she asks, turning to look at him.

It's just as well she did. Or maybe it isn't, given the strained look on his face, which is washed out in the blue of the screen. His eyes have gone glassy, and he's leaning forward, like he's trying to put himself closer to the forest. Laurel understands the inclination, but she also understands the concept of streaming video versus actually being in a physical location. She thought he did, too. "James—"

"I was there," he says. "I remember the way the path turned. There's a fork up ahead. One of the trails goes by a little creek, and there are a bunch of these plants with massive leaves and purple flowers and little seeds that get stuck on your clothes . . ."

Laurel swallows. "Burdock, maybe. Captain?"

Smith purses her lips, then takes the camera off of whatever's been holding it and flips it to show them where she's walking. The camera shakes a bit as she moves away from where the other officers are working. In a few seconds, it becomes clear that the path out of the area branches off in two directions, just like James said it would. Several large burdock plants are waving in the breeze off to one side, their huge green leaves bobbing pleasantly over a thin stream of water.

Smith turns the camera back to her face, which has gotten even stonier—impressive, since Laurel didn't realize it could do that any more than it already has. "How did you know about this?" Smith demands.

"I told you. I've been there." James turns to Laurel, eyes now bright. "Come on, let's stop wasting time and *go* there already!"

"Bastian and Henry aren't back yet," Laurel reminds him. "And we need to—"

There's a knock at the meeting room door. Laurel turns to the snake plant. "Are you expecting someone?" she asks. When it doesn't offer an opinion on the situation, she turns back to James. "Are you?"

"Assistant Director?" comes a voice from the other side of the door. "I'm sorry to interrupt, but do you have a moment?"

"We have to go," Laurel tells the screen. "Thanks for the update, Captain. You can finish up there and then head back."

James frowns at her as she cuts the feed off, leaving the screen in gray limbo. "What about—?"

"Go get together everything we have on those paths and your memories of your healer," Laurel says with the firmness of a leader on a mission. "We're going to shove it all in Henry's face as soon as he's back. Then he'll *have* to let us mount an expedition." She pauses, then adds, "Do you need horses if you're going to mount an expedition? I don't even know where we'd get horses. Or if they'd fit in the budget. I'll have to ask Irfan."

"Laurel, we don't need—"

"Assistant Director?" comes the voice in the hall.

Laurel drags James to his feet and over to the door. "Make sure you get the stickers, too," she says. "There's no way he'll be able to resist the stickers. Oh! Hello, Major. James was just leaving."

Major Alexis is standing outside of the meeting room, tablet tucked under one arm and cane with its strap around the opposite wrist. "Sorry for the interruption," he says again, "but I could use your help with this report that I need to get out in the next half hour . . ."

He tips his head, probably because he hears James's sigh, along with everyone else in a five-mile radius.

"Never mind James," Laurel says firmly, holding open the meeting room door a little wider. "I've got the door open for you, if you'd like to come in. Then James can be on his way to do some very important things without complaining even a little bit about them."

"Oh, I don't think we've met," the major begins.

"Bit busy," James says. As soon as the major is through the doorway, James slips past him and into the hall. Laurel frowns as she catches sight of a black coat watching him head toward the elevators. No matter how many times she explains that James has an ID just like any other compound guest and therefore doesn't need to be stalked, the black coats still act like he's going to sneak into top secret areas or go rummaging through their underwear drawers or something.

"Don't mind him," Laurel says, closing the meeting room door and wondering if Chloe would count this as another apology on James's behalf. "He really *is* busy. But I'm sure he didn't mean to be . . . like that about it."

"He's an asset, isn't he?" Major Alexis asks. "The firestarter from your compound."

"Yes." Laurel isn't sure why it makes her uncomfortable to admit it, but maybe that's just what happens when you stop sleeping like a normal person: Your emotions get all stupid and jumbled up. Maybe she'll ask Bastian to explain it when he gets back. "Can I help you with something?"

"I wanted to ask about James, actually, and the initiative to recover his memories. Any progress?"

Laurel glances at the darkened screen. "Maybe. Probably. I think so."

"Would you care to elaborate? I ask because I have to finish off this report, and I think the committee will want to know. And I have a related matter to run by you, too. Is there a place in here where I can set this down?" He waves his tablet.

"Yes, sorry. Table's just a few steps straight ahead of you."

Once the major is settled, she sits down next to him. "The scouting team just reported in," she says. "It looks like they found a place in the forest that James remembers, and it matches our records, too."

"Excellent. So what's the next step?"

"James will give Henry our extremely impressive report, and then Henry will send him and Bastian out there, and—"

"Bastian?"

Oh. She wasn't supposed to mention that part. "Or I'll go," she amends. "After all, I'm one of the most important people here, so—"

"Isn't that a compelling argument for why you *shouldn't* go? I'm sure the compound needs you here to help manage the asset program."

Stupid logic. "Yes, well. I'm sure we'll have a nice argument about who gets to go on the field trip, and Henry will give us all some very stern warnings about staying safe, and then James will get a team of some sort to go with him and figure out how to get his memories back."

"And the hope is that just being in that area will trigger something?"

There's nothing in his tone to imply any sort of judgment, but Laurel can't stop herself from feeling a little stung anyway. "Dr. Rowe's team thinks it's possible, yes. At the very least, they want to take some measurements and observe him once he gets there."

"It's unfortunate that there aren't any memors on the asset program roster," Major Alexis says, shaking his head. "Well. Aside from the young lady the director brought in a few weeks ago. But I assume she hasn't been pressed into service yet."

"No," Laurel says a bit stiffly.

"And you haven't found her parents yet, I understand?"

"No," Laurel says a bit more stiffly.

That one is a little weird, she has to admit. Angelica's been at the compound for a little over two weeks, and Kent has run all the information they could get out of her about her family, but still nothing. There's no record of her parents living where she says they live—no record of them existing at all, which is even weirder. No next of kin, no school records, no medical records, nothing. Laurel knows the hackers have had a lot of trouble finding assets' families—Dr. Wright and Major Valentine did everything they could to separate potentials from their outside connections, which makes tracking them down after the fact more difficult, particularly for assets who have undergone experiments with memory-related side effects. But to turn up so little on a child who wasn't even officially registered as a potential, let alone an asset, is more than a little odd.

"Hmm." Major Alexis appears to consider this for a moment. Then he smiles again. "Well, I'm sure you'll keep me updated. In the meantime, I wanted to ask you about this file I found."

He pulls over his tablet and runs his fingers along the keypad at the bottom until a file opens on the screen. Then he pushes it slightly toward her so she can have a look. Which she does.

And her heart stops.

Well, not really. But it gives a good stutter, and she feels her face heat up, and she forgets how to speak for a moment.

"I'm not really sure what it is," the major says, frowning, "but my tablet certainly can't read it. As far as I can tell, it's just a bunch of letters and numbers. I thought maybe it would make sense to you."

"Where did you get this?" Laurel asks, her voice wobbling a bit on the vowels.

"I accidentally clicked on it when I was trying to finish up my report. I'm not sure where it originated; it certainly wasn't there yesterday, although I admit I might have missed it. I would have simply brought it up with the hackers, but they seem a bit busy now. And if I'm not mistaken, at least some of those letters and numbers are in the order of an asset ID."

The screen on Major Alexis's tablet isn't big enough to show as much of the file at once as Laurel's tablet does, but she knows that if he scrolls just a little bit, he'll hit the image of the dead officer. Not that she needs to see it. She could describe the exact colors and position of the body with her eyes closed.

"I'm not sure what that is," Laurel says carefully. "Kent might be able to tell you more about it, though."

"You've never seen anything similar?"

Lying is bad, Laurel reminds herself.

"No," she says.

Major Alexis taps the table thoughtfully, then nods and closes the file. "Well, I can speak to Henry about it when he gets back. And perhaps Kent, when he's less busy." He pushes back his chair and stands.

She wants to ask if he's going to put it in his report—dreads thinking about what would happen if he did—but she's got to play it cool. If only she had a cucumber plant around to ask how to do that. "Sorry I couldn't help. Let me get the door for you."

When Major Alexis is gone, Laurel goes back to the table and picks up the snake plant, which is giving her the side-eye. "Oh, hush," she tells it, even though it hasn't said anything. "Let's go see how James is doing on that report."

The snake plant wisely says nothing.

Chapter 27

WHEN THEY GET back to the compound, Henry orders Bastian to call it a day and head to the suite. That Bastian goes silently with only a sour expression and a slight sag to his shoulders is a testament to how far he still is from full health.

Henry himself takes another few hours to get there. He checks in with Kent (compound mainframe is stable, but they're still tracking down any extraneous files) and Michaels (several messages from Donnigan demanding a call tomorrow, which Michaels has arranged, plus a disturbingly vague note from Major Alexis saying he's sent off his latest report to the committee and may need to follow up).

Henry thinks he's managed to wrap things up for the day and is leaving his office when Laurel practically tackles him in the hallway. "Henry! Have you talked to Captain Smith yet? Did you look at the information James and I sent you?"

Right; the reconnaissance mission. As if there weren't enough potentially life-altering developments on his plate already. "Not yet," Henry says. He can hear the exhaustion in his own voice. "What happened?"

Laurel grabs his hand, her eyes somewhere between excited and manic. "They found it. The dead zone, I mean. It's just where we thought it would be, and James remembers it. *Remembers* it! And I found more evidence of some sort of incident with an asset that took place there. So we should send James right away—"

Henry rubs his eyes with his free hand. "Laurel, it's late. The asset program committee will need to review the data Smith's team is collecting before we do anything. If you want to stop by tomorrow—"

"*Henry*." Laurel squeezes his hand tightly. "This is *it*. This is the thing that could help them both. James could get his memories back and be just like he was, and Bastian won't . . ."

As her voice trails off, Henry realizes how still and quiet the hallway is. In the silence, he keeps expecting it to sink in, that there might be hope left. That they might not have to watch as Bastian's power slowly kills him.

He can practically hear John Doe's voice again, scratchy and low; see the derision in his eyes as he gleefully told Henry that he'll lose more than anyone, that he'll know there was something he could've done to save Bastian, but not what. Henry should feel relieved and hopeful that they've found another solution.

Instead, he's just tired.

(Because a woman is dead, and compound security has been compromised, and Major Alexis is likely reporting to a subcommittee working directly against them, and a part of him can't help but wonder if it's even worth getting his hopes up because what if this is just like all the things they've already tried, and he's not sure he can handle losing Bastian on top of everything else—)

Henry closes his eyes briefly to steady himself, then opens them and gives Laurel a small smile. "I know," he says quietly. "Let's talk about it tomorrow."

She frowns at him. "You're not excited, are you? I mean, I'm not an empath, but I know what excited looks like, and it's not . . . whatever you're doing now. Unless you're just very bad at it."

"After a day like today, it's safe to say I'm bad at everything."

"Well, that's just silly. No one's bad at *everything*. And if they were, they'd be good at being bad at everything, so it's a moot point."

She looks at him for another moment, then purses her lips and drops his hand. "All right, I'll allow the lack of excitement this once, but only because you look like you need a nap. Go tell Bastian we need to meet first thing tomorrow. *First* thing."

She gives him a cheerful little wave, then hurries around the corner and disappears from sight.

***

They've firmly established that no matter how quiet Henry is when he comes back late, Bastian always knows when he gets in. Emotional signatures are apparently a dead giveaway even if their owner attempts to be stealthy.

Still, Henry tries anyway. His efforts turn out to be unnecessary tonight, though: Bastian is still up—and working, if the way he's frowning at his tablet is any indication. Henry would start a pointed conversation about bringing work home except that he was just debating whether he ought to track down his copy of Alexis's report, so it's not like he can talk.

Bastian doesn't look up when Henry enters. Instead, he shifts his weight slightly, like he can't quite find a comfortable position on the couch, and keeps his eyes on the screen. Henry assumes he doesn't want to be bothered and starts toward the kitchen to get a glass of water.

He stops short when Bastian clears his throat and says, "How was your day?"

So that obsession is still a thing, then.

Henry sighs and rubs his eyes. "Well, you know. A woman got herself killed trying to send us information we can't understand, the compound mainframe may not be as secure as we thought, and the liaison committee has likely been working against us this whole time. So I guess that makes it a normal weekday, really."

"She was a potential," Bastian says, gesturing to his tablet. "Emily Tezuka. One of the other compounds had been monitoring her until she moved to the city to become Nunez's aide a few months ago."

"Let me guess: Cyberreader?"

"Yup."

"And they hadn't sent us her data because . . . ?"

"They're incompetent. Or someone didn't want us to have it."

Forgoing the water, Henry sits down at the other end of the couch. "So someone just happened to find a potential working at the Hall, realize she was sending us information, and arrange to have her killed?"

"Convenient how they got hold of her information in the first place, isn't it? Almost like they had access to the Compound Network's system from the start. Or someone was feeding it to them."

Henry frowns. "You think someone on the Council did this?"

"Nunez said the committee's been playing us. The committee was set up by the Council. Why wouldn't they work together to kill someone who got in their way? You're going to tell me Carter's never done anything that gave you pause?"

Henry thinks of how quickly Carter jumped on the idea of placing John Doe under surveillance in the Council HQ medical facility to see if they could collect more asset data. And he's the one who helped them put away Major Valentine last year. He's certainly never seemed to have a problem with going against the grain when he could see the possible benefits. But would he really have a woman killed just because she was sharing information he didn't want shared?

"There was someone with her," Bastian says quietly. "It was poison, but they sent someone to follow her and make sure it did its job. It was important enough that they didn't want any loose ends."

"You read that at the scene?"

"Yes. But . . ." Bastian hesitates, then makes a face. "There was something else. It was like someone put something down ahead of time to keep the emotions from sticking. It was a hard read."

Henry raises his eyebrows. "Is that even possible? Keeping an emotional signature from registering in the first place?" He wants to ask what a "hard read" might entail, too, but he manages to cut off that line of inquiry. If Bastian hurt himself, it's not like he's going to admit it.

"I've never felt anything like it, but clearly it's possible."

"So it was premeditated in more ways than one. Great." Henry sighs. "However it happened, we can't prove that anyone on the Council or the liaison committee had anything to do with it. Not yet, anyway. And even though Kent seems relatively certain our system is safe now, we can't confirm that Emily didn't do any more damage, inadvertently or not. Or that nothing else got in with her files."

He blows out a breath. "There's one bit of not-awful news, at least: I ran into Laurel just now. She said she talked to Smith today, and they found the dead zone. James remembered it."

Bastian, who's been looking at his tablet again, transfers his frown from the screen to Henry. "He's sure?"

"Laurel was sure enough for him. She was ready to send you and James out right this minute, but I convinced her to start with a planning meeting tomorrow."

Bastian sets aside his tablet with more care than is absolutely necessary. "This is the last one," he says quietly.

"The last what?"

"The last thing we'll try. I'll go with James when the time comes, but if it doesn't work . . . You can't afford to waste any more time on this."

Henry frowns. "You think trying to save your life is a waste of time?"

"Yes. Did you forget the part where you have a compound to run? You need to focus on that."

"What makes you think I can't do both?" When Bastian doesn't answer, Henry's frown deepens. "Bastian?"

"You're worried," Bastian says, clearly going for evasive maneuvers. "About this?"

"About everything. You're not?"

Bastian gives him an odd look, then shrugs and says very carefully, "I think . . . it will all work out."

Henry suddenly wonders if he needs to get his hearing checked. "Okay, now I'm even more worried. That doesn't sound like you at all."

"You're not even more worried; you're—laughing at me. Forget it."

"You don't have to pretend that everything's all right, you know." Never mind that he has no idea why Bastian would bother in the first place, as amusing as it is to see him try. "You were in the car with Senator Nunez. You know how much trouble we're in."

Then he adds, mostly to himself, "But we have to keep going. We have to figure out what those file fragments mean. See if Nunez was right about what the committee really wants. We can't ask her to go public with anything until we have proof. It's the only way we can stop anyone else from getting hurt." He sees the look on Bastian's face. "What?"

Bastian shakes his head, smiling slightly. "Nothing. It's just . . . *That* sounds like *you*."

"Here's another thing that sounds like me: Are you going to tell me what you're sitting on so I can't see it, or am I supposed to keep pretending I haven't noticed?"

"It's nothing," Bastian says quickly, shifting his weight.

"Bastian, you asked how my day was. Again."

"I know. Isn't that how you're supposed to—?" Bastian cuts himself off.

"How you're supposed to what?"

The silence stretches out long enough that Henry starts to wonder if he should've kept his mouth shut. This is no time to be poking at the whatever-it-is that's happening with them—not with everything else going. And yet . . .

Bastian gestures vaguely at the space between them. "How you're supposed to do this," he says.

"This? You mean . . . us?"

"Yes." Bastian's gone back to not looking at him.

"I'm not an expert," Henry says carefully, "but I think there's more to being in a relationship than asking how someone's day was."

"Right, I just—"

"And anyway, I don't think you're really 'supposed to' anything. You don't have to follow some weird set of rules or . . ." He catches the expression on Bastian's face. "You're trying to follow some weird set of rules, aren't you?"

Bastian coughs and looks miserable. "Laurel gave me a book."

So *that's* what she meant the other day. Henry just barely manages to keep a straight face. "Did it have anything useful in it?"

"No," Bastian says irritably, taking it out from under him and throwing it over his shoulder. (Henry is definitely going to have to get a hold of that later, before Bastian can figure out a way to destroy it.) "Completely useless. I don't care about Cultivating Positive Discussions or Being Appropriately Supportive or Showing Interest in Your Partner's Daily Life."

"Where did she even get it? Please tell me I don't need to have a discussion with Anna about collection development for the Level 20 library."

"There's an officer who supplies her with ridiculous books whenever he goes into the city. She's doing an experiment to see if she can talk to different kinds of paper, since it used to be trees."

"And?"

"I didn't ask. Do you know how much paper there is in this compound? If Laurel can get it to do her bidding, I don't want to know."

"Point taken. I'll curtail it if I have to before things get too apocalyptic."

The silence stretches out again. The smart thing would be to not push it any more than he already has, but Henry is past being smart about this. He might not be able to fix any of the threats to the compound—at least not tonight— but he can fix this. Maybe. "So Laurel gave you a useless book that told you to ask me how my day was. What else?"

Bastian crosses his arms over his chest and pulls his legs up. "What makes you think there's anything else? Isn't it enough that I made an idiot of myself?"

Careful. "Look, I know the thing with John Doe was . . . bad. And I know you don't want to talk about it, but your health is obviously getting worse. Then there's the pressure of figuring out what's going on with the liaison com-mittee and everything else we learned about today. Given all of that, I just thought . . . I can't always tell with you, especially lately, so I wanted to make sure that this"—he gestures awkwardly between them like Bastian did—"is okay with you."

"Of course it's—" Bastian cuts himself off again, clamps his mouth shut, and looks away. "It's not that it's not okay," he says after a moment. "I'm just trying not to . . . distract you."

Henry half-laughs. "I've seen you in swimming trunks, and I have to work with you every day without getting any ideas. There's really no way you could *not* distract me at this point."

Bastian flushes slightly and rolls his eyes. "That's what I mean. That shouldn't—if you don't focus on the bigger issues, the liaison committee will notice. And now with the murder and everything else . . ."

He's not wrong. Still. "I don't want to talk about everything else."

"See? You're doing it right now. You can't just ignore the more important things."

Henry's heard this one a million times by now, but it still sets his teeth on edge. "Fine, I get it. I need to focus on the compound. It's not like I can't see how precarious our position is right now. But can you stop acting like *you* aren't important, too?"

"I'm not," Bastian says quietly. "Not compared to the work."

That sounds like . . . "Who told you that?"

"I'm capable of coming to logical conclusions by myself."

"Who, Bastian?" If Henry's right, it would explain why and how this started.

For a long while, it seems like Bastian isn't going to answer. Then he says, "At the Council HQ hearing, when I read Valentine—"

Henry's on his feet and pacing without knowing when he decided to stand. "I told you if she—"

"I'm not so pathetic that I just sat there and believed everything she said," Bastian snaps. "But she was right about this."

"No, she wasn't." A sudden thought occurs to him, and he turns back to Bastian. "What she said to you—have you been worrying about it this whole time? Ever since we were at Council HQ?"

Bastian picks at the couch fabric and doesn't look at him, which is answer enough.

"Listen, I don't give a damn about what Major Valentine thinks," Henry says firmly. "I want to know what *you* think. Are you saying we can't be in this relationship and run the compound at the same time?"

(Because Henry remembers sitting in that med bay room, holding Bastian's hand and realizing that none of the work matters if he can't—no, that's stupid, of *course* it matters, Bastian's right, it has to matter more than anything else, except . . . except he can't remember anymore if that's what he actually thinks or if that's what he's *supposed* to think, because he can't possibly be expected to just ignore what he—)

Bastian runs a hand rather savagely through his hair. "I'm saying being in this relationship means they have one more thing they can use against you."

He's not wrong. Henry considers this briefly, then comes to a very succinct conclusion. "So what?"

Bastian frowns at him.

"No, really. So what? If they didn't use this, they'd use something else. We knew this wasn't going to be easy—and if Senator Nunez's intel is right, they were planning to do everything they could to work against us from the start. So why should they get to keep us from having what we want?"

He pauses, then adds, "Assuming this is what you want."

"Of course it is," Bastian says quickly. "I just—I don't know how. You've done this before, but I—"

Henry snorts a bit self-consciously. "Just because I occasionally fraternized during training doesn't mean I have any idea how to actually build a life with someone I love."

Shit, that's a little . . . intense. Well. It's not like Bastian can't already tell how Henry feels. Although from the expression on his face, hearing it seems to have startled him anyway.

"And for the record, you don't have to look stuff up in a book on the sly," Henry hurries on. "You can just talk to me."

Bastian gives him a look that's part glare, part awkwardness. "I don't know when to—we talked about the cameras, but sometimes, I still . . . I don't know when it's okay to touch you."

"The book didn't say?" Henry smothers a smile and pretends to ignore Bastian's look, which is definitely on the glaring side of things now. "You could try asking."

Bastian gets up off the couch and comes over to Henry, leaning in. "Can I touch you?" He sounds tentative, but there's a hint of amusement in his eyes.

Henry clears his throat. "Yes," he says. "But if you're just talking about poking me in the arm or something, that would be a disappointment, frankly."

Of course Bastian immediately grins and pokes him in the arm. But he follows that up by cupping Henry's face and kissing him senseless, so Henry decides it evens out.

"I should—I don't know why I don't—" Bastian is making the very poor life choice of trying to talk and kiss Henry at the same time.

"Don't—what?" Hypothesis confirmed: Talking and kissing are not conducive to multitasking. Better to focus on the one that matters more.

Except he can't because Bastian pulls away slightly, still touching Henry's cheek. "I love you. I'm sorry I don't—I should say it more often."

Henry's pretty sure he shouldn't forget how to breathe every time Bastian says it. But to be fair, he's right that he doesn't say it much. Maybe it's just as well; walking into walls every time Bastian says those three words in that order would probably be considered unbecoming for the leader of a compound.

"Did the book tell you that?" Henry asks.

Bastian makes a face. "Yes. One of the few things it was right about."

"In that case, I think we need to make it the centerpiece of any further decorating we do."

"Absolutely not."

"I'll have someone build us a fancy alcove, and we can set up a shrine—"

"Shut up and kiss me."

The advantage of an open floor plan, Henry thinks vaguely, is that he doesn't have to worry too much about smacking into something as Bastian backs him into the bedroom. Unfortunately, there are other things to worry about. Like the way Bastian starts undoing the buttons on Henry's shirt and then flinches when his hands come into contact with more skin.

"Gloves?" Henry asks, somewhat incoherently. He tries to clear his head enough to check on his negation field. Maybe he can head off some of the emotional overwhelm with the right level of negation . . .

Bastian laughs a little breathlessly. "You want me to go get them?"

"I'd be lying if I said they weren't sexy," Henry admits. "The reason for them, not so much. Are you sure this isn't too—?"

"Yes," Bastian says quickly, closing his eyes. "Just give me a minute."

Henry can tell the exact moment when he gets the negation field balanced with Bastian's power: Bastian takes a deep breath, lets it out, and relaxes his shoulders. When he opens his eyes again, Henry smiles at him. "Okay?"

"Hmm. Better test it," Bastian says. Then his mouth is on Henry's, and they both get back to rectifying the button situation.

Henry can't help but continue to be concerned for a little longer—past experience has shown them both that even their best attempts to make this work aren't always successful, given the way Bastian's power can unexpectedly flare up. But he forgets how to be concerned by the time Bastian has finished undressing him, eased him onto the bed, and started kissing down his chest. Henry is vaguely aware that one of them is far more dressed than he should be, but he loses interest in pointing that out once Bastian gets to where he was going and takes Henry in his mouth.

The (very small) part of Henry's brain that's still coherent wonders if Bastian's book had a few tips—*hell*, speaking of tips—because Bastian's tongue is everywhere, his hand stroking where it can, and Henry's gasping and clenching his fist in the duvet—

"Sh—Bastian—"

He meant to give more warning, but there's really no time for it before he's coming.

He loses track of things for a moment, just trying to catch his breath. Then he becomes aware that Bastian is crawling back up the mattress and settling in beside him. He looks a little self-conscious, but also rather pleased with himself. And still almost entirely dressed, the jerk. "All right?"

It would be funny if he didn't seem genuinely worried about it. "Definitely all right," Henry says, rolling over and kissing his forehead. And then, because he doesn't miss the slight hitch in Bastian's breath when they're almost lying flush, he adds, "Can I touch you?"

Bastian's hand tightens on Henry's arm. "Yes."

This way makes it a bit easier for Henry to keep tabs on his negation field, though that's absolutely not the most important thing on his mind as he undoes Bastian's fly and begins stroking him. Bastian clings to him, rocking slightly into the movement of Henry's hand, hiding his head against Henry's shoulder, breath hot against Henry's skin as he starts to make quiet gasping noises. (Neither of them are going to win any awards for longevity tonight, Henry thinks a bit wryly.) "Still okay?"

"Yes—*please*—"

Henry barely has time to speed up and go harder before Bastian groans and comes.

Lying there afterward, Henry tries to formulate a plan for how they can do this several times a day every day and still pretend to be functioning compound leaders.

Although if he's being completely honest and incredibly sappy, Henry might admit that this is the part he likes best: Bastian curled up against him, calm and sleepy and allowing himself to be vulnerable in a way Henry's never seen him be anywhere else. He'd be happy to spend hours doing what they just did, and a lot more besides, but this . . .

"What are you thinking?" Bastian asks.

"You can't tell?"

Bastian rolls his eyes. "Empath. Feelings, not thoughts. Don't you know how this works by now?"

"Then what am I feeling?"

To Henry's surprise, Bastian hesitates. "Are you sure you don't want to just tell me?"

"Do you have a headache?" Henry asks, suddenly worried. "Maybe we shouldn't have—"

"It's not a headache, and we absolutely *should* have. I just thought reading you might be considered . . . rude."

Henry laughs. "I have it on good authority that you're always rude." Then, seeing that Bastian looks genuinely uncomfortable, Henry sobers up and kisses his nose. "Sorry. Want me to just tell you what I'm thinking instead?"

"That's why I asked."

"I'm thinking it's a travesty that we don't spend more time in bed together like this. I'm thinking that that book might've been useful after all, but we probably shouldn't tell Laurel, or she'll be smug for weeks. I'm thinking that I can't believe you've barely taken off any of your clothes yet."

"And?"

Henry raises his eyebrows. "I thought you weren't going to read me."

"I can't help it when you're projecting this much. You're upset."

"Not . . . exactly." Henry runs a hand through Bastian's hair and tries to figure out how to explain. "Is there anything you actually like about being an empath?"

Bastian blinks at him. "What?"

"I just . . . I know it hurts you to use your power. Even before it got as bad as it is now, that was pretty clear. And I know it makes a lot of things more difficult for you. So I just wondered . . ."

"Is this your way of trying for the millionth time to convince me to let you permanently negate my power?" Bastian has tensed, but he isn't pulling away yet.

"No," Henry says quickly. Then he amends, "Not exactly. I was just thinking—last year, before the Council hearing, I asked if you'd want to give it up, and you said you didn't. Do you still feel that way?"

Bastian is quiet for a while. Then he says, "I don't know."

"If there isn't anything good about it," Henry continues, aware he's pushing his luck but unable to stop, "I don't see why you wouldn't let me—"

"Because we don't know what would happen."

"To you?"

"To *you*."

Henry opens his mouth to argue, then closes it. Because Bastian's right; they really don't know.

"Anyway," Bastian continues, "there *might* be something about my power that I like."

"Yeah? What's that?"

"You."

Henry isn't sure what to make of that, but before he can ask, Bastian rushes on, not looking at him. "Feeling you. It can be . . . a lot. But I *want* to feel what you're feeling. It makes a difference if it's my choice."

Henry swallows, then reaches out to touch Bastian's cheek. "If you can feel what I feel, do you get why I don't want to run this compound without you? Do you understand why it drives me nuts when you act like it's no big deal if you die? Because it matters to the rest of us. It matters to me."

Bastian looks at him with an unreadable expression—and not just because it's getting dark, and they didn't bother to turn the lights above dim. "That's why you're upset."

Henry lets out an exasperated noise. "Yes."

"It's not that I don't think it's a big deal," Bastian says after a moment. "I just—in the asset program, you're only worth saving if you're useful. You remember Johnson. He wasn't going to be useful, so Wright let him die."

The officer Henry tried and failed to save isn't exactly the greatest subject for pillow talk. Stay on target. "So, what, you think you're only worth saving if you're useful?"

"I . . . don't know. Maybe part of me believes it."

"And what does the rest of you believe?"

Bastian meets Henry's gaze. "That I want to be here when you show all of these liaison committee assholes how wrong they are about you and us and this place."

Henry blinks, then laughs and kisses Bastian's forehead. And his nose again, for good measure.

Later, drifting off with Bastian in his arms, Henry decides he really is going to have to thank Laurel for that stupid book.

Chapter 28

"ARE YOU SURE you don't want to promote me?" Bastian asks.

Henry, who's been frowning at the door for at least twenty seconds, finally tears his eyes away and looks at Bastian. His trepidation-concern-anxiety is even easier to read than it normally would be—he must be going to extreme lengths to keep the negation in check. "Why would I want to promote you?"

"Because you love me?" Bastian suggests.

Henry rolls his eyes. "You're not an officer, so I can't promote you to anything that would prevent you from having to wear a tie."

"Guess I'll have to try mass homicide instead."

"That might get you out of this meeting, but not out of the tie."

Bastian makes a face and slumps back in his chair, tugging at his collar. "No one said I had to wear it *well*," he mutters.

It's probably good that they got to the Level 3 meeting room early this time, Bastian thinks. Better not to have people overhear him talking about homicide, even facetiously. Not right before a meeting where the committee is going to make some big decisions about the future of the compound.

They didn't *say* that's what they're doing, of course. Officially, the reason for this meeting is to discuss Major Alexis's findings and recommendations so far. Unofficially, Laurel warned them that Alexis found one of the file fragments Emily Tezuka sent, which is the opposite of good—though Laurel didn't seem to think he'd come to any specific conclusions. In fact, she was quick to change the subject, like she didn't think it was a big deal. Which means she's more spooked than she wants to admit.

Given that Alexis hasn't actually shown them his report, Bastian suspects they might all have good reason to be a little spooked.

They're not going to be able to keep all these secrets much longer, though. Too many to keep track of. What they need is a good distraction, something big to keep everyone's mind off of the things Henry needs to have their minds kept off of.

Bastian's got an idea about that.

The door slams open, and both Henry and Bastian snap their heads up. But it's not the senators, and it's not General Carter, either.

"Oh, good! You waited for me!" Laurel hurries over to the table where Henry and Bastian are seated, grabs a nearby chair, and starts to shove it between them.

Bastian frowns at her and makes no effort to move. This is going to make things more difficult. "What are you doing here?"

Henry, ever the polite one, shuffles his chair off to one side, giving her room to get her chair in. "Laurel, you don't have to be here," he says. "We're just getting some updates from the committee and Major Alexis. I'm sure Bastian can fill you in afterward." His words are the complete opposite of his tension-worry-frustration, which goes straight to Bastian's temples.

Laurel smiles and pats Henry's arm. "I'm here for moral support. And because Michaels sent me a note from Major Alexis telling me to be here. His exact words, in case you're wondering, were that 'everyone in important compound leadership roles should be at this meeting.'"

She holds out her hand without looking at Bastian, and he takes off his tie and hands it to her.

"You see, Henry," Laurel says while putting it around her neck, "I am a very important part of the leadership of this compound. As I'm sure you know, nothing gets done here without my approval."

Bastian snorts. "That's not true."

"As I was saying," Laurel says, ignoring him and sitting down between them, "I've earned my place at this—wait. How come General Carter gets a better chair? Do you think he'd notice if I switched it out?"

"Generals always get the best chairs," Henry says, his voice a bit strained. "Laurel, I really think—"

"Anyway, the *real* reason I'm here is because it sounds like something unpleasant is going to go down, and I want to be available in case physical violence becomes necessary. You'll just start shooting things, and Bastian will get angry at people, and neither of those things are as effective as my punch to the gut. Or my parlor palms, which I'm sure you've noticed lying in wait in every corner of this room. Nothing gets past me and my parlor palms. You're welcome!"

Henry pinches the bridge of his nose. "Look, I may have . . . understated how important this meeting is. Might be. We need to look as professional and capable as possible."

"I'm extremely professional," Laurel assures him, continuing to poke Bastian in the shoulder despite the fact that he's made it very clear he's not going to move and give her more room. Having her here is going to make what he has to do even more complicated, and anyway, isn't someone supposed to be babysitting the asset program?

"If we give anyone on the committee an excuse to think we're incompetent," Henry continues, "it could ruin everything we're trying to do here—whether or not Major Alexis's report is in our favor. And we have reason to think it might not be, given what you've told us. And . . . other things."

Bastian stops kicking Laurel under the table. "Henry. We know what's at stake."

"Yeah," Laurel agrees. "We'll show them what's what. What *is* what, by the way? I mean, if bad things go down, does that mean we get to use thumbscrews on General Carter or the committee in order to make them comply?"

Bastian makes a face at her. "No thumbscrews."

"But there are some people who really deserve thumbscrews, don't you think? Did you ever use thumbscrews when you were an interrogator? I guess you wouldn't have had to, but—"

"Okay, can you two *stop*?" Henry says sharply. "This is serious. Major Alexis has never kept me completely in the dark about one of his reports, which means we could be in trouble. If he's decided—"

He presses his lips together firmly, then says in a low voice, "If you could just give me a minute to deal with the very real possibility that we're about to lose all the work we've done over the past year, possibly putting hundreds of potentials and assets in danger, that would be great, thanks."

Laurel gives Bastian a pointed look, which isn't fair, since even he knows what to do.

She scoots her chair back, and Bastian leans over to touch Henry's arm. "We understand what's at stake," Bastian says again quietly. "What this means. Not just for us, but for everyone here."

"We believe in you!" Laurel says. "What? Just because it's cheesy doesn't mean it's not true. And don't look at me like that, Bastian. You believe in Henry more than anyone else in this entire compound."

"*Anyway,*" Bastian says, trying to pretend he can't feel his cheeks heat, "I—we won't let you down."

"This isn't about me. It's about—"

"Everyone. We need to protect them. I know." Bastian hesitates, then adds, "And I told you, sometimes you need to let someone else do the protecting."

He knows as soon as the words are out of his mouth that he shouldn't have said them. Henry gives him an odd look, but the doors to the meeting room open at the same time. Bastian has never been quite so pleased to see a med tech, not to mention the senators filing in behind him.

Bastian gets to his feet and walks around behind Laurel's chair. When he passes behind Henry's, he feels something tug at his sleeve, pulling him to a stop. "What did we say about you making plans without telling anybody?" Henry says quietly.

"I can honestly tell you that I have no plan whatsoever except to go over there and let that guy stick a needle in my arm." It's not even a lie.

Laurel frowns. "Oh. Do I need to go do that, too? Or can I just promise not to talk to any plants during the meeting? They're usually very polite, so I think they'll understand."

Bastian doesn't wait to hear Henry's response. He unbuttons his cuff and rolls up his sleeve as he walks over to the med tech, ignoring the man's brief greeting and holding out his arm so they can get this over with.

Just as the needle goes in, he sees Nunez enter the room. His power is already going fuzzy, so he only gets a swiftly fading determined-cautious-tense as she walks by. Not that he needs it; her brief look his way says enough about her state of mind. Her eyes shift away almost as soon as they've landed on him, but he catches the firm set of her mouth and the lines around her eyes. Still not sleeping much, then. But also not murdered yet, which is a plus. Probably.

General Carter comes in just as Bastian gets back to the table, and everyone stands up. Major Alexis is next to him, cane tapping gently on the floor as he guides himself to a chair. Once Alexis is settled, Carter sits as well, which means the rest of the group can sit, too. Laurel, having hurried over to get her shot of serum, quickly returns to her seat as well, frowning and rubbing her arm.

"Good morning," Carter says, though his tone doesn't indicate that there's anything remotely good about it. "We'll be discussing the details of Major Alexis's summary report today, but first, he's going to give us an overview. Major?"

"Thank you, General."

Alexis stands to address the gallery. "As most of you know, I've been staying at this compound in the role of observer, as requested by this committee. I believe General Carter suggested me because of the many years I've spent running my own compound, which, if you'll indulge my need to brag for a moment, has an excellent reputation as a training facility for officers."

Some polite smiles and nods from the gallery.

"My experience as an educator put me in Major Mortimer's path as far back as his initial recruitment," Alexis explains, "which means we've known each other for nearly twenty years. So I'm sure you understand that I am in no way biased when I say he is loyal, brave, and hardworking. I think we've all seen that based on how much this compound has achieved in such a short amount of time."

Bastian doesn't need his power to know that there's a giant "but" coming. He clenches his jaw and forces himself to sit still. He even manages not to look over at Henry to see if he's impressed with the restraint. The mess of vague emotions he's getting through the serum says probably not.

"Unfortunately," Alexis continues, "those traits aren't quite enough to effectively manage a compound, particularly one in transition. While I certainly believe that great progress has been made, the fact of the matter is that this compound has made some mistakes—in particular, with the handling of the asset program—that show its leadership isn't up to the task just yet."

Bastian supposes it's better for his brain that he's not fully able to feel the tension from Laurel and Henry through the haze of the serum in his bloodstream. But even blurred emotions that produce a slight twinge of pain rather than a full-on headache are bad enough. "Now we know what the report was about," Bastian mutters to Henry, who shakes his head sharply in the universal sign for "Shut up and let me listen to our death sentence in peace."

"To be clear, I'm not saying anyone has failed here," Alexis says over the quiet murmurs coming from the gallery. "I'm merely saying that I believe this compound requires more guidance and training in order to ensure its success."

"Do you have an official recommendation, Major?" Carter asks.

"I've provided more insights in my report," Alexis says, "but I'll give you the short version here, for the sake of discussion. I believe this compound would benefit from more oversight, at least temporarily, to prevent any current issues from developing into something that might endanger the officers and assets here. I recommend a small on-site task force be formed to coordinate with Major Mortimer and his staff. All information used by this compound should be made available to this task force, and all major decisions should be run through it in order to vet actions taken and ensure the best possible outcomes."

Alexis raises a hand to cut through the increasingly animated whispers in the gallery. "I want to reiterate that I do believe Major Mortimer and his team are capable of leading this compound successfully. I'm only suggesting that they receive closer supervision for a short period of time to ensure that they can operate efficiently within the structure of the Compound Network."

Carter nods. "Understood. Thank you, Major." His eyes scan the rest of the committee. "Does anyone have anything else to add?"

"General," says Senator Donnigan, getting to his feet, "if I might—"

"Excuse me."

Nunez rises stiffly, ignoring Donnigan and everyone else in the gallery. Donnigan keeps his mouth going for a moment, but she's having none of it, speaking over him like she's stepping over a piece of garbage on a sidewalk. "General, would you say the purpose of this committee is to 'discuss the work being done at the compound in an open, aboveboard manner that facilitates cooperation between the Compound Network and the broader city government'?"

Carter raises an eyebrow. "Yes, Senator. Your recitation of our bylaws is impressive. I assume the explanation of your point will be, too."

"I wanted to confirm that what's written in those bylaws is still accurate."

"And you're checking on this now because . . . ?"

"I was hoping you could explain how redacting significant portions of Major Alexis's report and refusing to provide details on his accusations fits with the rules established for this group. This is leaving aside the fact that we were given insufficient time to review the report before this meeting."

Insufficient time is still better than no time at all, Bastian thinks.

"Not accusations, surely, Senator," Alexis says mildly. "As I just said, I only—"

"Your report didn't include any specific instances of the mistakes you just alluded to. Unless those examples were part of the large amount of redacted information."

"Certain precautions must be taken to—"

"Yes, I'm sure you're very well-versed in the use of the passive voice to avoid responsibility, Major. But if the Compound Network can't be trusted to uphold its end of the bargain—which, as you'll recall, is to openly discuss issues that affect both the city and the compound—I don't see how we can trust your recommendations."

"Did I just hear Nunez *defending* us?" Bastian says under his breath. "Is that her idea of lying low?"

Laurel elbows him in the side. "Shh!"

Major Alexis frowns. It's the first truly serious frown Bastian has ever seen on his face. "Senator, while I appreciate your concerns, this situation is far more complicated than you're acknowledging. My report provides as many details as possible without endangering top secret programs. I'm afraid this is one of those instances where you'll have to defer to the experts."

"We are *all* experts in our fields, Major," Nunez says, her voice especially sharp. "And our job here is to pool our knowledge and prevent revisiting past communication issues that put all of our communities at risk."

It's so small, Bastian almost misses it: a slight deepening of the frown on Alexis's face and a shift in the way he's holding his shoulders. Even if Bastian were at full strength, it would be hard to read through Alexis's purposefully unassuming facade, but he can get enough through the fuzziness to know that Alexis is . . . angry? Annoyed? Anxious?

No, wait. He's *scared.*

Alexis's shield swallows it up almost immediately, not giving Bastian any time to figure out where the fear comes from.

"Very well, Senator," Alexis says, pleasant smile back in place. "I'd be happy to answer any questions you have. General?"

Carter is also frowning, but it's just his usual frown, the one that says he'd rather stomp on people than have to listen to them. He waves a hand. "Within reason."

"Let's start with the asset program," Nunez says. "What are your concerns, exactly?"

Alexis doesn't answer right away, obviously considering his words carefully. Then he says, "In my reports, I've alluded to a . . . guest who has been here at the compound for over a month now. While I haven't observed anything that would imply this guest is a threat, and I've been told he's working closely with the medical team, his long-term status hasn't been clearly communicated to me, and I'm given to understand that he regularly visits areas of the compound that are off-limits to people without security clearance."

Nunez narrows her eyes at Alexis. "Are you saying there's an undocumented asset wandering around the compound unchecked?"

"I'm saying I believe this compound has some potential security issues, specifically with regard to assets."

"And are these security issues likely to affect the city as well? Or the rest of the Compound Network?"

So much for Nunez being in their corner. Bastian suspects she's going to conveniently avoid mentioning how her own aide breached compound security on her orders.

"Don't be silly!" Laurel says. "It's true that we have a guest, but he doesn't just wander around and get into things. Not that we keep an eye on him all the time. I mean, people deserve their privacy. But—"

"I'm not certain you're completely aware of your visitor's actions, Assistant Director," Alexis says. "And that's part of the problem."

Laurel frowns. "What do you—?"

"We were told the new program would include visitors, but not that you might not be able to handle the security risks involved," Nunez interrupts. "Why wasn't the committee kept apprised of this situation?" She makes sure to provide Alexis, Carter, and Laurel with equal opportunity glaring.

"Because it doesn't have anything to do with the city!" Laurel says. "We're just trying to help someone."

"You see my concern, Senator," Alexis says calmly. "While I'm sure the assistant director has the program's best interests at heart, I can't help but think there's a way to prevent this kind of situation. With proper oversight and further training, I'm sure—"

"This isn't just about oversight," Nunez says. "This is about how neither you nor this compound's leadership have been forthcoming with information this committee needs to determine whether this organization is a threat to the surrounding community."

Now Henry is leaning forward, too. "The compound takes security very seriously, Senator, as you'll remember from the screenings you've gone through every time you've entered the building. There's no reason to think that a member of the asset program—or anyone else in this compound—is a security threat."

"No reason that you've seen fit to share with us, you mean."

Alexis holds up his hands, placating. "Clearly, the asset program at this compound needs some work. But with the plan I've outlined, I see no reason why it can't be—"

This is it, Bastian thinks. Time to do something stupid.

"I resign," he says loudly.

It takes a moment for everyone to shut up and realize he said something. "Just trying to speed this along," he adds.

"Bastian," Henry says out of the corner of his mouth, "what the hell—?"

"If you have issues with the asset program, that's on me," Bastian says, standing so that he can make sure everyone gets it. "Not my staff, not the other assets, and certainly not Major Mortimer. Everyone else has been doing their part to meet this committee's impossible standards, not to mention putting together a program that actually gives a damn about the people it's supposed to be serving. If you don't like the way things are going, that says more about you than it does about anyone who's been doing the work."

He turns to Alexis. "I can't stop you from assigning Henry a babysitter and second-guessing his every move. But I can ask you to separate whatever problems you have with the way I've run the asset program from the work he's done. You claim you know him and what he's capable of. So prove it."

Alexis's head tilts Bastian's way. Nothing in his body language betrays any sort of emotion, and Bastian doesn't get much of anything through the fog of the serum and Alexis's impeccable shield.

"I think this is a wise decision," Alexis says at last.

"I don't," Nunez snaps.

Bastian swallows his surprise. "You were just saying you think the asset program is a mess. I'm taking responsibility for that. What more do you want?"

"I want to avoid a change in leadership right now, when things are in flux," Nunez says pointedly. "More openness in communication would help as well, but—"

Henry cuts them off. "Then let me communicate openly. I need to confer with my staff before we can continue this conversation. With the general's permission, I'd like to take a short recess."

Carter heaves a sigh and sits back in his chair. "Make it quick, Mortimer. We'll reconvene in an hour and come to a decision on all of this."

Bastian doesn't even have time to figure out his next move before Henry grabs his arm and says into his ear, "My office. Now." He leans over and spares a glare for Laurel. "You, too. Move it."

Bastian and Laurel exchange a glance. Then they silently follow Henry out of the room.

Chapter 29

WHEN THEY GET to Henry's office, Michaels glances up from her tablet, takes one look at Henry's face, and goes very still.

"No interruptions," Henry bites out, yanking open the door to the meeting room and gesturing for Bastian and Laurel to go through.

"Yes, sir," Michaels says.

He doesn't quite slam the door, but it's debatable. He reaches into his jacket pocket and flips the switch on his jammer. With the boosters in his office, they ought to be fairly safe.

Turning to the others, he finds Bastian is leaning against the table, frowning deeply, rubbing his right temple like he already has a headache. Laurel is standing awkwardly next to him, clenching a fist and not quite looking anyone in the eye.

"What the absolute *hell* was that?" Henry demands.

When no one says anything for several moments, Laurel clears her throat. "Um. You may need to be more specific."

"Did I really just hear you tell the entire committee that you've been letting James wander around unchaperoned the entire time he's been here?" Henry says. "Did you even bother to get him an ID? Did you follow any protocol at all?"

"Of course I did!" Laurel says. "James sees Dr. Rowe every other day, and he has an ID and everything. If he's not with me, he's training with the other assets or in the Level 20 library doing research. I have no idea what Major Alexis was talking about. And in case you forgot, the med techs said he's *fine*. His power is stable, and he hasn't been breaking any rules or putting anyone in danger."

"You're lying," Bastian says.

Laurel glares at him, then glances at Henry and away quickly. "I mean—he left his room at night once, but it was *once*, and just to have some tea, and—"

"You're lying about him putting people in danger," Bastian says. "What about Angelica?"

"She offered to help!"

"You used her. She's just a kid, and you—"

"*She offered to help*, and when it looked like it wasn't going well, I told them to *stop*."

"Oh, so you're letting James do whatever he wants around the compound *and* letting him make use of any asset in the program?"

"Don't make it sound like—"

"*Enough.*" Henry realizes he's been pacing the last few seconds without knowing he was doing it. He forces himself to stop and turn back to them. Not like he's going to be able to out-pace the way his gut is twisting up. "I shouldn't have trusted you two to handle this," he says. "You're not trained to deal with assets who—"

"Assets who what?" Laurel asks, her face flushing with anger. "Want to live their lives like normal people? Need the compound to help them and not treat them like prisoners?"

"What do you think we've been trying to do, Laurel? What do you think is in danger now if they decide we've mishandled the program? They were looking for any little crack, any way in, and you gave it to them."

"No, she didn't," Bastian says. "They would've found something no matter what we did. And weren't you paying attention back there? I resigned. Pin all of this on me, and you can start over with the program."

"What happens to you, then?" Henry demands. "You can kiss your little vacation to find James's healer goodbye. There's no way they'll let me just send you anywhere you like without supervision. Especially with this task force Major Alexis suggested. You have no idea how closely they'll be watching us now."

"Neither do you. But that's not important." Bastian is in full-on glare mode now, but there's a fragile edge to it that makes Henry's anger stutter to a stop.

"This is what you meant," Henry realizes. "When you said I need to let other people save me."

"They'll be busy obsessing over the future of the asset program," Bastian continues, ignoring him. "That buys you the time you need to figure out what Emily Tezuka's files mean and if Nunez is right about the Council. That's all that matters."

Laurel narrows her eyes. "Bastian, are you trying to be selfless again? You know you're really bad at that, right?"

"I never said I was—"

Henry takes a breath. "Okay, here's what we're going to do.

"Laurel, you're going to pull together a record of all the work you've done with James. *All* of it, from the moment he showed up on compound grounds. Leave nothing out. That includes what memories he's regained so far and Bastian's read on him."

Laurel frowns. "Bastian's read was wrong, though. James definitely has emotions. He emotes all over the place."

"Find a more professional way to say that, and put it in the report. I want it by the end of today."

He turns to Bastian. "I don't accept your resignation, but I'm putting you on a leave of absence."

"The committee won't—"

"I don't give a damn what the committee will or won't. I'm the commanding officer of this compound, and until they remove me, I have the right to assign roles as I see fit."

"What do you mean, 'until'?"

Henry rubs his eyes. "Alexis's task force will have access to all of the information we have. All of the personnel files. Everything. On all of us."

Bastian catches on immediately. "We've never found anything on you here. Dr. Wright destroyed his notes."

"Yeah. Except he didn't, did he? Emily Tezuka showed us that. In files that won't be secure anymore."

"Do you still think they'd remove you if they knew you're a negator?" Laurel asks tentatively. "I mean, think about all the work you've done! And there's nothing anywhere saying an asset can't run a compound, right?"

"An asset who can theoretically negate everyone around them? Maybe permanently? And that's not even counting the part where there's never been a registered negator in the history of the Network, which means there's no data to back me up if I say I won't use my power to hurt anyone."

Henry sighs. "We've had this conversation before, Laurel. We knew it was only a matter of time. And with everything blowing up, now seems like as good a time as any. But while we've still got access to information and the ability to help people, we're going to do what we can."

"Maybe we should mutiny," Laurel suggests. "Again."

Bastian frowns. "I still don't think that's the right word."

"Maybe not. But it's a good word, right?"

"There's one more thing we're going to do," Henry interrupts.

"What's that?" Bastian asks.

"We're going to sneak you and James out of the compound so you can go find James's healer."

Laurel blinks at him. "Um. Weren't you just angry about James wandering around the compound without supervision? And now you want to sneak people out of the compound?"

"Yes. To both of those things."

"Now isn't a good time," Bastian protests. "Like you said, they'll be watching even more closely, and you have other things to—"

"We can't wait around for permission on this one." Henry meets Bastian's gaze and tries not to sound too desperate. "We don't know how restricted our actions will be, and we don't know how much time we have. So tell me you'll do this. Please."

Bastian swallows, then nods and looks away.

Henry blows out a breath, letting the last of his anger dissipate in favor of focusing on the mission. "All right. Here's how we're going to do it."

Chapter 30

"I'M CALLING THIS Operation White Nettle," Laurel explains under her breath as she and James walk down the Level 8 hallway. "Because no one will suspect we're trying to sneak out if we avoid security and pretend everything is normal. It's like how white nettles look a lot like stinging nettles, only they aren't, but people don't notice that because—"

"Why did we wait so long?" James demands. His voice sounds too loud in the quiet hall, and Laurel cringes before she can stop herself. "It's been a week since your friends totally lost control of this place. They've probably already put up more cameras everywhere and started sticking assets in cages."

That deserves a glare, so Laurel gives it to him. "First of all, *rude*. Second of all, Kent said there are exactly the same number of cameras as there were a week ago. And speaking of cameras and what gets caught on them, stop looking like you're escaping."

"But I *am*—"

"No, you're not. You're taking a slightly-off-the-books stroll with the assistant director of the asset program to the loading dock in the middle of the night. Completely legitimate. Now hush."

"Why would I hush if there's nothing wrong with us being here?"

"Because we don't want to bother the black coats while they're very busy keeping other parts of the compound safe. It would be silly of them to waste their time on us."

James grunts and falls silent.

He has every right to be worried, Laurel supposes. Nothing significant has changed in the compound since Major Alexis and Senator Donnigan formed their task force, but the overall ambiance has started to shift. More black coats in the halls. More officers getting short with each other and with the assets. More awkward silences during Laurel's garden training sessions, especially after she told Mariah, Ezekiel, Reva, and Gabe that they were going to be doing a presentation for Senator Donnigan and Dr. Rowe's med techs.

Laurel and James make it to the elevator without incident, although Laurel keeps her hand closed around the jammer in her pocket. She turned it on as soon as they left her room, more as a precaution than a necessity. Kent gave it to her last time she visited hacker HQ, which is also when she learned that Bastian and Henry have each had one of their own for months. She's been trying not to be upset about how completely unfair that is.

Standing in the elevator, she looks over at James, who's rocking slightly on his heels, like he can't stay still. Of course he doesn't bother to hit the floor button, so Laurel does it as the elevator doors close.

"Have you been having weird dreams lately?" James asks suddenly.

Laurel definitely does *not* think about the dead officer and her green face. "What?"

"Nothing. Never mind."

The awkward silence stretches out as the floor numbers on the digital screen go down, and they get closer to the surface.

"It's just—I keep dreaming about our compound," James says. "The stuff I remember. Only it doesn't quite seem like what I thought I remembered. At first it's like everyone is there, and they're all happy, and then they're"—he swallows—"they're dying. In the fire. And I get outside somehow, and you're there, and you're angry with me. And then there's this voice in my head saying it'll all be okay. I thought it was Wright at first because he used to say that when he ... But it's not. Except it still sounds familiar, like it's someone I should know."

He shakes his head a little too hard and acts like watching the numbers go down is suddenly the most interesting thing in the world. "Never mind," he says again. "I don't know why I asked you that. Forget it."

"Yes," Laurel says quietly, before she can think better of it.

"Good."

"No. I mean—you asked if I've had weird dreams lately. The answer is yes. Not exactly like that, but ... yes."

He looks at her with an unreadable expression and starts to open his mouth just as the elevator comes to a stop at Level 1. She quickly steps off and hurries down the hall in a move that is in no way meant to forestall having to talk about things she doesn't want to talk about.

The problem, of course, is that he's taller than her, and it takes no time at all for him to catch up. "Laurel—"

"Shh!" she says. "Operation White Nettle isn't over yet."

They make their way through nearly empty halls, detouring here and there to avoid patrolling black coats and the occasional officer pulling a late nighter. Laurel makes a note to discuss the importance of a full sleep schedule and time off—no one should be wandering around their workspace at this time of night. And not just on nights when she's trying to do something not-entirely-legitimate and doesn't want to get caught.

Pushing through the main door and out onto the grounds is a relief. Not that there aren't still security cameras, but they're more spread out and easier to avoid without having to rely on the jammer. Plus, out here there's the quiet susurrus of the grass getting comfy for the night, not to mention the honey and floral scents coming from the nearby moon garden. The night-blooming jasmine in particular is showing off; Laurel may need to have a word with it before someone's asthma gets activated. A sneezing officer with watering eyes and a large gun won't do anyone any good.

Laurel is struck by the sudden urge to take off her shoes and socks so she can be touching the ground, but she curtails it. The mission objective is to get James to the loading dock, and there's no deviating from the mission. Even on a nice night like this.

"Listen," James says, matching her steps, "I don't know when your idiot friend is going to show up, so I need to get this out now."

"Takes an idiot to know an idiot," Laurel says.

"What?"

"Never mind. You were saying? Quietly, so it won't draw any attention?"

James grabs her arm, pulling them to a stop. "Yeah, I know, we need to keep going. Just gimme a minute." He takes a breath and gives her a very serious look. "I'm not going to be here to watch your back—not for a while, anyway. So you're going to have to watch it for me."

"I watched it for over a year when you were dead," Laurel says before she's had a chance to think about how rude it sounds. "Metaphorically, of course. You can't actually watch your own back. Well, *I* can't. Anyway, why would I even need to?"

James waves a hand at the compound. "Because this place is *wrong*. It's only a matter of time before they figure out that they liked assets better when we were drugged up for experiments and locked in our rooms at night."

"Henry wouldn't—"

"Henry isn't an asset. He wouldn't understand. And he's barely in charge anymore, anyway. Not from what I've heard."

Laurel decides now isn't the best time to tell James that Henry actually *is* an asset. Sort of. If you count the ones that no one believes exist. "Why are you still like this?" Laurel demands, yanking her arm away. "Did you miss the part where we've all been trying to help you ever since you got here? Why do you think we're going to so much trouble to help you find your healer right now? Because the compound wants to keep you locked up?"

"They're letting me go because the major cares more about saving his dying boyfriend than playing by the rules. And you're letting them let me because you're too nice to care about covering your own ass."

"It's not about being nice," Laurel says, not sure why she feels stung. "We can save Bastian and help you at the same time. That's what friends do for each other. Did you forget about that?"

James sighs. "How can you be so—?" He stops, then shakes his head. "Look, I know I'm not saying this the right way, but I just … You're my friend, and I don't want you to get hurt, all right? So I really don't think you should trust anyone. Other than me, of course. I'm very trustworthy."

"Yes, because trustworthy people tell you not to trust anyone but them." Laurel narrows her eyes. "Are you saying this because you're scared about going into the forest? The trees are really nice, I promise."

James looks at her for a moment, then laughs in a way that's hardly a laugh at all. "I'm just nervous about taking a vacation with someone who hates my guts to find someone we're not completely sure exists."

"Oh, don't worry about traveling with Bastian," Laurel says brightly. "I'm sending someone else with you to balance things out."

James frowns. "Who?"

"Come on. Let's get to the loading dock before anyone notices us standing here in the middle of the night having a completely normal conversation."

"Laurel—"

"Shh! Operation White Nettle is almost complete!"

James clamps his mouth shut and makes the appropriate choice to follow her silently across the moonlit grounds to the loading dock.

Chapter 31

BASTIAN STOPS JUST outside the suite, hand on the door. He needs to duck in and grab his things before he meets Laurel and James at the loading dock, and there's no time to mess around, especially if he wants to leave without drawing attention to himself.

But he can feel Henry inside, emotions muted in what seems like a fitful sleep.

Bastian quickly tries to gauge the best way to get in, grab his travel bag, and be out without disturbing him. Or having to talk to him.

One way—and he's ashamed he's even thinking of it—would be to use his power to convince Henry he doesn't feel like getting up. Even if Henry woke up enough to properly negate, it's not like Bastian isn't strong enough to push through it. Might end in a bloody nose, depending on how much Bastian's power decides to irritate him this evening, but with enough emotional manipulation, he could—

What the hell is he even thinking?

Bastian shakes his head (bad idea; there's a headache simmering under the surface) and enters the suite as quietly as he can.

Henry is sitting at the kitchen table, head resting on his hand as if he's reading something on the tablet in front of him. It's clear as Bastian passes him on the way to the bedroom that he's fallen asleep, the screen casting a blueish tint on his face and setting off the dark circles under his eyes. Not that Bastian lingers for a moment to look at him or anything.

He's barely made it to the bathroom when he hears movement: a quick curse and the sound of something dropping to the floor. "Bastian?" Henry calls, sounding groggy.

Bastian doesn't answer. It somehow seems far more important to recheck everything he stashed in his travel bag days ago and has been unpacking and repacking ever since. He thinks of all the bags of supplies he stashed around Laurel's clearing after he ran away from the compound two years ago. How he thought that if he stole enough stuff and put it in enough places, he'd never have to worry about being caught unprepared. Like he was playing some stupid game of hide-and-seek with the compound officers who wandered into the area. As if he weren't constantly thinking about how easy it would be for Valentine to decide she'd had enough, and it was time to bring him back.

Which she did. Though not at all how he'd thought she would.

Is that what this is, too? Running away? Pretending it's no big deal to just leave Henry and Laurel to deal with everything while he takes a stupid pilgrimage to find some strange asset who can solve all his problems? If he stays, he'll just be in the way; but if he goes, and things get worse . . .

(The way Dr. Rowe looked at him earlier today at his check-in, the lines around her mouth deepening; the way she's entirely stopped saying things like "we need to do some more tests" or "nothing is definitive yet"; the way her concern-concentration-sadness drives nails of pain into his skull—)

"Bastian?" Henry says from the other side of the door. "Are you . . . ?"

Bastian zips up his bag with more energy than is really necessary, then opens the bathroom door and nearly smacks Henry in the face with it. "Sorry. I—"

Henry holds out an unopened bottle of painkillers. "I stopped by the med bay earlier," he says. "I wasn't sure how much you had left or how much you'd need while you're . . . away."

Bastian swallows. Then he takes the bottle and stuffs it into his pocket. "I should go meet James," he says. "Stop working and go to bed."

"I was waiting up for you," Henry says, rubbing his eyes. "Should've known reading an email from Donnigan would put me to sleep."

"Don't forget to give yourself overtime pay. Double it every time you find a typo."

It's a dumb joke, but Henry half-laughs—the one where his eyes do the crinkly thing, and he gives off a soft wave of wry-amused-tired—and suddenly, Bastian has trouble breathing.

(This is stupid, nothing is more pathetic than being floored by someone not-even-really laughing or getting distracted by the way their hair sticks up at odd angles when they've been sleeping in a weird position or wanting to touch someone and knowing you shouldn't because it'll only make things worse, and it was so much easier when this didn't matter, when it was just interrogating people and hating Valentine and not thinking about what his power was doing to people—)

"Bastian."

(Don't look at him don't—) "I have to go," he says, maneuvering around Henry.

"Wait—"

"Do me a favor? At the next meeting, tell Donnigan—no, you know what, just kick him in the—"

"Bastian—"

He's gone maybe three steps toward the doorway before he drops his bag with an annoyed grunt, goes back, grabs Henry by the back of the neck, and kisses him.

All sense of exhaustion and hesitation coming from Henry immediately vanishes. He kisses Bastian back desperately, pulling him closer and squeezing all the breath out of him—as if he'd have any breath left, with Henry's tongue—but it's too much, the fear-anger-helplessness-*want*, and—

"I can't," Bastian chokes out, mortified but unable to stop. "I don't want to go. What if it doesn't work? I want to be here with you when I—"

"Don't." Henry's arms are still around him, still tight but not too tight.

(Like when they found the room on Level 49, and Henry held him even though he was being pathetic, he's *still* being pathetic, he can practically hear Valentine laughing at him for being so weak, for letting his emotions get the better of him, and how can she still be in his head when she's *gone*—?)

Bastian shudders, then makes himself be still. "Never mind," he says, struggling to keep his voice even. "It's fine."

"No, it's not."

"You said you wanted me to go," Bastian reminds him, pulling back just far enough to see that Henry's mouth is set in a grim line.

"I lied." Henry takes a shaky breath. "Okay, not a lie, exactly. I think it's clear that this is our only option, so of course I want you to take it. I just . . . I don't like sending you out there alone."

Bastian raises his eyebrows. "I didn't realize you think James is as useless as I do."

"No, you idiot. I mean I want to go with you and help you figure it out, not be stuck here dealing with Donnigan's aggressive misuse of commas."

"They *are* pretty bad. I can see why you'd want to escape." He makes the mistake of meeting Henry's gaze right then, and whatever other joke he was going to make immediately dies unspoken. He almost wishes Henry were fully negating at this point because everything coming from him *hurts*, even through the usual low-level fog. At first, Bastian thinks it's his own power still trying to self-destruct until he realizes all the hurt is coming from Henry.

"Listen," Henry says, his voice a bit unsteady, "I need you to—" He swallows and tries again. "I need you to be careful, all right?"

"We made a deal," Bastian reminds him. "Careful is my middle name. Anyway, that's not what you're really asking."

"I thought you said you couldn't read minds?"

"Only yours. Sometimes. When you're being obvious."

"And what am I being obvious about this time?"

Bastian pats down an errant patch of Henry's hair, deciding not to mention the few strands of gray, barely visible in the dim light. "I promise I'll do everything I can to come back here to this horrible place. To you."

Henry does his half-laugh thing and leans his forehead against Bastian's (relief-worry-exhaustion). "I'll take it. I think."

He hesitates, then adds, "I'm morally obligated to ask you one more time, so bear with me. Are you absolutely sure you don't want to try the negation? You really want to do it this way instead?"

Bastian closes his eyes. He could agree right now and change everything. He wouldn't have to worry about dying somewhere in the forest in the company of a firestarter who nearly killed Bastian's best friend and *did* kill nineteen other assets and an unspecified number of compound staff members. Even if Henry's power doesn't work, Bastian could count on being with him when time runs out. Which is really the best he's hoped for since Dr. Rowe first made her pronouncement.

He can't imagine a life where he isn't an empath, though. It's part of who he is. A disgusting, irritating, frustrating part, but still a part. He meant what he told Henry at the beach a year ago: that he wants to see what he can do with his power when it's his choice. Not Valentine's or anyone else's.

Maybe that was a mistake. But if he's going to figure out a way through this, it needs to be on his terms.

"Bastian?" Henry's anxious-curious-concerned is starting to put unpleasant pressure on Bastian's temples.

"Yes," Bastian says. "This is the way I want to do this."

Henry takes a deep breath and lets it out. "Okay."

"I really do have to go," Bastian says after a few moments.

"I know," Henry says.

Bastian forces himself to move away and pick up his bag again. He hesitates, feeling like an idiot, but says it anyway. "The deal goes both ways. You have to be careful, too. Don't let the committee or Carter or anyone else convince you that you have to . . . do what you do."

Henry raises his eyebrows. "What do I do?"

"You know what I mean. All the stupid heroic stuff." He rushes on before Henry can do much more than open his mouth. "I know, you need to protect this place, hero complex, blah blah blah. I'm not asking you to change. I just need you to be more careful about it now. They'll be looking even harder for reasons to trip you up. Have Kent destroy evidence if necessary—"

"I'm not going to do that."

"—or maybe try not being so conciliatory where the liaison committee is concerned—"

"Also not going to do that."

"—or at least stop reading Donnigan's emails instead of going to bed."

"That one's doable." Henry walks over to Bastian, takes his hand, and kisses his palm. "I promise I'll be careful."

Of course this couldn't be one of those times when Bastian forgot to wear his gloves. "Okay. Right. Then I'll just—"

But Henry is kissing him again. It's good, but it's also not. The fear-frustration-anger-worry-desperation-love practically splits Bastian's head open.

(Like he has no shield at all, like he's back to being a child in an alley, overwhelmed by everything, only this is different because it's not just random people's emotions bombarding him, it's all coming from someone right in front of him, someone he—)

"I love you," Bastian says. Because that's far more important than trying to catch his breath.

"I love you, too," Henry says. "Go."

So Bastian does.

***

Laurel and James are waiting at the loading dock, standing next to a particularly dingy vehicle. The back is open, and James is rummaging around in a duffel bag. Laurel, on the other hand, immediately notices Bastian approaching and puts her hands on her hips. Her anxious-irritated-worried is easy to read. James, of course, still reads as a whole lot of nothing.

"You're late," Laurel says. She's obviously trying to be quiet because she's managing the exact opposite.

"Busy saying goodbye to the major, I bet," James says in a way that makes Bastian want to punch him in the face. Well. Makes him want to do that more than usual, anyway. Never mind what happened last time he punched someone in the face.

Bastian maneuvers around them and shoves his bag into the vehicle's storage area. "Are we just going to stand around wasting time here, or what?"

"We're not wasting time; we're taking a moment to set some very important ground rules." Laurel frowns. "James, stop messing with that bag."

"I'm just making sure you packed all the essentials."

Bastian raises his eyebrows. "You packed his bag for him? What is he, a five-year-old?"

"You're just jealous she didn't do yours, too."

"I didn't do yours, either," Laurel tells him. "That's just stuff that was left over in this vehicle from the last mission it went on. If you wanted something else, you should've packed it yourself. Anyway, stop stalling."

James looks some approximation of affronted. "Seriously? If you didn't pack this, how can we be sure it has what I need for my hair?"

"Shut up and listen." Laurel holds out a finger. "Rule number one: No killing each other. I'll add that this is a very basic rule, and I can't believe I'm having to address it for two adults."

"Do you usually have to address it for two children?" James asks. "Because if so, I'm having even more doubts about this asset program of yours."

Laurel ignores him and holds up a second finger. "Rule number two: If you meet a plant along the way who tells you to do something, you do it."

"We don't speak plant," Bastian reminds her.

"Yes, I've told them you're idiots, and they'll have to be really obvious about whatever they're trying to communicate. I hope you realize what a burden that is, by the way. Plants don't like to be obvious. They're usually really slow and thoughtful and quiet. I had to call in all my favors."

"Laurel—"

"What part of 'shut up' don't you understand, James? I'm mission debriefing here."

"Debriefing is afterward," Bastian mutters. "You're briefing. Unnecessarily."

"It's *extremely* necessary, thank you very much." Laurel holds up a third finger, then switches to her whole hand, which she raises in a wave at something behind Bastian.

He turns to find Chloe hurrying toward them, wearing a backpack and exuding a sharp burst of embarrassed-nervous-tense.

"Sorry," she says when she gets closer. "I had to wait until the black coats near the teen dorm switched shifts."

Laurel holds up three fingers. "Rule number three: You're taking Chloe with you."

"Forget it," James says at the same time Bastian says, "Laurel, you can't just ask—"

"I didn't ask! It's an official mission. Well, a highly classified, off-the-books mission, anyway." She narrows her eyes. "In case you forgot, you're about to go into the forest into an area we don't have completely mapped to find an asset we're only pretty sure exists. Uncharted territory all around, right? So who better to have with you than a tracker? Especially a tracker who's already been to the dead zone?"

Bastian frowns. "What did Henry think?"

"I'm sure he wants this mission to be successful as much as the rest of us do."

"That's not what I asked."

Laurel looks away (guilty-embarrassed-determined). "Yeah, well . . . sometimes you need to keep secrets. Temporarily. For a good cause."

There's an edge to the way she says it that Bastian decidedly doesn't like. "Give us a minute," he tells the others, taking Laurel's arm and leading her far enough away that they won't be overheard.

"She really wanted to go," Laurel says.

"Do you honestly think now is a good time to break the rules?" Bastian asks. "More than we already are breaking them, I mean. It's going to look pretty bad if someone finds out you've helped three assets sneak out of the compound, including a teenager."

"I think now is a *great* time to break the rules because the rules are *stupid*." She pokes him in the chest. "We don't have time for this. You all need to get going. We can ask for forgiveness later."

"This isn't really a mission," Bastian reminds her. "It's—I don't know what it is. Not something we can risk an asset's life on."

"Oh, come on! Going through the forest isn't as death-defying as all that. And anyway, what are you going to do if the vehicle autodrive cuts out? We can't exactly send a driver with you, and neither of you can drive."

"And Chloe can?"

"She hasn't been barred for life from all compound vehicles, which is more than can be said for you. And if James ever knew how to drive, he definitely doesn't remember now. At least, that's what he said when I asked. Besides, you two seem like you could use a babysitter. Honestly, I still don't understand why you don't at least *try* to get along."

"Because he's an untrustworthy asshole who has no emotions and likes to make you apologize for him rather than acting like a grown-up. But, you know, pick your own friends."

She gives off a tiny jolt of defensive-hurt-annoyed, but before he has a chance to feel bad about it, she says, "I picked you."

Bastian smiles in spite of himself. "Yeah, you did. Regretting that choice now?"

"Hmm . . . Nope." She grins and walks back over to the others. "Ready?"

"Always." James smiles brightly at her—an attempt to be suave, maybe, but it's completely at odds with his lack of emotion. "Chloe and I were just chatting."

Chloe is standing with her shoulders hunched and her eyes cast down, more or less just like she was a moment ago. Only now, Bastian notices, she's got her shield tightly wrapped around her. She's clearly uncomfortable around James but doesn't want to move away or make any fuss about it.

Bastian presses his lips in a thin line and goes to stand next to her. "Are you sure about this?" he asks. "Never mind what Laurel told you. You don't have to come with us if you don't want to."

Chloe's hands are tight on the strap of her backpack when she looks at him. "Can I help? My power, I mean?"

Bastian hesitates. But it's not like lying will do any good. "Yeah."

"Then I want to come."

"See? All set!" Laurel claps her hands, then goes over to James and throws her arms around him. "Don't die. Again."

James pats her on the shoulder. "Of course I won't. The world barely survived without me the first time."

The flippant way he says it sets Bastian's teeth on edge. (Surely he can see her pain, how much it means to her that he's there, the strength it takes to let him go again—Bastian may be shit at this friend thing, but even he can see she's doing the keep-a-bright-face-for-the-crowd act, which James should know better than Bastian, having been her friend for longer, but here he is cracking jokes and barely even hugging her back, maybe just because it's the right thing to do, not because he actually feels—)

"Hey, stop spacing out." Laurel is frowning at him. "Do I need to go over the not killing people rule again?"

"No."

"Good." She hugs him, too.

He has a sudden thought, and it's out of his mouth before his brain catches up. "I never thanked you. Back then, when you found me in the clearing . . ."

Laurel blinks at him. "That was two years ago."

"Yeah, well. I wouldn't have had those two years if it hadn't been for you. So. You know. Um. Thanks."

Her eyes go wide. She flicks a glance over at James and Chloe. "You know there are other people here, right?" she whispers loudly.

He sighs. "Forget it."

"You're welcome."

"This is touching and all, but can we get on with it?" James says.

"You're just jealous because I didn't hug you longer," Laurel retorts.

"Well, yeah."

"Shut up and get in the car," Bastian tells him. Then he turns back to Laurel. "There's something else I need you to—"

Laurel smiles. "I know. Admit it: You're a romantic."

"Don't be stupid."

"I promise to look after him."

Bastian swallows. "Thank you."

"I mean, he's not really going to let me, but I can be very tricky when I want to be. There will be so much looking after, and he'll never even guess it. I'm just that good."

"Maybe spare a little bit of the looking after for yourself?"

"Aw, why are you saying such nice things where I can't record them to blackmail you later?"

"Bye, Laurel."

"Really? That's how you want to—?"

Oh, what the hell. He puts an arm around her in a half hug, kisses the top of her head, and then moves away quickly before she can do anything other than sputter in surprise.

James looks up when Bastian opens the front passenger-side door. "Ready now? Or do you still need to look back longingly at the only home you've ever known?"

"Get out."

"You realize it's going to be difficult for you to find this healer without me, right?"

"Get in the back seat. I'm sitting here."

James stares at him for a moment, then shrugs and gets in the back. Bastian takes his place next to Chloe and does his best to ignore the confused-grateful-relief shouting off of her.

"Should I start the autodrive now?" she asks.

He nods.

As the vehicle begins to move, he finds he *does* want to look back. But he doesn't.

Chapter 32

BY THE TIME he grabs his briefcase and leaves the suite for his meeting with Senator Donnigan and Major Alexis, Henry can't remember anymore whether he got any sleep after Bastian left. He knows he spent most of the night debating which confidential files he might have to give up today, not to mention going over how he's going to spin James and Bastian's hasty exit.

But he must have slept at least a little because he remembers dreaming about the hidden room on Level 49 where Bastian underwent his last experiment. When they finally managed to open it during inventory—after Henry was sure Bastian had left the floor—there was nothing there beyond the same kind of disturbingly clean gurney and storage cabinets they'd seen in all the other rooms. But in the dream, Henry saw a label on one of the drawers that read FSP6342867, and when he looked at the corner of the room, he saw a med tech disappearing through a dimly lit doorway . . .

He's just gotten onto the elevator up to Level 1 when he hears Michaels's voice in his earpiece. "Good morning, sir. Senator Donnigan is waiting for you in your meeting room."

Henry grimaces. "He realizes he's twenty minutes early, right?"

"Would you like me to bring him some coffee while he waits?"

"I don't think we need to go that far, Michaels."

"Excuse me, sir. Some other beverage instead?"

"Let him stay parched. I'll be there shortly."

"Yes, sir."

Henry considers taking longer than necessary out of spite, but that doesn't seem like a very auspicious way to begin the day. Plus, it would be just one more thing for Donnigan to complain about to the liaison committee and the Council, which is the opposite of what they need right now. Particularly since he's one of the leading members of the new oversight task force.

The other task force leader, Major Alexis, is approaching the office just as Henry gets there. Which means it's time for Henry to act like a professional and not a cranky, sleep-deprived mess of tension. "Good morning, Major."

Alexis turns toward the sound of his voice and smiles. "Hello, Henry. How are you? With the loading dock issue, I imagine you've had a bit of a night."

Henry frowns and stops in his tracks, both literally and metaphorically. "What are you talking about?" It's not terribly convincing, but the edge of annoyance he got in there without even trying helps sell it a bit.

Major Alexis's facial expression seems sympathetic, but Henry isn't entirely sure. He's not sure of anything anymore where Major Alexis is concerned. Maybe he never was.

"The task force's access to the compound's security feed went into effect this morning," Alexis says. "I checked in with hacker HQ on my way here, and it sounds like a vehicle has been missing since late last night. They're in the process of tracing what happened."

One of the mechanics must have come in early and noticed the missing vehicle ahead of schedule. Would've been nice if Kent had let him know Alexis was snooping around, but Henry supposes there wasn't enough time. "I'll explain in my office. Senator Donnigan is already waiting for us, so let me just get the door."

He holds it open, but Alexis stays where he is, hand tightening slightly on his cane. "Henry—"

"The senator is waiting."

Alexis hesitates for a moment longer, then nods and goes through the door without saying anything else.

Michaels greets them as they come through, exchanging pleasantries with Major Alexis and showing him to the meeting room while Henry goes over to his desk to drop his briefcase and get out his tablet. Michaels comes back to check in. "I've sent you a list of your meetings and other agenda items for today," she says. "Will there be anything else?"

"No, thank you."

A flicker of something he can't quite read flits across her face. "If I might ask, sir . . . Did last night's events proceed as expected?"

Given that Michaels did most of the arranging, it seems only fair to tell her, even though knowing might not be in her best interest. "I understand that a vehicle left the loading dock," he says. "The rest is classified."

"Of course. I understand." He might be imagining things, but it seems like her movements are slightly less tense as she returns to her desk.

Henry tucks his tablet under his arm and goes to the meeting room door. Then he pauses, takes a deep breath, and lets himself in.

Major Alexis and Senator Donnigan cut off their quiet chatter as soon as Henry enters.

"Good morning," Henry says politely as he sits down across from them at the conference table.

"The major tells me there was an incident at the loading dock last night," Donnigan says without preamble. "I'm sure you realize the liaison committee is very concerned about this compound's security—it's part of why this task force was formed, after all. Perhaps you'd like to fill us in?"

Henry's pretty certain he wouldn't, but he's not about to share that. "The vehicle that left yesterday did so under orders," he says.

"Whose?" Donnigan asks.

"Mine."

When Henry doesn't offer anything further, Alexis leans back in his chair with a small, thoughtful noise. "You'd better explain," he says.

"It was a small reconnaissance mission. Three assets are going into the forest to gather time-sensitive information and bring it back to the compound." It was only supposed to be two, but Laurel blindsided him with a call very early this morning to explain her late addition to the team, so he gets to deal with that, too.

"And they needed to leave in the middle of the night?" Donnigan says dubiously.

"Yes. For security reasons."

"Which assets? And why the urgency?" Major Alexis is always hard to read, but Henry gets the impression that he's somehow disappointed.

"It's a classified mission, so I'd appreciate your discretion."

Donnigan frowns. "Major, in case you've forgotten, our purpose here is to—"

"I'm very aware of your purpose, Senator. I'm also aware that mine is to protect the people in this compound. I don't classify missions or materials on a whim; I do it because the situation warrants it."

"And the situation is . . . ?"

Henry steels himself. "If you'll recall, we have an asset who's been suffering from severe memory loss. I know you had some concerns about his actions here at the compound, but we've reviewed his case and cleared him. Meanwhile, our ongoing research has turned up a healer who might be able to help him."

"A healer?" Donnigan's frown gets deeper. "That seems unlikely. Valentine kept very careful data on the assets in this area."

"Yes, but she wasn't always forthcoming about that data, was she?"

"This has to do with the team you sent into the forest not long ago, doesn't it?" Alexis asks. "I didn't realize you'd already settled on a follow-up course of action." He makes it sound like Henry's a teenager who went out after curfew and just got caught.

"Based on my discussion with Officer Smith and my review of the data her team collected, it seemed like the logical next step. And because we're dealing with a significant unknown entity, I've made the details need-to-know only."

"You didn't say who you sent," Alexis reminds him. "Aside from—what was his name?—James."

"A tracker." Henry's still not pleased about Chloe, but Laurel was right: She's already been to the dead zone once with Smith, and she's the only tracker in the compound right now. If her chaperones act like adults, she should be fine.

So she's probably not going to be fine.

"And?" Alexis prompts. "You said there were three assets."

Henry sighs inwardly. "Bastian went with them, too."

"I thought the director was on leave," Donnigan says. "Now you're saying he's on a mission?"

"He's still on leave in terms of his duties as the asset program's director. But if our intel is right, and they run into an asset who isn't familiar with the program, they'll need someone who can read the situation and help navigate their interactions. Bastian's power and experience are suited to that."

The corner of Alexis's mouth quirks upward. "So you sent him to be a negotiator? Or an interrogator?"

"Neither. I sent him as someone who knows the worst of what a compound can do, which makes him the best person to talk to an asset who might not trust outsiders. He'll know how to convince the healer that it's safe to help James."

"Sending him as your diplomat seems unwise, given his ... disposition," Donnigan says. "And the fact that you have an entire committee full of trained diplomats you could've called on."

"He also ought to be under stricter surveillance," Major Alexis says gently. "He stepped down for a reason, Henry. His mishandling of the asset program—"

"If you'd like to lodge a formal complaint with the Compound Council regarding the director, that's your right," Henry says, surprised at how calm his own voice sounds. "In the meantime, as the commanding officer of this compound, I retain the right to assign my officers and staff as I see fit. There's nothing in the arrangements for this task force that states you have veto power over my decisions, only that you want to advise me and to be kept informed about what's happening at the compound. I've just informed you."

The room is filled with an awkward silence, broken belatedly by Alexis shifting in his chair. "Of course we trust your judgment on this," he says. "If you feel the mission needed to happen now and in this manner, we'll defer to you."

"However, we'll need access to all communications between the compound and this team," Donnigan adds. "It would be difficult to advise you without knowing what's happening."

He gives Henry a stern look. "And I would suggest you consider your actions from here on out very carefully, Major. I'm sure I speak for both Major Alexis and myself when I say that while we're dedicated to seeing this compound succeed, success depends in large part on you and the choices you make. I would hate to have to tell the liaison committee that protocol isn't being followed."

"We understand that this is a difficult situation for you," Alexis says quickly, "and we appreciate your cooperation. There's a lot of ground to cover, and with your asset program in flux, it must be quite a strain."

"The compound has had quieter periods," Henry admits.

Donnigan leans forward. "But for you personally—"

"Senator. Major. Let me be very clear." Henry can't quite keep the sharpness out of his voice and, for once, he also can't be bothered to feel bad about it. "I'm here to discuss matters related to the running of the compound and to provide you with whatever information you need to take back to the liaison committee. I appreciate your concern, but my personal life isn't relevant to this discussion. I'm sure neither of you will have any trouble keeping things professional."

Donnigan looks like someone slammed a door in his face, and it squashed his nose before he could get out of the way. But the look passes quickly, as he seems to come to terms with not being able to catch Henry in a moment of weakness. "Of course, Major."

"Sensible," Alexis murmurs.

(And for a moment, Henry is back in the doorway of his parents' house, staring at two adults in uniform who claim to be there for him, who don't care that he's got a black eye and a long list of schoolyard fights on his record, who are telling him he's sensible for not letting them into his house without knowing who they are and what they want, and it turns out that what they want is to train him and give him a place where he can belong and do some good, except—)

"So." Henry raises his eyebrows at Donnigan. "Senator? What do you need to cover today?"

"Yes, well." Donnigan glances at the clock on the wall. "Our list of officially requested documents should be in your inbox by now."

Henry flips over his tablet to look. The legalese is burdensome—impressive that Donnigan could use so many words to say next to nothing. Still, the gist of it is the same as previous requests: They want more records of intake protocols and numbers (extra work for Smith and the other retrieval captains; they'll be thrilled), updates on the results of the latest asset experiments, and . . .

"What are these 'extraneous files' you want to look for?" Henry asks. He has the sneaking suspicion that he already knows, and that suspicion isn't making his morning any more pleasant.

"Anything out of the ordinary," Alexis says. "We briefly discussed the one I found just before I sent in my last report—you remember."

"I remember you found some sort of corrupted file that was likely a misplaced mission report," Henry says carefully. "But you have that already."

"Yes. And I found it concerning. The assistant director didn't seem to know anything about it, and neither did anyone at hacker HQ. You're probably right that it's just an erroneously placed file, but it may indicate a larger security issue. We'll need your hackers to do a sweep and report their findings, just to be sure. We'll provide them with some updated software to use."

Kent and Sybil will love that. "And who would be reviewing the findings?"

"At the moment, just the two of us. If we come up with something we feel needs to be released further, we'll let you know."

"Is there any particular reason you don't want us to do this, Major?" Donnigan asks lightly.

Henry can't see a way to stop it. If he doesn't let them have their sweep and whatever it turns up—which will almost certainly include Emily Tezuka's file fragments—Donnigan won't be the only one to accuse him of trying to hide something. And if he just stands back and lets them do it, they'll find out exactly what he's hiding.

He might be able to have Kent and Sybil work something up to protect what's in the files, but any augmenting they do is likely to be traced back to them, which would defeat the purpose.

Anyway, *he's* the real problem, isn't he? The details aren't clear, but the biggest issue seems to be that the fragments indicate that Henry is an asset. With a side of possible evidence that the Council knows. Or at least that they were somehow involved in this Fail-Safe Protocol.

Could Major Alexis really not know what Henry is and what those files mean? It's never been safe to ask, but now Henry wonders if not asking is what's going to destroy this compound. Alexis might've been willing to negotiate some sort of agreement, some guarantee that the assets here would be protected no matter what. Now he'll have proof that Henry's been hiding things from the committee. And if he's actively working with the Council as well . . .

"Major?" Donnigan asks.

"Excuse me. Of course I want to make sure you get everything you need. I'll have my team get started on pulling the records you requested, and I'll have the hackers run the sweep as soon as you get us that software. Anything else?"

"That's all for the moment, thank you," Major Alexis says.

As if Henry had any other option. "Of course."

Donnigan makes a quick exit after that. Alexis is a little slower, and when Henry moves to open the door for him, he stops entirely.

"Be careful, Henry," he says, his voice low.

"About what?"

Alexis taps the grip of his cane. "This level of scrutiny can be … difficult for someone new to command. You need to take special care that you're cooperating and following protocol to the letter at all times. It's the only way to protect yourself."

Henry frowns. "There are a lot more important things to protect, Major."

Alexis shakes his head and smiles a bit sadly. "Always willing to do whatever needs to be done, no matter what the cost." He sighs. "I really do want to help, Henry. But there's only so much I can do."

Henry distinctly remembers Bastian saying after their dinner with Alexis that Alexis's top priority was *not* to help them. And yet … this sounds an awful lot like a comment from someone who wants to help. Sort of. After he's already gone and publicly torn down this compound's autonomy and any chance Henry has of staying in power long enough to do some good.

So … what does that mean?

"I've got the door," Henry says.

Alexis sighs again and passes through.

Chapter 33

THE VEHICLE DRIVES for hours, its headlights cutting through the dark in hazy beams that catch on brush and ancient trees. Bastian doesn't recognize the path as one of the ones that goes to Laurel's clearing—those would be too narrow for a vehicle traveling without a plantspeaker to tell things to get out of the way. And they seem to be keeping to the outskirts of the forest where the trees are thinner. So maybe it's the route Henry and his team took last year when they were ordered to find Bastian. If Bastian had spent less time fighting headaches and more time reading mission plans, he might know for sure. Hopefully, the vehicle knows enough for all of them.

James tries a few times to start up a conversation, but when neither Bastian nor Chloe show much interest, he falls silent, leaving them with just the hum of the vehicle and the occasional call of a nighttime bird. Some interminable time later, Bastian glances at the rearview mirror and sees that James has leaned his head against the window and fallen asleep.

"I think I used to go on car trips like this," Chloe says quietly. "Someone drove, though. I mean, someone other than the car."

Bastian stares out the windshield and doesn't respond.

"I think it was my dad. It was just the two of us, and . . . Is it weird that I can't remember?"

Bastian looks over to find her frowning at her hands in her lap (embarrassed-confused-melancholy). "How long have you been at the compound?" he asks.

She seems startled to hear him answer, but she recovers quickly. "Three years."

"You're a little young to be having memory problems, but you were in Wright's program long enough to be entered into one of his memory experiments. That seems like a dumb memory to erase, though." Her startled-alarmed-stricken pierces his skull almost instantly, so he quickly adds, "Dumb as in, it's important to you, but it wouldn't have been to him. Which means he wouldn't have tried too hard to get rid of it. So it's probably still in your head somewhere."

"But I never even met Dr. Wright."

"He always had some sort of long-term experiment going in the background. And he didn't care who he used so long as there were enough bodies to fill the quota. If you never met him, it means you were pretty far down the food chain. Which is a good thing."

Chloe is silent for a moment before she asks, "Were you part of that experiment, too?"

It's just as well that it's so dark; Bastian doesn't want to know what his face is doing right now. As it is, he has to force himself to unclench his fists. "I don't think so," he says. "But I also don't remember much of anything from before the compound, and I spent a lot of time with Wright. So."

He knows from all the assets he's met over the past year that an unnervingly large number of them are missing chunks of their memories—often a lot more than whatever he and Chloe have lost. And then there's Angelica, whose pre-compound life seems to have just inexplicably vanished, despite the details she's given Kent. The hackers have been working since day one to piece things back together, but it's been slow going.

James shuffles a bit in the backseat, and then things go quiet. Bastian thinks the sky might be lightening a bit by the time Chloe speaks again, her quiet voice startling him. "You're different."

Bastian tears his eyes away from the vehicle GPS. "What?"

"You're not like Dr. Wright. I mean, I never met him, so I don't really know anything, but—everyone was afraid when he was in charge. Now, it's different. The assets aren't scared anymore. At least, not the ones I've talked to." She looks at him, then quickly away.

Bastian shrugs. "Yeah, well. Laurel's much better at working with assets than Wright ever was."

"No, I mean—she's really great, of course, but . . ." Chloe presses her lips together for a moment, then meets his gaze. "I think it matters that it's *you* who's in charge of the program now. I think the assets know you understand what they've been through, so they trust you and what you're trying to do with the program."

She falters and adds, "I just. Um. Thought you might want to know."

Even though it syncs with what Henry said, Bastian still can't quite wrap his head around it. "I don't—that's what they're saying?"

Chloe nods. "That, and that you and the major are . . . you know."

Bastian rolls his eyes. "They don't have anything better to talk about?"

"Well—"

The vehicle suddenly jerks to a stop, throwing them back against their seats and eliciting a yelp from the back seat.

All of the instruments have gone dark. Bastian tries the door and finds it's stuck shut.

"What the hell?" James asks helpfully.

"Um," Chloe says. "I think we're here."

Bastian realizes he can't feel her anymore—and he can't feel anything else around here, either, although he can hear a few early morning birds starting things up in the trees around them.

He takes a moment to really focus, carefully feeling out, and . . . still nothing. It's not quite the comfort of Henry's negation, although it feels close: a heavy blanket over everything, just this side of uncomfortable, like he's woken up too hot after piling on the layers the night before. Except he can't get out, and it makes his skin itch.

There's something else about it, too; something he can't quite . . .

"Hey, I can't get a light," James says. The sound of snapping fingers comes from the back seat.

"Dead zone," Bastian reminds him. "But just in case, can you maybe not try to make the vehicle explode while we're trapped in it?"

Chloe, who has undone her seat belt and spent some time shuffling around in the glove compartment, sits up. In the dim light, Bastian sees she's holding a long, orange tool with a metal head in one hand. Her fingers tighten around it as she turns around to look at Bastian. "You should probably stay back as far as you can."

"What are you doing up there?" James demands.

Neither of them answer. Chloe stares intently at her window, then takes a deep breath, shifts her weight, and slams the metal top of the tool against the glass.

Bastian flinches away, then raises his head to find that the window is now covered with a network of cracks.

Using her shoulder and elbow, Chloe pushes against it until the glass falls out onto the ground. Then she turns back to Bastian and hands him the tool. "I'm going to get out and see if I can open your doors from the outside. If I can't, use this like I just did. Aim for somewhere at the top of the window."

Bastian looks at the tool in his hand, then at her. "Do I need to ask why you know how to break out of a car?"

She smiles awkwardly. "My dad taught me. I think. That's called a safety hammer."

Bastian considers the tool again. "We're definitely going to have a talk about adding this to the asset program curriculum."

"Hey, if one of you is going to rescue me, could you get on with it?" James says. "We still have a healer to find."

After quite a bit of shuffling and rearranging herself, Chloe manages to struggle out of the passenger-side window. She also manages to get the other doors open from the outside, meaning James and Bastian don't have to worry about using brute force other than to push a bit from their side of the vehicle.

The back of the vehicle doesn't want to open, either, but instead of resorting to more property damage, Chloe offers to get their bags by going in from the back seat. It takes awhile, and by the time it's done, the forest area has lightened up considerably.

"The clearing where Officer Smith and I went is just ahead," Chloe says.

James immediately heads off without another word.

Bastian hesitates for a moment—he's really not sure what compound protocol is on leaving a damaged vehicle in the middle of nowhere—but it's not like there's anything they can do about it for now.

As they walk into the clearing, the odd feeling of nothingness bears down on Bastian's temples hard enough to start him on the day's first headache. He grits his teeth against it, unsure why the sensation is so familiar.

The path continues through the open area, which is full of patches of grass and dirt with a few white wildflowers poking out of the ground here and there. Smith and her team did a good job of cleaning up when they were done: Other than a few footprints, nothing's been disturbed.

On the other side of the clearing, James comes to an abrupt stop at a split in the path. One part of the fork breaks off toward a small creek lined with several plants with huge leaves. The other fork goes deeper into the forest.

"Jaunty little stream or dark forest path?" James mutters. "Sure would be nice to have a tracker about now."

Bastian frowns. "Or you could use your memory. Does any of this look familiar?"

"Sure. The plants. Laurel said they were . . . I don't know. Something forest-y."

"Burdock," Bastian says.

"Yeah, that." James waves a hand. "I guess we just choose one at random."

Chloe makes a small noise, then clears her throat when the others turn her way. "Um. Does being here remind you of anything else that happened in the forest? Maybe we can reconstruct enough of where you went that we can follow it until our powers kick back in."

James heaves a loud sigh. "We tried that for weeks back at the compound, remember?"

"Yeah, but we're here now. Maybe something will trigger another memory."

James still looks skeptical, and Bastian finds he doesn't have any more patience. "Stop complaining and *think*."

"I'm not one of your asset program cronies," James snaps. "You can't tell me what to do."

"What are you, a toddler? Do you want to find this healer or not? Chloe is our fastest way of getting out of here. Anything you've got, tell her."

James scrunches up his face in an approximation of irritation. Then he lets out a breath and turns away, running a hand through his hair. "I remember . . . fire. A lot of it. Everywhere. I remember stumbling through the forest on paths like this for . . . days? Weeks? Everything sort of blends together. There was rain once, and I started smoldering. More than I usually do."

He waggles his eyebrows at Chloe, who looks at him blankly, making her Bastian's favorite person of all the people he can currently see.

"Do you remember anything about what you saw?" she asks. "Landmarks or other plants? Quality of the dirt? Time of day?"

"Quality of the dirt? Really?"

Chloe shrugs. "Dirt is different, depending on where you are. If you remember, it might help us figure out which way to go."

"Huh. I didn't think anyone other than Laurel cared about dirt."

It doesn't take an empath to see that Chloe is pleased by the comparison. Just what Laurel needs: hero worship.

"Anyway," James continues, "I don't remember much else. I think I could see the mountains through the trees—I was going north, like I said before."

"You told Laurel and Chloe that there were other people, right?" Bastian says. "What were they doing?"

James shrugs. "Walking with me? Holding me up? I don't really—" He pauses, then turns to look down the darker path. "There was something . . . They had a way of blocking their path so no one could follow. That was really important. They didn't want anyone following them back to the—the safe place. The . . . caves. We had to keep going north, but first . . ." He starts walking quickly into the trees.

Bastian and Chloe exchange a look, then follow after him.

They walk for at least half an hour, the brush getting deeper and the trees harder to maneuver around as they go farther into the forest. There's still a muted quality to the air, constantly reminding Bastian that someone has figured out a way to keep this entire area power-free. In between the dull throbs of pain at his temples, Bastian considers the very real possibility that that someone is the same someone they're heading toward right now. After all, if James is right, and the people who saved him wanted to stay unnoticed, it would make sense for them to come up with a way to defend against asset powers, right?

But Bastian has never felt something like this, the dulling of his power that's similar to negation but also somehow different. It's not just that he can't feel anything; it's like there was nothing to feel to begin with. Like something prevented emotions from leaving residue in the first place. Almost like—

Almost like the crime scene at the Hall.

"Here!" James has stopped in front of a large pile of logs blocking the path. "We need to get on the other side of this."

The logs are enormous, jaggedly cut off at odd angles, roots sticking up like unkempt hair. They've clearly fallen from higher up—Bastian can just make out the broken stumps up on the hill. Lightning strikes, maybe.

The brambles covering the area are definitely unnatural, at least in terms of how they're growing. They snake around the logs and rise high enough to block most of the view of the other side. Bastian is no plant expert, but he's fairly certain brambles aren't supposed to grow so tall or coil around each other tightly enough to form a wall that looks like something out of a fairy tale.

It's clever, Bastian thinks. Physical barrier plus negation barrier equals no uninvited guests. Doesn't explain how they got access to whatever weird negation they used to create the dead zone—or why it's so similar to whatever was used to mask Emily Tezuka's murder. But it shows they mean business.

"Could we get around?" he asks Chloe.

She shakes her head slowly. "I'm not sure. But with all the plants and the hills, I think we'd lose a lot of time."

"I've got this." James has thrown his bag down and is approaching the brambles on the right side of the log obstruction. At first, Bastian has no idea what he's talking about; then he sees that James is holding a small container of lighter fluid.

Bastian lunges forward and completely fails to grab it out of James's hand. "What the hell are you thinking?" he says. "If you start a fire here—"

"—I can redirect it once I'm on the other side. My power will come back."

"You can't know that."

"I can and do." James grins in a way Bastian finds extremely unsettling. "I *remember*."

"And on this side? It's not going to burn a nice little tunnel for you to skip through. That's not how normal fire works."

"I just need to weaken it enough to push through. Then when I've got my power online again, I can use the fire to make something you two can get through." James opens the bottle of lighter fluid and takes a lighter out of his pocket. Because of course the firestarter keeps a lighter in his pocket.

"And that's how you did it last time you were here?" Bastian asks, eyes still on James's itchy trigger finger.

James frowns. "Yes. No. There was someone who asked the brambles to . . ." He gets an odd look in his eyes. "One of them was a plantspeaker."

Which just makes Bastian wonder how much Laurel will kill them if she finds out they burned a bunch of plants. But it's not like she's here to ask the brambles nicely to move.

Bastian turns back to Chloe. "How much water do you have?"

"Seriously?" James frowns at them both. "You're going to waste time—?"

"Never mind. Whatever we have isn't enough. Before James burns the entire forest down, we're going to go back to that stream and collect as much water as we can."

James rolls his eyes. "Thanks for the vote of confidence. You realize that's not going to do much good if the fire gets out of control, right?"

Bastian looks up from rummaging around in his bag to collect all of the containers he has. Not many, but it'll have to do. "Are you telling me you *can't* redirect it once you're on the other side?"

James frowns. "I just said I could."

"Then all we have to do is keep it contained until you get through. Which means we need more water."

They lose an hour to retracing their steps, collecting the water, coming back, and getting set up. At least it gives Bastian a chance to down some painkillers without anyone noticing. It also gives him plenty of time to imagine exactly what Laurel would have to say about potentially endangering the forest this way.

"Now, can we get on with it?" James asks.

Bastian looks over at Chloe, who nods. "Go ahead," he says. "And try not to get us all killed."

James douses a small portion of the brambles with the lighter fluid, then tosses the container away and sets the plants on fire.

They burn surprisingly quickly—fast enough that Bastian and Chloe are throwing water around the edges in minutes. James grabs his jacket from where he dumped it on the ground earlier and uses it as a shield as he starts pushing against the weakening brambles. Whereas a normal person would be afraid of getting close to the heat of the fire, James clearly isn't. That lack of self-preservation is either going to save them or get him burned to a crisp.

Bastian decides now is not a good time to remind James that firestarters aren't exactly flame resistant—or retardant—when their power isn't working.

James is partway through, the burning leaves giving way to his relentless pushing. His hair is getting caught in the thorns, but he doesn't seem to notice, even though he must be losing some as he goes.

The flames are spreading, flickering from leaf to leaf, and they're running out of water. "Hurry up!" Bastian yells, but he breaks in the middle for an involuntary cough, so he's not sure James heard. Doesn't seem to matter much, though; James grunts and pushes another inch. The smoke and thorns obscure the rest of his movements.

And then the fire stops spreading.

It's still burning, but it's like someone hit the pause button on the combustion process. After a moment, the fire rearranges itself into a perfect circle, burning more of a tunnel through the brambles.

The smoke clears out, and James, now on the other side, pokes his head back through. "Well?"

Bastian turns to Chloe. Her hair is in complete disarray, and she's got a mixture of sweat and soot all over her arms, but she doesn't look injured. "Okay?" he asks.

She starts. "Oh! Yeah, let's go."

They bundle up the rest of their things—including James's bag, which he left behind—and cover their upper bodies with their jackets as they make their way through the smoldering bushes. Bastian makes Chloe go first, figuring that if James drops his power at any point, the fire will restart closer to where Bastian is rather than where Chloe is.

He's pleasantly surprised when James does a very good job of keeping everything contained until they're through, though he does stop holding the fire back just slightly too early, and the flames singe the edge of Bastian's jacket.

They're barely clear when Bastian feels his power come back, and he gets a slap in the face of relieved-weary-anxious from Chloe. His headache immediately spikes, and he has to bite back a curse. At least he doesn't fall flat on his face, which was a real possibility.

James brings his fingers together, and the flames go out. He turns to them and grins. "Pretty cool, right? Or, well. Hot, I guess. If you want to get technical."

"Where to now?" Bastian asks. At least his voice sounds level.

James shrugs. "Follow the path, I guess. Unless you want to find some more brambles to wander through."

"You mentioned a cave, right?" Chloe crouches on the ground, hands in the dirt, head tipped slightly in the direction of the wind.

"Yeah. So? We didn't see any caves on the maps back at the compound."

Chloe screws up her face in concentration. "The dead zone and the bad maps made it hard to tell," she admits. "But now that we're on the other side, maybe I can . . ." She stays like that for a minute, obviously going through their trail options.

James paces while she works, flicking his fingers and bringing up small sparks of flame. He's got a good imitation of impatience going on.

Eventually, Chloe gets to her feet and shoulders her bag. "I found it," she says, her voice tinged with the vague tone of an asset in the midst of using her power. She starts walking away without another word.

"Hey, what gives?" James demands.

"Shut up and let her work," Bastian tells him, shoving James's bag at him.

"Yeah, but where is she going?"

"Somewhere we need to be. So move."

Of course, Bastian has no idea if that's true. But anything has to be better than standing around waiting for James to come up with another reason to burn something.

Chapter 34

THE FIRST STRIKE against Senator Donnigan isn't that he made someone bring him a chair. Laurel is quite ready to encourage people who want to sit in her garden; it's a lovely garden, after all, and perfect for sitting, if you don't mind the grass sighing in that long-suffering way grass does when it feels it's not being appropriately appreciated.

No, the problem isn't the chair. The problem is that once he's in it, he closes his eyes. Like he's *bored*. Like he might *fall asleep* in *her garden* in front of *her students*.

Asleep is, of course, not the appropriate way to view a demonstration that's being put on primarily for your benefit. The best way is to stand at the ready so that you can jump up and down and cheer at the appropriate times. Falling asleep shows an unacceptable lack of enthusiasm, given how hard these assets have worked to be able to show off today.

"Never mind him," Laurel tells her small group of students after she's done gaping at the senator's rudeness. "You're all very clever, and your powers are very exciting. There's no way they won't be impressed, and I'm sure Senator Donnigan will wake up once you get to the finale." She considers. "Do you think he's just tired from constantly nagging Henry? I mean, that would be his own fault, but maybe we ought to make allowances. Very small allowances because we are nice people who only mostly hate him but are otherwise super tolerant and forgiving. What do you think?"

The four teenagers standing in front of her look at her like she's nuts. Also like they're nervous and can't really be bothered to think about much else.

"Why do we have to perform for these losers anyway?" Ezekiel already has tiny sparks of electricity dotting his dark skin as the muscles in his hands twitch.

"We don't electrocute people just because they're annoying, remember?" Laurel gives him a stern look until he stills, and the electricity dissipates.

"I can make the wind knock him out of his chair if you want," Gabe offers pleasantly.

"Then I can drown him," Reva adds. "Well. I can probably dump some pond water on him, at least."

Laurel frowns. "You're all being very violent. Have you been talking to the azaleas? They're really cranky today, and I'm beginning to think they're leading you down some dark paths. Which is weird, since they prefer direct sunlight."

"I don't want to do this," Mariah says. "They don't care about us. They just want to see what we can do so they can figure out how to use us."

"Don't be silly," Laurel says with more than a little forced cheerfulness. "Senator Donnigan is representing the liaison committee, which is full of people who care a whole lot about the assets here and want to make sure we have the resources we need. We're just going to show them what you've been working on so they give us lots of money to keep learning neat things."

Mariah blows a strand of hair out of her face and sighs. "Whatever you need to believe, I guess."

Laurel opens her mouth to respond, but she's interrupted by a med tech who's peeled off from the small group standing on the other side of the pond. "Assistant Director? We're ready when you are."

"Roger that." Laurel salutes, which he doesn't seem to appreciate much, as he just gives her a weird look before hurrying back over to where Dr. Rowe and the other med techs are standing ready to take notes.

Laurel turns to her charges. "All right, are you ready?"

"No," Ezekiel says.

"That's the spirit!"

Dr. Rowe clears her throat and calls, loudly enough to startle Senator Donnigan into wakefulness, "Let's begin!" She throws a nod over her shoulder, and several med techs start up their recording devices.

Gabe goes first, building the natural soft breeze into a stronger wind that whips through the group before dying down again. Every time the med techs finish fixing their hair and clothes, the wind picks up again. Laurel decides to pretend it's not on purpose, since Gabe solemnly swore to behave, and they would never go back on their word.

Gabe's wind finally settles in a small cone hovering and rotating over the pond. They have the pattern carefully contained, waiting for the next step.

Reva takes a deep breath and moves forward. Her long brown fingers reach out toward the pond. She moves her hands up, palms out, and then down quickly. The water just below Gabe's wind funnel slowly rises in a thin stream that coils itself around the gusts.

Esther would love this, Laurel thinks, her mind drifting back to her compound. Maybe even more than getting back at James. She'd turn the water to ice, then shatter it into a million pieces, and they'd scatter on the wind like—

(—shards dropping to the floor, Esther's hands still outstretched as she breathes heavily, sweat rolling down her cheeks—or is it tears?—and she turns to Laurel and says—)

Dr. Rowe is frowning thoughtfully as a med tech whispers something in her ear. She catches Laurel's eye and nods slightly. Next to her, Senator Donnigan is finally paying attention—still sitting, but sitting up, at least.

Gabe and Reva take their funnel a bit higher, lengthening it in the process. Gabe is grinning, while Reva is determined but struggling a little.

Laurel shakes her head to clear it and turns to Ezekiel, who has started to sparkle again. All right, maybe not "sparkle"—he doesn't like it when Laurel uses that term. It's not terribly accurate, anyway; his power is less sparkle and more eruption of small bolts of electricity all over his hands and face. He's crackling now, even in his eyes, and he raises his hands—

(—the way Xavier raises his hands and pulls the pipes out of the ceiling, drawing the metal to him like a magnet. A scream is cut off at the same time as the alarms, and Laurel tries to remember when she last breathed. She's never been afraid of Xavier, but when he looks at her, she can't see any of the patient kindness in his eyes anymore. "If you're not going to help, get lost, Pipsqueak," he growls. She gulps and turns and runs, tripping over debris and things that look an awful lot like dead bodies, all the while feeling a tickle of heat on the back of her neck, the voices of the plants just outside, warning her—)

Ezekiel's electricity shoots from his hands into the swirling vortex of wind and water, adding blinking lights around the edges. Laurel hears him grunt quietly as he tries to hold it. On the other side of the pond, the senator and the med techs jump back a bit.

"Time for the finale!" Laurel says, her voice shaking for reasons she doesn't quite understand. "Mariah?"

Mariah steps forward, her mouth set in a firm line, and Laurel suddenly knows with jarring certainty that it's all going to go wrong.

The sky above them begins to darken, and there's a rumble somewhere in the distance. The med techs start whispering to each other, and Senator Donnigan's hands tighten on the arms of his chair.

The rumbling gets louder, and the clouds knit together, casting the entire garden in shadow. Laurel feels the air thicken as she turns to Mariah. "*Localized* storm, remember?" she says, raising her voice a bit to be heard over the increasing howl of the wind.

Wind. Right. She looks over and sees that Gabe, Reva, and Ezekiel are still holding their funnel, except—oh. It's getting bigger and moving much faster. Almost like—

Mariah raises her hands toward the sky, and a torrential rain begins falling. In a few seconds, the rain turns to hail—sharp pinpricks of frozen moisture that dig into any exposed skin.

Laurel makes a quick downward gesture with her right hand, asking the nearby maples to bend over and protect Dr. Rowe and the others from the worst of the growing storm. She sends them a silent thank-you as they spread their branches, then turns to the assets near her. "*Stop!*" she says, grabbing Reva's arm.

Reva falters, and the water inside the whirling tornado drops back into the pond. But Ezekiel, Gabe, and Mariah keep going, the wind, electricity, and storm all coming together into a funnel cloud that moves far too quickly to the other side of the pond. The maples try to hold out against it, but Mariah yells something that gets lost in the wind, and a giant lightning bolt shoots down from the sky, cracking the largest maple in two—

(—hurry hurry hurry the trees are practically screaming at her, and she's tripping and running up the stairs and out into the clearing just as everything explodes into fire and smoke, her shirt is on fire, her hair is on fire, and she's still running and stumbling, and the grass is wailing as it bursts into flames, thin voices that call out sharply and go silent almost at once, and she looks back to see a wall of fire where the compound used to be, where her friends used to be—)

Someone is shouting, and Laurel realizes the wetness on her face is rain and hail mixed with tears. The maple isn't dead yet, but its scream of pain is sharp and hot, cutting through her chest and twisting so that she can barely breathe. Numbly, she watches Dr. Rowe and the med techs scurry around trying to extract equipment from beneath the destroyed trunk. She can't see Senator Donnigan, and she can't seem to care.

Mariah and the others are standing still a few paces away, their powers fading as the sun comes back out. Reva, Gabe, and Ezekiel look stunned by what they've done. Mariah, on the other hand, meets Laurel's gaze with no trouble at all. "They deserved it," she says, her voice low and hard. "We're not trained animals. We're not—"

"How long have you been planning this?" Laurel demands.

The teenagers exchange glances, but before they can say anything, Laurel continues, "Never mind, I don't want to know. Get out."

Reva hesitates, then begins, "Laurel—"

"*Get. Out.* You're no longer allowed in this garden. Or the asset program. Maybe. Ask me again later, if I'm still speaking to you." She turns to the black coat standing nearby. For a certain definition of "standing"—the woman is looking a little woozy, and her hair is sticking up in weird patterns. "Make sure they go straight back to the dorm."

Without waiting to see what happens, Laurel hurries over to the other side of the pond. Dr. Rowe tries to get her attention, but Laurel only has eyes for the maple. Its scream has become more of a dull, echoing ache, and looking at it, Laurel can see why: It's beyond saving. This particular maple is self-absorbed and old and tough, and it will be dead by tomorrow. All that's left is for it to suffer until it can't feel pain anymore.

Laurel swallows, forces the tears back, and wraps her arms around as much of the maple as she can reach. "I'm sorry," she mumbles into the bark.

"Assistant Director?" Dr. Rowe is standing a few feet away.

"What?" Laurel asks sharply.

"We need to take Senator Donnigan to med bay, but I thought you might want to—"

"What? Why?"

Dr. Rowe looks back over at her team, and Laurel follows her gaze. Someone's brought a stretcher, and they're strapping in the senator, whose leg is bleeding profusely. He must have gotten caught under part of the maple when it fell. Laurel's pretty sure she should feel bad about that, but she's not feeling much of anything at all.

"He'll make a report," Dr. Rowe says quietly. "Apologizing might mitigate the potential fallout."

(Apologize if they catch you doing anything wrong, make sure they don't know we're doing this—it has to be a secret, the biggest secret, the only one that matters, the one that will keep them from ever being able to keep us a secret, everyone will know what they've been doing, but only if we apologize and pretend to be docile and cooperative, never let them see we're really—)

"Assistant Director?" Dr. Rowe is frowning at her. "I'm sorry; I know you'll want to do something about your friend. But—"

Laurel wipes her face and stands up straight. "I'll talk to him."

("I'll talk to him," James says soothingly. "We'll figure out a way to make it less obvious. We'll say it was an accident." But Laurel looks at the dead officer on the floor, the mottled green of her face, and she realizes that even if they get through this, James will ask again, and she'll know exactly which plants will be willing to offer up their leaves and tell her she's doing the right thing by making the poison, and she feels sick to her stomach just thinking about it—)

Assets don't hurt non-assets, Laurel reminds herself. Not in training exercises, and not in . . . whatever that was. (Not a memory; never a memory.)

She takes a deep breath, then plasters on her best concerned and conciliatory smile before walking over to the senator to see if she can salvage the situation.

Chapter 35

THEY WALK THE rest of the day and well into the next in relative silence, only stopping briefly to sleep when they're all too exhausted to move anymore. James fishes around for sympathy about his aching feet a few times, but Chloe is too busy tracking to take much notice, and Bastian doesn't care on principle. That, and his head seems to hurt a little less if he focuses on nothing other than putting one foot in front of the other.

When James starts whining for the eighteenth time on the second day, Bastian snaps. "When you got to the compound, you'd been wandering around barefoot and injured for who knows how long. You didn't complain then. Why is this any different?"

"My feet are just as delicate and important now as they were then," James says, wiggling his toes in his sneakers and frowning. "Maybe more delicate and important, actually. I've had time to get soft."

"Why would your healer let you wander around like that, anyway? That doesn't seem particularly healer-ish."

"How should I know? I told you, I don't remember." He glances at the back of Chloe's head and adds brightly, "Are we talking now? Does that mean I can mention how weird she looks when she's using her power? It's like nothing else exists."

Bastian watches Chloe moving steadily forward and mumbling to herself a bit. "It's not like that for you?"

"Nah. I just do it and look cool." James snaps his fingers and produces a tiny flame. "See?"

"Not the looking cool part, no."

James waves his hand, and the flame goes out. "Isn't it your turn to impress us with your power? Chloe and I have already done it, so I think it's only fair."

"You should be able to do some of what I do," Bastian reminds him. "You've been spliced with my blood, right?"

"Nope."

Bastian stops and frowns at him. "What?"

"I mean, yes, I was spliced with your blood. At least, that's what Laurel tells me. And I remember Wright's notes, the ones I hid before . . . you know. The last experiment. But I don't think I could ever do anything really empath-y no matter how much they messed with my blood. Laurel got the empath link, and some of the others got bits and pieces. But not me. The only thing your blood did was make me unstable enough to do what I did to the compound."

So Bastian's blood made him go nuts. Great.

"Hey, don't worry about it." James claps him on the shoulder. "I don't need anything else to make me attractive or charismatic; I've already got that covered."

Bastian flinches away from the touch. It's worse than having someone's emotions shoved in his face without warning; it's a skin-crawling *nothing* that threatens to swallow him, the sense that James is more of a human shape pretending to be alive than a real person. Henry's nothing is strange and soothing; the negation in the dead zone is odd and uncomfortable; but James's nothing is downright *wrong*.

"Did my blood do that, too?" Bastian asks without thinking.

"Do what?"

"Make you not feel anything."

James looks at him like he's crazy. "What are you talking about?"

Damn. Shouldn't have said anything. But it never seemed like the right time to ask, and none of Dr. Rowe's tests ever showed anything, so Bastian was starting to wonder if it's somehow all in his head.

"You don't have any emotions," he says, even though it makes him sound like an idiot. "You do a good job of mimicking them, but you don't actually feel them."

A pause. Then James laughs loudly, startling some nearby birds out of a bush and into the sky. "Are you serious? Look, I know you're sick, but I didn't realize it'd turned your brain to mush."

"What do you mean, he's sick?" Chloe has turned around and come back to where they stopped.

"He's an idiot," Bastian says. "Ignore him."

"What, is it a big secret? What does she think we're doing out here, any-way?" James gives Chloe a very solemn look. "Your director is dying. I'm not the only one who needs this healer."

Shit. "It's not—"

"Is that true?"

Bastian sighs and tries to ignore the slowly increasing throb at his temples. "Yes."

(stricken-worried-confused) "Why didn't Laurel tell me? She said we were doing this for James. She said—"

"It doesn't matter." Bastian frowns at James. "And you never said how you found out."

James shrugs. "I saw it in a dream."

"Don't be—"

"That's why Laurel seemed so sad!" Chloe says. "I wanted to ask, but I didn't want to pry, and there was so much else going on, I—"

She swallows whatever else she was going to babble and looks at Bastian, a firm set to her mouth and determination in her eyes. "We'll find something to help you. I promise."

She makes it sound like it's so easy.

"What were you tracking?" Bastian asks.

Thankfully, she takes the hint and moves onto a different topic. "The cave James mentioned is this way. I think we'll be there in a few hours."

"Really? You found it?" James does a good approximation of genuine surprise.

"Tracker." Chloe gives him a tentative but still somewhat cocky smile, then turns and starts walking through the brush on the tiny animal path they've been following for about an hour.

James blinks, then looks at Bastian as the two of them follow her. "I mean, I get that it's her power, but how is she not lost yet? I barely gave her any directions, and she hasn't even looked at the maps we brought along. I'm the only one of us who's ever been here, but she's the one who knows how to get where we're trying to go?"

"How do you make fire?" Bastian asks.

James shrugs. "That's easy. You just focus all your energy on where you want there to be fire, and then there's fire." He snaps his fingers and ignites a flame as proof.

"Trackers do the same thing. They focus their energy on visualizing where they want to go and the fastest way to get there, and then the route is there. Data can help, but they don't need it. There's something about the path itself that shows them which one to pick."

"Hmm." James gives him the side-eye. "Is that your professional analysis based on being the director of the asset program?"

Bastian grimaces and steps around a pile of muddy leaves. "I'm not the director anymore."

They walk in silence for a blissful few moments before James starts up again. "Would you like me to share a meaningless platitude about how you'll be back at the compound in no time?"

"No."

"Or I could inspire you by telling you there's no way Laurel and the others are going to be able to keep the program running, so you'd better hurry home."

Bastian narrows his eyes. "Aren't you supposed to be Laurel's friend?"

"Oh, sure." James grins. "Laurel is great. She's funny and smart and not bad to look at. But she's never going to be a leader. She doesn't have what it takes."

"So who does, then? You?"

James laughs loudly, causing Chloe to start and turn quickly.

"Are you kidding?" James says. "I never want to have anything to do with another compound ever again. Every compound in existence should be burned to the ground."

"And who would do the burning, I wonder?" Bastian mutters.

There's a flash of something in James's eyes that's almost—*almost*—an emotion. "I would. In a heartbeat."

"And the people who live there?"

"Better get out of my way."

James brushes none-too-gently past Bastian and glares at Chloe. "Well? Don't we have to actually move if we want to get anywhere?"

"Um. Yes." Chloe starts walking again.

When both their backs are turned, Bastian takes out his bottle of painkillers and dry swallows several. He can't do much about the company, but at least he might be able to get some relief from the pounding in his head.

***

"Does it look familiar?" Chloe asks as James sticks his head into the darkened cave entrance several hours later.

"Well, it's dark. So even if it looked familiar, I wouldn't really know for sure, would I?"

Bastian wants to tell them to stop debating and just go in already. But he's hampered a bit by having to sit on a large boulder and cover his nose with his jacket so he doesn't bleed on things.

As nosebleeds go, it's not a very bad one, all things considered. But it's accompanied by a ringing in his ears and a weird, stuffy feeling in his head. All of that makes it hard to walk in a straight line, never mind exploring a dark cave.

The cave makes it worse, actually.

True to Chloe's word, it only took them a few more hours of walking before the trees started thinning out, and the path steadily inclined until they hit a rocky area covered in moss and brush. Not long after that, the path forked again, with one route continuing back into the forest and the other going up another incline to this cave.

The cave shouldn't be causing Bastian to have this reaction in and of itself. He isn't actively using his power, and the only other times he's experienced this sort of immediate physical reaction were when he was purposefully overextending himself. This time, his nose just decided to explode as soon as he got closer to the damned cave.

"You sure you're ready for more adventuring, Director?" James says with a smirk.

"Yes." Bastian manages to get to his feet with only minimal wobbling. "Any chance you want to be a firestarter now?"

James snaps his fingers and produces a flame large enough to light their way. The mixture of light and shadow casts an eerie pall on the stone walls. "Happy to help," he says cheerfully.

Chloe and James go first, and Bastian follows closely. Or at least, he tries to. But he makes the mistake of steadying himself by touching the wall, and his mind is completely overrun by the echoes of *fear-dread-anger-hate-desperation* and then—

—nothing.

It's almost like the dead zone, except he can clearly still use his power because he feels intermittent bursts of *rage* and *pain* in between the *nothing*. It's like someone made an effort to keep emotions from seeping into the cave walls, but they failed miserably, and now the emotional residue is pissed off about it.

Bastian doesn't realize he's on the ground, blood dripping freely from his nose, until Chloe is kneeling next to him, almost but not quite touching. "Bastian? Are you—?"

"We need to hurry, not take a nap." James's frown is illuminated by the play of the firelight against his face. "Look, I know it's tough going, but—"

"You don't feel that?" Bastian asks stupidly. "I mean, you can still use your power?"

James waves his fire, spreading sparks. "Obviously. Look, if you're too weak to—"

"You?" Bastian asks Chloe.

Chloe hesitates, then shrugs (awkward-embarrassed-worried-*owthathurts*). "I'm fine. Um . . ."

Not negation, then; it's just him. Lovely. "Never mind. I can—"

But he has to stop talking because *they were hurt and afraid when they came this way but they came anyway because there was nowhere else, he was the only one who could help them, the only one who could keep them safe, keep them from being taken, and their hope-anxiety-desperation soaked into the walls because they had to believe so strongly that he could help, that he wasn't just a story—*

"Bastian?" The concern-alarm-determination is still clouding up Chloe's face as she crouches next to him. Vaguely, Bastian thinks she reminds him of Laurel. Except that Laurel would be smacking him right now for trying to hide how awful he feels.

He should probably stop staring blankly at her, but he can't seem to move just yet. Not that it seems to bother Chloe too much. She sets her bag down, unzips it, rummages a bit, and takes out a small bottle, which she hands to Bastian. "Drink this."

Bastian squints at it, knowing it looks familiar but unable to place the memory. "What is it?"

"Laurel gave it to me in case . . . She said it was in case anyone got really hurt, but she must've meant it for you."

Which means it'll be both disgusting and effective.

Bastian downs it in one swallow and tries not to gag. Laurel's concoctions continue to prove their worth: He starts to feel better almost instantly. The ringing in his ears dissolves into something that sounds like laughter before it fades entirely.

He tries getting to his feet, which works fairly well. Then he takes a deep breath and fortifies his shield. It's not much against the powerful emotions in here—not to mention the way they've been manipulated—but it helps a little bit. And Laurel's tincture has him thinking straight for the first time in hours.

"Thank you," he says to Chloe.

"Well, that was fun. Are we ready to go now?" James is tapping his foot, like empaths collapsing in emotion-laden caves is a personal affront to him.

Bastian doesn't have the energy to bite James's head off, so he just nods, and they start off again.

After they've been walking for several minutes down the narrow tunnel, he senses more emotional residue coming from multiple directions. Fear-hope-desperation, but the timbre is slightly different—different people, different times, all overlapping each other. All flowing toward a central destination.

Chloe leads them into a cavern with branching tunnels. It's about the size of the room where Bastian gave his speech to the new assets—which is to say, it could probably fit a few hundred people. It doesn't look exactly like a natural cave: The stone is there, and the walls look a bit damp, but it's all smooth and open, more like the lobby at the Hall than a secret cave at the edge of the forest. It doesn't have any of the Hall's finery in terms of couches or benches, but there are a few makeshift wooden chairs positioned here and there, like someone did their best to make it seem like a place where you might sit down and chat for a while. The combination of archaic torches and sketchy-looking light bulbs combined with wiring on the walls adds to the low-budget ambiance of it all.

James lowers his hand, and his fire goes out. "This is . . ."

"You recognize it?" Bastian asks.

"I think so. Those tunnels . . ."

"There are six, including the path we took in here." Chloe narrows her eyes. "I can't quite tell what's at the end of them, but it's all part of a system of pathways. Like a highway with lots of exits. There are doors all up and down, and rooms that branch off."

"This is a crossroads," James says slowly. "People stop here on their way to—somewhere else. They're sort of . . . pilgrims. They come to him for help."

"Terrified pilgrims," Bastian mutters. Then he tenses because—

"Of course they're terrified," says a voice from behind them. "That's when you go searching for help, isn't it? When you're terrified."

Bastian, Chloe, and James turn to see a man come out of the shadows, smiling at them. His stringy, salt-and-pepper hair is a little too long, and his shirt and pants have been patched too many times to be trendy; but otherwise, he looks unassumingly normal, like someone you might see on a city street and forget about a moment later.

(Bastian knows that voice, has felt it press into his skull without warning, but how—?)

The man's smile is friendly as he takes a moment to show it to each of them in turn. But there's something off, something that isn't quite apparent until he looks directly at Bastian.

He doesn't have any emotions.

"Hello, Bastian," he says.

Chapter 36

IT'S BEEN AWHILE since Henry's taken to roaming the compound halls rather than sleeping.

There's something almost nostalgic about worrying himself further and further away from rest until it finally seems pointless to keep trying. In the past, when it got bad enough, he would throw on enough of his uniform to look presentable and go try to find something useful to do—training room exercises or paperwork or checking the cafeteria for his team getting up to nonsense. He usually let that one go unless Valdez and Alexander were getting too close to an altercation, in which case, no one seemed to mind if Henry broke things up and sent everyone back to the barracks.

Mostly, though, he did something similar to what he's doing tonight: wandering from level to level and trying not to think.

There are always officers and staff working at all hours in different parts of the compound, but by the time Henry hits Level 16, they've thinned out to the point where he has most of the hallways to himself. The only noise is a quiet buzz from the lights and the occasional opening and closing of a door as someone hurries along to their next task.

There are lots of things to not think about as he walks. Like Laurel's report on her disastrous asset program presentation. Or how he hasn't heard anything yet from either Donnigan or Alexis about the files he sent them. Or how empty the suite feels with Bastian gone. Or how he can't stop thinking about the door on Level 49 that he imagined but definitely wasn't there when they did inventory . . .

Coming around another corner, he's distracted by a shuffling and several low voices. The door to the children's dorm is partially open, and there's a staff member speaking firmly to a small child in a robe and slippers. She's half in, half out of the door and looks like she might make a dash for it at any moment.

At least they caught her before she got anywhere this time, Henry thinks with a sigh.

The children's staff aide looks up as Henry gets closer, and Henry vaguely recognizes the face, though he can't quite find the name. "Problem?"

The aide lets out a quiet little laugh laced through with frustration. "Sorry, sir," he says. "We've talked about how wandering around without supervision isn't what we do after bedtime, but Angelica seems to forget."

"I don't forget; I just don't want to stay in bed." Angelica turns to Henry. "It's okay if you go with me, right?"

"Angelica, we can't ask the major to do that," the aide says. "It's very late, and he's probably very busy."

"It's all right," Henry says. "We'll take a quick walk around the floor, and then I'll bring her right back."

The aide rubs his eyes and smiles wryly. "Thank you, sir. And I'm sorry for the trouble."

"It's no trouble . . . ?"

"David."

"David. I can recognize a fellow insomniac when I see one." Henry gives Angelica a moderately stern look. "We'll walk for a little bit, but then you're coming back here and going to bed without giving David any more problems. Got it?"

Angelica considers him with her large, dark eyes, then nods. "Got it."

They walk in silence for a while, and Henry wonders yet again how a little kid can be so quiet. She's a pro at keeping her slippers from making any noise as they hit the floor, and she doesn't seem particularly interested in starting a conversation. Did she pick up a tendency toward that level of quiet from her home life before the compound? Not that they have any way to be sure, since they *still* haven't found any trace of her family.

None of that appears to be troubling her, though—she seems happy enough to be walking next to him. He almost thinks they're going to forgo conversation altogether until she says in a low voice, "I can help."

"I'm sure you could," Henry agrees immediately. "With what?"

"Your memories."

Henry frowns. "What about them?"

"They're messed up. Like James's. Sort of." Angelica hops from one floor tile to another. "I can fix it."

Don't even think about it, Henry counsels himself severely. This is the very definition of *not okay*. No matter how much he wants to know about whatever it is that he can only barely remember.

"Angelica," Henry says carefully, "Laurel said you tried to help with James, and it didn't go well. I don't want you to hurt yourself."

"But I didn't know how to do it right then. Now I do."

Shut up, stupid flutter of hope. "What do you mean?"

"Dr. Rowe showed me. Or I showed her, I guess. I remember when I touch someone, but it's easier if I'm near where the memories are. James didn't know where his memories were, but you do, don't you?" She stops walking and gives him an intense look.

He tries to decide if he's grateful or disturbed. Or both. "Have you been using your power on me?"

She looks away. "No. Maybe. Not on purpose. It's just, sometimes I remember things even when I'm *not* touching someone. Sometimes it's just if they're close by." She hesitates, then adds, "Bastian didn't like it, either. Is that why he went away?"

"No," Henry assures her. "He had to—do something, but he'll be back soon. Then you can show him what you've learned."

Henry remembers watching Bastian and Angelica practice shielding in the garden. Her power had seemed quite strong then, too. It's not unheard of for memors to be sensitive enough to pick up memories without touch, but it's unusual, as far as Henry recalls from the research. In most of the documented cases, the asset couldn't consistently maintain that level of sensitivity. If Angelica can do it now, though, even for just a short while, it could be . . .

Could be what? Could be *useful?* He can't possibly ask a little girl to—

"I want to help," Angelica says. "Aren't you sad to not remember things?"

(The lights are too bright, and his eyes are too heavy, but if he closes them he won't see the needle they put in his arm, and he has to see it because he has to remember, he has to tell someone—)

"Major?"

Henry realizes he's pressing his hand against the wall. He feels dizzy, like he's got a fever. "We should get you back to the dorm," he says.

Angelica reaches for his other hand, then pauses before she touches him. "I can help," she says again. "Can we go to the place? I can help more there."

She probably could. If she read him in that Level 49 room, maybe they could trace what happened there. Maybe he would remember something about this Fail-Safe Protocol, something they could use against the Council, if it comes to that. Something they could bring to Carter and use to demand an explanation, at least. Nunez did say they should look for evidence that might help them fight back. The answer could be somewhere in his memories. Somewhere he can't get at, unless . . .

Henry takes a deep breath. "All right," he says. "But I need to make some calls first."

***

"This is . . . a jammer?" Michaels asks, turning the device over in her hand.

"Yeah. And don't hit the switch on the side unless you want to bring the entire compound down on our heads." Kent's voice through Henry's comm is practically vibrating with agitation. Michaels, her comm set to the same frequency, clearly gets the picture and sets the jammer down carefully next to the machine she's calibrating.

"Are you sure about this, Major?" Kent adds. "I don't want to second-guess you, of course, but in my experience, nothing good comes of wandering around the compound in places you're not supposed to be. Uh, I mean, from what I've heard."

"He means we're ready when you are, sir," Sybil's voice says calmly.

Henry, Michaels, and Angelica are standing in a large experimental recovery room on Level 49. There's something eerie about the relative silence, punctured only by a barely audible hum from the energy-saving lights and the occasional clicks as Michaels works on setting up the machine. Henry feels like a little kid up late, sneaking around and trying not to get caught. Using the jammers to prevent the security cameras from recording any of this late-night activity doesn't do much to dispel the idea.

He frowns at the wall panel in front of them. It took a fair amount of work from the inventory team to even find it, never mind how long it took for the hackers to crack the code. When they finally did, they confirmed that Bastian was right: There was a small, aggressively sterile experimentation room on the other side with no notes to be found about its function. At the time, Henry thought he felt sick being in there just because of how easy it was to imagine Bastian two years ago, lying on the table in the middle of the room, slowly bleeding out from a botched experiment. Now he wonders if it was also because he's been there before. Maybe.

Michaels finishes setting up the machine and turns to Henry. "Ready here as well, sir."

"You're sure it'll record Angelica's read on me?" Henry asks again.

"It's designed to be used with the director's power," Michaels admits. "However, the adjustments I've made should make it viable for a memor as well. Once she's brought up your memories, we should have a short window in which to record them."

Henry nods and turns to Angelica. He's still not convinced it's right of him to ask her to do this, but there's no going back now. "Okay?"

"Okay." She's eyeing the machine warily. "That thing is going to remember memories, too?"

"We're going to use it to record what you help me remember," Henry explains. "Then Kent and Sybil will put the record somewhere safe. In the meantime, they're going to make sure we can take as long as we need without anyone interrupting us."

"Actually," Kent says, "we can only give you a head's up, and even that's potentially iffy. The jammers we gave you and Officer Michaels will probably keep your movements off the security recordings, but we haven't finished setting up our system on the lower levels, so—"

"We'll do what we can, Major," Sybil says firmly. "No need to worry."

"Ready for us to open it up?" Kent asks.

Henry presses his lips together for a moment, then nods. "Go ahead."

There's a soft beep, and the door slides open.

It looks just like it did before: a much smaller room than the one they started in, but still with all the essentials—cabinets, drawers, a refrigerator for samples, a gurney off to one side, and a single operating table in the center of the room. It looks sterile but unassuming; just another experimentation room. Nothing worth hiding.

Unless he can remember something worth hiding.

Henry checks his negation field to make sure he's got it pulled back as far as possible to keep it from impeding Angelica's power. Then he turns around and holds out his hand to Angelica. Wordlessly, she steps forward and takes it.

"You remember seeing Bastian do it the first time," she says after a moment, her voice vague and quiet. "Use his power, I mean. He was going to fall into the pool, but you stopped him. You knew something was wrong then, but you didn't know what until later. There were a lot of things you didn't know until later."

Henry clears his throat. "We need to go back further. Was I here?"

Angelica scrunches up her face, then relaxes it with a sigh. "Yes. But this isn't where it happened."

"Where what happened?"

Angelica points to the far wall with her free hand. There's a pristine off-white cabinet and nothing else.

"Kent?" Henry asks.

"There's nothing from our inventory that suggests there's anything over there. Sybil's doing a quick check of the compound blueprints—"

"Nothing," Sybil reports.

Well. If Henry could navigate through a burned-out compound to find evidence last year, surely he can move a piece of furniture and see what's behind it now.

He drops Angelica's hand and walks over to the cabinet. It looks flush with the wall—and attached, as far as he can tell. He goes back and forth, pushing at each side; no dice. So much for moving it, then.

The several rows of drawers at the bottom—a large one on the right and three small ones on the left—open easily enough and prove to be just as empty as they were during inventory. Nothing on the counter, either. The two glass doors on the top open easily as well, although Henry manages to give himself a shallow cut opening the one on the right. The shelves inside are empty, too.

"Are you sure about this?" Henry asks Angelica, who has been standing silently and watching him.

She nods once, so he turns back to the cabinet and purses his lips. Maybe if he tries pushing at a different angle . . .

He hears a clicking noise and jumps back, startled, as the entire cabinet slides to the left, revealing a dimly lit opening and metal stairs going down.

"Secret passage!" Kent says. "Neat! Also not neat because it implies that our blueprinting program sucks. Uh. Does this mean you're going to dock our pay? If so, I should mention that I didn't code this one. Gimme a sec; I'll think of a minion to throw under the bus."

"Never mind that. Are you saying you can't tell me what's down there?"

Kent huffs in irritation, and Henry hears some rapid clacking on keyboards. "No cameras, Boss. Sybil and I can look for any historical data on the compound's architecture, but we went over all of this during inventory. How did you get it open, anyway?"

Henry frowns and looks for some sort of switch he might've inadvertently hit. Then he realizes there's a panel on the wall that would've been almost entirely hidden behind the cabinet in its original position. It doesn't look like any other lock mechanism he's seen in the compound. There's no slot for an ID; just a small rectangular recession set in a cracked white plate.

A cracked white plate that now has a bit of his blood on it.

(He's sitting on the table, the lights burning his eyes no matter how much he blinks, and the med techs are talking around him, like he's not even there—"We have plenty of the synthetic stuff; why do we have to keep draining this guy?" "Shut up and help me with the sample. We need more blood for the security system."—and then there's a sharp jab to his thumb, and one of them takes something over to the cabinet—)

His first step into the darkened area causes a shock of sickly yellow lights to spring to life. At least he won't have to worry about falling down the stairs into nothingness. Like the stairwells in the rest of the compound, this one turns at right angles and is accompanied by concrete walls. But these stairs look rickety and rusted, and the walls are devoid of security cameras. He won't need to use the jammer, but he might still trip on debris and crack his head open.

"Sir?" Sybil asks.

"I'm going down. Michaels, Angelica will wait with you while—"

"No." Angelica is at his side, peering down the stairs. "I'm coming, too. I want to help."

"You've already helped."

"I can help more. I told you, I remember better when I'm in the place. What they did happened down there, not here."

Henry swallows and holds out his hand again. Angelica takes it. "Leave the line open," Henry tells Kent and Sybil. "And keep looking at those blueprints in case we missed something."

"Yessir."

They've made it down less than one flight when Angelica flinches and stops short. "It's gone."

"What's—?"

There's a grating noise in his ear, then silence. "Kent? What was that?"

Angelica is turning her free hand over, palm up, palm down, like she can't quite make sense of what she's seeing. "Gone," she says.

Henry gives up trying to raise Kent—his comm is completely dead—and turns to Angelica. "Are you all right?"

"I can't use my power anymore."

Henry immediately checks his negation field, but nothing seems to be different about it, as far as he can tell. If something's affecting Angelica's power, it isn't him. And he's not sure exactly how he'd know if whatever-it-is is affecting his power, too.

"Let's go back up," he tells her. "I need to find out what happened with Kent."

"No." She gives him the full force of her determined mouth and accompanying stubborn glare. "Keep going."

Henry hesitates. It's not like Angelica can help much if she can't use her power, and she'll be safer up top with Michaels. And he really should figure out what happened with the comm connection. But with the level of scrutiny the compound is under now, they may not have another chance to figure out what this area was used for.

He squeezes her hand. "Be careful going around corners."

They walk down several more flights, the lights getting dimmer as they go. Henry is viscerally reminded of descending further and further into the lower levels of Laurel's compound. At least he's not dealing with burned stairs and leftover rubble this time. The only real issue here seems to be moderate disrepair: dust, rust, and decay in abundance, but no danger of putting a foot through a stair. Probably.

"Oh," Angelica says when they reach the bottom. Her hand tightens around his. "It's back."

Henry frowns. "That's good, but—"

"You remember the door," she says, her voice going dreamy again. "The big room. That's where it happened."

The door in front of them looks like any other door at the end of a staircase in the compound: dull gray and thick with a panel to the right of the door frame. But this one, like the one behind the cabinet, has a crushed white plate and a tiny rectangular hole rather than the usual ID reader.

"They used your blood to make the doors open," Angelica says. "They put it in things, and the things made the doors move. It was to keep it safer. So only the people who knew could get in."

Henry peers at the lock. He's never seen an ID card that could fit in such a tiny slot, although the shape looks like . . .

(One of the med techs is holding him up with a firm grip on his arm, and the world is still tilting, and they're still talking to each other like he's not there— "They'll take enough for the rest of the tests, right? I hate doing this, especially with a teenager." "Just get the door open."—and the other med tech pushes something into the door, a small rectangle that looks a bit like a slide for a microscope, like the ones he's seen them use to study asset blood—)

Henry grimaces and looks at the cut on his finger, which has long since stopped bleeding. Unless he wants to get out his gun and shoot off a limb . . .

He sighs, lets go of Angelica's hand, and takes a look around the stair-well, which eventually offers up a better alternative—for a certain definition of "better." A closer look at the stairs they just came down reveals a jagged edge on the underside of one of the steps. Without giving himself time to consider whether this is worth the risk of tetanus, he swipes the pad of his finger against the edge and reopens the cut.

Just like before, touching the panel with his blood opens the door. He gets a handkerchief out of his breast pocket and wraps his finger. Then he takes Angelica's hand again and goes in.

Their movement starts up another set of lights, though these barely illuminate the gloom of the long hallway they've just entered. It's covered in cobwebs and dust. Evenly spaced doors line both sides of the hallway, each with an ID reader. Henry suspects his ID wouldn't work on any of them, but if he can get the hackers down here, maybe they can—

"That way," Angelica says, pointing to the end of the hallway. "You remember . . ."

(—walking down the hallway, hearing shouts from the rooms on either side, followed by soothing voices, then nothing—if he didn't feel so woozy, he might turn and run the other way—except that's not what he's supposed to do; he's supposed to follow orders, do what's best for everyone, Major Valentine said—)

Henry shudders. "Let's go."

The door at the end of the hallway has the same security panel as the others, which means it's up to his poor finger again, which is increasingly unhappy with its treatment but still manages to give up a tiny bit of blood he can press against the broken white rectangle. The door slides open.

This room is bigger, with desks and carts for med techs positioned throughout and various sections curtained off. Like the other areas, this one clearly hasn't been in use for quite some time. A few of the smaller carts have been knocked over, and some of the curtains have been pulled partially off their hooks, as though someone ran through trying to do something in a hurry.

Something like hide evidence. Or destroy it.

Angelica points to a curtained area to their right. "That one. There were others, but that one—"

(They say it won't hurt, and it doesn't, but maybe that's just because he can never quite remember what happens, only that they have him sit in a chair while someone attaches something to his arm, and today, he's supposed to nod when the man in uniform talks to him—not just nod; he's supposed to say "yes, sir" as needed, and maybe salute, but he can't quite remember because this part always makes him sleepy—)

Uniform, Henry thinks. Four stars. A general. Why would Carter . . . ?

"You remember the day he came to watch," Angelica says. "He talked to the lady about it. You weren't supposed to hear them, but you did. He was angry and worried about what would happen if it didn't work. They'd been trying for a really long time, and she kept promising it would work, but it didn't. Until they found you."

Henry doesn't realize he's walked over to the curtained area Angelica pointed to until he finds himself standing there. He reaches up to pull the curtain aside—

"He really won't remember?" Carter says, his booming voice bordering on marginally quiet.

"Anna's taken care of that," Valentine assures him.

"So you say." Carter grunts. "If it doesn't stick, we'll have to rely on Alexis's observations about the kid's dedication to the cause."

"As I said, General, everything is—"

"I hope you weren't going to say 'all right,' Major, because it clearly isn't." Carter's voice gets even lower, to the point where Henry can barely make it out over the ambient noise of the med techs hurrying around. "The Council is getting impatient to see results. I can only hold them off for so long, and if you keep making ridiculous proposals about things like artificially manufacturing a backup empath using someone you pulled off the street—honestly, Valentine—"

"I have high hopes for Sebastian. But he—"

"—is a pain in the ass, by all accounts. I understand. He's also barely more than a child. If you can't handle him, I'll have him transferred to someone who can. Alexis trained us a negator. Maybe he'd like a chance at an empath as well."

There's a very long pause. Then Valentine says stiffly, "That won't be necessary, sir."

"Good. Then let's get this show on the road. How many samples are you taking today? The last report said the serum made from his blood took out a fully powered psionic in ten minutes. Any permanent damage?"

"None. The effect continues to be temporary."

"Hrmph. Not much better than the synthetic stuff we've been making do with, then. Keep testing. Take more blood if you need to. If the protocol can't be used in a permanent capacity, the Council will lose interest. We're trying to prevent a war, not give a few assets minor headaches."

"Understood, sir."

"They wanted a way to make it stop," Angelica says. "In case it got too bad."

"A fail-safe," Henry says grimly. They wanted to use his blood to stop any asset who got out of line—and not just temporarily. Were they really so frightened of what people in the asset program could do? Did it never occur to them that maybe locking up powerful people and experimenting on them for years might make them less inclined to play nice if they ever had full control of their powers?

Henry supposes it *did* occur to them. Only instead of curtailing the human rights violations, they figured they'd engage in a few more.

Angelica shakes her head and looks up at him. "Not just that. You heard other things. You remember . . ." She frowns. "It's stuck. The lady who made you forget things made it so I can't—"

"It's all right," Henry assures her gently. "Let's go back upstairs now. Michaels can—"

"They said what they'd do if it didn't work," Angelica continues, as if to herself. "They were worried about the other assets, about what they could do. They told you that you were helping. But then you heard them say that if it didn't work, they'd just bury it. Pretend it never happened." She looks up at him, eyes wide. "Pretend *you* never happened. They could make it stop that way, too. So they wouldn't get in trouble."

Because there had to be a fail-safe built into the project itself, too. Come up with something that could wipe out an asset's power permanently, and every compound in the entire Compound Network would be clamoring for it. Fail for years trying to make that happen, and the Council would start looking for a scapegoat. At which point it would've been in Major Valentine and General Carter's best interest to disavow the whole damned thing.

Henry clenches his free hand into a fist. He knows he shouldn't be surprised about the confirmation that Carter has been involved this whole time, but he can't shake the frustration and sense of betrayal. Carter was supposed to *help* them. If he was working with Valentine from the beginning, why fight to use the evidence Henry, Laurel, and Bastian found to put her on trial? And how did helping Henry with John Doe fit into the agenda? Or giving command of the compound to Henry in the first place?

Henry wonders if he'll get a chance to ask.

"Come on," he says to Angelica. "We shouldn't stay here too long." If the recording process for Angelica is anything like it is for Bastian, they'll need to get her back to the machine as soon as possible to record the most accurate read.

"There's more," Angelica tells him. She's sagging into him a bit, and her eyes are half closed. "You remember . . ."

"Angelica." Henry crouches down and waits for her gaze to clear before giving her a small smile. "I appreciate your help, but that's enough for now. Let's get you back upstairs so you can go to bed."

She blinks sleepily at him, then nods.

He doesn't have to carry her back up the stairs, but it's close. Near the smaller experimentation room where they moved aside the cabinet, Henry's comm comes back online suddenly with a sharp noise that startles both him and Angelica into alertness.

"Major? Are you there?" Sybil's voice is laced with a level of concern that implies she's been trying that line for quite a while now.

"It's all right," Henry tells her. "We're fine. We just have to record—"

"You need to come to hacker ops right away."

Henry frowns as he opens the door into the main room where Michaels is waiting. "What's wrong?"

"Sir?" Michaels has the machine ready.

"Sybil?" No answer. Henry's frown deepens, but he nods to Michaels.

Getting Angelica hooked up to the machine looks almost exactly like when Bastian does it. The only real difference is that Michaels makes a particular effort to be gentle and explains everything she's doing, waiting for Angelica to nod before moving on. Just like Bastian, Angelica seems a little uncomfortable when Michaels switches the machine on, but she stands very still throughout, including when Michaels flips the switch and takes the electrodes off of Angelica's skin.

"Thank you," Henry says to both of them. Then, into his comm: "Sybil? Kent?" Nothing.

Henry turns to Michaels. "Make sure Angelica gets back to the dorm. I need to find out what's going on with the hackers."

"Yes, sir."

He hesitates, then adds, "And make sure no one sees you coming back or putting away the machine. The jammer ought to help with that."

"Of course, sir." She says it like he's asking her to go get some paperwork, not try to hide activities that could get them all court-martialed. Or worse. He considers promising her another raise, but at this point, she's probably due a higher salary than anyone in the entire Compound Network. And he has some hackers to find.

Henry nods once, then turns on his heel and hurries to the elevators.

Chapter 37

"YOU PREFER 'BASTIAN,' right?" the man says, smiling with nothing behind it.

"Who are you?" Bastian demands. "How do you know my name?"

The man ignores him and turns to James. "You look well, James. Better than you did last time I saw you."

"I was here, wasn't I?" James sounds confused, like he's trying to remember a dream he had months ago. "You helped me."

"Yes. You were here for quite some time, actually. More than a year."

"Since . . ."

The man nods. "You were very hurt when you came to us. We did our best, but healing your physical wounds didn't change the fact that you'd had a traumatic experience. Then you disappeared, and we looked desperately for you, but . . ." The man shakes his head. "All we could do was hope your memory would eventually lead you back to us."

"Hang on," Bastian interrupts. "James destroyed an entire compound when his power went haywire. You're saying after all that, he somehow managed to stroll through the forest, stop by here for a chat, and then wander off again while no one was looking?"

The man turns back to Bastian. "Not exactly. James's injuries were very severe when we found him, and he barely survived the trip here. Luckily, he had people to look after him on his journey. A bit like how he got here today, actually."

He looks over Bastian's shoulder and smiles. "Chloe, right? These boys have you to thank for their safe arrival, don't they?"

"Um. Yes, I suppose." Bastian can see her eyes flitting here and there, probably looking for an exit. She's holding her ground, though.

"Excuse me," the man says, shaking his head. "I should've started with introductions. I'm Quentin. You're in a sanctuary, of sorts. We take in anyone who needs help and can't find it elsewhere."

Bastian thinks of the emotions in the walls on their way in. Those desperate people must have been coming to Quentin. Except some of that emotional residue felt old—*really* old. How long has this guy been here? And how has he managed not to be picked up by a retrieval team, if he's really an asset?

A man and woman appear out of a side tunnel and hurry over to Quentin's side. They're dressed normally enough in t-shirts and loose pants, though their clothes have definitely seen enough washes to lose most of their color. The same might be said of their skin, which has a dull tone to it that matches the blandness of their mutual solicitous-polite-deferential.

"Quentin? Can we help?" the man asks.

"Yes, thank you, Tom. Please show Bastian and Chloe to our guest rooms. And Dana, if you'd take James back to his old room, I think he might like to see it. I'll be along shortly."

Dana leads James away down one of the tunnels. Tom starts to herd Bastian and Chloe the other way, but Quentin stops him.

"I know why you came, Bastian," Quentin says, "and I know you must have questions. I promise we'll talk soon. But it's late, and you've had a long trip. Get some rest, and know you're safe here."

The trouble with people telling you you're safe, Bastian thinks, is that it only makes you feel less safe. "Sure," he says, since Quentin seems to be expecting an answer.

Tom takes Bastian and Chloe down a dimly lit tunnel not unlike a compound's residential floor. There are doors on either side, all closed. Everything looks clean, if minimal—this place is clearly more about function than form. A little more natural-looking than a compound, given that everything is carved out of stone rather than concrete (an asset's power, maybe?), but it has some of the same kinds of generators and wires tucked into corners that Bastian remembers from Laurel's compound. He can't help but wonder how Quentin and his people managed to get even this rudimentary level of technology out here without being seen.

Unless, of course, they had a way to keep hidden. After all, what is the dead zone if not evidence that they had some sort of compound technology to create it? A way to cover their tracks, so that the only remaining evidence of their existence consisted of vague notes in mostly redacted reports and a collection of inaccurate forest maps?

Except that was fifty years ago. Which would make Quentin a *lot* older than he looks.

As they take a turn, Bastian touches Chloe's arm. She starts, then glances at him.

"You're tracking all right?" he asks in a low voice.

"Yes. Why?"

"You need to be able to get yourself out of here, if it comes to that."

Her eyes widen. "Do you think it's dangerous?"

Yes. "I don't know. But if you need to get out, do it. Leave me and James if you have to."

"No."

Bastian frowns and opens his mouth to give the proper retort, but she doesn't let him even start on it. "I told Laurel I'd make sure we all come home," she says, like that settles it.

"Here we are," Tom says, stopping in front of two doors. "One for each of you. I'm sure Quentin will want to speak with you tomorrow, but for now, please make yourselves comfortable. Someone will come get you when it's time."

Bastian doesn't like the dullness around Tom's emotions. He's not completely without them—the calm-passive-hospitable is definitely there—but it's muted. A bit like when Bastian was first trying to feel through Henry's negation field, and everything had a thick fog around it. This doesn't feel like a natural output of an asset's power, though; it's more like someone's turned down the volume on the emotions. Or stopped them from existing in the first place.

Like the crime scene, Bastian thinks. Like the emotions have been sucked out before they could fully manifest. Makes it harder to figure out emotional motivations or likely next moves.

Which is the excuse Bastian decides to use for why it comes as a surprise when, a moment after entering his room, he realizes Tom's locked him in.

***

It doesn't take long to get the gist of the layout: a small bed with threadbare sheets that are a step up from the ones in the jail block back in the compound, but only just; a beat-up wooden chest for belongings, currently empty; a light bulb hanging from the ceiling, wired awkwardly enough that Bastian's surprised it's getting any power at all. No windows, no adjoining rooms, no bathroom (that last could get awkward if they decide to keep him locked up too long).

He drops his bag on top of the chest and paces the room a few thousand times. When it turns out pacing isn't making the time go any faster, he sits down on the bed, lets out a loud sigh, and decides to take the most comprehensive empathic tour he can of this place.

Chloe is easy enough to feel through the wall. Her anxious-worried-confused stays active for a long while, but it begins to fade as she finally drops off to sleep. He lets it go after he's sure she's all right; no need to intrude.

To his surprise, most of the other rooms seem to be empty. He tries to pinpoint anything unusual about the few emotions he can sense in this part of the sanctuary, but they're all too indistinct to determine much. A little calm-peaceful-sleepy here and there, but nothing that tells him anything about whoever's feeling it. The weirdest thing is that all of the emotions seem to have the same signature—no differentiation by individual. The unnatural sameness makes Bastian's skin crawl.

He searches for James and Quentin, even though he knows he won't be able to feel either of them. Whereas Tom and Dana and the other threads of emotions he's felt so far have been muted, it's not the same as James and Quentin. Muting something implies that it's still there, just quieted. For James and Quentin, the emotions don't exist at all. They wear the right facial expressions, but there's nothing behind them.

Bastian remembers the first time he felt Henry's negation. It was a sudden sense of *nothing* that was alarming—and interesting—because it was different. Not a threat, exactly, but not what he was expecting. It was the first time Bastian had ever experienced the calm, peaceful silence of not having to feel everything at full blast for once.

(Bad idea, don't think about Henry or his laugh or the crinkle-around-the-eye thing or how it feels to wake up next to him or the way he's probably fighting to keep the compound together right now, and Bastian just left him to it—)

Bastian makes an irritated noise in the back of his throat and tries to quiet his mind enough that he can feel out even more. Maybe there's something he missed . . .

The sharp smack of the headache almost makes him miss the fact that he's started bleeding profusely from his nose.

Keeping up a steady stream of swearing, Bastian flails for his bag, trying to staunch the blood with a sleeve while using his free hand to search for something better. There isn't anything much other than a few bandages and the rest of his clothes. And his bottle of painkillers, which is nearly empty.

It'll have to do.

He tries to balance pinching the bridge of his nose, using an extra shirt to keep from bleeding everywhere, and downing the rest of the pills. Then he curls up in a tight ball and waits for something to work.

In the meantime, although he knows it won't help with the pain, he sets about strengthening his shield. At least it gives him something to focus on that isn't how pathetic and wretched he feels.

He's not sure how long he stays there, trying to remember to breathe and keeping his attention on the shield and nothing else. He thinks he might be dozing off sporadically, but never long enough to feel like he's actually slept. Every time he comes back to himself, he shoves all of his energy into the shield again. He definitely doesn't think about how the painkillers are having no effect whatsoever.

With the pain in his head, his bleeding nose, and his grim determination to pretend that shoring up his shield is going to help, he doesn't feel the other presence in his mind until it does the equivalent of clearing its throat.

Hi! Laurel says brightly enough to make him cringe. *I thought I'd just check in and—wait. What's wrong? Tell me right now.*

"Nothing," Bastian says immediately. "When did you decide to use this link thing again?" He knows he won't be able to hide his relief that it's her and not—well, it has to have been Quentin in his head those other times, right? That's why his voice is so familiar. But it makes no sense because Bastian felt emotions through the link—emotions Quentin doesn't have. And how could Quentin have made the connection in the first place? The only reason Laurel can do it is because she was spliced with Bastian's blood.

I decided to use it when you went on an adventure without me, and Henry said you couldn't bring along a phone because we couldn't risk anyone tracing the tech. Anyway, whatever's bothering you doesn't feel like nothing. 'Fess up or else!

"It's nothing you can help with," Bastian amends. "Why are you awake?" He's not sure what time it is, but it feels very late. Or very early.

(hesitation-anxiety-determination) *I'm an extremely busy person doing extremely important things at—um—very unusual hours. Anyway, let's talk about you. Did you find the healer yet?*

"Yes. Maybe. It's complicated." He frowns. "Why are you lying about—?"

Good! So you and James are all fixed up now?

"I don't—"

Because I'm thinking maybe you shouldn't come back right away.

"Wait, what? Why?"

I bet the forest would let you stay for a while. Oh, you could go to the clearing! James might like that. Unless you've already killed him, but I know you haven't because I made it very clear how unacceptable that would be.

Bastian rolls his eyes and tries to ignore the slight lurch of dizziness that produces. "He was alive the last time I saw him."

What do you mean, the last time you saw him? Did you leave him in the forest somewhere? I told Chloe not to let you two be stupid!

"We're all fine, Laurel. Tell me what's happening at the compound."

It's nothing. I mean, I had a really weird training presentation yesterday, and Senator Donnigan was—

Something in their connection shudders to a stop as her attention is abruptly pulled away. Bastian feels her spike of alarm but can't figure out where she's directing it. "Laurel?"

I have to go now; there's someone at the door. Listen. Don't come back to the compound yet, all right? I really think it's better if you don't.

"Laurel—" But he can feel that she's gone.

He stays curled up on top of the bed for some indeterminate amount of time before a sound drags him out of his stupor: knocking, and then the turning of a lock.

Bastian gets carefully to his feet, noting that the bleeding seems to have stopped. His headache has gone down to manageable levels of pain, too—at least for the moment.

The door opens, and Tom sticks his head in. "Good morning. I apologize for bothering you so early, but Quentin wanted to speak with you before break-fast." He gets a good look at Bastian's face and frowns. "Are you all right? Do you need a healer?"

Bastian realizes he's got a bit of blood on his collar, and his extra shirt is lying on the bed looking a little redder than it should. "I'm fine," he says, trying to ignore how thick and congested his voice sounds. And the way Tom is wearing the right facial expression for worried-sympathetic-concerned, but the feelings are vague enough to be non-existent.

Then he registers what Tom just said. "Healer?"

"Yes. Sandra has a clinic in Tunnel 3. She's healed all of us at least once since we've been here."

"She's a doctor?"

"Maybe she was at some point—that's her story to tell. I believe she came here when she realized she didn't need medicine to do her job."

That answers the question of what sort of people inhabit the sanctuary, then. "You mean she's an asset."

Tom frowns again. "We don't use that word here, but yes. We all are."

Because of course they all are. That must be what Quentin meant by calling this place a sanctuary: It's where assets on the run come to find safety. And given that there's no record of it anywhere that Bastian's ever seen, they've been doing a damned good job of staying hidden, despite being so close to a compound. Whatever they did to set up the dead zone in the forest is working really well.

"Take me to Quentin," Bastian says.

***

Quentin is sitting on a pillow on the floor, legs crossed, like a spiritual leader about to give a lecture. Bastian notices his turnout isn't so great, though: There's no one else in the room until Bastian and Tom enter.

"Good morning," Quentin says, smiling at them. "Sleep well?"

"Yes, thank you," Tom says. Bastian doesn't say anything.

Quentin takes a good look at him, eyes lingering on Bastian's bloody collar. The smile slowly drops off his face. "You'd better come sit down."

To Bastian's surprise, Tom comes with him and sits a few feet away, also cross-legged.

"You're nervous," Quentin says as Bastian sits down. "Don't be."

"Are you going to explain everything now?" Bastian asks. "Like what this place is and how you've hidden it from the compound for so long?"

Quentin is smiling again. "You're so good at reading other people's emotions, but not your own. I can help with that, too. But let's start with the most important part: You're dying."

"It's just a bloody nose."

"And the pain, right? It's always there now, isn't it? Sometimes you can ignore it or push past it, but last night . . . not so much."

Bastian knows it's pointless to try to strengthen his shield; it's already as firm as he can make it. Even so, it feels like Quentin is reading him somehow. Only Bastian can't pinpoint exactly what he's reading or how he's doing it. He has to be an asset, but what kind? It's almost like—

"I didn't see any cameras in my room," Bastian says slowly. "You've got some other way to spy on your guests? Bit of a voyeur?"

"You know it wasn't cameras, Bastian. Would a camera tell me that you were communicating with someone outside of the sanctuary earlier this morning? And I don't mean you called or texted."

Valentine's compound tech never caught the empath link, despite its other ways of monitoring asset powers. And Bastian's never heard of an asset whose power is to eavesdrop. Not on empath-based communication, anyway. The only kind of person who might be able to overhear something based on an empath's power would be—

Bastian narrows his eyes. "There aren't any more empaths."

"What about John Doe?"

"He wasn't—How do you know about him?"

Quentin sighs. "We found him in the forest last year when he was looking for the clearing. We tried to help him, convince him to come with us. But he was . . . resistant."

"So you just left him there. Where he could come and go and kill more people whenever he wanted."

"You have to understand, Bastian. This place is a safe house for people like us. We need to be careful about letting others know we exist. When John Doe made it clear that he had no intention of accepting our help, we weren't about to force him."

"But he'd seen you. He could've told someone."

"He wouldn't have remembered enough to tell anyone, even if he'd wanted to."

Bastian stares at him. "You didn't force him back here, but you erased his memory."

"*I* didn't. But we had an erasi guest at the time who was happy to—"

"Mess with his memory. On your orders. You know he'd already had his memories tampered with, right? And you just—" Bastian pauses. "Is that how you found out so much about the compound? By rooting around in his head?"

Quentin smiles slightly. "Yes. And no. I'm very familiar with your compound for a variety of reasons."

"Then you know that hiding is pointless now. Things have changed. You're not in danger of being locked up and experimented on anymore."

"Are you sure about that? What about the Compound Council? What about the rest of the Compound Network? I applaud the attempts at change, and I truly hope you're able to make a difference. But for now, people who have escaped that life have to be cautious. Frankly, I'm surprised you're involved at all, after what they did to you."

Clearly, Kent and the hackers have more of a security problem than just letting a few encrypted files sneak in. "I think this is the part where you tell me why you know so much about everything."

Quentin's smile widens. "Have you considered that I might just be very smart?"

"No."

The smile becomes a laugh. "I'm sure you realize there's only one way I could've contacted you in the compound. And I'm sure you *also* realize that not everything Valentine told you was true. After all, how could she have been telling the truth about you being the only empath if she knew John Doe existed?"

"He was an experiment made with my blood. Not a real empath. The last natural empath manifested over two hundred years ago." Bastian raises his eyebrows. "You've aged well."

"Thanks."

"You're not serious."

"I'd ask you to read me and see if I'm lying, but I know you can't right now. At least, not without hurting yourself. Because, as I mentioned earlier, you're dying." Quentin's face grows thoughtful. "You've lasted longer without intervention than I did. It's been interesting to watch."

Well, that's not creepy. "Are you going to tell me how you've been spying on the compound?"

"Yes. But not now. I think we have more important things to discuss, don't you?"

"Like how you've managed to live for over two hundred years?"

Quentin leans forward, hands on his thighs. If it weren't for the blankness where his emotions are, he might almost be excited. "Would you like me to save your life?" he asks.

Bastian knows what he's supposed to say. What Laurel and Henry would want him to say. After all, this was the point of everything, right? To come find this healer and let him heal. Except clearly Quentin is hiding things, and Bastian isn't sure how he's supposed to trust someone he can't feel.

"That depends," he says after a moment. "How are you going to do it?"

Quentin leans back and lets out a long, quiet breath, his eyes never leaving Bastian's face. Without consciously intending to, Bastian feels out toward him, trying to get a read. It's useless, of course; even if Quentin didn't have the odd nothingness all over him, he'd still have what feels like an impenetrable shield—one of the strongest Bastian's ever felt.

"Let me try to explain," Quentin says. "Then, if you decide you want to live, I'll show you how."

"Why?"

Quentin blinks. "Why what?"

"Why would you help me?"

Quentin looks taken aback for a split second. Then his small, increasingly unnerving smile pops back into place. "I help people, Bastian. I didn't always, of course. When I was younger, I was a lot like you: angry, distrustful, misanthropic. When you feel everything all the time, it becomes a burden, doesn't it? Like people are shoving their emotions at you without even thinking about it, and all you can do is build up your shield and wait for the pain to stop. Only it doesn't. So all the horrible things in the world—fear, despair, fury—it all gets stuck in your head. And you can never get it out. Sometimes you can't even separate what someone else is feeling from what you're feeling. The only thing that takes the edge off the pain is deciding you're not going to feel anything at all."

Bastian swallows. "And?"

"And all that feeling becomes not just a psychological burden, but a physical one. Any asset's power has an effect on their brain chemistry, though the compounds haven't figured out precisely how it all works. But for an empath, it's too much. The power is too big. The brain can't handle the energetic flow, so what you experience emotionally begins to affect you physically. Your body starts attacking itself, trying to get away from it. Eventually, you self-destruct."

"You didn't."

"Yes. I managed to reverse the effects of my own power. I didn't realize what I'd done at first, but once I did, it got easier and easier to do, and I knew it was the answer."

Quentin is looking at him intently, like he's making mental notes about Bastian's posture, his clothes, the expression on his face, recording it for something. It reminds Bastian of the way Wright looked at him. Like he was an experiment. A toy. A curiosity. It takes every ounce of strength Bastian has left to keep himself from shuddering.

"What was it like when you first did it?" Quentin asks. "I always wanted to see it from someone else's perspective."

"When I did what?"

"Took someone's energy."

Bastian frowns. "I've never done something like that."

Quentin smiles. "You don't know, do you? Of course you don't; there wasn't anyone to explain. I didn't understand at first, either. I just knew I was dying, and I knew I had to escape the compound before it happened. There was an officer guarding the experimentation room, and I just . . . *pushed*. I thought I was planting a feeling, an idea, but it was more than that. She opened the door for me, but she had this glassy look in her eyes. I always wondered what happened to her."

(Snyder's face during the interrogation, the first one after Bastian's power started to change; the dead look and confusion that later became madness in the jail block when Bastian saw him again; the knowledge that he'd done it before, that so many of the suspects he interrogated under Valentine's orders became mindless and died rather than going to the authorities like Valentine said they did; the way John Doe took Bastian's energy to attack the others in the forest, leeching it while Bastian lay on the ground, unable to stop it—)

"Now you remember," Quentin says quietly. "It's happened before, probably without you realizing what it was. But you felt better for a while, right? I mean, after the initial exertion faded. It wasn't until you stopped doing it that everything went downhill."

Bastian hasn't tried that level of read since last year, it's true. Nothing that involved that kind of manipulation of someone else's feelings. But he'd never—

"The problem," Quentin continues, "is figuring out how to keep that energy rather than letting it dissipate."

"Emotions aren't the same thing as energy." Bastian's mouth is dry, and his head is starting to throb again.

"Aren't they? Emotions drive us to action, color how we see the world, what choices we make. They have the power to completely change our thoughts and how we see ourselves. Scientists may not agree on precisely what emotions are, but there's no doubt that they affect us all. And that effect—that energy—is what can save you."

"You're saying . . . what? I need to steal someone else's energy to live?"

Quentin looks at him and says nothing.

Bastian laughs. "That's ridiculous. It's not how empathy works, for one thing. You don't go around sucking people's souls out."

"Just like you don't go around attacking people with emotions?" Quentin pauses. "It's interesting that you associate emotions with the soul. If we had time for a philosophical debate—"

"Look, I get that there are parts of an empath's power that we don't understand yet. The emotional attacks were new, and not just to me. But this idea of stealing energy—"

"It's not stealing if it's offered freely." Quentin nods to Tom. "Now, strictly speaking, you can do it with anyone, since everyone has emotions. But I've found that taking the energy of someone with powers lasts quite a bit longer. Not forever, of course, but . . ."

"You mean I'd have to keep doing it."

"Yes." Quentin pauses, then adds, "It's unfortunate that it requires that level of effort, but I think you'll agree—"

"How many?"

"Excuse me?"

Bastian fights to keep his voice level. "How many people have you done this to? You know it kills them, right?"

Quentin's eyes go wide. "You think it—? Oh, no! Not at all! Not once you understand how it works. People regenerate their energy over time, so what we take is replaced. In the meantime, it merely reduces the amount of emotional energy in the body."

"So they act like they don't have any emotions," Bastian says slowly. "You can't read them. Like James."

"They *act* like they don't have emotions because they don't. They can *mimic* emotions, of course; their bodies remember what to do physically. But until the energy regenerates, they don't experience anything that might be considered a genuine emotion."

Bastian feels sick. Not a good combination with the headache and his testy nose.

"It's quite relaxing, actually," Quentin continues. "Like getting a day off from the worst of the world. I think that's why Tom and the others offered."

"Did James offer?"

"Yes. Although his role is a bit more complicated than that. You asked how I know what's been happening at the compound? James has been instrumental in making that possible."

"You mean he's been spying for you."

"Not spying," Quentin says. "Not precisely, anyway. James did provide me with information throughout his stay at the compound, although he won't remember that he did. And, perhaps more importantly, he served as an anchor for the empath link I used to contact you."

"James said he didn't get the ability to form an empath link from the experiments with my blood. And what do you mean, he won't remember? Just how much did you mess with his head, anyway?"

"He may not be able to form a link himself, but he still has your blood in him—or whatever concoction the med techs made from your blood. I only needed a little extra boost to make the link work. They're harder when you don't have a previously established emotional attachment to the other person. I expect it'll be much easier now that we've spoken both through the link and in person. It was important to me that we forged that connection, and I hope you'll come to value it as much as I do." Quentin smiles. Like they're pals.

Bastian must be doing a crappy job of hiding the revulsion from his face because Quentin quickly sidesteps. "Through my connection with James, I could see what was happening in the compound. Not literally, of course, but being connected with his emotional energy meant I could experience much of what he did. And I could . . . persuade him to acquire information and share it with me."

"You were controlling him." That would explain Alexis's accusations about James sneaking into places he shouldn't have been. It might also explain how he knew about Bastian's health. All those times Laurel was allowing James to wander around the compound without supervision, he was collecting information to send to some weirdo in the forest. All because he was being manipulated—just like John Doe manipulated the senators into killing themselves last year.

Quentin frowns. "'Controlling' isn't the term I would use. James knew what his mission was, and he was glad to help us learn what we needed to learn about the compound."

"And you couldn't have just picked up a brochure somewhere? You really needed to go to all the effort of putting a sleeper agent on the inside?"

"I needed more information than just what I have in my own memory," Quentin says. "It's been quite some time since I was in the compound myself, after all."

He fixes Bastian with an intense look. "I take the safety of the sanctuary very seriously. The people here depend on me. We depend on each other. Remember when I told you that you've created a symbiotic system for yourself, one worth protecting? Well, the sanctuary is mine. I've spent years doing what I can to keep it safe and off of the compound's radar."

"The dead zone," Bastian says, trying to ignore the increasing pressure on his temples.

"Is that what you call it?" Quentin tips his head to one side as if considering. "That's quite atmospheric! Yes, I created that area years ago as a way of discouraging any compound scouts. When I escaped, I took an experimental aerosol with me that negated the problem quite nicely. And literally. Add to that a little encouragement for the officers to rework the maps, and the sanctuary has been left relatively undisturbed for nearly fifty years."

Negation? As in, Henry's sort of negation? But Henry wasn't alive fifty years ago, so how does that work? Did Quentin steal some sort of concoction that they used before they had a real negator's blood available?

Bastian shakes his head. "So when you said yesterday that James just wandered away from here, and you've been looking for him ever since . . ."

Quentin sighs. "A lie, but a necessary one. We needed James's help to gather information, but we also needed his memory to be unclear enough to protect the sanctuary until he was ready to return to us. Even if it's starting to come back now, we still need to be careful. An erasi's work can't be undone too quickly, or it will cause damage to the person whose memory has been erased."

Bastian thinks of the massive wall he felt in James's mind during that first questioning. "If it can be undone at all."

"Yes. James was aware of the risk he was taking. Even if he's forgotten that now."

Bastian's pain is edging toward high alert, pounding on both sides of his head in rhythmic pulses matching his heartbeat. Which is speeding up. Because he's an idiot. (It's not as bad as collapsing in the hallway, calm down, never mind what happened to James, not now—)

"I could feel you then," Bastian says, annoyed that his voice sounds a little wobbly. "I can't now, but when you were using the link . . . How did you . . . ?"

"Ah." Quentin looks down at his hands, then back up. "I think you know how much of a burden emotions can be. They make an empath exceptionally strong, but they also take their toll. Periodically, it's good to have a break."

He looks into Bastian's face like a doctor assessing a patient and frowns. "I know you still have questions, and I promise to explain more in time. But now I believe you have a decision to make."

Bastian's skin feels hot, and he's having trouble processing everything he's hearing. Sitting still is becoming more complicated, like he physically needs to be moving in order to perform the mental gymnastics required to file all of this information where it needs to go. Or maybe he just wants to bolt.

(All these assets hiding here in the caves, all these people somehow escaping the compounds or maybe even getting here as potentials, all this for over a hundred years—all being fed off of by a parasite who's apparently the world's oldest living empath, who might also be the only person who can—)

"I can help you, Bastian. If you'll let me." Quentin has moved closer and is leaning forward. He's too close, but Bastian can't seem to move away.

(He said they offered, he said it was all right if—)

Quentin says something quickly and quietly to Tom, whom Bastian vaguely realizes hasn't moved or spoken this entire time. Then he turns back to Bastian. "I know you don't trust me yet," he says gently, "but if you'll just let me show you, I can help you get back to the people who are waiting for you."

Bastian thinks of Laurel's fierce determination to fix everything, her aggressive cheerfulness, her willingness to believe in the goodness in people, no matter what. He thinks of Chloe's awkward but endearing need to help. Angelica's inexplicable decision to latch onto him. Kent, Sybil, and Michaels finding stupid excuses to come visit him when he was in the med bay.

And Henry.

Bastian closes his eyes against the growing dizziness and clenches a fist. There's no way to know what's happening at the compound right now, but if he collapses here, if he lets this thing take its course, he can't find out. He can't make sure the others get out of here safely. He can't make sure the assets he left in the compound are safe. He can't make sure Donnigan and Carter and the whole damned Council get what's coming to them.

(He can't make sure Henry keeps his promise to not do anything stupid, that Henry knows how important it is that he's still trying to change things, and that even though Bastian's never been good with people, he's desperate to figure it out where Henry's concerned, even if it makes him look like an idiot, so anything it takes has to be worth it—)

"Bastian. Please."

Bastian takes a shaky breath and opens his eyes. Then he takes off his gloves. "Show me."

Chapter 38

SYBIL DOESN'T EVEN look up from her screen when Henry gets to hacker ops. "Someone's trying to break into the maze," she says, her fingers flying across her keyboard.

It's two in the morning, and Henry is in no mood for riddles. "What does that mean? And why did you and Kent disappear?"

"We took extra measures to protect the compound system after"—she glances up at the security camera, then back at her screen—"I mean, as part of our latest updates. With the task force needing to get into our files, we figured we should do something to make that easier and more secure for them."

Henry narrows his eyes and wonders if that's supposed to be code for "we found a way to hide information from Donnigan and Alexis even though they now have full access to everything in the compound." Which means there might still be files they haven't seen. Like anything about the Fail-Safe Protocol. Not something Henry asked the hackers to do, and it'll probably come back to bite him in the ass, but it might also be what earned them the time to get into the hidden experimental area tonight.

"And now someone's trying to break in," Sybil continues, frowning at her screen.

Time's up, Henry thinks. "And?"

"And they're going to get through in about forty minutes. I thought you should know."

Mindful of the camera, Henry lets the appropriate amount of irritation take over. "You said you could keep our system secure."

"I know!" Sybil throws her hands up in an unusual display of frustration. "It was supposed to be unhackable! Someone would have to know everything about our system in order to be able to—" She stops.

Henry didn't realize the sinking feeling he's been having for the last few seconds could involve any more sinking. He makes a snap decision. "Show me how you're tracing it."

Sybil glances sideways at him. "Sir, with all due respect, you don't really know much about—"

"Show me." He leans over the back of her chair and peers at the computer screen.

"Um. Well . . ."

In this position, he blocks most of the security cameras' views. And now that he's audibly given a reason for them to be looking at the screen and talking together, it won't raise any flags when he surreptitiously reaches into his jacket pocket and turns on the jammer.

"—and here's where the firewall—"

"We have about fifteen minutes. Tell me what's actually going on."

Sybil clamps her mouth shut without turning her head toward him. After a moment, she says, "Kent designed the jammers. If it's his code that's trying to break down our security system—"

"I know. So keep your voice down. Where is he?"

"He stepped out to get some more tech. We thought we could make up a relay and get a visual on the undocumented area where you were. He didn't come back, and he's not responding on the comm channel."

"Did you track his ID?"

"He's turned it off. Or someone else has."

Henry frowns. "ID tracking chips are never turned off."

"And security feeds are never jammed." She hesitates, then adds, "This can't be him breaking the system, sir. I mean, it has to be because no one else could, but he wouldn't—"

"What if you were in danger? Or the compound was?"

Sybil shakes her head. "You think he's destroying the code we built together on someone else's orders? Even if that's true, who would do that? And why would he be taking so long? He could dismantle it in five minutes if he really wanted to."

Henry has a sneaking suspicion he knows exactly who would do that—or at least who's shown the most interest lately in getting as much compound information as they can. But she does have a point about how long it's taking. "Maybe he's trying to do what he's been told but also give you time to circumvent it. He likes to think he's tricky."

Sybil's reflection in the monitor smiles slightly. "Yeah, he does."

"So what can we do?"

"I can try to fight it, but honestly, it's only a matter of time before he gets through. Forty minutes, tops."

"There's nothing you can do to stop him?"

"Kent likes to think he's tricky because he *is* tricky. He's definitely the best hacker in the compound, anyway. Don't tell him I said that."

Henry looks intently at the screen, which is a jumble of letters and numbers he doesn't understand. The countdown clock in the bottom right-hand corner is pretty self-explanatory, though.

"All right, here's what we're going to do. You're going to stall whatever this is for as long as you can. If there's any way to move the files Emily Tezuka sent us to somewhere more secure, do that as well. I'm going to figure out where Kent is. If you need anything from me, get in touch on the most secure channel you can—the one Kent set up for us at the Hall, maybe, assuming that still fits the definition of 'secure.' I'm going to leave you the jammer as well, so make sure to recharge it when you need to."

"But sir—"

"We want it to look like you're pulling an all-nighter and just reported a false alarm. That explains why I'm in here and why you're staying this late."

"I can see if there's another jammer for you . . . ?"

"Better not. There are enough of them floating around already." He glances down at her. "Ready?"

She nods.

Henry flips the jammer switch and slides it onto the table in such a way that it's hidden from the cameras, as best as he can tell. Then he stands up straight and sighs loudly. "Look, I appreciate that you're trying to stay on top of things, but how about you do a full system check before calling me in the middle of the night for a false alarm?"

"Yes, sir." She adds just the right amount of frustration and contrition to her voice. "Sorry, sir."

"Don't apologize. Just get it right next time."

He walks out of hacker ops without looking back. When he's far enough down the hall, he switches frequencies on his comm. "Michaels? Sorry to bother you, but I need your help again. Meet me at my office in ten."

***

"Sir," Smith says carefully, "This really isn't my area. Or my team's. Maybe the black coats should . . . ?"

She still hesitates on possessive pronouns when she's talking about the team. Like she suspects he's going to demote himself back to captain and take them away from her. As ludicrous and impossible as that would be, Henry can't say he's never thought about it. Especially on bad days like this one.

"I need a small group on this," he tells her. "People I can trust. Consider it an in-house retrieval."

"Yes, sir." She's still dubious but obviously ready to get to work. "What do you need?"

He hands her a tablet with Kent's picture and all of his personal information. "Have your team canvas the compound and find him. I know you've worked together, but the others haven't, so make sure they have all the details they need from his file. And keep communications minimal, including within your team. If you think you've been compromised in any way, come back to this office immediately."

She scrolls through the file. "How long has Kent been missing?"

"A few hours. The time is less concerning than the fact that his ID chip has been turned off."

Smith looks up from the tablet. "You think he's in danger?"

"Possibly. He was in the middle of a job, and he's not the sort of person who skips out on work. Assuming he hasn't left the premises, we'll find him quickly enough. If he's not here, though, we need to know."

She's still looking incredulous, but she's also been an officer long enough to know when to focus on the mission parameters. "One team won't be enough to canvas the entire compound," she says. "And with the lowest levels still being rebuilt . . ."

"I know, but we have to do what we can with what we've got. Michaels and Laurel will coordinate additional manpower. For now, your team's job is to check all public areas, starting on Level 40 and working your way back up."

Smith frowns. "Additional manpower? You mean assets?"

"Yes."

"Wouldn't it be easier to bring in other officers? More reliable ones?"

The last thing Henry needs right now is to deal with Smith's distrust of assets. "This isn't open for discussion. We need to bring Kent in, and we need to do it in the least disruptive way possible. Get going."

"Yes, sir."

On the way out of the room, Smith passes Michaels coming in, and they exchange quick nods. Once Smith is gone, Michaels turns to Henry and begins, "I've let the assistant director know—"

Laurel barges through the door and around Michaels, who calmly closes it once she's in. "I can't believe you tried to run an entire secret operation without me!"

"Keep your voice down," Henry says sharply. Not that it'll matter. If Kent's already hacked through the security defenses in Henry's office, they could scream out seditious plots for all it would matter.

"Sorry," Laurel says more quietly.

"Did you get them?"

"I found a few assets who can help, yes. Two of them were about to sneak out of the teen dorm, so it turns out they're very eager to help, especially if it means they won't get in trouble. Don't worry; I plan to write up fifteen pages of angry tirade about breaking rules and make them read it at least seven times. Right after we finish breaking some rules here."

"Laurel—"

"Yes, I know it's dumb to tell you about assets breaking rules. But it helps us this time because Karl and Sam suggested we talk to Imogen, and she's a hyran, so she'll hear more than we would otherwise. Anyway, the point is, we're ready to search and destroy. Or is it search and help? Are we actually destroying anyone tonight?"

"First of all, it's morning. Second of all, no destroying."

"You're no fun."

"I'm extremely fun when one of my staff isn't missing."

Laurel purses her lips. "How worried do you think we should be?"

"I don't know." Henry sighs and runs a hand through his hair. "Someone would've caught him if he tried to leave the compound grounds, so he must still be here. That's probably a good sign. I just don't like the idea that our best digital security expert is breaking down his own system, and we can't find him to ask why he's doing it."

They're both quiet for a moment. Then Laurel says, "Senator Donnigan and Major Alexis can have whatever information they want now. So there's no reason for them to be blackmailing someone into getting into the system, right?"

"They requested an additional security sweep for any 'extraneous files,'" Henry reminds her. "If they think we've found a way to hold out on them, they might decide to just help themselves."

Laurel picks at a nail, then looks up at him. "Senator Donnigan seemed really upset about what happened in the garden, even though he's *completely fine*, whereas the trees are—" She swallows. "Anyway. Maybe being cranky made him want to go sneaking around without telling us."

"We need to find Kent," Henry says firmly.

Laurel nods but makes no effort to go. Instead, she crosses her arms over her chest. "You know, I told Bastian I'd look after you and make sure you don't get into trouble. He hugged me and everything, so now I have to do it. Even if you're not making it easy with all this sneaking around stuff."

Henry blinks. "He hugged you?"

"I know, right?"

"Did you get any of it on camera?"

"If anything got through the jammer, he'll have figured out a way to bribe Kent to get rid of it."

The mention of Kent's name makes their smiles fade.

"I'll go get the assets," Laurel says. "You want us to start on Level 1, right?"

"Right. And go easy on the residential areas. We don't want a bunch of alarmed compound staff taking to the halls."

"Got it." She turns and hurries out the door.

The room falls silent for a moment. Then, from the corner: "Sir?"

Henry jumps; he forgot Michaels was still there. "We're good for now," he tells her. "Let me know if any of them contact you."

"Yes, sir."

"And the . . . other thing you were working on for me? That's all taken care of?"

"Yes, sir. Everything is back in its place."

Meaning both Angelica and her read are safe. For now. "Good. Thank you."

Michaels nods and leaves the meeting room. Henry sits down in a chair and adjusts the volume on his earpiece. He's not likely to miss anything, given that he's told everyone to stay quiet as much as possible, but it gives him something to do.

There's a brief comment from Smith to her team, and then nothing. Now for the waiting.

Henry manages it for about two minutes before he sits up and switches to a different comm channel—the most secure one he knows of. "Sybil?"

"Busy." She adds after a slight pause, "Sir."

"He hasn't gotten in yet?"

"Not yet, but—damn, that took a whole month to set up, and he took it out in five minutes!"

Henry pinches the bridge of his nose. "You said he was going to pick up more tech. Where?"

"We've been tinkering with a few new prototypes in my room. As far as I can tell, that's where he was when his ID went offline."

"You took materials out of hacker ops and into your personal space?"

"Um . . ."

"Never mind. What level are you on? I'm sorry to intrude, but I'm going to need the override code for your room."

"He's not there anymore, sir. I set up a search algorithm as soon as I realized he was missing. It started there."

That gives Henry pause. "You had time to program and set a search algorithm, start protecting the security maze, and call me within the space of a few hours?"

He can practically see her bemused face. "Of course. I had a few more things in the works, but then it looked like the maze situation was getting bad, so I set everything else aside to focus on that. Was I wrong?"

"No. Not at all." He shakes his head. "I'd still like to check out your room and see if Kent left any evidence we can use. What level?"

"Seven." She's just about done giving him a long string of numbers for the override when there's a loud beep on her end.

"Sybil?"

"Two-eight-three," she finishes quickly. "I have to go; he's almost—how did he even—?"

Henry probably ought to be irritated by the way she abruptly cuts the connection, but he'd rather have her attention there than on him.

The smart thing would be to wait for any news from the teams already canvasing the compound rather than to follow up on what's probably a dead lead. But if he manages to find something, he could cut down the time it takes to locate Kent before the rest of the compound starts in on morning rounds. Because Smith was right: There's no way they'll be able to cover the entire compound fast enough.

But they have to do what they can. And Henry can't just sit around while other people do all the work.

Michaels's head pops up as he enters the main office area and heads for the door. "I'm going out," he tells her. "This office is off-limits to anyone except you and me until further notice. Understood?"

"Yes, sir."

Sybil's room is just a few halls over from Henry and Bastian's on Level 7. It takes him awhile to get the code into the ID reader (at least there's no blood required this time, he thinks, shuddering), but eventually, it opens.

Sybil's room isn't a suite, which means no kitchenette or open living space; just a bedroom, bathroom, and small study area. Better than an officer's room or a team's barracks, but not much room to spread out. Luckily, Sybil appears to be a minimalist: Her room is practically barren. The only immediate evidence that someone lives here is a huge computer monitor surrounded by several smaller ones on a desk in one corner. There are three keyboards that Henry can see, as well as a stack of books and a forest of cords snaking toward the wall.

The bedroom is more lived-in, although it's clear no one's slept in the bed for quite some time. The bedside table has a precariously stacked collection of books on coding languages and security protocols that don't exactly look like pleasant nighttime reading in Henry's opinion, but then, tech isn't really his area. There are a few silver rings lying near the books that look similar to the ones Sybil wears on every finger.

No sign of an ID or any evidence that Kent was here.

Henry takes a breath and goes through everything anyway.

A thorough search doesn't reveal much beyond what the cursory one did, although he does discover that Kent's earned himself a drawer in the bathroom. By the time Henry makes it back to the desk and its large collection of wires, it seems pretty clear that he's not accomplishing anything other than invading Sybil's privacy.

He grimaces and is about to stand up from where he's been crouching behind the desk when he catches sight of something attached to the underside of the chair. Frowning, he gets himself at the right angle to pull away a small metal tin. Whatever logo was on the top has faded beyond recognition, and it's dented a bit in the middle, which makes it hard to pry open the lid. His fingernails prevail, however, and he manages to get the lid off to find an archaic USB drive. No label or other identifying information, but having worked with Kent and Sybil long enough and seen their disdain for outdated tech, Henry knows they wouldn't bother to use something like this unless they were being overly cautious about having multiple backups. Like if they had some really important, highly classified documents they couldn't afford to lose. Even if their superior officer told them not to keep anything that might put them in danger.

Henry glares at the USB drive, starts to stick it in his jacket pocket, then pauses. Clearly, he's going to have to have a talk with Kent and Sybil about how to follow orders. And yet . . . If this is the data he thinks it is, it might be a good thing to have it stored somewhere no one else knows about. Dangerous if someone finds it, of course, but potentially useful to have something completely separate from the compound mainframe.

He glares at it for a moment longer, then puts it back into the tin and makes sure the tin is secured to the chair.

He finishes his search, which turns up exactly nothing that might tell him where Kent is. Sighing, he heads for the door and is barely through it before a skinny woman collides with him.

"Henry!" says a familiar voice from not far off. "Why were you in Sybil's room?"

Laurel is standing in the hall with several assets, including two identical boys with glowing hands. They take one look at the rank noted on Henry's jacket and snuff out their lights, sticking their hands behind their backs. They're completely in sync and completely failing to look innocent.

The woman who bumped into Henry has continued to move along slowly, her head tipped to one side. "There's someone a few halls over," she says in a low, melodious voice as she drifts by.

"There are lots of someones on this level. It's a residential floor." Henry's voice comes out less patiently and more sharply than he intended. He turns to Laurel. "Asset?"

"Imogen's the hyran I mentioned. She said she heard something weird coming from this area, so we skipped some of the upper floors to get here faster. We should probably hush and let her get on with it."

"Most people are quiet now," Imogen says, her long white-blonde hair waving back and forth as she tips her head in different directions. "But there's noise coming from over there. The kind of noise you make when you're trying to keep quiet. They're moving around and talking a lot. Something about"—she squints—"a maze?"

Laurel and Henry exchange a look.

"I'll save my questions about why you broke into Sybil's room for later," Laurel says. "Which way, Imogen?"

The woman starts off down the hall, and everyone else follows.

The route is familiar—so familiar, in fact, that Henry figures he really shouldn't be surprised when they stop in front of the suite he shares with Bastian. The one only he and Bastian should have access to.

Laurel frowns. "Why would—?"

"Stand back." Henry takes out his gun with one hand and his ID with the other.

"You're scaring the assets," Laurel says, glaring at him. Behind her, Imogen and the boys are poised like they're ready to scramble away the moment anyone moves too quickly.

"Around the corner," Henry tells them. "That's an order."

Her frown gets deeper, but she does as he says, taking the assets with her.

When the hall is clear, Henry holds his gun at the ready and taps his ID to open the door.

There are several compound security officers standing around the living area. Henry can't place any of the faces and finds himself wishing that his power was eidetic memory rather than negation—it'd be more useful for remembering the hundreds of compound personnel who might break into his suite.

At least they seem well-trained, given that they immediately go for their weapons when they see his gun.

"Hey! Don't disturb the maestro with any potential shooting. You dragged me here against my will, so I can only assume you were serious about wanting me to—"

Surrounded by laptops and tablets, Kent is sitting on the couch, the blue glow from the screens casting shadows on his face. Unlike the officers, he didn't even look up when Henry walked in. He does now, though, and his eyes widen. "Oh. Uh. Hello, Major."

"Kent. You all right?" The officers must have recognized him by now, but none of them are lowering their weapons, so Henry doesn't, either.

"Sort of. I mean, I'm not dead."

"Who are your friends?"

"They're—"

"Security," says a voice to Henry's left. "It seems I was justified in calling them."

Henry turns sharply and realizes his gun is now pointed at Senator Donnigan, who immediately holds his hands up. Henry notices a large scratch and some bruises on the side of his face. He also seems to be limping a bit.

"Goodness, Major! Pointing a gun at a representative of the people?"

"A representative of the people who somehow broke into my living quarters and is coercing my lead hacker into dismantling our security system."

Senator Donnigan raises his eyebrows. "Is that what you see here? I see a group of compound officers doing their duty after they've come upon their superior working with a hacker to hide information from an approved task force member. In the dead of night. In unmonitored personal quarters, where they won't be seen."

The black coats don't seem particularly concerned about any of these accusations, Henry notes. And he really doesn't recognize them. At all.

"And now that you've been discovered in the act, you're threatening me with bodily harm."

Henry lowers his gun. "I haven't—"

"Officers," Donnigan says, "I'm going to have to ask you to take the major into custody."

Chapter 39

THE MAN STANDING outside of Chloe's door clearly doesn't want to let Bastian in, which is very unfortunate for him, since Bastian has no intention of going back to his own room quietly.

"I'm sorry," the man says with just the right amount of vague apologetic-polite-embarrassed. "We respectfully ask that guests not mingle outside of—"

"You mean you don't want us conspiring without supervision. I get it. I also don't care."

"Well, that's a little—"

"Rude, I know. I've been told it's one of my better qualities. Now move."

"I'm afraid I can't do that. I'm also afraid I'm going to have to ask you to return to your room like Quentin asked."

He's *not* afraid, of course, because he's not really feeling much of anything. But he *is* starting to look ever-so-slightly alarmed. The discrepancy between body language and emotion doesn't give Bastian a headache, exactly—his headache was gone when he woke up in Quentin's room, and it hasn't shown any sign of returning—but he still shudders slightly before he can stop himself.

(He came to with no idea how long he was out, and Quentin looked calm and pleased, almost how Wright looked after an experiment that gave him the results he wanted, and Bastian knew he had to *get out now*, only Quentin shushed him like a wild animal he was trying to tame, told him to go back to his room, assured him Tom was fine—)

"Chloe?" Bastian calls. "You all right?"

"Yes." It's muffled, and it's followed up with a burst of confused-concerned-worried. She's holding it down pretty well, but it still stands out against the blandness of the guard and the other people in nearby tunnels.

(Don't think about what causes it, how Tom must be doing right now, lying in Sandra's clinic and thinking, feeling, seeing nothing because—) "You can't kick the door open or anything?"

"Um. I don't think so."

Bastian turns back to the man. "Sorry."

"What . . . ?"

It's easy to close his eyes and feel out, much easier than it should be. No more pain or blinding effort. He doesn't even have to think about the extra *push* into the man's mind. He slips in quickly and very carefully places a suggestion of ambivalence-calm-disinterest, a passing desire to hand over his key and move off down the hall to see if he can help with the setup for lunch . . .

For once, the woozy sickness in Bastian's stomach has nothing to do with the physical effects of using his power, so he forces himself to ignore it.

The man doesn't even look at Bastian as he hands over the key and wanders off down the hall.

"What happened?" Chloe asks as soon as he opens the door. "I didn't see you at breakfast, and no one would tell me anything before they locked me up again—"

"Get your bag. We're leaving." He pauses, then adds, "Although Laurel will kill us if we don't find James, so I guess we'd better do that first."

"He's gone," Chloe says. "I heard some people say he left yesterday."

Bastian frowns. "We just got here yesterday. Why would he leave?"

"I don't know. They seemed excited about it."

"Happy to see him go, probably," Bastian mutters. He tries not to think about everything Quentin told him and what that might mean for the current state of James's mind.

"Maybe." Chloe looks dubious.

"We'll keep an ear out for more on that, then. You ready?"

"Are you sure you want to leave? Did you . . . get what you needed?"

Bastian grimaces. "Sort of."

"That's good! I mean, it *is* good, isn't it?" She frowns. "You don't, um, look like you think it's good."

(Vague memories of Tom's deadened eyes as Sandra helped him out of the room and the way Quentin seemed to think Bastian had passed some sort of test; the pain receding as the energy entered his body, the way he felt sleepy but better, more whole, less fragile and useless—but it's only temporary, and if he wants to stay alive, he'll have to—)

"Let's get out of here," Bastian says.

Chloe shoulders her bag and doesn't say anything else.

The key works on Bastian's door, too, so he's able to get back in and quickly grab his own things. When he comes out of his room, Chloe points down the hall. "That's the fastest way out."

He narrows his eyes and feels out again. There's a bit of diffused content-busy-focused in that area, but far less than in the opposite direction, the one Bastian came from. No telling if there's an asset here in the sanctuary who could actually stop them from leaving, but he can't make out anyone feeling aggressive anywhere around them, at least.

Bastian doesn't quite follow the circuitous route Chloe takes them on, but it does a good job of keeping them away from other people, which is all that really matters. Eventually, they come back around to the area where they first entered, and Bastian is dismayed, if not surprised, to see more people lounging around. He and Chloe pause before entering.

"They'll notice if we just walk through, won't they?" Chloe shrugs her shoulder. "The bags."

She's right, of course. Bastian can't feel any curiosity or alarm right now, but if two strangers carrying duffel bags stroll in, it's going to cause a ruckus. "There's no way around?"

She shakes her head. "Too many people blocking the other paths."

There's nothing for it, then. "I've got this."

It would be easier if he only had to do one person at a time, but they don't have that luxury. At any moment, someone could decide to head this way—or someone could come up behind them. So he's going to have to do this quickly and all at once. And he'll have to think of multiple places to send people; it'll look odd if they all leave by the same tunnel.

And no matter what he does here, the amount of power he'll need to use will almost certainly alert Quentin.

"You need to shield," he tells Chloe. "Make it the strongest one you have. Keep close, but stay back. We'll need to move quickly."

"Um. You realize keeping close and staying back are kind of opposites, right?"

It would be easier with Henry, Bastian thinks. He could negate and protect Chloe, so there's no chance for Bastian to do yet another awful thing and get someone hurt. (Definitely don't think about this or the look on Henry's face when he finds out what Bastian's done—)

Bastian closes his eyes and focuses on dispersing the *push* of his power through the room, not letting it get too close to Chloe. He's never done it like this, trying to get people's emotions to change slowly rather than all at once, just a hint that they might like to do one thing and not something else. The bored-restless-curiosity to push a few people down a tunnel to meander a bit and see what's going on. The amused-excited-thoughtful that makes them want to grab a few friends and find someplace to chat. The irritated-combative-energetic to make the younger ones want to go practice their powers on each other. The concerned-worried-resigned to send a few adults after them.

Dividing his attention isn't so bad at first, but the more he does it, the more everything starts to ache. He pushes harder, but while some people start moving, others don't budge. He's starting to feel dizzy even with his eyes closed, so he tries to steady himself with a hand on the wall.

Bad idea. The helplessness and fear he felt coming in is worse here, even though he's wearing his gloves and working with a new reserve of energy. He manages to move his hand away before the nausea reaches the point of no return.

"Bastian?" Chloe says quietly. "Whatever you just did, it worked. They're all going away."

He's been clenching his teeth so hard, it takes a second before he can get his jaw working again. "We need to move. Come on."

Marching off with determination, Bastian learns, is less impressive when the first thing you do is stumble and nearly fall flat on your face.

Chloe grabs his arm and steadies him without saying anything. When he's less wobbly, she lets go. "Okay?"

He's in no shape to feel out with any real accuracy right now, but a cursory sweep says—shit.

"Hello," Quentin says, appearing from a tunnel to their left and coming to stand in front of them. "Were you thinking of leaving so soon?"

"Not as soon as James, apparently." Bastian shifts the weight of his bag and starts walking. After a brief hesitation, Chloe joins him.

Quentin smiles, making no effort to move out of their way. "Is that concern I feel from you? No, of course not. It's—"

Bastian bolsters his shield so quickly and decisively, he nearly knocks himself over again. He's spent most of his life trying to perfect his shield, but he's never come up with something this solid in seconds. He can practically feel Quentin smash his metaphorical face against it.

"Well," Quentin says, blinking several times. "I guess we can have the conversation about the importance of letting people in later."

"Where's James?" Bastian demands.

Quentin tips his head to one side thoughtfully. "I don't suppose you'd agree to stay here and rest for a while before I tell you?"

"Not a chance."

"Very well. He's gone to do something for me. For all of us."

"What the hell does that mean?"

Quentin gives him a very serious, almost painful look. "It means that it would be best if you didn't return to the compound right now."

(Laurel's thoughts through the empath link, her hesitation and not-quite-fear, like she could sense something bad was on the horizon—) "Why?"

"Because there are changes coming, and you need to be prepared for them. Racing off into the forest isn't going to help anyone. If you stay here, we can continue your recovery, and I can show you how to heal yourself safely whenever you need to." He smiles at Chloe. "I'm sure you'll both be quite comfortable. We have an excellent stew on Monday nights."

"What exactly is James doing, and what does it have to do with the compound?"

Quentin gazes at him silently, then says, "Sometimes, we need to break down the past in order to build the future."

(James getting that look in his eye when they were talking about the compound, about how no one was good enough to run it because it needed to be stopped, that every compound in existence should be burned to the ground—)

Bastian stares at Quentin. "What did you tell him to do?"

"Nothing. I merely planted the suggestion." Quentin's face changes, somehow. It's not showing emotions, exactly—whatever he did to himself to block them seems to still be there, and even if it weren't, his shield is probably too strong to let anything through. But his face darkens somehow, and while Bastian's still not sure he quite believes Quentin is over two hundred years old, he can't deny that there's something in there that's too much for a normal face to handle.

"I've seen what the Compound Network does to assets," Quentin says, voice quiet but sharp. "What it did—or tried to do—to everyone who comes here. You felt the emotions in the caves on your way in, right? The compounds did that to those people, and nothing I've tried can get their dread out of the walls. But I can't help everyone who needs help in this sanctuary. We need bigger change."

"James," Bastian says.

"In a lot of ways, he's been our strongest soldier, even if he doesn't remember most of it."

"This isn't a war."

"Isn't it?" Quentin gives him a penetrating look. "You grew up there. You know what Dr. Wright did to you. You know the obstacles you've faced with the Compound Council. Do you really think change can come any other way?"

He knows what Henry would say, and he opens his mouth to say it, except nothing comes out. Because all their work has only led to the committee taking over the compound and blaming Henry for everything. So how is that progress?

Quentin nods. "You see why we have to do whatever it takes."

"Are you going to hurt people?" Chloe asks. Her voice makes Bastian jump slightly; he almost forgot she was there.

Quentin seems to have forgotten for a moment, too. He blinks and looks over at her, putting on one of his calm, almost sad smiles. "I hope not. I hope everyone will cooperate and agree to work together toward our freedom from the system that's hurt us all for so long. But I suspect a certain amount of force might be necessary."

"There are assets at the compound," Chloe says, her voice timid but still surprisingly forceful. "You said you want to help the assets, so what about them?"

"We'll have to hope they make the right decision."

Something in Bastian's chest tightens.

(Every time on the gurney, every time on the table, whenever he protested—back when he still thought it would work—Wright would look at him with exasperation-irritation-anger, and then the words, sometimes alone and sometimes accompanied by needles or restraints to hold him down—*I know you'll make the right decision, Sebastian*—)

"We're going," Bastian says. "Get out of our way."

Quentin meets his gaze for several seconds, then steps aside. "You won't make it in time, I'm afraid. But please go ahead, if you think it's important. We'll be here to welcome you back when you're ready."

The sharp jolt of Bastian's own anger startles him, and he has to take a moment to stuff it down before it can show up on his face. He suddenly, desperately wants to hurt Quentin, wipe that careful approximation of smug benevolence off his stupid face.

(And he *could*, he knows what he's capable of, the kind of anger that he used as an attack in the forest a year ago, the kind that cuts through anything in its path—if he really wanted to, he could—)

But if Laurel's anxiety is anything to go by, and if James is already this far ahead of them on the way back to the compound, there really isn't any time to waste. Not if there's still a chance to keep people from getting hurt.

Bastian clenches his jaw and storms past Quentin, hearing Chloe close on his heels. He almost expects Quentin to follow them, but he doesn't.

They head back down the tunnel where they entered yesterday, the only noise a faint dripping from somewhere. Bastian keeps himself away from the walls and sticks to stony silence. He's not sure he could speak around his frustration and fear even if he wanted to.

Some indeterminate time later, they come out of the mouth of the cave.

"Is James really going to do something to the compound?" Chloe asks, her voice barely above a whisper.

"Probably." Bastian considers what Quentin said about planting a suggestion in James's mind. "Although I'm not sure it's entirely his choice. Either way, we still need to get back as fast as possible."

Chloe takes a breath and scans the area. "Okay," she says. "I know where to go."

Chapter 40

HENRY SUPPOSES HE ought to be glad they didn't cuff him to anything, but it's hard to feel thankful when he's spent most of the last twenty-four hours pacing the suite while a black coat who isn't a black coat refuses to let him out of sight. No access to his tablet or his comm or the outside world, and bathroom breaks have been awkward.

He's exhausted enough at this point that he's nodded off a few times, but it never sticks, in part because it's hard to sleep with a stranger staring at you from across the room, and in part because his brain keeps dredging up odd flashes of the hidden area on Level 49. He can almost remember conversations he overheard, med techs running around and muttering about oxygen levels and test results and deterioration rates . . . but it all blends together. How many times was he down there? What exactly did they do to him? And why did they think he needed to forget about it?

That one is easy, at least. If last year taught him anything, it's that Major Valentine was perfectly happy to keep him in the dark about pretty much everything, so it's no surprise that she had his memory regularly wiped. He and Bastian already assumed as much, given how she had Wright taking Henry's blood for the serum without him knowing.

But it was more than that, wasn't it? Because if Henry's shoddy memories and Emily Tezuka's files are any indication, he was being kept around for more than just blood donations. Somehow, he was supposed to be the backup plan for dealing with assets who got out of line. A fail-safe that could remove the powers of everyone in the compound at its commanding officer's whim. Never mind just keeping one cranky empath from running; he could keep anyone from running ever again.

Theoretically, he reminds himself. The book on negation didn't say exactly how to do it, only that it was possible. For all the times he offered to negate Bastian to save him from his own power, there was never any guarantee that Henry could actually do it.

But Major Valentine and General Carter clearly believed in the possibility and were prepared to do whatever it took to make it an option.

From his seat on the couch, Henry looks over at the not-a-black-coat, who's sitting at the kitchen table, eyes glued to his phone. Henry's learned two things about him so far: He only speaks in grunts, and he's always aware of everything going on around him even when he seems distracted. Henry is less interested in holding those things against him than he is the fact that the man is sitting at Bastian's place at the table. That, and he took Henry's gun.

There's a knock at the door, and Henry looks up to see Major Alexis entering with another probably-not-a-black-coat. Henry's guard goes over and confers with his compatriot for a moment in a low voice. Meanwhile, Alexis guides himself over to the kitchen chair where Grunty was and takes his seat. "Hello, Henry."

Henry sits up but doesn't respond.

After an awkward silence, Alexis calls to the officers, "Can we have a moment, please? I'll let you know when we're done."

Grunty clears his throat. "The senator said we're not supposed to leave the major alone." His voice is higher pitched than Henry would've expected.

Alexis smiles, a tiny bit of sternness around the edges. "I appreciate the senator's concerns about security, but he isn't actually a member of compound leadership. I'm sure he'll be happy to defer to my expertise."

The two guards glance at each other, then nod and walk out, letting the door close behind them.

Alexis sighs. "This isn't how I wanted to do this," he says quietly. "I hope you know that."

"How you wanted to do what?" Henry demands. "Bring unknown and potentially dangerous officers into the compound? Threaten my people? Remove me from office?"

"Those guards are members of the Hall's independent security force, and I agree that Senator Donnigan overstepped by inviting them here." Alexis makes a face. "He said he felt unsafe requesting further information from your hackers. I tried to explain—"

"He accused me of withholding information, and he did it by kidnapping my head hacker and breaking into my personal space to make it look like I was actively trying to destroy evidence."

"Donnigan is overly dramatic, I agree. But can you honestly say he's wrong about you withholding information?"

Henry can't, of course. So he doesn't say anything.

Alexis taps a finger against his cane. "Do you know why I was really sent here?"

"To spy and report back to the committee," Henry says. "You still owe me a copy of your last report, by the way."

"I was sent to report back to the committee, yes. And as I said at the time, I was sent to see if any of the new programs and procedures you were implementing could be used at other compounds." He pauses. "And I was sent to protect you."

Henry frowns. "Protect me? From what?"

"From the committee. And the Council." Alexis leans forward. "They know what you are, Henry. They've always known. And they have plans for you. Just as soon as they get enough proof."

Henry's mouth goes dry. "What proof? What are you talking about?"

"The Fail-Safe Protocol documents. Wright scattered most of the data just before he was arrested, but Carter and the Council hackers were able to trace some of it within the Compound Network systems. He needs as much data as possible to convince the rest of the Council to move forward with his plans. Once it's officially enacted, the protocol will change the future of the entire Compound Network. And you're standing in the way of that."

Of course it's stupid to play dumb at this point, but Henry honestly doesn't know what to say. He stares at Alexis for a moment before he finally manages, "If you knew about me all along—if you knew what they wanted—why didn't you say anything?"

Alexis's smile is smaller and sadder this time. "I told you. I wanted to protect you." He takes a breath, then adds, "So you need to tell me everything."

Henry blinks, then lets out a loud laugh. "Are you serious? You haven't even told me what you're supposedly protecting me from. The people who put me in charge of this compound with no intention of letting me actually do my job? The people who had Nunez's aide killed? The people who were secretly experimenting on me for years and made me forget about it?"

Alexis sighs. "Henry, I've been a teacher for longer than you've been alive and the commanding officer of a compound for nearly as long, and I can tell you with certainty that this job takes more than just hard work and goodwill. I meant it when I said I have faith in you and your abilities as an officer, but you have to understand that pleasantries and good intentions will only get you so far. I waited and hoped you'd figure out that by playing nice, you were putting your compound in danger. But you didn't, and now we're here."

He leans forward and hurries on before Henry can protest. "There will always be people like Carter and Donnigan, making demands and maneuvering resources for their own benefit. Being good and just means nothing to them. You have to—"

"What, be clairvoyant? I'm well aware of the need to keep Donnigan on a short leash, but how the hell was I supposed to know about Carter? He was there when Bastian and I gave testimony. When we showed him the evidence of everything Major Valentine and Dr. Wright did at Laurel's compound, he acted like he gave a damn, like he *hated* what he was hearing. Like he cared about the people whose rights had been violated."

"And then he allowed you to go against the Council's wishes and monitor John Doe's deterioration," Alexis reminds him. "Why do you suppose he did that?"

Henry frowns. "How do you know about—?"

"I'll tell you why. There's no telling what Valentine might have told John Doe, and Carter needed to make sure he didn't share anything that would be detrimental to Carter's plans—an overheard conversation, a misplaced file, whatever. The best Carter could do was use your hopes for Bastian as an excuse to monitor what, if anything, John Doe had to say before he died."

Henry suddenly wants to punch things. "It wasn't about collecting medical data to help the assets," he says. "Of course it wasn't; not if he's been playing us from the beginning. But if that's the case, why would he bother to remove Valentine and put us in power?"

"In my experience, General Carter makes whatever move most benefits him. Valentine was drawing attention to an unsanctioned experiment that would make the Compound Network look bad, if it ever got out. People died—powerful, prominent people. She had to be stopped, if only to contain the damage. And it gave Carter the power to choose her successor."

"What for? He could've just taken over from the beginning."

"You put a good face on it, Henry. You truly believed that this compound could change. That kind of idealism had the capacity to improve the way the Compound Network was perceived."

"I was a good PR opportunity, you mean," Henry spits.

Alexis shrugs. "Maybe. Or they thought they could control you. You've proved them wrong, and now they have to pivot. Perhaps if you'd been able to approach the job with a little more finesse and a little less naivete—"

"I'm not naive," Henry snaps. "I've been an officer in this compound for sixteen years. I understand that the asset program was fatally flawed and needed a massive overhaul. I've spent the last year reading every report and tracking down every detail about the people who have suffered and died here. I knew what we were up against."

"Clearly, you didn't," Alexis says carefully.

"Only because you and the others kept things from me! If we'd all worked together, we could've actually helped the assets who are relying on us. You know, like we all promised to do when we took our oaths and became officers."

"Change doesn't come so easily, Henry. And idealism only goes so far. Particularly in the Compound Network."

"Yeah. Particularly when people are too busy furthering their own agendas to bother doing their jobs. That's why we all have to admit that this compound— the entire Network—absolutely *needs* to change. And enacting that change is our responsibility. Funny thing: It's not so hard to do your damned job if you just get your head out of your own ass."

In the brief silence that follows his tirade, Henry supposes he ought to be embarrassed for yelling at a fellow officer, but he finds he doesn't care. Not anymore.

"Have you considered," Alexis says quietly, "that maybe it's too late for that?"

"Have *you* considered that your refusing to speak out is the reason at least one woman is dead?"

Alexis frowns. "Nunez's aide? That's hardly—"

"You didn't call out Carter or the Council for their actions because you figured it wasn't worth it, right? Because you figured that's just how things are? Being resigned to the way things are isn't a badge of honor. It's a choice you make to absolve yourself of guilt when things go wrong and you do nothing to fix it."

Alexis sets his mouth firmly, tapping his cane against the floor. "Where are the files with the details about the Fail-Safe Protocol?" he asks at length.

"I don't know."

"Have you had any contact with the assets you sent into the forest?"

"No."

"What were you doing before you came back to this suite yesterday?"

"Taking a walk."

Alexis taps his cane a few more times. Then he gets to his feet. "If you don't tell me the truth, I can't protect you," he says.

"I didn't ask you to." Henry crosses his arms over his chest. "Are we done?"

(He wants to ask Alexis if he knows about the secret area on Level 49, if that's why he was asking about it during dinner at the suite—or maybe he was just fishing to see if Henry and Bastian knew, to see if they were going to be a danger to Carter's big scheme, the one Alexis is somehow a part of, the one where people get hurt, and no one who claimed they were committed to helping actually does anything—)

Wordlessly, Alexis heads for the door. When he brushes past the couch where Henry is sitting, he says very quietly, "I wish you'd trust me. Believe it or not, I know what's best for—"

"I'm done letting someone else decide what's best for me. Or for the people who are my responsibility."

"They won't be your responsibility much longer," Alexis says. "Surely you can see that."

Henry swallows and says nothing.

"I don't know what their plans are for you just yet," Alexis continues, "but I'll do what I can when I find out. For what that's worth. It would be best if you cooperated until then. No grand, sweeping gestures of rebellion, if you please. Not if you want to stay alive."

Henry laughs humorlessly. "They won't kill me. They need me."

"They need your power. That's not the same thing."

Alexis moves past, goes to the door, and has the guards let him out before Henry can figure out what exactly he meant by that.

Chapter 41

LAUREL HAS GOTTEN antsy from being cooped up in her room under house arrest, particularly since no one's said anything about Henry for more than a day or bothered to answer her questions about why she, Imogen, and the boys were scooped up from the hallway and handily escorted away by black coats. Based on what she's overheard since then, Laurel thinks Imogen, Karl, and Sam have been locked up in their rooms as well, but she doesn't like that she doesn't know. She's supposed to know this stuff as assistant director of the asset program, but everyone's too busy being all shady to explain.

At least she managed to send Bastian a warning before everything went down. Of course, she didn't know then what she sort-of-doesn't-really know now, which is problematic.

She's finally gotten them to let her come out to the garden, although they were reluctant—probably because they assumed she'd plot as soon as their backs were turned. Which, to be fair, is exactly what she was planning to do. The white oaks are always up for plots to smack people around.

Except it's been hard to plot because they stuck her with a syringe full of serum before letting her go in. It didn't hurt, but the way it made the subtle hum of the plants around her go dim made her skin crawl.

(It feels like when she's inside too long, when there aren't any plants to talk to, when it's just stone and metal and cold, and she can feel herself withering and dying—)

Even if the plotting has to wait, it's good to be out of her room and sitting next to her pond, the gnarled trunk of the hornbeam against her back. Maybe if she can just relax for a few minutes, she can figure out what to do next . . .

The sudden hand on her arm—the one where she just got the shot—doesn't help with the whole relaxing thing at all.

"Quiet!" a voice hisses, and when Laurel turns, she sees that the hand on her arm is attached to a crouching figure hiding in the shadows. A crouching figure with a very familiar face.

"You need to come with me," James says.

"What are you doing here?" Laurel demands. "Where are Bastian and Chloe? How did you even get into the garden without them seeing?" She flicks a worried glance at the entryway and realizes that the guards are out of her line of sight.

"They'll be busy for a few minutes. Enough time for us to get out the back way. Come on." He tugs at her arm.

"Not until you tell me what's going on. I've spent a whole day cooped up with no one telling me anything, and I've decided I really don't like it. So start talking."

James sighs. "Can't you just trust me?"

"Trust comes with details. Talk. Also, don't think I didn't notice that you haven't answered my question about Bastian and Chloe."

"They're fine. Probably. Look, there are some big changes coming, and I can only protect you if you come with me right now." He pauses and gives her an odd, penetrating look. "You really don't remember, do you?"

"Remember what? Oh! Does this mean you got your memory back?"

"Yeah. And now there's something I need to do. I was hoping you'd do it with me, for old time's sake."

There's something about his face now—eager like a kid but also like a predator ready to pounce—that makes Laurel suddenly wish he weren't touching her. She can't seem to move away, though. "I don't understand. What do you want to do?"

"Change things. Make things better. Ugh, this would be so much easier if you'd just *remember*! Alice really had no idea what she was doing, messing around in our heads. A memor shouldn't try to be an erasi."

"What do you mean? She was—she was trying to help. We had to remember and write it down so that . . ." Laurel trails off, frowning.

"That's not all we did. You weren't cooperating, though, so we had to do most of it without you." His face scrunches up in annoyance; then something shifts, and he's giving her his most winning smile. "But you're smarter now, and you've been through so much. I know you'll want to help. If you'd just—"

(The dead officer on the floor and James promising it wouldn't come back on her; the compound in disarray and Xavier telling her to get lost; Alice's large blue eyes locking onto Laurel's, her hands reaching out—)

"Hey, are you listening to me? I said we need to go."

Laurel shakes her head. "Something's not right. Kent went missing yesterday, and then they locked me up, and then the black coats said Kent wasn't missing after all, and no one will tell me what happened to Henry—"

"Who *cares* about them, Laurel?"

"I do! You should, too, after everything they've tried to do for you. I'm glad you got your memory back, I really am, but it'd be rude to wander off right when something bad is happening."

"Something worse is *about* to happen." James grips her arm tighter—tight enough that she winces. "I'm trying to give you a way out, Laurel. Are you going to take it or not?"

She looks at him—at his earnest, slightly terrifying face—and swallows. "No."

There's a noise from the garden entryway, and Laurel looks over to find the black coats hurrying back in, heading right for her. She whips around to warn James, but he's already let go of her arm and disappeared into the shadows. And of course she can't ask the trees to track him right now.

"Recess is over," says the male black coat, slightly out of breath. "Get up. We're going back inside."

Laurel gets silently to her feet and brushes grass off of her pants. The black coat reaches out to take her arm, but she sidesteps him and marches out of the garden, not looking back.

***

Laurel spends a very long time not sleeping that night. She probably should've been productive and redone her nails or something, but she was too busy composing screeds to throw at whoever opened her door first. It's clearly a wasted effort, unfortunately, because as soon as her clock reads something resembling morning, one of her guards knocks loudly and says she has a meeting in ten minutes. This is news to Laurel, but at least it gets her out of her quarters.

They take her to a meeting room on Level 3. Not the large one where the liaison committee meets, but a smaller one with a rectangular table, uncomfortable chairs, and a projection screen. All of the chairs but one are full when Laurel gets there, mostly with people she doesn't know, but she sees a few familiar faces: Senator Donnigan, General Carter, Major Alexis, and—

"Henry!" Seated at the far side of the table, sandwiched between Carter on one side and Major Alexis on the other, he looks like he's had an even worse night than she has. Laurel decides she's going to march right over there to give Henry a hug and Carter a very large piece of her mind, but before she can do it, someone sticks a needle in her arm.

"Seriously?" Laurel snaps, trying to ignore the slight wooziness of the serum entering her bloodstream. She glares at the med tech who has just appeared

330

behind her. He hastily lets go of her arm as soon as the syringe is empty and backs away.

"Standard precautions," Carter says, probably because there's a snake plant in the corner behind him. "Sit down." He nods to the chair in front of Laurel, which would put her at the head of the table. Not, she suspects, because anyone wants to give her the seat of honor, but because it means everyone else can get a good look at her. Like she's a dangerous animal on display in a zoo.

Well. Just because she's expected to sit, doesn't mean she has to be graceful about it.

"Thank you for joining us, Laurel," Donnigan says as she flops down under the watchful eyes of the black coats who brought her in.

"It's Assistant Director, actually," Laurel reminds him.

"I'm afraid it isn't," Donnigan says. "Given our observations, Major Alexis and I have recommended, and the rest of the task force has agreed, that current compound leadership be temporarily disbanded while a full investigation is—"

"What recent events? Is this about Kent? Because that was—"

"Your involvement will become clear in a moment, I think, so there's no reason to waste time pretending ignorance." He gestures to the other people sitting at the table. "As you might recall, these senators make up the rest of our task force. We thought it would be beneficial to come together and review the events of the past few days so that we can decide how to present the facts to the full liaison committee, and from there, the Council. Before we do that, though, we have some questions for you."

Laurel sneaks a glance at Henry. There's a firm set to his jaw that she doesn't like, mostly because it implies he's imagining inflicting damage on other people. His knuckles are white where he's clenched his hands and set them on the table. She wonders what questions, if any, they've already asked him.

"All right," she says, giving Donnigan an unfriendly smile. "Since everyone's been so kind about locking me in my room and sticking needles in me and not telling me why you have the right to do any of that."

"You'll confine yourself to answering the senator's questions from here on out," Carter booms. He normally booms, of course—he seems incapable of speaking quietly—but there's an edge to it now, like he expects to be obeyed immediately, and there will be consequences if he isn't.

Laurel's eyes go to the snake plant behind General Cater. She can't ask right now if it's as displeased with the rudeness as she is, but she thinks maybe it's making an unamused face. Insofar as plants have faces. It hurts not to be able to commiserate, though.

Donnigan clears his throat and picks up a tablet from the table in front of him. "Perhaps you could start by telling us when Major Mortimer first asked you to lie for him."

Laurel stares at Donnigan. "What are you talking about?"

"The senator is getting ahead of himself," Major Alexis says. His calm tone doesn't quite match the tension in his shoulders. "Let's start with more recent events. You were found wandering the compound halls in the middle of the night with several young assets who were actively using their powers. Were you doing that on orders?"

"Yes."

"And what were those orders?"

"What does this have to do with lying for Henry?"

"Just answer the question," Carter growls.

Laurel resists the urge to stick her tongue out at him, but just barely. And mostly because Henry shakes his head slightly at her, which is Henry speak for "I already have a headache; please don't make it worse."

"We were looking for Kent," she tells Alexis. "I know I'm not supposed to ask questions, but is he all right? No one ever said."

"Yes," Donnigan says dismissively before Alexis can answer. "Mr. Turner is fine. Which begs the question: Why were you searching for him in the middle of the night?"

"Because he was missing. That's usually why you search for someone, right?"

Donnigan frowns. "Do you mean a staff member with access to highly classified information could become completely undetectable within the compound itself?"

"Well, Kent *is* very good at what he does. But I don't think he was completely undetectable because we detected him. We had to look for quite a while, but Imogen heard his voice, so we just followed, and—"

"You didn't have any idea beforehand where you might find him?" Major Alexis asks.

"No. If we did, he wouldn't really have been missing, would he?"

"And your superior officer? Did he have any idea where Kent might be?"

"I don't think so. Did you ask him? He's sitting right next to you."

"As I mentioned earlier, your role here is to answer the questions put to you, not ask them," Carter says sharply.

"Okay, but seriously, what does any of this have to do with—?"

"Let's talk about Major Mortimer for a moment," Senator Donnigan interrupts. "He has access to all of the asset program data, correct?"

"Yes."

"Including highly sensitive data?"

Laurel gives him the side-eye. "Yes. Why?"

Senator Donnigan taps his tablet, and a file appears on the projection screen. "Can you tell us what you see here?"

Laurel squints just to be sure, but it's pretty clear. "That's a roster of the assets currently in the program."

"Is anyone missing from this list? Anyone currently on the grounds?"

Oh. That's not good.

It's not a lie to say every asset in the program is on this list, right? Henry doesn't really count; he's never officially been added to the program. And the healer Bastian, James, and Chloe went to find doesn't really count, either. They may be assets, but they're not *assets*.

"Every asset I know of is on this list," she says at last, not letting herself even glance at Henry.

"To be clear. You know of no asset presently in the compound who isn't on that list?"

Laurel looks him straight in the eye. "That's correct."

She absolutely, positively, very much does *not* like the glint in Donnigan's eye as he looks back down at his tablet and swipes to another file. "You asked what this has to do with lying for the major? I'd like to explain by showing you some security footage. I should mention that it was in the process of being deleted when Mr. Turner was found in Major Mortimer's quarters the day before yesterday."

The others shift in their seats to be able to see the screen—all of them but Henry, who glares at the table and says nothing.

Laurel opens her mouth to protest—there's no way Kent would delete things the way Donnigan clearly means—but the video starts playing, and the words die in her throat.

It's footage of a nondescript compound hallway. There are a few officers walking up and down, but nothing much seems to be happening . . . until two very familiar figures come rapidly around the corner.

Henry is saying something, and Bastian looks like he's trying to ignore it. He's walking quickly, slightly ahead of Henry, until he suddenly stops. He makes a face, barely visible on the video, and reaches for the wall. Then he shudders and collapses to the floor.

Laurel swallows, clenching her fists in her lap. This must be from when Bastian had the fit that landed him in the med bay.

(She doesn't want to see this, the way he's curled up on the floor, obviously in pain, like the pain she felt not so long ago from the empath link, the pain she can't do anything about because it's his power trying to kill him, and if that healer can't fix him, he'll be just another one of her friends she couldn't save—)

In the video, Henry rushes to Bastian's side and crouches down next to him. "Bastian, what—?"

"D-don't—"

Donnigan pauses the recording and points to the bottom right-hand portion of the screen. "This is the interesting part. Pay attention to the numbers here."

Laurel considers telling him that he's an absolutely horrible human being for playing this security footage in front of an audience—in front of *Henry*—like they're watching a movie instead of witnessing someone suffering. But she doesn't have time to say anything before he's gotten the recording going again.

"Get the med techs here *now*," Henry is saying into his comm. "Yes, it's an emergency. Stop talking and *do it*." To a nearby officer, he says, "Find Laurel and send her to the med bay as well."

(It took her so long to get there, and even when she did, it was only with a last-ditch idea, and she still doesn't know if it worked, and even if it did, he'll come home to all of this—)

Bastian grabs Henry's jacket. "S-stop—"

Henry's voice, almost too quiet to hear, comes out soothing and earnest. "I'll be careful. Just—"

"S'not working."

He's negating, Laurel realizes with a sinking feeling. Or trying to. Which is dumb because they're in the middle of the hallway, and the cameras are on.

Senator Donnigan is pointing to the bottom of the screen again. "I'm told compound security systems have the capacity to track the use of asset powers within a certain range," he says. "Major Alexis, are you familiar with this feature?"

Alexis is tapping a finger gently on the table. "Yes. The newest Compound Network security cameras monitor and record the use of asset powers in public areas to varying degrees. It's meant to be a way of noting any potential conflicts and deescalating them before anyone gets hurt."

"Those numbers are large enough to indicate that an asset was acting in the hallway when that footage was taken," Carter says, leaning forward.

"Bastian is an asset," Laurel reminds them. Her eyes are back on the screen, where Henry is holding Bastian protectively and yelling something down the hall as the med techs arrive with a stretcher.

"True," Donnigan says. "But we have records of the former director's power signature to compare with this footage, and while he does appear to be using his power here, the reading is too intense for only one asset."

"There were other people nearby," Laurel tries. "Any of them could have—"

"Also true. But the additional signature is one we have on record, albeit in a highly classified group of files. Files that Mr. Turner was erasing when he was found in the major's suite."

"But why would he—?"

"Perhaps he was deleting the files because he was ordered to."

"He wasn't," Laurel says firmly.

"You don't know that," Donnigan says in a tone that implies she's a little girl who doesn't know any better.

"I know Henry," Laurel tells him. She waits for Major Alexis to say something—he's known Henry longer than she has, after all—but he stays silent.

"The major seemed reluctant to hand over the files we requested," Donnigan says. "And now we find that he was attempting to hold some back. Why do you think that is?"

It's not really a question, but she answers it anyway. "I mean, he's been bending over backward to do everything you all ask of him for months, so when you and Major Alexis decided that wasn't enough, I'm sure he just wanted to get you what you needed and not bother with anything irrelevant. Because that's what he does: He works really hard, and when people tell him that's not good enough, he works even harder to prove them wrong."

"Or," Donnigan says, that glint in his eye again, "he wanted to *appear* to be cooperating while giving himself enough time to order his hacker to destroy anything compromising. Such as evidence that he's an asset himself, and he's been lying about it. And asking his staff to lie for him, too."

Laurel wants to explain that Henry wasn't *lying*, exactly; he was just hiding some details because other things like saving the compound were more important for now. But that sounds pretty bad in her head, which means it'd probably sound pretty bad out loud, too. So she tries something else. "Did you ask him what was happening in his suite when he got there, or are you just assuming that was it?" A sudden thought occurs to her. "Or do you know because you were there?"

"Do I need to repeat my instructions regarding questions yet again?" Carter booms.

"But he wasn't asking questions for me to answer; he was just making rude assumptions!"

Senator Donnigan taps his tablet a few more times. The security footage of Henry and Bastian changes to a collection of crime scene photos. The colors are slightly off, like the images have been corrupted, but the basics are clear enough: Bodies lying in burned-out hallways, covered in shattered glass. Something dark smeared across the white floor of what looks like an experimentation room. An officer lying on the floor next to a gurney, her face mottled and green.

Laurel knows that face.

"These images are also from the batch of files that were in the process of being deleted by Mr. Turner," Donnigan says. "As far as we can tell, they were originally recovered from the decommissioned compound that was the subject of a Compound Council investigation last year. That investigation, as you might recall, led to the sentencing of Major Valentine and Dr. Wright, as well as the formation of our liaison committee. At the time, we believed that all relevant information had been given to the Council, but it turns out there was evidence missing. Incidentally, you'll remember that Major Mortimer and Director Lucas were the ones who provided that information."

Laurel tears her eyes away from the image of the dead officer. "Wait. Are you saying Henry and Bastian kept this from—?"

"It's horrible, isn't it?" Donnigan says to the others, ignoring her. "All that pain and suffering . . . However, the actual facts are different from what we were led to believe."

(The officer is lying dead on the ground, and James is looking at her like she's an experiment gone wrong, just like the look Dr. Wright gets when something doesn't go his way—but that's not how James is supposed to look; he's supposed to be clever and funny and conceited but not really, and now he turns to Laurel and shrugs and says, "Don't worry; we'll figure out a way to make it less obvious. Wright won't know. I'll talk to him, say it was an accident—")

"We're still validating the rest of the files," Donnigan is saying, "but it seems clear that the victims here were not the assets, as we originally thought. Rather, the assets rose up against the staff and murdered them. The destruction of the compound appears to be an unintended consequence of their actions."

(Standing in the hallway with the sirens and the fires and the screaming, all of her friends scattered every which way, the staff not even bothering to keep them in line anymore, and Xavier's voice, his eyes as he glares at her—"If you're not going to help, get lost, Pipsqueak"—)

"That's not true," Laurel hears herself say. "What about Vanessa? She died alone in that room after everything Dr. Wright did to her, and . . ." Her throat closes up.

"Are you sure about that?" Donnigan asks. "A moment ago, you were sure there were no unregistered assets in this compound, and yet we have evidence that Major Mortimer himself is an asset. How can we trust anything you have to say?"

"Because I was there!"

"Yes, you were. But you survived. And your firestarter friend did as well, with no charges brought against either of you. Why do you suppose that is?"

"Is that a question you want me to answer, or is it one of those questions you ask where the point is the misleading question itself and not the answer? I'm honestly having trouble keeping them straight at this point."

Donnigan jabs a finger at the screen. "This officer was poisoned not long before your compound was destroyed. According to forensics notes taken at the time, it was a unique, extremely deadly poison that would have killed her in seconds. There were twenty-one assets in the compound at that time, and only one of them had a power related to plants and fast-acting herbal concoctions."

Laurel stares at him. "You think I—?"

"I think you lied to protect the assets at your compound, who violently rebelled and senselessly killed the hardworking staff who spent years—"

"The hardworking staff who spent years torturing assets? Who beat us when we didn't do what we were told? Who did things to James that made his power go haywire and—?"

"I think it's clear that we don't really know what happened, and we can't trust you to tell the truth about it. Just like we can't trust you to tell the truth about what's been going on at this compound."

"What do you mean?" Laurel demands.

"I mean you knew that the major is an asset, and you said nothing. Just like you knew what really happened at your compound, and you said nothing about that, either. You've endangered the lives of hundreds of officers, staff, and assets by not revealing that you were a party to a crime."

"That's not—"

"And then you allowed the prime instigator of this horrific crime to leave this compound without any kind of oversight."

"If you mean James, he's with Bastian—" Oh. Except he isn't, is he? Laurel has no idea where he is or what he's doing. But she *does* know he's around here somewhere, and he said something big was coming, something he wanted to save her from . . .

Donnigan is looking disturbingly triumphant. "And now, we find that your silence has kept all of your coworkers and charges in the dark regarding the fact that their commanding officer is an asset who could destroy this entire compound."

"Henry would never destroy this compound! Haven't you been paying attention to anything we've been telling you? He's trying *fix* it! To *save* it!"

"By lying about his power? By putting his friends in positions that allow them to manipulate the information disseminated from this organization?"

"Well, that last part is just dumb and wrong, since the Council agreed to all of our appointments. As for the first part, there's nothing wrong with being an asset, you know. If he is one."

"That's debatable, given his power."

Because of course they know that, too, Laurel thinks, her heart sinking. If they've read the file fragments—even just a few of them—they probably know enough to piece together what the Fail-Safe Protocol is. What Henry is.

Donnigan looks around the table. "According to the files we managed to salvage before Mr. Turner destroyed them, Major Mortimer is a negator—a rare, never-before-documented asset with the power to negate other assets' powers, possibly permanently. As such, he is a danger to the liberty of every asset in this compound—even more so because he was willing to lie about it. I recommend that he and his entire staff be removed from office permanently."

Chapter 42

A NEW CONTINGENT of black coats is patrolling the Level 15 jail block, lingering at each intersection and at Prison Officer Templeton's desk. Henry's cell is too far away for him to see how she's doing right now, but whenever she makes one of her frequent trips over to his general area to "check on things," he can tell she's living in a perpetual state of nervous agitation. She's also been shooting him sympathetic glances behind the black coats' backs, and it makes him uncomfortable. It's like she knows just how monumentally screwed he is, and she's waiting for a chance to ask what he'd like for his last meal.

His questioning with the task force was about as awful as he expected, but the part where he had to sit and watch them do the same thing to Laurel was worse, especially Donnigan's finale. He certainly didn't need to relive the agonizing moments in the hallway where Bastian collapsed, either, but he wasn't really expecting his comfort to be the top agenda item on that sort of meeting.

He wasn't given the chance to ask how the hell Donnigan got into the suite and what he actually had Kent doing, not to mention why the Council resorted to poisoning an aide to keep information on a top secret project from getting out.

Poisoning. Like Laurel did to that officer.

Henry grimaces. Those images weren't part of any file fragment he saw, which means Donnigan must have found them somewhere else, or . . . what? Did Laurel know about them? She certainly seemed stricken when Donnigan played them on the big screen, but that doesn't mean it was the first time she'd seen them. Then again, hiding them doesn't sound at all like her.

He looks up at the sound of voices coming toward him: Templeton and—he cranes his neck a bit more—a black coat holding Laurel firmly by the arm. No one looks pleased about the situation, least of all the black coat guarding Henry's cell.

"What's going on?" Henry's black coat demands. "Why are you bringing this prisoner over here?"

"This is still my jail block, thank you," Templeton says, her face pinched into what can only be described as Stern Mom Mode. "I'll decide who goes in what cell." She nods her head at the one next to Henry and takes out her ring of keys.

The black coat restraining Laurel looks pained. "But—"

"I'm sure you have better things to do than quibble about housing arrangements. Put her in here."

"Should the prisoners be so close together?" the black coat asks dubiously, not letting go of Laurel's arm. In that moment, he looks awfully young.

Templeton puts a hand on her hip and raises an eyebrow. "Are you saying your fellow officer can't look after more than one prisoner at a time?"

The black coat looks quickly between Templeton and his coworker, clearly realizing he's put his foot in it. "Uh. No, ma'am."

"I thought not. In here, please. Then get back to your post."

Henry's at the wrong angle to see precisely how things go down, but he hears the door open and close. Templeton locks it and turns to the remaining black coat. "I trust there won't be any problems, Foster?"

Henry's black coat regards him for a moment, her facial expression unreadable. Then she turns back to Templeton. "I think we're good here."

Templeton nods. She catches Henry's eye and gives him something that looks an awful lot like a wink before going back down the hall.

There's a squeak of springs as Laurel sits down on the bed in her cell. The silence stretches out, but he can't think of anything to say.

Just as it's starting to get awkward, Laurel clears her throat. "Okay, this looks bad."

Henry lets out a humorless laugh. He half expects Foster to shush them, but she's stepped a few feet away, her back to their side of the block. Almost like she's purposefully giving them a little space to talk.

"But—I mean, it could be worse," Laurel continues. "Let's not forget that." When he doesn't respond, she says tentatively, "Henry?"

"Bad. Right. Listening."

He's not, really. Mostly, he's pacing and thinking about Bastian being in this cell last year and for years before that. He spent so much of his life locked up, just because he was a rare asset, someone Major Valentine needed to control as much as possible. Someone to experiment on and study like he was an interesting problem rather than a human being. Like Carter and the Council could decide to do all over again with the other assets, the people Henry was supposed to protect. Like they could decide to do with Henry himself.

"You're moping, aren't you?"

Henry rubs his eyes. "I think the situation warrants a little moping."

"No, it doesn't." Laurel taps on the wall. "There are people counting on us. Counting on you."

"I know," he snaps. "But it doesn't matter anymore, does it? We can't help anyone in here."

He doesn't mention the worst part: that he may not be able to do much of anything at all, once they decide what to do with him. Ship him off to the Council HQ medical facility for testing, maybe? They could stick him in the same room where John Doe withered away. Or maybe he'll go back into the hidden area of this compound, away from the other assets. After all, negators don't officially exist, so there's no precedent. They could do whatever they want.

"Don't be like that," Laurel says. "You have to keep your chin up. For one thing, it terrifies other people to see you walking around with your chin at a weird angle. Also, it's supposed to be good for you or something."

They fall silent for a while. Henry wants to ask about the security footage from Laurel's compound, but he can't quite figure out how to do it with a black coat potentially hanging onto their every word. "Laurel . . . About what Donnigan said . . ."

Laurel doesn't respond for a few very loaded moments. Then she says, "You know when you think you know things, only someone shows you that what you know isn't what you actually know, and now you don't know anymore?"

"Sorry, is that a question or just a grammatical massacre?"

"It's not a massacre! There are nouns and verbs and everything, and they're even in the right order. I think." She sighs. "I don't know what happened back then, but I know it was bad. And I know it wasn't what I thought it was."

"Did James know?"

"I—"

She's interrupted by the sound of a scuffle down the hall, and then shouting. Foster perks up and moves closer to Henry's cell, her hand reaching for the gun on her belt.

That's when the sirens start.

Henry claps his hands over his ears and moves quickly to the jail cell bars. "We're not going anywhere," he yells. "Go find out what's happening."

Foster is still hesitating when the younger black coat from earlier comes racing down the hall toward her. "Foster! Get over here!"

She glances at Henry once, then hurries away.

As soon as she's out of sight, Henry removes his hands from his ears, gritting his teeth against the noise, and starts searching the cell. Bastian once said he hid things in the cells where he was locked up. If something like that hairpin of his is still lying around . . .

"Henry?" Laurel's voice is barely audible over the howl of the sirens.

"Check your cell for anything we can use to get out of here," Henry calls. No sense in bothering to be coy, now that the black coats are all preoccupied.

"What?"

"A loose brick, a piece of metal, anything!"

"Don't you think this would be easier, Major?"

Henry jolts upright to find Templeton standing in front of his cell, holding up her keyring.

He frowns at her. "I can't ask you to—"

"I've made an executive decision based on the situation," she says, opening the door and waving him out. "Any minute now, some of those black coats are going to come back to escort the prisoners outside, per emergency protocol. It would be unfortunate if some of those prisoners escaped in the ruckus."

"Cameras," Henry says, keeping his voice as low as he can while still being heard over the sirens. It may not matter much now, but if anyone gets hold of the security footage in the aftermath of whatever this is, Templeton could find herself in serious trouble.

She doesn't seem particularly concerned, though. She puts a pair of cuffs on his wrists—nowhere near tight enough to actually close. "I'm taking you to the front end of the jail block to wait for security," she says. "You might get lost in the crowd after that."

"Crowd? What crowd?"

Templeton is opening Laurel's cell when the sirens abruptly go silent.

"Does that mean it's over?" Laurel asks, rubbing her ears.

"Maybe." Henry shakes his head in an attempt to clear it. "Sirens mean a security breach—and not the kind Kent or Sybil can deal with digitally. Someone must've entered the compound illegally. I suppose they could've caught whoever it is already, but—"

A stream of yelling comes suddenly from somewhere outside of the jail block. Then a sound Henry can't quite place: whooshing, like something being thrown. Impact. Then more yelling.

Then gunshots.

"Go." Templeton presses his own gun into his hand.

Henry gives her a lopsided smile. "You know this is the opposite of what a prison officer is supposed to do in an emergency, right?"

"You can certainly reprimand me later, Major. After I've locked down the jail block, and you've secured this facility."

"Thank you, Templeton."

"See that you don't get shot this time, young man. I won't be there to patch you up."

Henry and Laurel hurry away, while Templeton goes in the opposite direction to check on the rest of the prison area.

They ditch their cuffs in the hall, which turns out to be a total mess—far beyond anything Henry was expecting. Black coats and officers are running and shouting, moving in waves that make it clear which of them did well in training and which didn't. No one notices two escaping prisoners, and once Henry reaches the intersection with another hallway, he realizes why.

Dozens of assets are attacking dozens of officers. The armed officers ought to have the upper hand, but the assets are holding their own, covering each other with masses of wind, fire, ice, and psionic forces. As Henry watches, a magnetizer uses her power to pull the metal casing of an overhead light out of the ceiling and down toward an officer who barely manages to get out of the way in time.

"*Ezekiel!*" Laurel yells at a teenager hurrying past them. "What are you doing?"

"What's it look like?" Ezekiel calls back. His hands are crackling with electrical energy, which he shoots at a woman in a med bay uniform as she ducks around a corner.

"You can't just go around electrocuting people!"

"Sorry, Teach! New rules!" He laughs and disappears down another corridor.

Laurel looks at Henry and sputters, "He's not—I told him to—"

"Laurel—"

But she's taken off after the kid, and all Henry can do is follow.

At least the officers are using tranqs, he thinks as they rush through the crowds. And he knows exactly what kind of tranqs, too: the kind that knock the assets to the ground and make them unable to use their powers. Negation serum, just like the retrieval teams use.

A familiar face goes by, and Henry grabs her arm without even thinking. "Smith! Report!"

She turns toward him, surprised. "Major? What are you doing out of your cell?"

"Nice to see you, too. What's going on?"

Her face darkens instantly. "Mutiny."

"What are you talking about?"

Smith presses her lips together, throwing a quick glance at the mayhem behind her. "The assets are rebelling. No one knows how it started, but we're containing it. You should get back to your cell and leave it to us. If you go now, I won't report you to the black coats."

"The assets wouldn't just do this," Laurel says, suddenly at Henry's elbow. "You must have done something. What did you do?"

"Laurel." Henry turns back to Smith. "You have no idea what might've caused this?"

"I can't really discuss it with you. All you need to know is that we have things under control."

So much for showing deference to a superior officer. "Smith, I need you to—"

"Excuse me, but you're not in charge anymore—"

Henry almost doesn't hear the noise, and by the time he does, it's too late. The heat hits him in the face, even with Smith between him and the source. She cries out and stumbles into him, and he can see that the back of her shirt is on fire.

"Roll!" Henry says immediately, helping her to the ground.

She's taken orders from him for too long to do anything else on instinct. The flames go out quickly enough, and he takes off his jacket and wraps it around her to protect the wound. Then he reaches for the comm he doesn't have anymore to call for a med tech. Grimacing, he starts to look around for other options, but he's distracted by a shout from Laurel.

"James!"

She throws herself at him, and at first, Henry thinks she's trying to hug him. Then he realizes it's less of a hug and more of a body slam. Not that it does much; she's too willowy to put much weight behind it, and James is still holding a large flame in one hand.

"Get out of the way," he growls.

"Don't be stupid! What are you even trying to—?"

"I told you: Changes are coming."

"That doesn't—"

"Shut up, both of you," Henry says. "Smith needs a med tech."

James looks down at her. "She's going to need a lot more than that when I'm done. And so are you."

"Where are Bastian and Chloe?" Henry asks, tensing.

"You're not in any position to ask questions, Major," James says. He somehow makes the honorific sound like an insult.

Henry gets to his feet, drawing his gun as he does. "You realize that if anything's happened to either of them, I will personally shoot you, right?"

"Really? You'd kill an asset?"

"There are plenty of places to shoot someone where they'll be in excruciating pain but won't die."

"*Stop.*" Laurel is glaring back and forth between them. "No one is shooting or otherwise harming anyone else. Are we clear?"

James laughs—a slightly uneven, wobbly sound. He lowers the hand holding the fire. "I'm doing what needs to be done. We all are."

"You're *hurting people*," Laurel says. "Assets don't hurt people."

James stares at her, then laughs again. "Are you serious? How can you still not remember? They hurt us, we hurt them back. We all agreed. Even you did, at first."

She flinches like he struck her across the face. "I was wrong," she says after a pause, her voice small enough to nearly be lost in the ruckus around them. "We all were."

"No, we weren't. We would've taken them all out if Wright hadn't pushed the experiments too far and made me—" He swallows, looking lost for a split second before the simmering anger comes back. "Your empath friend and his stupid blood ruined everything."

"It wasn't his fault! They—"

"He should've fought back like we did. Like we are now."

"Is that what this is?" Henry asks. "You're fighting for your freedom?"

"Yes. We're taking this place down." James's eyes narrow. "You had a good run, pretending like you give a shit. But now it's time for something that'll actually work."

"This is what you were trying to tell me in the garden," Laurel says slowly. "You were warning me that you were going to do this. That you'd convinced the other assets to do this."

"Not a whole lot of convincing required, actually. We all know what happens to assets in a compound."

"Things are different now," Henry says, hearing how insufficient it sounds but not knowing what else to do. "Assets are here because they choose to be here. We're trying to—"

"You're failing." James sneers. "Did you really think anything was going to change just because you claim it's all better now? The Compound Council isn't going to suddenly decide we're people. Vanessa was right: They call us 'assets' because we're commodities. Investments. They bring us in, train us, then sell us to the highest bidder. Lucas was a tool for Valentine and the police, and who the hell knows what you are?"

James gives him an odd sort of grimace. "I bet you don't even know what they're going to do with you now, do you? Stick you like a pin cushion? Siphon off enough blood to kill you? You're so special, I bet they'll come up with something new, just for you."

Henry resists the urge to glance back at Smith. The rumors about the reasons for his incarceration are probably already rampant, so if she doesn't already know he's an asset, she will soon enough. They all will. Though that doesn't explain how James knows already—or why he seems to know some specifics.

"We've all been trying to help," Henry says carefully. "I know it's not enough. It may never be enough. But—"

"You're right," James agrees. "It isn't enough."

He turns to Laurel. "Last chance. Are you with us or not?"

Laurel looks at him and swallows. "There are good people in the Network," she says. "There are horrible people, too, but—"

"Don't be an idiot, Laurel. There aren't any good people."

"Not even you?"

Something flickers through James's expression too fast for Henry to read. Then he sighs loudly. "I don't know why I thought this would be any different than before. You're still a coward, Laurel. Your call, I guess; just don't expect me to cover for you poisoning people this time."

Laurel pales considerably. "I didn't—"

"That officer died because of you," James says, a terrible edge to his voice. "And there would have been more. Lots more. It would've been so much easier than what we ended up having to do. But you wouldn't make us more poison. Instead, you let me lie to Wright about it to keep you out of trouble, and he took it out on me instead in the next experiment, and . . ." He shakes his head. "Never mind. Time to decide who I'm gonna fry next."

"No one," Henry says.

He doesn't even have to think about it, to his surprise. It feels like breathing out, just a quick breath, and all the tension he's felt for the past months dissipates. He doesn't have to hold it in anymore. Even when he could stop worrying about negating in the suite, he always knew it was temporary, that he'd have to start hiding it again as soon as he left.

Now it doesn't matter anymore.

The fire in James's hand goes out. The shouting closest to them stops abruptly as the assets realize they can't use their powers anymore.

James blinks, staring at his empty palm. "Quentin told me, but I didn't think you'd actually—I didn't think you had the guts."

"And I didn't think you were stupid enough to try to kill the people who want to help you. So color us all surprised."

James looks around the hallway. "How far does it go? Not the whole compound, right? Maybe we should test your range."

He smiles, backs away a few steps, and then turns and bolts.

Instinctively, Henry shoots—and misses. So much for focusing on negation and negotiation at the same time. He drops the negation field entirely and starts running, ignoring Laurel's yell.

***

If he stops to think about what he's seeing and hearing—people running and screaming, things catching fire or freezing solid, no one listening to anyone else—he won't be able to keep going. Which would be bad, since that's not a problem James seems to be having.

James hasn't been in these compound corridors long enough to know them as well as Henry does, but that doesn't hinder him much. He's taking lots of twists and turns, clearly doing his best to keep as many people as possible between him and Henry, never mind how injured or armed they might be. As soon as he has the opportunity, Henry slows down enough to grab a comm off a stunned officer. It means losing ground, but it also means Henry now has access to better communications. Assuming they're still up and running . . . and willing to talk to him.

"Kent? Sybil? I need you to track a firestarter on Level 15. Not sure if he still has his guest ID on him, but it looks like some of the security cameras down here are still—"

"He's at the north stairwell," Kent's voice says in his ear, uncharacteristically clipped and efficient. "Not sure where he's going yet, but I'll keep an eye on it. Which you didn't hear me say because I am in no way doing anything General Carter hasn't asked me to while waiting for the black coats to let me out of my room."

Henry tries to ignore the stab of guilt for potentially getting Kent into even more trouble. "Thanks," he says as he dashes for the stairs.

Maybe this is what failure really looks like, he thinks, passing hallway after hallway of officers and assets at each other's throats. Officers going back on their word to protect, and assets lashing out in fear. James was correct about one thing, at least: There's no way they can trust the Council to do what's right. Not when their idea of "right" ends up looking like this.

He switches to another channel on the comm. "Michaels? You there?"

A pause, and then a throat clearing. "Yes, sir. Are you safe?"

"More or less. What the hell is going on? Do we know how this started? Is there any sort of coordinated evacuation effort happening? The answer to that last one looks like a resounding 'no' from where I'm standing, by the way."

"I'm . . . not at liberty to discuss the details at present."

Oh. Right. Because he's not in command anymore, and asking her to give him any information at all could put her at risk of court-martial, and then some.

"Sorry, Michaels. I didn't mean to—"

"Yes, sir," Michaels says a little too loudly. "General Carter is leaving now to assess the situation on the grounds. In the meantime, his orders are to contain the threat by any means necessary."

Henry grimaces and turns a corner just in time to catch the tail end of a psionic blast that lances through his temples before he can throw up a negation barrier strong enough to block it. Staggering slightly, he pushes forward toward the elevator bay. "Michaels—"

"Excuse me, sir. What do you need?" Her voice is much less guarded now.

"Was General Carter just there with you?"

"Yes, sir. As you may have heard me say, he's gone to check the grounds. I thought it best to let him carry on without getting distracted by our conversation."

"Very stealthy, Michaels."

"Thank you, sir. You needed something?"

He hesitates for a split second. Asking Kent for help, and now Michaels, is dangerous for them, especially if Carter is wandering around. But he can't afford not to do it. People are getting hurt—quite possibly dying, if this goes on long enough. There's no time to think about anything other than trying to diffuse the situation and get people to safety. "We need a better exit strategy than just 'smack people around until the fighting stops.' Evacuation above everything else. Coordinated sweeps on each level for threat assessment and de-escalation. Eyes on whatever security cameras we still have to find the ringleaders and subdue them first. There's no reason for this level of chaos."

"Actually, I believe there is, sir. My understanding is that the general is . . . hoping for a particular outcome."

"What the hell does that mean?"

"I understand that collateral damage is expected and even welcomed so long as the assets are shown to be the clear aggressors."

That explains why the officers don't seem concerned at all about who they're hurting or how much. Henry swallows the swell of anger and frustration. "We can play political games later," he snaps. "Get people organized and secure. Now."

"Yes, sir."

He takes a quick breath. "Thank you, Michaels. I owe you at least seventeen macchiatos when this is over."

"I believe we're up to twenty, sir."

"Make it twenty-one."

"Very good, sir."

***

By the time he gets to the northern elevator bay and stairwell, it's clear that the damage is getting more intense. The elevators should have shut down automatically when the alarms went off, but given that the doors of each elevator are heavily dented, sporting intermittent sparks, and making odd groaning noises, Henry thinks it's more likely an asset's power got to it first. Just as well he's taking the stairs.

He's barely gone a few levels before Kent's voice is suddenly in his ear, nearly making him trip backward and break his neck. "Level 1."

"That's a lot of floors," Henry says once he's steadied himself. "Are you sure?"

"He punched it into an elevator on Level 12."

"You mean one of the elevators that shouldn't be working right now?"

"Yup. An electrocutor must've gotten it running again for him. Or one of the other assets he's with."

So James has picked up more friends. Great. "There's no way I'm going to beat an elevator with stairs."

"No, but you can beat an elevator with an elevator. Go to the south bay on Level 11."

It must be the stupid part of his brain that made Henry expect a residential floor to be faring better than the jail block level. He's disabused of that notion as soon as he shoves open the stairwell door on Level 11 and gets blasted with a thick wave of smoke and screaming. He can't see any fire, but then, he can't see much of anything, and he's a little too busy doubling over and coughing to be sure. There's more yelling and the sound of guns being fired in every direction, but there's no way he can help any of them when he can barely see straight.

He makes his way toward the elevator bay mostly by sliding along walls and bumping into things. One of those things is a black coat, lying on the ground with a large gash in his chest. Henry stops to feel for a nonexistent pulse before forcing himself to keep moving.

"Get in," Kent says when Henry finally makes it to the elevators. Henry realizes the one to his right is slowly opening, groaning against its hinges. Not exactly reassuring, but he gets in anyway and reaches for the button for Level 1.

"Never mind that," Kent says as the doors slide shut painfully slowly. "Hang on."

"What—?"

But there's no time for talk as the elevator lurches and bolts upward at a much higher speed than it was designed for.

"Got here just before he did," Kent says cheerfully as it comes to a jarring stop. "You're welcome."

The elevator pings, and the doors open on Level 1.

Henry staggers out and takes a quick look around. The chaos here is even worse than it was on the lower levels: more people running back and forth, most of them heading toward the exits, as far as Henry can tell. Both assets and officers, so it looks like James wasn't able to convince the entire asset population to join him.

Henry catches sight of a staff member hurrying several children down a side hall, and he wonders with a sudden jolt of anxiety if Angelica and the other kids in the children's dorm on Level 16 have made it out yet.

The elevator next to him pings and begins to open. Henry turns, raising his gun, just in time to be knocked off his feet by a huge rush of heat.

The amount of fire bursting from the elevator car seems like more than could possibly fit, and it keeps coming even as several figures step out and disappear into the billowing smoke. Screams and unpleasant smells fill the air.

Sitting on the floor, dazed and with his heart trying to beat its way out of his chest, Henry tries to figure out why he's not burning like everything—and everyone—around him. He was right next to the blast, so why . . . ?

Then he realizes he's negating.

(Why didn't he make a bigger field, there are people in agony all around him, trying to put out the flames if they're still capable of movement, and he's just sitting here like an idiot, when he could have—)

The walls are burning, too.

Henry has met firestarters before, including potentials who couldn't control their powers yet. He's done his due diligence, too: Firestarters are common enough assets that it's good practice for retrieval teams to be aware of what they might come up against. So he knows that firestarters can burn anything, and he saw as much at Laurel's compound. But he's never seen anything quite this bad. And the weirdness of burning stone is nothing compared to the knowledge that James is still out there, ready to set off more fireballs and kill more people. Or convince others to do it for him.

Henry gets painfully to his feet and starts scanning the area, forcing himself to ignore the chaos around him. "Michaels!"

"Sir?" She sounds harried, which is completely out of character for her. "Excuse me. There are fire-related incidents on Levels 1, 5, 8, 9, 16, 32—"

"Get the damned alarms back on and *evacuate*! And where the *hell* are the emergency teams? Is Carter doing anything at all?"

"I haven't heard anything from the general. I believe he's still outside. As for the alarms—"

"Sybil and I are on it, Boss!" Kent says. "Well, I'm on it; Sybil is trying to get the emergency doors open. They're locked on some of the floors, and—"

"Just get it done," Henry says, distracted by movement in the smoke. "If any officers actually remember emergency protocols, send them wherever you need them to help anyone who's stuck. Otherwise, get everyone out. And make sure the city's sending emergency support. We're going to have more than a few injured."

He hurries after the faint sound of footsteps.

There's enough fire and debris to dodge that he suspects James must have coordinated fire attacks across compound floors—probably pulled in at least some of the other firestarters in the asset program. The damage to the compound structure is bad, but Henry passes med techs and the occasional officer or black coat still doing their best to move people toward exits. If anyone notices a commanding-officer-cum-convicted-criminal running around with a gun in his hand, they aren't mentioning it.

Kent's voice comes over his comm. "Hey, are you still looking for a firestarter? Because I found one—"

Henry doesn't need Kent to tell him what he can see for himself. He skids to a stop in front of James, who's standing over the crumpled body of an officer, his hands smoldering.

Henry immediately points his gun at James's head, but before he can say anything, James turns and laughs. "We both know you're not really going to—"

"Try me."

James shuts his mouth and looks silently at Henry for a moment. "I heard the rumors about what happened to you. This isn't going to get you back into the Compound Council's good graces, you know. They'll still have a set of cuffs for you no matter what you do."

"As long as we're not in the same cell. Move."

James ignites a ball of flame in his hand. "You know a gun isn't going to work on me—I'm faster with my fire than you are with your moral hesitation. I suppose you could try negating me again, but I'll just find somewhere outside your range and get going again."

Henry frowns. "How do you even know about—?"

"Imogen is a fantastic eavesdropper, it turns out. Not surprising for a hyran, but she really went above and beyond, figuring out a way to get out from under house arrest so she could bring me more information. It'd be a shame if she doesn't make it."

"People are already dead," Henry says sharply. "Assets, too. In case you were wondering."

"Collateral damage. You know about that, right, Major? Happens in war."

"This isn't a war. This is one asset involving hundreds in his personal vendetta and potentially getting them all killed."

James narrows his eyes. "It was never just about me. You have no idea how many of us want this. Even Laurel wanted it, back in the day. Before she chickened out."

Laurel. Who hid potentially vital information by holding back those files. Who probably killed at least one person, if James is to be believed. Who is going to give Henry a well-deserved earful for running off and leaving her with Smith.

"I'm not an asset," Henry says, "so I can't really—"

James snorts. "Seriously? You're going to deny it even now?"

"I mean, I was never actually entered into the program. I don't know what it's like. I can guess, based on having been a retrieval officer, but I never had to suffer through anything like what you did." Henry takes a breath only slightly clogged with smoke. "So you're angry? All right. That makes sense. This organization has done a good job of screwing you over. But how is killing a bunch of people going to make anything better?"

"I'll feel better knowing their lives have been destroyed, too." James raises his hand. "Maybe especially yours. No one should get to have it both ways."

Henry lowers his gun slowly. "You're right."

Not what James was expecting, obviously; he's blinking at Henry in confusion. "What?"

"You're really going to destroy this compound? Even if it means killing assets, too?"

"Yes."

"Okay." Henry takes another breath. "You don't get to have it both ways, either. Murderous freedom fighter or asset. Not both."

"What are you talking about?"

"I told you there would be consequences if you did anything to threaten the safety of the compound or anyone in it. I think this more than qualifies."

Everything is screaming at Henry that this is the stupidest idea he's ever had, that this is going to be the end of more than just his career, that he's going to be locked up permanently, *and he'll deserve it*—

—and if he doesn't do it, more people are going to die.

James clearly realizes something is happening because he throws the fire in his hand. Henry instinctively ducks out of the way, putting up a stronger negation barrier as he does it. His momentum slams him against the wall, bruising his shoulder, which he also ignores. Right now, all that matters is closing his eyes, clearing his mind, and reaching out to his mental shield.

And *pushing*.

The book didn't say what it would feel like, since it was only a theory to begin with. Henry's vaguely aware of a dropping sensation in his stomach, like the time he fell off the climbing wall during training. He gets the subsequent sharp pain in his back and inability to catch his breath, just like he did then. Like the wind's been knocked out of him.

Dazed, he opens his eyes and looks over at James, still standing in the middle of the hallway.

James seems startled but not harmed. He straightens up, shakes himself, and turns to Henry. "What the hell was that supposed to be?"

Henry can't speak yet. He feels his negation barrier dissipating on its own, and he sags against the wall. It occurs to him that if this didn't work, he's about to be burned to death.

James appears to be having the same idea. He raises his hand as if to ignite another flame . . . and nothing happens.

Frowning, he tries a few more times. Shakes his hand. Tries again.

When nothing works, he turns to Henry with eyes that are slowly widening. "It doesn't—It feels different. What did you do to me?"

Henry wonders if it would ruin the moment if he threw up right now. There's something deeply disturbing about seeing James become increasingly panicked. About knowing he did something to cause it.

He forces his shaking muscles to cooperate as he straightens, picks up his gun, and trains it back on James. "You're done hurting people. Let's go outside. Now."

"Holy shit. You actually—Quentin said you'd never—"

"I don't know who that is, but he doesn't know a damned thing about me. Like how much I want to shoot you right now. Move."

James stares at his hands, then up at Henry, then back at his hands. "I mean, it's just temporary, right? You wouldn't actually—"

"Yes, I'd actually. You're never making fire again. You're not an asset anymore. That just leaves murderer, which is plenty for one person."

"But—you can't just take away an asset's power!"

"I don't see why not. Are you going to move, or am I going to shoot you?"

James starts walking, possibly because he's too shocked to do anything else. Henry's probably doing a very bad job of hiding the fact that he's pretty much in the same headspace. At least he has the wherewithal to keep the gun pointed where it should be—and to grab a pair of cuffs from the body of an officer as they pass (don't think about that).

Outside the compound, officers, staff, and assets are milling around a safe distance away. Henry doesn't see Laurel, but he does see Smith being treated by a med tech. No sign of Carter.

He finally spots Templeton with a few black coats and starts to herd James in that direction, but they don't get very far.

The compound explodes.

Henry gradually becomes aware that he's lying on the ground, stunned. Everything around him is heat and screaming and smoke. There's a terrible smell in the air, and little patches of grass are burning all around him.

At least the sirens are back online, he thinks dimly.

Chapter 43

TRAIPSING THROUGH THE forest with nothing but an exhausted yet determined tracker to guide him isn't exactly how Bastian wanted to be spending a day and a half of his life. Particularly since he's pretty sure they went through poison ivy at some point, and his skin isn't happy about it. That said, he can't deny that Chloe's paths have gotten them back faster than they otherwise would've managed, especially with the vehicle still trapped in the dead zone.

As soon as they come through the brush and onto compound grounds, he's good and distracted from the slog they've just been through.

The compound is on fire.

That's ridiculous, of course; it's made of mostly stone and concrete. Except clearly, that doesn't matter: There's no mistaking the flames that are completely engulfing the main building, not to mention the ones creeping out toward Laurel's garden and the loading dock.

Bastian starts running. The jumble of fear-pain-shock-fatigue-terror coming from the people milling around pounds against his shield, but it holds. For now.

"Michaels!" he shouts, spotting her in the crowd. "What the hell is going on?"

She turns, her ever-present tablet in her hands and a look of mild surprise on her face. Which means she's in total shock. "There's been an incident," she says.

"No shit. Firestarters?"

"Yes. And others. We've gotten most of the compound evacuated, and city emergency services is on its way to transport the more severely injured. In the meantime, we're doing what we can to deal with the emergency."

"And?"

She hesitates. "There were . . . fatalities. More injuries than anything else, but—"

Bastian suddenly can't breathe. "How many?"

"I'm afraid we don't have the exact numbers yet. However—"

"A lot." Laurel is walking toward them. Her hair is a mess of soot and ash, and her arms have been dressed for wounds—probably burns, given the state of things. Her messenger bag, precariously slung over her shoulder, is bulging with what looks like even more herbs and poultices than usual.

Or rather, it *was* precariously slung over one shoulder. She drops it on the ground with a startled noise when Bastian hugs her.

"It must be bad if you're hugging me in public," she says, her voice muffled against his shirt. It's probably supposed to be funny, but nothing about the situation makes him want to laugh.

"Where's Chloe?" she demands, pulling away after a moment and rubbing her eyes. "You didn't leave her in the forest, did you?"

"No, I'm here." Chloe comes up behind them, her face drawn but determined. "What do you need?"

"I need to hug you immediately, if that's okay."

"Um. All right."

Laurel swoops in and hugs her without further ado. "Thank you for bringing him home," she says quietly. "And for bringing *you* home. You're the more important one, obviously, but he's nice to have around, too."

Bastian rolls his eyes, and Chloe laughs. "You're welcome. Only I didn't bring everyone."

"I know." Laurel straightens up, her face darkening. "James is already here. Or he was."

"Is this his handiwork?" Bastian asks, jerking a thumb at the burning compound. "Because if it is, we don't have time to talk about it. I need to go find him and kill him."

"You've always wanted to kill him. What's so different now?"

"Laurel."

She looks away (worried-confused-hurt). "I don't . . . It's complicated. I'm not sure how to explain."

"How about you start by telling me what happened?"

"James may have sort of . . . started an asset rebellion. And before you ask, yes, I regret introducing him to the other firestarters. And all the other assets. And basically everyone he convinced to help him do this. But he's not—he wasn't *like* this before! He was arrogant and charming and idiotic sometimes, but he wasn't a murderer! When he showed up yesterday, it was like—"

"Like he doesn't have any emotions. Like nothing affects him. Like people don't matter anymore." Bastian doesn't add "like he's been manipulated by a

200-year-old empath" because she probably gets the point, and now doesn't seem like the right time to explain how empaths can apparently defy the progression of time.

Laurel bites her lip. "Well, yes. I mean, you said ages ago that he didn't have any emotions, but I didn't believe you. I thought if he just got his memories back, everything would be . . ."

There are shouts as another part of the compound structure caves in, and a group of med techs hurries over.

Bastian turns to Michaels. "So are we just going to let the compound burn itself out, or are we going to do something to help? And what about city assistance? They're supposed to send us more than just a few stretchers if something like this happens, right? That's one of the liaison committee documents I actually read."

"Compound staff have been doing what they can to extract anyone still inside," Michaels says, "but with city emergency services held up—"

"Held up by what?"

"I . . . couldn't say."

"Yes, you could," Laurel says grimly.

Michaels's jolt of awkward-concerned-embarrassed quickly goes under wraps in favor of careful politeness. "Based on a brief conversation I had with the general, I believe the intended outcome of this emergency is to show that the compound is unable to deal with the threat of an asset uprising."

"Which it will be, without city help," Bastian says. "Where's Carter now?"

"Not long after the attack began, General Carter went to check the grounds and hasn't communicated since. I haven't been able to raise either him or Major Alexis, although they were both spotted leaving the building. Without anyone in command at the moment, the situation has gotten a little . . . out of hand."

"What do you mean, without anyone in command?" Bastian demands. Then he steels himself to ask the question he's been too terrified to ask: "Where's Henry?"

Michaels and Laurel both give him looks that make his stomach twist unpleasantly. "Officially, the major has been removed from office," Michaels begins.

"Unofficially, he's been going back in to find trapped people and bring them out," Laurel adds. "Because he's an idiot. And because there aren't enough other people to help. Never mind that if someone sees him, they'll throw him to the black coats, and then where will we be? It's hard enough for me to heal people and keep myself from being locked up again. Henry's being extremely rude to make me have to worry about him, too."

Bastian isn't quite tracking how the hell both Henry and Laurel got themselves on the most wanted list, but that doesn't matter now. Nothing else matters except the flames and the people caught in them. And one person in particular who completely fails at keeping promises about being careful.

"How many more are still in there?" he asks Michaels.

"We're hindered by a lack of technology, unfortunately. Mr. Turner and Ms. Tassos have already been evacuated, and we no longer have access to the hacker HQ facilities. That said, they've been able to trace one remaining asset ID. That's the one the major went in after."

Bastian looks at the burning building, then turns to Laurel. "Don't let anyone else die."

She frowns. "You're going to do something stupid, aren't you?"

"I can help." Chloe is staring at the compound building like she's trying to assess it—or to assess pathways into and out of it. Because of course that must be exactly what she's doing.

"I'm not asking," Bastian says quietly.

"You can feel him, right?" Chloe asks, ignoring the comment. "Or do you have to get closer?"

There's enough noise and energy all around them that it ought to be hard—maybe even impossible. But he can usually feel Henry better than anyone, and now that he's stronger ... there. He knows that brand of determined-angry-worried even when it's buried in smoke and noise and fear.

"Level 16," Bastian says.

Chloe gives him a determined look. "I know you're not asking; I'm telling. Let's go."

"What she said." Laurel picks up her bag again.

"Laurel, you don't have to—"

"Yes, I do. I've seen what happens when you try to be heroic by yourself. It ends with you lying to people and then breaking your hand. Which I had to fix, if you'll remember."

"A lot of the paths are closed off because of the fire, but I think I can get us through," Chloe says, narrowing her eyes. Given the level of terror-concern-focus coming off of her, it's pretty impressive that she's managing to look so calm.

(He can't take them, not if things go sideways, they matter too much—and anyway, he's responsible for Chloe, and being responsible means not leading people into a fiery death, so far as he knows—but he can't stay here, not while Henry—)

"I won't be able to communicate with you while you're inside," Michaels is saying. "The system has sustained too much damage. The hackers may be able to track your IDs if you still have them, but I'm not sure we could get you any assistance before—that is, in a timely manner."

"Don't worry about it, Officer Michaels," Laurel says with forced cheerfulness. "We'll be out before you know it."

Michaels hesitates, then nods and says to Bastian, "Please give the major my regards when you find him."

"You can give them to him yourself," Bastian says.

Then he's running again.

***

The heat and the blaring alarms slam him in the face, followed by the smoke and the sickly sweet smell of something burning that he's definitely not going to think about.

Of course, he's not the only one familiar with this kind of situation. For him, it was walking through a hidden compound in the forest that had been nearly burned to the ground. Laurel, on the other hand, has first-hand experience. Her grim-stubborn-purposeful indicates she'd rather not talk about it, though, even if they could hold a real conversation over the sound of the alarms.

They stay low as they move quickly toward the stairwell, stepping over debris and being careful not to touch anything. The further in they go, the worse the emotional residue gets—not to mention the heat and smoke.

"Chloe?" Bastian asks—shouts, really—when Chloe stops them in front of the stairs.

She coughs, then jerks her head toward the door. "This is the quickest way for now."

It's jammed shut so tightly that it takes all three of them to open it. Good to know the compound's automatic emergency protocols weren't at all prepared for this level of damage. Although if Laurel and Michaels are right about the reason behind the delayed city emergency services, it could be part of Carter's sabotage effort. That would be in keeping with the idea Nunez floated in the car at the Hall five lifetimes ago.

They stumble down a few flights before Chloe stops again. Bastian, focused on trying to find Henry's emotional signature, loses his concentration and nearly bowls her over. "He's not on this floor."

"I know. But the stairs farther down are blocked. We have to get out here and cut across to the other side."

Bastian can tell before they even open the Level 5 door that there's someone there. The anger-fear-revulsion is sharp, a sudden pinpoint of energy that gets cut abruptly. Bastian pushes open the door far more aggressively than is necessary and practically falls out into the hallway.

In addition to the same sort of debris they came across on other floors, this one also has what looks like a standoff between two people. Or rather, what *was* a standoff. Now it's just a black coat lying on the ground in a heap and a man tossing aside a gun. He looks up as they enter, shoulders heaving as he pants.

The alarms, which must have drowned out the gunshot, go abruptly silent.

"James," Laurel says.

He's covered in sweat and dirt like the rest of them. And, Bastian realizes with surprise, he's got burns on his face and arms as well. Has he really been so caught up in destroying the compound that he hasn't even bothered to protect himself from his own element?

"Get out of my way," James says, low and guttural. He's pissed off and suffering from more than a little smoke inhalation, apparently.

Wait.

Bastian narrows his watering eyes and tries to focus past Laurel's sadness-frustration-anger (a physical pain in his chest for more than one reason) and . . . there. It's faint and easy to miss, but James really *is* angry. And something else: a vague sadness, maybe. For the first time ever, Bastian can feel real emotions from him.

Quentin must have been telling the truth about that much, at least. It's taken awhile, but James is getting his emotional energy back. What Quentin did to him doesn't seem to be permanent.

(That shouldn't make him happy, shouldn't make him think that maybe it's all right for him to have done what he did, like it's somehow less awful just because the person he hurt will be fine—it's Valentine all over again, telling him that he's helping, that interrogating criminals is about justice, that it's only an occasional misfortune that he destroys their minds—)

Laurel doesn't respond to James's implied threat. Instead, she looks at the gun on the ground and then at the dead black coat. Then back at James. "You killed her."

James coughs—or maybe laughs. "At least it was quicker than poison."

Bastian doesn't have time to ask what the hell that means before Laurel's shame-hurt-disgust flares, and she takes a step forward. "You—"

"We need to go," Chloe says, a little louder than necessary. "I don't think the paths on this floor are going to stay open much longer. If we want to get to the major—"

This time, James definitely laughs. "Yeah, have fun with that. He and that kid are probably squashed by now, unless the smoke got to them first."

"What are you talking about?" Bastian demands.

James finally looks at Bastian. Everything about him, from the tension in his muscles to the slightly manic glint in his eyes, says fear-fury-hatred, although the emotions themselves are still muted. Bastian instinctively takes a step backward.

"I wouldn't have come back into this hellhole, but it's impossible to get around your stupid security. Gave me a chance to see the major get what's coming to him, though. And now I'm heading out." James narrows his eyes at Laurel. "*Move.*"

The fire is getting hotter, and it's becoming harder to breathe. Bastian glances at the gun on the ground. He has no idea how to use it, but if Laurel and Chloe can distract James, maybe . . .

James apparently has the same idea. His eyes latch onto Bastian's. Then they both start to go for it, except that Bastian is distracted by a hand yanking him backward. A split second later, there's a loud *crack* and a rush of heat. He realizes with a start that Laurel pulled him back just as the fire ate through a large portion of the ceiling, which has crashed to the ground where black coat was, cutting off the rest of the hallway.

"*James!*" Laurel screams, even as she clings to Bastian's arm. It feels like she's practically pulling it out of its socket.

It also feels like her anguish-anger-helplessness is going to break him in half.

He tries to find James with his power, feeling out as far as he possibly can, but he's lost the thin emotional signature underneath everything else in the hall. He thinks he might be able to hear footsteps, but that could also just be his heartbeat hammering in his ears.

"You were right about him," Laurel says, voice barely audible. Tears are streaming down her face and leaving tracks in the dirt on her cheeks. "You said we shouldn't trust him, and you were right."

"No, I wasn't. At least, I think it's more complicated than that." Bastian turns to her. "He was sad when he looked at you. For what it's worth."

Laurel swallows once. "Do you think he's—?"

"If anyone can get out of a burning building safely, it's a firestarter."

Chloe clears her throat and says hesitantly, "Um. I've found another way around to the other stairwell, so . . ."

Laurel takes a quick breath, then nods. "Okay. Let's go."

***

Coming out of the Level 16 stairwell with enough adrenaline in his system that he's started shaking, Bastian stumbles to a stop when he realizes he can't feel Henry anymore.

That could mean loads of things, Bastian reminds himself even as he starts running. People's signatures dim or even go out completely when they hit REM, or when they fall unconscious, or even sometimes if they're just dazed or incapacitated.

Or if they're dead.

"Hey!" Laurel yells after him, but he doesn't stop.

He knows he can't possibly cover the entire level, especially since portions of it are probably too damaged to get through, per Chloe's comments on upper floors. But every moment they take things too slowly means one more moment they haven't found Henry yet, which might mean—

Bastian stops abruptly, pulls off his right glove, and slams his hand against the wall. The sharp, stinging pain probably means a second-degree burn is imminent, but he ignores it as best he can, closing his eyes and trying to focus.

(He's stronger now, stronger than he's ever been, so surely he can find Henry quickly, even if the emotions are dim—or at least he should be able to feel where they *were*, assuming he's allowing himself the past tense here, which he is *not*, so it's just a matter of—)

There. The echo of worried-determined-frustrated should be enough to get him to the right hallway.

He starts running again, picking up speed when he hears what sounds like someone crying. The crescendo of fear resolves itself into a huge pile of burning debris and a small girl crouching to it, sobbing.

"It fell," Angelica says. She's covered in dirt and ash and sweat, and she's hugging her arms to her chest, rocking back and forth. "He pushed me out of the way, but—"

"Angelica!" Laurel appears right behind Bastian and rushes over, Chloe close behind. "Are you all right?"

Bastian barely registers anything they say or do. He left one of his gloves back there, and his hand is throbbing, but he drops to his knees and starts digging through the burning pile anyway.

Wordlessly, Chloe kneels next to him and starts to dig as well.

"I am going to need so many burn salves after this," Laurel mutters. To Angelica, she adds, "Stay back a bit, all right? We'll be out of here soon."

The pain is getting worse, and Bastian's right hand is turning an alarming shade of red. The left one isn't doing much better. Not that he cares; the only thing that matters now is digging and lifting and burrowing his way deeper into the pile of stone and wood and concrete, looking for anything that resembles—

—an arm.

He doesn't have the energy left by this point to call out to the others; he just starts digging faster, pushing past the pain that's spreading from his hands to his knees to his back. He becomes vaguely aware that Laurel and Chloe have gotten closer and are digging just as quickly.

The arm becomes a shoulder, which is connected to a neck, which is connected to a very bruised and bloodied face.

Bastian can't breathe for a split second. (He's too still; why is he so still?) Then he snaps out of it and works swiftly and carefully to remove as much of the debris as he can.

"Henry." He doesn't recognize his own voice. "*Henry.*"

There's a brief moment where all Bastian can hear is the crackling of the fire around them. Then a small, pained cough starts his heart beating again.

"Ow." Henry's voice is thready, and he's extremely slow to open his eyes. "I think . . . I broke a rib . . . Bastian?"

Bastian makes a noise somewhere between a laugh and a sob. "Trust you to think of yourself before anyone else. And we need to have a serious talk if this is your idea of keeping your promise to be careful."

"Angelica . . . ?"

"I'm okay," Angelica says. Her braid is looking more than a little worse for wear, and her face is wet with tears, but she's standing a little ways off and looking relatively uninjured.

"You scared her, which was extremely rude of you," Laurel says sternly. Then her face softens. "Are you . . . ?"

"I'm fine." He actually starts to sit up before Laurel and Bastian yell at him in tandem. Whatever pain he's experiencing is probably more effective at getting him prone again than their warning, though.

Bastian turns to Laurel. "We need to get him out of here, but he's not going to be able to walk."

"You could . . . carry me."

Bastian gives him a withering look, which is hard to maintain when Henry is smiling at him. "You carrying me down a flight of stairs isn't the same thing as me dragging you up fifteen while everything is burning around us." To Laurel: "Any ideas?"

Laurel frowns. "I think we can get him out from under all this stuff—the biggest pieces missed him, so we'll only have to work around them rather than figuring out how any of our powers could translate into super strength. As for his injuries . . . I think I have something that could get him walking again, at least temporarily. Hang on." She scuttles away to where she left her bag and starts rummaging through it.

"Bastian," Henry says quietly, "did you find . . . ?"

"Drink this." Laurel is back, shoving a tiny vial of something at Henry. "Wait; you shouldn't move yet. Bastian, make him drink it."

Henry makes a face as it goes down—as with most of Laurel's concoctions, it probably tastes awful—but even Bastian can see that it works quickly, getting rid of some of the dazed vagueness in Henry's eyes. A moment later, he sits up, wincing but mobile. Bastian immediately grabs onto his arm to steady him.

There's a bit more contorting and awkward movement as he, Chloe, and Laurel work to get Henry out from under the debris and over to where Angelica is standing, but they manage it. Bastian doesn't want to imagine how much it would hurt Henry to be doing this without whatever Laurel gave him.

As soon as Henry's clear, there's a loud groan from the ceiling, and another pile of debris crashes down, setting the entire pile on fire.

They all look at each other for a moment, then head quickly for the stairs.

***

Chloe leads them on a convoluted path through smoke-filled hallways, gaping holes in the walls, and precarious stairwells. Eventually, they end up back on Level 1, which is not looking any better than it did earlier. At this point, they're all keeping as low as possible and covering their faces with hands and sleeves. The combination of emotional residue and smoke is giving Bastian a headache that, while it isn't quite as bad as the ones he got before, is still bad enough.

Henry is starting to droop in Bastian's arms, and he's let a small negation barrier form—not enough to interfere with Chloe's tracking, so far as Bastian can tell, but enough that it's noticeable, if you know what to look for. Just to be safe, Bastian gently reminds him to pull it back as they get closer to the exit.

"Doesn't matter," Henry mumbles, stumbling slightly. "They know."

Bastian frowns. "What do you mean, 'they know'?"

Before Henry can answer, Laurel moves ahead of them and starts to push open the door, allowing in a blast of crisp early-morning air. The door is partially jammed, so Chloe hurries forward to help keep it open, and Angelica joins her, bracing her tiny body against the door, the determination-fear-worry clear in her face as she looks at Bastian. He wants to say something, to thank her for being so brave, but all he can manage is a small nod as he helps Henry through the doorway.

Once they're outside, they head toward the large group of assets, officers, and staff members milling around a safe distance away from the compound. Bastian certainly isn't thinking clearly enough to take a head count at the moment, but he's pretty sure there are far fewer assets here than are actually enrolled in the program. Either the others were working with James and got away . . . or they didn't.

Michaels hurries over to meet them, her relief-alarm-concern louder than anything Bastian has ever felt from her. "Sir," she says to Henry, "I'm very—"

Henry starts coughing. Not surprising; they've just come out of a burning building. Coughing up blood, though, probably isn't a good sign.

When his legs buckle, sending him unceremoniously to the ground, Bastian goes with him. "Henry—please—"

"S'okay," Henry says around another cough. "I just need a minute ..."

Michaels grabs a passing officer. "We need someone from emergency services. Immediately."

"Yes, ma'am." The officer races off.

Bastian doesn't bother to ask how long it ended up taking the city emergency staff to get here. Instead, he focuses on Henry, who's starting to look as dazed as he did when they found him, if not more so. Laurel's tincture must be wearing off. "You need to stay awake," Bastian says, though he has no idea if that's true. "I need you to—"

Henry takes his hand in a weak grip. "Did you ... find it?"

(Tom's dead eyes and Quentin's triumphant ones, the surge of energy that cleared his head almost at once, the disorientation of losing time and waking up and realizing what he'd done—)

"Bastian?"

He doesn't want to lie, but there's no time to explain, and he can feel Henry's blurred desperation-hope-concern overlaying the pain.

He swallows. "Yeah. I found it."

"Good. Come here."

Bastian leans in toward Henry, who gets hold of Bastian's shirt to gently pull him even closer. "I thought you should know that ... I'd really like to be kissing you right now, but ... I'm sort of bleeding everywhere, so that would be disgusting."

Bastian laughs, a painful sort of laugh that gets stuck in his throat. "Definitely the most romantic thing I've ever heard." He leans the rest of the way in and kisses Henry's forehead.

"Please move aside, sir." The city emergency team has finally gotten the memo and brought over a stretcher and some oxygen. Out of the corner of his eye, Bastian sees Laurel, Chloe, and Angelica already getting checked out. Laurel has a very judgmental look on her face, but she's also letting the EMT fit her with an oxygen mask. Given the kind of day she's had, Bastian supposes she's allowed a bit of dubiousness for mere mortals who dare to practice medicine that doesn't involve plants. So long as she still gets herself taken care of.

"Sir?" The EMT is clearly already in assessment mode, only her eyes are on Bastian, which means they aren't on Henry, like they should be.

Bastian forces himself to get back to his feet and move away. It's physically painful to stop touching Henry, but even in his wrecked state, Bastian knows that being pathetic isn't going to get Henry the medical attention he needs.

Once they've gotten Henry strapped in, the EMT turns to Bastian. "You should let us check you out as well. We can—"

"You can do it on the way to wherever you're taking him. I'm going with you."

"No, you're not."

Bastian whirls around to find General Carter standing there, a professionally concerned look on his face. "Thank you," he says to the EMT. "You can go ahead and take the major."

"Not without me. And where the hell have you been?"

Carter regards him coolly. "All you need to know right now is that this compound is officially under my control, per the Compound Council's wishes. I'll be making any and all decisions about the major's future, not to mention yours."

"What does that have to do with—?"

"That means you won't be leaving the compound grounds unless I deem it appropriate." He gives Bastian a quick once-over. "You don't look seriously injured, so I suspect the med techs can take care of you here. Once they've cleared you, I suggest you take some time to prepare yourself for an intensive investigation into the mishandling of power during your tenure here."

"*What?*"

Carter frowns at him. "I understand that the events of this past evening might have confused you, so let me bring you up to speed. Major Mortimer is no longer in charge of this compound, and you are no longer a member of its leadership. Clearly, the Council and I were mistaken when we thought we could trust you and Mortimer to effectively reorganize and oversee the work being done here. Your only role now is to answer questions put to you by myself and the liaison committee as we try to sort out this mess."

His gaze softens slightly, though it remains stern. "I understand that you've just been through a lot, but I'm afraid you won't be going anywhere anytime soon. You need to be held accountable for your actions."

Bastian feels his chest tighten, particularly when he catches a glimpse of the emergency services team rolling Henry away.

He whips back around to glare at Carter. "Are you going to be held account-able, too? Say, for having a woman killed? Or hiding the Fail-Safe Protocol experiments? Or magically disappearing while the compound burned down?"

"I suggest you keep your unsubstantiated theories to yourself," Carter growls. "We've just gotten a very explicit example of why assets can't be trusted, and we plan to react accordingly. If you'll pardon the overly apt metaphor, it would be in your best interest to not add fuel to the fire."

(It feels like it did at the sanctuary and in the forest a year ago, the anger welling up inside of him, too much for him to control—all of the things he keeps locked down because he knows it's not safe, because feeling this much could hurt not just him, but everyone around him—but he can't hold it in, not if they're going to destroy everything Henry fought so hard for, not if they're going to take him away—)

"Bastian." Laurel is at his side, not touching him but standing near enough to break his concentration.

She's been hurt enough, he thinks. He can't risk doing anything that might hurt her more. Or anything that might hurt Chloe or Michaels, standing a bit behind her, looking worried. Or Angelica, sitting on the ground with an oxygen mask over her face and ash in her hair. Or Kent and Sybil, standing with a group of hackers, holding hands and looking singed but all right.

These people matter. And they're his responsibility now.

"General Carter is slime, and he'll get what's coming to him," Laurel says, smiling dangerously before turning back to Bastian. "But the slime is right about one thing: You can't go anywhere. We need you here. The compound needs you here."

Bastian looks at her for a moment, and a tiny bit of her determined-tenacious-compassionate sneaks through his shield. Just enough that he can tell she means business.

He nods, turns his back on Carter, and starts walking away.

"We'll find Henry," Laurel adds in a low voice as she catches up. "Wherever they take him. I promise."

He can't speak, so he just nods again and takes her hand as they head over to the rest of the survivors.

About the Author

Katy Morgan is an indie fantasy author and fiction editor with an eye for detail and a heart for supporting the creative community. When she's not writing or editing, she can be found cross-stitching something sassy, daydreaming about hedgehogs, or drinking far too many mochas, usually all at once.

Keep up with Katy on BardicFool.com.

***

Thanks for reading *Fail-Safe*!

If you enjoyed this book, please consider letting others know by leaving a review on Amazon and/or Goodreads. Reviews are one of the best ways to help new readers find indie work—and we can't do it without you!